Tammy Hoey

BLACK KNIGHTS

A Rick Attison Novel
by Tammy Coulter

Contents

Dedication

This book is for everyone who said I could do this writing thing. For my parents who encouraged my love of reading, my sister who keeps saying I can do anything I want, for my "kids" who said hurry up and publish it so we can read it! Lastly for my late husband, Rob, who said kids don't talk like that. If it wasn't for all of you, this would never have happened. Thank you.

Chapter 1

It was the same, night after night. Oh, it would start out okay, but it never stayed that way. Tonight was the worst yet. Rick had come home around midnight, after a long night of partying with his friends. He had fallen into a deep sleep as soon as his head hit the pillow, despite the sounds coming from where his dad was "entertaining" his newest girlfriend. Almost immediately, he fell into what he had come to call "The Dream."

Rick Attison, 16, belonged to a gang he thought was pretty cool. The Black Knights were the best friends a guy could ask for – loyal and protective. If Rick was in trouble, Blade and the boys were always there. Well, usually always there. Rick had come to understand that sometimes he just didn't count, but, hey, that was okay. The same went for Rick – he was always there for his boys and Rick never, ever, backed down from a fight.

Lately, though, Rick was getting worried about Blade. The leader of the Knights was becoming increasingly violent and deliberately cruel, two things Rick wasn't. Blade didn't seem to care who he hurt, or what he did, even to his own gang. At times, Rick was sickened by what his leader did, but he never really questioned it. After all, Blade was their leader, and that meant whatever he wanted to do, the gang did. Rick never objected to Blade's "lessons" if whomever was being taught the lesson was being disrespectful. After all, the Knights had a rep to maintain, especially on the streets. But sometimes Blade went too far, and Rick was beginning to wonder what he was doing with the Knights.

Rick figured it was that doubt which had led to the brutal nightmares which had begun shortly after the Knights had attacked a new kid in school, almost killing the kid in the process. In the nightmare, the Knights would be hanging out, wandering the streets of town, horsing around. They would spray paint the walls of the high school or a shop downtown, ignoring the shouts from the owners to stop. Little punks who got in their way would end up lying in the gutter, bloodied and bruised, right where Blade thought they belonged. Sometimes, Rick led the way, but more often than not, Rick was the follower. Eventually the gang would end up in the neighbourhood park near Rick's house, laughing and congratulating each other. Everything was good, and Rick loved it. Now, if the dream had ended there, Rick wouldn't have had a problem, since that pretty much described how the Knights lived every day. And the first few nights, that *was* where it had ended. But gradually it had changed.

This version of the nightmare was something darker, more sinister. The Knights were sitting around in the park – Blade and Brain were sitting on a park bench, smoking and talking about something, while Crank and Rick wrestled around and Pup was standing guard, as usual. In the bushes, some movement caught Pup's eye; he whistled for the boys. All the Knights pounced on the intruder; punching, kicking, using whatever they found to beat up whoever dared to spy on them. Rick, like the rest, was caught up in the moment. Eventually, Blade stopped the brutal attack and hauled the victim into the open, while everyone else tried to catch his breath.

The victim lay there in the park's dim lights, halfway in the shadows. After the first couple of nights the nightmare's victim, at first a boy about Rick's age, changed, growing slimmer and slimmer. Horrified, Rick would bolt up, shaking, drenched in a cold sweat and his blankets tangled around him like a noose as he finally realized their victim was a young girl, but since he couldn't see the face, he didn't know if he knew her or not.

Tonight, somehow, he forced himself to stay asleep, kneel down beside the still form and brush the thick red hair away from the battered face. What he saw catapulted him awake, screaming in terror.

"Christ, boy! What the hell's wrong with you? I was asleep, dammit!" Rick's father demanded harshly from the door.

"It's nothing, Dad. Sorry," Rick snapped back, not sorry at all, especially when he heard a female voice murmuring in his dad's bedroom, wondering what all the noise was about.

After his dad slammed the door and stomped back to his room, Rick sat in the dark, shaking and dripping with sweat. The nightmare was so realistic, you couldn't pay Rick enough to go back to sleep. At least not right away. The sight of that face haunted him. *Man, I must be turnin' chicken*, Rick thought after he had finally calmed down. The more he thought about the dream, the more disgusted he was with himself. *Blade would laugh at me. After all, it's just a dream. Doesn't matter who's in it.*

Eventually, Rick fell back into a very troubled sleep, but he wasn't even close to rested when his alarm shrilled the next morning. With a groan, he rolled out of bed and staggered to his bathroom. He let the steaming hot water pound down on him for almost 20 minutes, trying to wash away the nightmare from the night before. He staggered back to his bedroom and stared at his reflection in the mirror. Dark circles rimmed his bloodshot eyes and he looked like he hadn't slept at all.

"Matches how I feel. Man, what a night," Rick muttered with another groan. He ran his fingers through his hair as he pulled out his clothes for the last day of school. Black jeans, white tee shirt, black, low-heeled cowboy boots, black bandana with the word "Money" stitched on it in silver and a black leather jacket with silver stitching around the cuffs and waist. Everything was the best money could buy, especially the custom-made jacket. He could easily afford what the others couldn't.

Thank God it was the last day of school. Rick couldn't wait to get out of school, away from the teachers and their watching eyes and he knew he'd be able to sleep in tomorrow, even if Blade kept them out all night, which was likely. Rick finished tying his bandana and shrugged into his jacket. He knew he looked good, especially in black. He preened in front of the mirror for a couple of more minutes, and then thundered downstairs, not caring who he woke.

"Hello. You must be Richard," the young woman sitting at the table said with a smile. "I'm Judy." She held out her hand, which Rick ignored.

He chuckled nastily as he got his breakfast. "And ya must be dreamin' if ya think it's gonna last. Yer the fourth one this month alone," Rick leered at her as he poured milk on his cereal. Judy flushed and lowered her head.

"Richard," his dad warned as he came into the kitchen clad only in his jeans.

"What? At least one of us'll tell her the truth," Rick snapped back. His few bites of breakfast sat in his stomach like a rock. "Screw this. I'll grab somethin' on the way," he groused as he pushed away from the table, ignoring his book bag just inside the front door.

He didn't wait for his dad to say anything, and most likely, he wouldn't've cared anyway. Seeing how his dad was dressed, Rick knew his old man had no intention of going to work. Fortunately, the Knights would split as soon as they could and he wouldn't have to be home for hours. By then, the playmate would be long gone. Probably his dad, too. He'd probably kick her out fairly quickly so he could head to one of his favourite watering holes where he could meet up with his bookie. *Man, my dad's lame*, Rick thought as he sauntered down the sidewalk.

It only took Rick a few minutes to get to school and, once there, he loitered in the lounge, just inside the main doors, waiting for the rest of the Knights. A couple of freshmen bumped into him and he sent them scurrying away with a growl, just as he heard someone coming up behind him. He sighed as he realized who it was, just from the sound of the footsteps. *What now? Why now?* he thought sourly.

"Ending Grade 10 on a good note, Richard?" a deep voice said, leaning in to speak quietly into Rick's ear.

"Look, Delaney, quit bustin' me. Blade and Crank're three times as bad as I am and ya never give 'em this much grief. And, for the last time, the name's Rick," Rick snapped without turning all the way around.

Principal Delaney moved even closer so he could whisper in Rick's ear. "This is your last chance, Richard. If you don't do something and quickly, they're gonna scrape you up off the pavement with Johnny's knife in you and *no one is going to care*. Not even your boys," he said softly, but emphatically. Rick just snorted.

He started to move away when a student at the front door caught his eye. "Then again, maybe she'll care. Think about it, son. What're you willing to lose?" With that, Delaney walked away without so much as a backwards glance.

Rick stared at the young redheaded teen-age girl who had just walked in. *The dream lives. What the hell am I gonna do?* Rick thought with a shiver. Walking behind her was her male version; both had fiery red hair and freckles and, with a groan, Rick realized both of them were about to get in some serious trouble. Because right behind them were the rest of the Knights. It looked like Blade was looking for some entertainment, and, much to Rick's horror, these two were it.

Rick strode quickly over to the group just as Blade reached out and grabbed the young girl in a vice-like grip. "Sweet Irish Cream," Blade smirked as she struggled against him. The harder she struggled, the more he laughed.

The rest of the gang quickly surrounded her companion and wrapped him up tight. "Let her go!" he grated as he fought with Crank. Again, Blade just laughed.

"When I'm ready, Mickey Mouse," Blade sneered and dragged the young girl closer. As he swung her around and pinned her to the wall, Rick stepped in and grabbed Blade's hand. The student lounge was suddenly as quiet as a tomb.

"Blade, don't," Rick said softly.

Blade turned to Rick. His eyes were as hard as steel and his voice was devoid of all emotion when he spoke. "What's that, Moneyman? Don't think I heard ya," he said, blandly, while glaring at the girl. Scowling, he wrenched his arm out of Rick's grasp and shoved the girl towards Brain who wrapped her up in a bear hug.

Blade grabbed Rick and slammed him against the wall, while the girl cried out from the pain of Brain's grip. Rick didn't even flinch, although he was having a hard time breathing. He knew he deserved whatever Blade was about to dish out. No one ever touched Blade and no one ever told him 'No.' Everyone was too scared of him. Everyone, that is, but Rick. Rick just respected the power his leader held.

"Look, Blade, chill, man. No matter what *you* did, *I'd* catch the heat, man. I don't feel like dodging her old man all summer. I don't need that. *We* don't need that. Leave her alone," Rick snapped hotly as he stared at Blade. The bell had rung for Homeroom and, despite the ongoing drama brewing between the Knights, the student lounge had emptied quickly. The only sound left was the sound of trickling water in the pond and Rick's laboured breathing.

Blade's eyes narrowed, then he laughed. "Wouldn't wanna screw up summer, right, boys?" he laughed over his shoulder at the rest of the gang. "Let 'em go." With a grin, Crank and Brain shoved the pair away. They fled, leaving the Knights alone in the lounge.

"As fer ya, Moneyman," Blade said softly, turning back to Rick, leaning in even closer. Rick tried not to cringe at the venom in his leader's voice. "Thought'cha knew better. Don't cross me. Ever. I don't care how much crap yer gonna catch from her old man. I come first. My pleasure. My fun. Got it?" Without warning, Blade's fist slammed into Rick's solar plexus, leaving him in a heap on the floor, gasping for air.

"Got it... Moneyman?" Blade hissed angrily as he leaned over Rick.

"Yeah, I got it," Rick gasped. He struggled to his feet and stood, wobbling back and forth. He adjusted his clothes and once more stood as a Knight. For the longest time, Blade made Rick stand there, just like he was in the principal's office, then sharply pushed him away, his point made.

Rick staggered toward his first class, feeling Blade's eyes on him the whole way down the hall. *What the hell was I thinkin'?*

Rick raged to himself as he finally stumbled around the corner and out of Blade's sight. *I know better than to challenge him!*

"Thank you, Rick," a soft voice, with a barely discernable Irish accent, came from a dark hallway.

Rick stopped and stared into the darkness. Out stepped the red-headed girl he had just saved. She stepped closer and after a quick glance down the hall, grabbed his hand, and pulled him into the safety of the darkness.

"You okay, Jor?" Rick asked softly as he wrapped his arms around the slender girl, giving her a long, tender kiss. He held his long-time girlfriend tight while he tried not to think about what could have happened, and what had just happened to him because of it. Jordan O'Reilly wasn't just any girl. She and her twin brother, Mickey, were the children of the local police chief, Inspector Seamus O'Reilly, a tough cop and a constant pain in Rick's neck, especially when it came to the Knights.

"I'm fine, love. What's his problem today?" she asked rhetorically as she leaned back against the wall, with her arms up around his neck and stared up at her boyfriend. With a sudden jerk, she pulled off his bandana and ran her fingers through his thick blonde hair.

"Much better. I can deal with everything but that. I love your hair," Jordan smiled. Her smile faded as Rick grabbed the bandana out of her hand and tied it back on with a grunt.

"Leave it, Jor. Full gear or I get my butt whipped. Again. I've already taken enough pain for you today, girlfriend or not. Trust me, I don't need him any angrier with me. Not today and not if I wanna survive the summer," Rick snapped. He clenched his fists as he tried to control a sudden, inexplicable surge in anger.

"I'm sorry, Rick...please? Don't be mad at me. I'll leave it alone, I promise. Please? I'm sorry, really, I am," Jordan begged softly. She paled at the quick flare of anger in Rick's eyes.

Rick counted to ten and sighed as he unclenched his fists. "Sorry, Jor. Forget about it. Look, we're already late for class, so I'm going to blow. Not like Delaney cares anyway. You'd better get back to Mick. He'll be frantic by now," Rick said, softly, anger gone. He gave her another quick kiss and led the way out of the hallway, checking right and left for the Knights.

"All clear, sweets. Now go. I'll try and call tonight," Rick said softly and watched her walk away. *Too close*, he thought as he sauntered towards the metal shop. *Gotta be more careful. With her* and *Blade*. He rounded the corner and walked straight into the Knights.

"Yer late," Brain snapped. "Ya gettin' some more Sweet Irish Cream?"

"And if I was, so what? Blew her off and here I am," Rick drawled, glaring at Brain long enough for the other boy to drop his gaze.

"Do I have to tell ya again, Moneyman?" Blade asked lazily. Rick heard a soft hiss and backed off a couple of steps.

"Drop it, Blade. She's *not* a problem. I am a Knight," Rick said emphatically, wondering what it would take to convince Blade Jordan wasn't the problem Blade was making her out to be.

"Let's roll, boys," Blade said with a jerk of his head.

All five sauntered past the office as if to point out they were above the rules. In Blade's mind, they were. In Rick's mind, he was...well, he may not have been above the rules, but he was damn tired of being hassled. *Why can't everyone just leave me alone?* he thought miserably. *I like being with the Knights. They're my family.* He sighed loudly as the passed the office.

"Delaney still bustin' ya, man?" Blade asked as soon as they were out the front doors.

"Hell yes. Every single friggin' day, and yer little go round with the O'Reillys this mornin' didn't help. By now, he's called their old man and he'll have someone dog me all day. That's why ya've gotta leave Jor alone, man," Rick griped as he fell into his spot to Blade's left. Pup was in the middle and Crank was right behind the smallest Knight.

"Why don'cha challenge O'Reilly, man? Yer good 'nough to take 'im," Brain asked from his spot at Blade's right as they sauntered along.

"'Cause I like my freedom, man, and my Gran'd skin me alive if I did. I'm more scared of her than of anyone and that includes you, Blade," Rick said blandly.

"If ya got the gold, ya make the rules...right, boys?" Blade chuckled dryly, looking back at Rick as they continued towards the pool hall.

"Yep and I'll get a nice chunk of change when I hit eighteen, man, so I'm tryin' to keep my nose as clean as possible. Or, at the very least, make sure she doesn't find out." With that, Rick put the beginning of summer vacation out of his mind.

The rest of the day passed quickly, between the pool hall and hanging out in front of one of their favourite convenience stores. By suppertime, Rick was exhausted, thanks to his bad night's sleep and was ready to call it a day, but the rest of the Knights decided they wanted to see a movie. By the time they got to the theatre, though, the gang had picked up a shadow. Rick saw the unmarked car first. He muttered a soft curse and nudged Blade.

"Tail," he said quietly, nodding to the car behind them.

Blade swore as he saw the unmarked cop car. "How long?" he demanded.

"I dunno. Just picked 'em up a couple of blocks ago. Coulda shown up at Mahoney's," Rick mused, trying to think if he had seen the car before.

Blade cuffed Rick across the back of the head, stunning him momentarily. "Yer on lookout. Why didn't'cha call out?" he snarled.

Rick rubbed the back of his head and bit his tongue. "'Cause, if it was there, it wasn't visible. Anyone see Mahoney on the phone before we split?" Rick retorted, looked at the others.

Crank reluctantly nodded. "Didn't think anythin' of it, Blade. Sorry, man," he apologized, avoiding Blade's angry stare.

"Great. So much fer sneakin' in," Blade muttered. He stood, fuming, hands shoved deep in his pockets and his shoulders hunched. Rick knew the problem. Blade, as usual, was broke. That was why he stole so much. He just couldn't afford it.

Rick could, and had no problem helping out his friends. He reached for his wallet. "I got the tickets, guys. Let's go. The movie's starting," he said and led the way to the ticket counter. After getting their tickets and snacks, the five settled in the back row, keeping to the shadows.

"Thanks, Moneyman," Blade said quietly, choking slightly on the words. Rick grinned viciously in the darkness. He knew how much that one word hurt Blade to say.

"Payback fer this mornin'," Rick shrugged and settled in to watch what turned out to be a fairly good movie.

Once the movie let out, the cop car was long gone, and Rick breathed a little easier. It was wishful thinking on Blade's part that Mahoney had seen them steal anything and had called the cops. No one ever *saw* Blade take a thing, and if they did, a midnight visit from him was more than enough to convince them to look the other way. It was more likely Delaney had called O'Reilly about the incident with Jordan that morning and the inspector had sent someone to watch Rick, not the others.

It didn't take long for the gang to end up in the local park near Rick's house. Blade liked it because it wasn't well lit, even in summer. There were lots of trees and shadows, perfect places to hide. Rick felt uneasy the moment he set foot in the park. It reminded him too much of his recent nightmares.

They all sat around a picnic table, talking, laughing and planning their summer vacation. As the darkness deepened, Rick became quieter. It was eerie the way his dream was coming back to him. He almost expected Pup to notice some movement or other and for the gang to attack.

"Moneyman, wake up! I just asked ya the same question three times!" Blade snapped suddenly. Rick jumped as a knife thudded into the table, barely missing his hand.

"Christ, Blade! Chill, man. I'm friggin' exhausted. My old man had another playmate over last night and they partied, loudly, until two or three. Not to mention we were out until midnight or one. Drop it," Rick snapped back. Blade just glared at Rick who glared right back.

"Screw it, man, I'm outta here. I'll catch ya boys at the pool hall tomorrow afternoon," Rick continued as he stood. Blade started to pull him back, but Brain quickly leaned in to talk to his leader and the two began to mutter quietly.

Rick left the park and headed for home with a bad feeling he was going to be spending a lot of time in the emergency room at the hospital this summer. He didn't need Blade mad at him. Blade was not a nice guy when he was mad. *Oh well*, Rick thought philosophically, *how mad can the guy get?*

Chapter 2

Even the trees're cryin', Aunt Di, Rick thought sadly as the minister finished up the graveside service. He hadn't heard a word of it. He leaned against a willow with his arms around Jordan who held the umbrella over them both. Rain fell softly from the grey sky and dripped from the overhanging leaves. The rain easily hid the tears he shed at his aunt's death. Diane Attison had been driving to work one morning about a week earlier when a drunk driver hit her at high speed, killing her instantly. On the other side of the grave, Rick's cousin Megan sobbed in her dad's arms as the casket was lowered into the ground and out of sight.

Poor Megs, Rick thought as he watched her and her dad, Ian, climb into a waiting limo, almost stumbling in their sorrow. The only other lady in Rick's life, Megan Emily Attison, whom everyone called Nana, held the door open. Megan was Nana's namesake and looked just like her. Rick smiled sadly as he watched the limo drive away. Nana was really the only mother Rick had had since he was six and he loved her very much.

"Aren't you gonna follow?" Jordan asked as she snuggled closer.

"Naw. I hate funerals, and I can't stand sitting around someone's house listening to them talk about the 'dearly departed,' even if it's family," Rick replied sourly.

He held Jordan closer and watched as everyone left the graveyard. He just couldn't understand how something like this could happen. How could someone be that drunk at that time of the morning and able to drive at all? He shook his head and pulled Jordan even closer. He could feel her shivering.

"Cold, sweets?" he asked softly.

"A little," she admitted, then looked around. "We're all alone," she said quietly.

Rick smiled. "Just the way I like it," he said and pulled her around for a slow kiss.

"Beast," Jordan giggled when Rick let her go. She glanced at her watch and sighed. "You'd better take me home," she said softly. Reluctantly. "Before Daidí calls out the troops," she said, using the Gaelic word for Daddy.

Rick chuckled at the old-fashioned language she spoke as the pair began to wind their way through the graveyard, hand-in-hand. Jordan studied the headstones as they passed.

"Rick, is this a private cemetery?" she asked suddenly.

"I guess. This has been the only place the Attisons have been buried, at least around here, since they arrived in this country, oh, 150 years ago or so. We apparently founded Collingwood and now there's only the five of us in this part of the country. Me, Dad, Nana, Uncle Ian and Megs," Rick shrugged. It was ancient history to him.

"Here's one of the oldest graves," he pointed out as they walked. "Bruce MacGregor Attison. Attie's Son's how it's apparently translated."

Jordan looked around. "Isn't your grandfather buried around here?" she asked, as she studied the tombstones while they walked.

Rick pointed to a simple headstone a couple of rows away with a horse and stable carved into the granite. "Right there," he said softly. *Hey, Pops,* he thought sadly. His throat tightened as he remembered the gentle giant who had been his grandfather.

"Would things've been different if he'd lived, Rick? I remember he was strict, especially with you. You couldn't get away with anything," Jordan said, giggling, as they continued through the rain to the car.

"Do you mean – would I still be a Knight? Probably. Pops couldn't be there 24-7," Rick shrugged again.

He pulled Jordan into another hug as they reached Rick's car. It was actually his dad's Corvette, but since Michael didn't want to come to the funeral, he told Rick to take it. They just stood there, taking what comfort they could from each other.

"Rick!" Jordan whispered suddenly, terrified.

"Crap," Rick swore as he pulled back. Passing slowly by the graveyard was Brain's black Camaro. The driver's window was rolled down and Rick could see both Blade and Brain glaring at them. With a sudden squeal of tires on the wet pavement, the car roared away.

"You'd think that today, of all days, he'd leave you alone," Jordan complained bitterly as she climbed into the car. Rick slid in next to her, gave her leg a squeeze and tried to explain the problem for probably the hundredth time since Rick had joined the Knights in Grade Ten. They'd also been formally dating since then, even though they'd been together a lot longer than that, no matter how hard her family tried to prevent it. He could tell Jordan wasn't convinced and was relieved when she didn't pursue it.

"Look, sweets, I know he scares you, but I just can't convince him I can love you and still be a Knight. He sees anything outside of the gang as a distraction," Rick explained.

"Rick, does your uncle live far away?" Jordan asked, switching subjects abruptly as they drove back to her farm.

"Um, half an hour, an hour. Depends who's driving," Rick replied with a chuckle. "Why?"

"How come I've never seen your cousin before?" Jordan asked.

"They lived in Dundee, Scotland, where Megs was born. They came back when Megs was around 5, I guess, and settled on a farm in the next county," Rick explained. "Believe it or not, I don't think I've ever met her. Dad tends to stay away from family functions, especially when Uncle Ian's around. Apparently he and Dad don't get along too well." *Who does get along with my dad?* Rick thought sourly as he drove.

"What about school? She's close enough to attend Colonial High, isn't she? How come I've never seen her?" Jordan pressed, not realizing she was making Rick mad at her.

"Private schools, I guess. Why?" Rick asked again, annoyed.

"No reason, Rick. I just didn't remember seeing her, so I was curious," Jordan replied, a bit defensively.

Rick sighed as he realized he'd snapped at his girlfriend. Again. He couldn't understand where this sudden anger was coming from, and it honestly scared him at times. "Sorry, sweets. Didn't mean to jump all over you. It's just I don't know Megs that well. She's had a better life than me," Rick said bitterly. *Everyone's had a better life than me*, Rick thought, even more bitter at the world.

Jordan fell silent and just enjoyed the drive home. As they pulled up in front of her house, her dad was waiting on the front porch, scowling as Rick climbed out of the car. He escorted his girlfriend to the steps and kissed her good-bye.

"I'm heading over to Glencrest for the weekend. Call me," Rick said to her.

"Not on yer life, boy. Get outta here. Now," Seamus snapped. He led a protesting Jordan into the house and slammed the door behind them.

Rick seethed as he strode back to the car. No matter what he did or didn't do, Seamus hated him and Rick didn't know what he had done to deserve it. He treated Jordan like gold and was respectful whenever he came over to the house, yet Seamus hated him.

As he climbed back into the car, Rick debated heading back into Collingwood to drop it off. Unfortunately, that would mean he'd have to get Michael to bring him back to the ranch, complaining all the way. Rick was in no mood for that, not today. *Screw it*, he thought angrily. *Dad has other cars.*

He peeled out of Jordan's yard and drove the short distance to Glencrest. As usual, it was a beehive of activity, even in the rain. He parked in front of a single-storey house, set apart from the main house, and climbed out. A tanned, well-weathered farm hand walked over.

"How come you're not at Mr. Ian's?" he asked bluntly.

"Hello, Frank," Rick chuckled dryly as he climbed up onto the covered porch to get out of the rain.

Frank smiled back. "Sorry, lad. Hello, Rick. The service go...okay?" he asked softly. Rick shrugged and pretended not to see the tears in the older man's eyes. Diane Attison had obviously been a favourite of Frank's, since Rick knew the long-time Glencrest employee had no children of his own. Rick leaned on the rail and looked over the ranch for a few minutes to give Frank time to get himself back under control.

"Megs is a mess, Uncle Ian didn't look much better, and I figured the last thing they needed was one more person telling them how sorry they were for Aunt Diane's death, y'know? Even if it's family," Rick explained without turning his head.

"Besides, I need to clear my head. Be alone for a while, y'know? Cherokee ready for a ride?" Rick continued as he looked towards the barn.

"You're gonna go for a ride in this rain? Whatever. Yeah, Cherokee should be okay for a ride. He was worked a little earlier, but he should be cooled off by now. Stay out of the north pasture, please, directly behind the barn. The fence is being redone and I don't want him cut," Frank said and walked away.

Rick quickly changed into some old jeans he kept at the farm and took his black stallion for a long ride, duly avoiding the pasture in question. A couple of hours later, he returned, wet and muddy of course, but much more relaxed. He cleaned up Cherokee and mucked out some of the stalls he noticed needed to be done, before returning to the house, his sanctuary away from the crazy life he led. The physical labour felt almost as good as the ride had.

A hot shower and change of clothes later and Rick was ready once again to face the world. He called over to the main house to see about supper and got a surprise.

"Your Nana decided to stay at Mr. Ian's to help out for a couple of days, and I didn't know you were here, so I didn't make anything. Will you be alright?" the housekeeper asked, sniffling.

Rick looked in the well-stocked fridge. "Looks like I'm good, Martha. I'll whip something up, no worries. Nana did mention I was going to stay the weekend, didn't she?" Rick asked tentatively. He wasn't sure what he'd do if he couldn't stay.

"She may have, Rick, but with Miss Diane's death, I've probably forgotten most of what she told me this week," Martha sniffled again.

"That's cool, Martha. I just needed some quiet. Dad's been 'entertaining' again, and I need some undisturbed sleep. Lemme know if Nana comes home early, 'kay?" Rick said and hung up. It didn't take him long to whip up some steak, potatoes and frozen peas. Cooking was something he had learned to do in self-defence. Even on a good day, his dad burnt water and Rick really did like to eat decent meals instead of always having take-out. So he learned to cook and cook well. *Better than at home,* he chuckled to himself as he settled in the living room to watch T.V.

Half way through his favourite show later that night, his phone shrilled and shattered the comfortable silence. He sat in his easy chair and tried to calm his pounding heart. After the third ring, he snatched up the phone.

"What?" he growled. He was pretty sure he knew who it wasn't. It was way too late for either Nana or Jordan to be calling.

"Moneyman, one of these days, yer gonna believe I'm damn serious," Blade snapped back.

"Drop it, Blade. It was my aunt's funeral, for chrissake. Showin' up with my boys wouldn't've been in any taste, let alone good," Rick seethed, trying to control that strange burst of anger again. *He's gettin' to be as bad as my old man,* Rick fumed. *Now I have to ask* his *permission to do anythin'?*

"So ya found comfort in yer sweet Irish lady's arms. Isn't that nice?" Blade cooed. Rick flushed as he heard the others roar with laughter in the background.

"Now, yer hidin' out at Granny's and won't be around all weekend. Did ya ferget 'bout the rumble with the Slayers, boy? How the hell're ya gonna get back? Ask Granny to drive ya? Frig, that's gonna look real good when ya get dropped off like a baby. Why the hell did I let ya in?" Blade ranted on for several more minutes while Rick just listened patiently. He knew Blade would run out of things to say soon enough.

"Are ya finished?" Rick asked dryly as Blade finally paused for breath.

"Why? Got some sob story 'bout not comin' tomorrow?" Blade snapped again.

"If ya'd zip it fer a minute, ya'd find out I gots Dad's 'vette and I'll meet y'all at the vacant lot by nine as planned, unless I come in early. Then I'll meet ya at the pool hall. Now drop it, Blade. I'm here fer some peace and quiet from my old man. Ya don't like it? Too bad," Rick snarled and slammed down the phone.

He stood in the kitchen, struggling to calm down. Every time Blade pulled something like this, Rick could feel a noose closing tighter and tighter around his throat. The tighter it got, the more Rick struggled and the more control Blade seemed to gain over him. Sometimes Rick wondered if he had any control left over himself.

Rick stormed to his bedroom, threw himself onto his bed, and fumed. He was getting tired of arguing with both his dad and Blade, seemingly about everything. He didn't know how he was going to sleep tonight. He was shaking with anger, and couldn't seem to do anything to calm down. He got up and began to pace, his mind going a thousand miles a minute.

Having his dad's Corvette, though, was going to be a big problem. Where they were going tomorrow, the car would be stripped faster than you could say "Corvette," if it wasn't stolen outright. But the more Rick thought about it as he calmed down, the more he realized he just had to go into town early enough to drop the car off and pick up one of his dad's trucks.

That'll work, Rick finally decided as he continued to pace. *Now how can I get Blade to lemme take on Ricardo? Wonder what the word on the street is?* A glance at his clock made Rick realize it was almost midnight and he would need to get some sleep if he was going to be any good to the Knights in the morning.

After a night of pretty restful sleep, and thankfully no dreams, Rick got up, took a long shower, and, once again dressed in his gear, was ready to face the world. He had breakfast, cleaned up the house and slid into the car around noon. He drove into town and parked out front of the house. He opened the front door and heard his dad entertaining again. Rick just snorted and grabbed the keys to one truck. He didn't even leave a note. *Not like the old man gives a damn anyway*, Rick thought as he punched a code into the door of the garage.

Climbing in, he went cruising. He found what he was looking for outside of Mahoney's. Opening the window, he whistled sharply. A tall, lanky boy peeled himself away from his friends and sauntered over to Rick.

"Yo, Moneyman," he greeted the teen with a nod.

"Yo, Jimmy. What's the word?" Rick asked his friend as he looked around.

"Word's out, so take care. The cops know somethin's goin' down, so they're watchin' the usual sites, includin' the vacant lot where you're gonna be. I'm gonna try and direct them away from you, if that's cool. Not like Blade'll care, but I'll help if I can. This is the biggest rumble since the Slayers took on the Hit Squad and word is Ricardo and Miguel're arguin' over Blade," Jimmy said with a grin.

"Who wants who?" Rick asked. His eyes may have been roaming and watching the world around him, but his ears and head were solely on what Jimmy was saying.

"Miguel wants Blade. Figures he can take him, blade on blade," Jimmy snorted.

"And Ricardo wants Blade 'cause he's lead?" Rick asked, nonchalantly. Inside he was jumping for joy. It would kill two birds with one stone, literally. He'd get Ricardo and Blade would take Miguel, the most troublesome Slayer, out. No one was better than Blade with a knife. *What the hell's Miguel thinkin'?* Rick wondered with a shake of his head. *No one's better than Blade, not even me and I'm pretty damn good.*

"Ricardo figures he's earned the right to take Blade, but Miguel's the better knife fighter of the two, even if he sucks compared to Blade," Jimmy continued with a chuckle.

"Could I take Ricardo?" Rick wondered idly, hoping Jimmy would know Ricardo's weaknesses. The other teen didn't disappoint.

"Easily, Moneyman, real easily. He always drops his left when he's fightin'. Somethin' to do with his shoulder. Another weakness is his left knee. Broke it a couple years back and it's never healed right. Take out either one of those, he's on the deck. Just watch your back tonight, man," Jimmy advised and walked away, slipping the twenty from Rick into his pocket.

Rick smiled as he headed over to the pool hall, looking for a couple of his other contacts. These were boys who wanted to be Knights, but just weren't quite right. They didn't have the look or the instinct, or whatever. Blade never really told Rick why he didn't tap them, but he didn't. They were so desperate to be a Knight, though, they would do anything to get noticed by Blade. It made some of them good contacts on the street, and Rick milked them every chance he got.

"No trouble now, y'hear me, Moneyman?" Antonio called, frowning, from behind the counter as Rick sauntered on in. Blade and the others were obviously playing in the back room if Antonio was already warning him about trouble, but Rick wasn't ready to join them yet. He wanted to confirm Jimmy's story. He slid up to another table and spoke quietly to a couple of older boys for a few minutes, then threw down a couple of bills on the table.

"Yo, Brain," Rick greeted Blade's second-in-command as he sauntered into the back room. Brain just nodded as he took his shot.

"He's over there, and he wants t' see ya," Crank said, motioning to a booth.

"Blade," Rick greeted his leader as he slid into the booth.

"Moneyman, do ya have any idea how stupid y'are?" Blade asked quietly.

It was going to be one of those meetings. Rick sighed and shook his head as he heard the anger in Blade's voice. "Look, Blade, yer old man never spent every night, all night, carryin' on with yer old lady, never mind a new playmate every night. After a while, between stayin' out with ya and his partyin', I'm exhausted and I need some place quiet to crash. Otherwise, I'm no good to ya and yer quick enough to point *that* out. So, I go to Nana's. What's the big deal, man?" Rick asked with a shrug, trying not to let on how nervous he was.

"Yer becomin' a pain in the ass, Moneyman. First the chick, then ya split out to Granny's and then yer hangin' up on me. Wha'cha think I should do, Moneyman?" Blade asked quietly, but with venom, as he leaned in to get right in Rick's face.

"Take it out on Miguel. Word on the street is he thinks he can take ya," Rick said as he leaned back. He didn't want to be within reach of Blade's steel or his fists for that matter.

Blade threw his head back and roared. "*He* thinks he can take me? He's the worst knife fighter they have," Blade chortled when he could finally talk.

"Gimme Ricardo. I can take 'im," Rick pleaded.

"He's Brain's," Blade snapped, back in control.

"Santana wants him. Tomas wants Pup and Julio's gearin' fer Crank," Rick said with a nod towards the door.

"Yer talkin' to the trash again?" Blade glared at Rick.

"Has Jimmy or his crew ever been wrong?" Rick retorted with a snort.

Rick turned his head as Pup and Brain came up to stand beside him. "Give 'im Ricardo, Blade. He'll get his butt whipped," Brain chuckled nastily.

Not likely, Rick thought as he hid a smile at what he knew. That's why he talked to the "trash" as Blade called them. Blade never did, and Rick would go to a fight with a distinct advantage. If Blade didn't give Rick the one he wanted to fight, well, more often than not, Rick would keep his secrets to himself. It might pay off later.

Blade fell silent, then waved everyone away while he brooded. With a shrug, Rick joined the other Knights at the pool table and proceeded to wipe the table clean. Several times.

That night, Rick followed Brain to the vacant lot on the south side of town. He was bouncing with excitement and anger. He was so ready to pound on whichever Slayer Blade let him have, he could hardly contain himself. The five Knights stood in the shadows and waited for the other gang to arrive.

"Blade," Ricardo nodded a greeting as the Slayers gathered around their leader.

"Yo. Match up," Blade replied with a sneer.

"I wan'cha. I can take ya," Miguel snapped as he shoved Ricardo towards Rick and pulled his steel, weaving back and forth, waiting for Blade to make a move.

"Moneyman, he's yer's. I'm gonna love this," Blade grinned viciously.

That was all Rick and the others needed. Rick's fist flashed out and caught Ricardo square in the jaw. The bigger boy stumbled back, but recovered quickly. His first punch caught Rick in the ribs, almost driving Rick to his knees. All around the two, the fighting raged, but Rick heard none of it. He was concentrating on Ricardo, watching and waiting for the Slayer's next move.

Two more solid punches landed in Rick's side and he felt something crack. *Must be a rib,* he thought as he grimaced in pain, then ignored it. He connected with two shots of his own and danced away. As he and Ricardo circled, Rick could see he was the only Knight left. The others had finished so quickly they had circled around the pair, cheering Rick on.

"What's the matter, boy? Am I too much fer ya?" Ricardo taunted.

Rick flushed as Ricardo continued to taunt him. Seeing his opening suddenly, Rick moved quickly. A solid punch connected with Ricardo's left shoulder, making him cry out in pain. With a vicious laugh, Rick spun and kicked solidly at Ricardo's bad knee. Ricardo screamed as his knee shattered, but Rick wasn't done yet. As the other boy was falling to the ground, Rick's last uppercut knocked Ricardo out and the Slayer leader lay in a crumpled heap, like the rest of his gang.

That last punch also cracked Rick's hand. "Don't call me 'boy'," Rick grated, then groaned. "Damn. I think I broke my hand on that jackass' hard head, not to mention the ribs he's broken." Gently probing, he winced as he found at least one. *Nana's gonna kill me*, he thought as he gasped at the pain in his side.

Blade came over and stood by Rick. "Good, Moneyman. Yer learnin'. Now split 'fore the cops show," Blade ordered as all five scattered to the wind.

Chapter 3

July passed quickly for Rick and the Knights. Word spread rapidly through Collingwood the Slayers had been thoroughly trounced by the Knights, whose reps just grew some more. Miguel nearly died from the stab wounds he had received from Blade, but steadfastly refused to say who attacked him. He wasn't stupid. Blade just laughed as the cops watched him. They knew what had happened – they just couldn't prove it.

Rick had indeed cracked his hand and broken a couple of ribs in the fight. Nana wasn't very happy when she saw him less than a week later at her store with his hand in a cast and his ribs taped up.

"Lad, when're you gonna learn?" she snapped. "Fighting's no way to spend the summer. Keep it up, and I swear I'll haul you out to the ranch and put you to work in the barns instead of here in the store," she threatened.

"C'mon, Nana, it was for honour. The Slayers were bragging they could take us and Blade wasn't 'bout to let that happen," Rick protested weakly as he squirmed under Nana's baleful stare. He hated when she was mad at him and he knew he was doing it more and more.

He got up and knelt by her side. "Nana, please don't be mad. I'm sorry. It wouldn't have happened if I had hit him right," Rick explained softly, trying to get her to understand. The last thing he wanted was Nana mad at him. If he didn't shape up, she would bring him to Glencrest and Blade would be really choked.

Nana smiled as she looked down at her favourite grandson. She sighed as she looked at the bandana covering his thick hair. She ran a hand over his head and pulled him close for a hug. "Get up, lad. I'm not really mad at you, just worried. I really wish you would get away from those boys before something horrible happens to you. They scare me, lad, especially that oldest boy, Blade? isn't it? What about Jordan O'Reilly? Are you still seeing her?" Nana asked.

"When I can sneak away from the Knights and she can escape her dad and her brother. Which isn't often," Rick snorted as he stood.

"Lad, she's a fine lady. Think about it – what're you willing to lose for this gang of yours?" Nana asked as Rick left for the day.

Rick wandered slowly back home, thinking. That was the second time someone had asked him that. *Did everyone think the Knights were that bad? Was he willing to lose* anything *for the Knights?* He was lost in thought until he heard the faintest scraping of a boot along the gravel on the sidewalk, just loud enough to catch his attention. He smiled. *When's Blade gonna learn? Those boots suck,* Rick thought, as he kept walking. He tensed as he heard the slightest scrape of Blade's knife on its sheath, then dropped to his knees. Blade's knife thudded into the post just millimetres from where Rick's head had been.

"Hey, Blade. Boys," Rick said, climbing to his feet as if nothing had happened and nodding a greeting to Brain, Crank and Pup.

"Five bucks, man," Brain chortled as he elbowed Blade in the ribs. "He heard ya comin'."

"Lucky guess, Brain," Blade snapped as he grabbed his knife and handed over the five bucks he had swiped from his mother.

Rick shook his head and grinned at Blade's discomfort. "Sorry, man. Heard ya. It's yer damn boots. The tread's too deep and they pick up little rocks. They scrape. And this time, I heard ya pull yer steel," Rick said as he fell into place, walking beside Blade.

"My place, guys? It's closest," Rick continued.

"Cool."

This became a regular part of Rick's summer routine. He spent the mornings working at the store with Nana and hung out every afternoon and night with the Knights. When Blade mentioned the amount of time Rick spent away from the gang,

Rick merely pointed out it was a summer job and he was getting paid to work.

"That money pays fer the movies, Blade. Y'know, the days when the ticket boy won't look the other way," Rick said softly. Blade growled, but dropped the matter.

August, though, began on a not-so-bright note. Rick got up that first Friday morning to the sounds of Michael and Judy laughing in the kitchen. Showered and dressed, Rick sauntered downstairs and grabbed his breakfast.

"Good morning, Richard," Judy said as she poured herself another cup of coffee.

"Wow, you must be really good, lady. He hasn't kept a playmate this long in, oh, five or six months," Rick said dryly, ignoring the rosy blush on her cheeks.

Michael flushed a deep red and backhanded Rick off his chair, swearing viciously at his son. Rick slowly peeled himself off the floor, wiped the blood from his lip and snarled, "Wanna try that again, old man?"

Michael raised his hand to do just that and suddenly found himself on the floor looking up at the barely recognizable face of his son. "Ya lay a hand on me again, ya bastard, and I'll make sure Blade leaves nothing identifiable," Rick snapped and stormed out of the house.

By the time he got to Nana's store, the blood had dried and he had calmed down. Somewhat anyway. "Morning, James," he called to the manager as he sauntered to Nana's office. She was on the phone when Rick came in. She waved him to a chair and continued her call.

"Yes, Martha, that's right. Tomorrow night. Since they're settled now, I wanna get everyone together. Tell Frank to mow and trim. See you tonight. Give my love to them." Nana hung up and stared at her grandson.

"Who hit you?" she demanded as Rick flopped into a chair.

"Dad," Rick said with a shrug.

"Wonderful. What am I gonna do with him?" Nana asked, exasperated. She was pretty sure this wasn't the first time

Michael had hit his son, but it *was* the first time she'd ever seen the proof on Rick's cheek.

"Nothing, Nana. Told him if he did it again, he'd answer to the Knights. *That's* why I have them, Nana. They'll protect me in a heartbeat," Rick said with a shrug, knowing Nana didn't really understand.

"Enough, " Nana said sharply. "You'll just have to mend your fences with your father. Tomorrow night, I want you both at the ranch to have supper with Megan and Ian," Nana said.

"They here for a visit?" Rick wondered. Now he'd finally get to meet his cousin.

"No, lad. They sold their farm and moved in with me," Nana said, sadly.

"Too hard after Aunt Diane died?" Rick asked, shrewdly.

Nana nodded. "Especially for Megan. They were so close. Ian's gonna take over managing Hollyhock's here and Jesse's gonna move onto running the feed mill. Megan'll be in your school and I expect you to behave tomorrow," Nana warned as Rick stood and clocked in.

"Tell that to Dad," Rick retorted good-naturedly as he left the office to begin work.

Saturday was warm and cloudless. Rick lounged in bed. It had been a late night with the boys and it had ended badly. Rick found himself in Emergency, again, for another 10 stitches, after Blade sliced his ribs for probably the third time that summer after he found out Rick was going to be at the farm.

Oh well, Rick thought philosophically, *Nana has the money so I'll do what she says.* He climbed out of bed and showered carefully. He changed the bandage over the stitches and dressed in sweats and a muscle shirt. His dad was alone at the table when Rick came down, but Rick knew he was heading to Judy's for the day.

"Be ready at four, boy," Michael snapped and left.

"Morning to you too, Dad," Rick said sourly to the empty room and got his breakfast.

He spent most of the day on the front porch, just listening to his favourite metal band and reading. It was so rare that he got any time alone, so when he did, he relished it. He knew he could've been with the Knights, but he also knew it would've been impossible to get away and Nana wanted Rick at this supper.

By 4 p.m., Rick was on the porch in full gear, waiting for his dad. Michael screeched to a halt in front of the house and honked the horn sharply. With a sigh, Rick climbed to his feet and walked over to the Corvette. He almost gagged at the reek of alcohol that wafted from Michael when he opened the door. After buckling himself in, Rick cranked open the window and held his hand out to his dad. *Christ, I'm not his kid, I'm his friggin' babysitter*, Rick thought sourly.

"Gimme the spare set, Dad. You've already had too many," Rick said blandly.

Without a word, Michael dug out the other set of keys and tossed them to Rick, then screamed away from the curb. He sped through Collingwood and headed out to the ranch. Judging by the reckless way Michael was driving, Rick knew this was going to be a long day. Not what he needed.

As Michael turned the final corner, Rick studied the farm as if seeing it for the first time. The two-storey white house with its wide veranda stood like a sentinel over a smaller, single storey house just to the east. The smaller house had been built for Rick a year earlier when things had become almost unbearable at home. Rick could see the blue and white paint had been freshened since he had last been to the farm almost a month ago and the swing which sat on his porch waiting for visitors who never came was new.

Nana's flower and vegetable gardens were in full bloom, and all around the finely-manicured lawns were flower pots and baskets filled to overflowing with a wide variety of plants, the flowers vibrant against the dark green lawns. Nana loved her plants, Rick knew, and took great pride in making sure everything always looked perfect.

He looked down the driveway at the barn. He thought the doors were new and it had a fresh coat of paint, also done since his last visit to Glencrest. *Didn't I help Frank do that just last summer?* Rick mused with a smile. The horses had been turned out into the paddock and Rick spied his beautiful stallion, Cherokee, standing next to the mare he knew was Megan's, a beautiful dun-coloured horse named Dundee Mystique. Both horses were part of the full blood American Quarter Horse line Nana raised on the ranch for show jumping and rodeos.

As Michael pulled up, Rick saw Nana standing on the veranda by the table, which was covered in a white and blue checkered tablecloth. She was helping Martha secure it with clamps so it wouldn't blow away in the gentle breeze. She turned at the sound of the car and waved before turning back to what she was doing.

Nana was wearing the only outfit Rick ever remembered her wearing at the ranch, whether working or entertaining visitors. It was her way of reminding people she worked on this farm, and didn't just give orders. The jeans were deep blue and her long sleeved cowboy-style shirt was also ice-blue and white checkers, Glencrest's colours. Her salt-and-pepper hair was braided, as usual, and hung down her back. Over it was a straw cowboy hat which also hung down her back by its string.

Rick swaggered around the corner. He could hear Nana talking to someone standing in the flower garden. He stopped at the foot of the stairs and slowly looked around; he sensed someone staring at him. He saw a slender, yet graceful, dark-haired girl standing by the edge of the garden, who quickly turned away from him. He didn't get a good look at her, but thought she seemed familiar. *Wonder who the chick is?* he thought as he sauntered up the stairs.

At the top, he gave Nana a hug. "How are you, lad?" she asked.

"Never better, Nana," Rick lied, hiding a wince at the sudden stab of pain her hug had caused. At 5'10" tall, he towered over Nana's 5'5" height. His electric blue eyes roamed the yard automatically, as if seeking someone or something. He knew his blonde hair was barely visible under the bandana and he shifted it slightly so "Money" was squarely in front. Under the hot sun, he was uncomfortable in his black jeans and the leather jacket, but he wasn't ready to take the jacket off yet. The silver stitching around the bottom which looked like a random pattern was actually the words "Black Knights" stitched over and over. His black cowboy boots echoed on the wood as he turned to look for the girl again.

He was startled to find she was right behind him. She was wearing a distinctive perfume which he *should've* been able to smell miles away, yet there she stood, just inches away. *She was close enough to touch me. I must be slippin'*, Rick fumed at his laziness. *I never even heard her move. Blade'll kill me. I never let anyone get that close, not even my boys.*

"Megan, lass, this is your cousin, Richard," Nana said, as Megan stuck the bouquet she had picked from the garden into a crystal vase on the table. She moved with the grace of a dancer and her long, dark hair, left hanging loosely down her back, fluttered in a sudden gust of wind.

So this is my cousin, she thought as she held out her hand. "Nice to finally meet you, Richard," she said with just the faintest trace of a Scottish accent. Her smile faded and her hand dropped limply to her side, as Rick just stood there, leaning against the rail, gazing at her. Suddenly, Megan felt like a bird who'd been caught by the cat.

So she decided to stare back at her cousin, trying to figure him out. She noticed right away there was the faintest sheen of sweat near the edge of the bandana, so he must have been roasting in the black leather jacket. His eyes would flicker back and forth between her and the rest of the yard. Megan finally decided Rick was cute, in spite of the icy hardness she saw in his eyes. He had the face of an angel, but it had hardened into a mask of granite. She suddenly knew not to make him angry.

So this is my little cousin, Rick mused as he studied Megan from behind half-closed eyes. She was shorter than he was, only about 5'6" or so, but her slender body moved so gracefully she gave the impression of being much taller. He could see the hurt in her hazel eyes at his lack of manners, but he honestly didn't know what to say to her. She brushed away a strand of hair that had blown into her face, just as his hand twitched to do the same thing. The longer he studied her, the more he felt the urge to grab her and pull her next to him. He wanted – no, *needed* – to protect her.

Nana cleared her throat discretely and Rick jumped. He had forgotten Nana was even there. "Name's Rick," Rick replied shortly as he turned away from those mesmerizing hazel eyes. The urge to protect his cousin grew stronger and Rick realized who he wanted to protect Megan from. At least right now.

"That's enough, Richard. Act your age," Michael snapped as he climbed onto the veranda. He ran an agitated hand through his dirty blonde hair and tried to look like he was happy to be at the farm. The sneer on his face and the barely-hidden disgust in his light icy-cold blue-green eyes told a different story, though.

Rick sighed softly as he watched his dad. He noticed a slight weave in his dad's step and was glad he already had the spare keys. It was gonna be one of those visits, Rick just knew, one where he would eventually want to crawl under a rock and hide. *Somethin' tells me my little cuz's gonna be in Dad's sights all day long,* Rick thought bitterly, though he couldn't really say why he felt that way. *Just friggin' wonderful.* He stepped up beside Megan and glared at his dad. Michael didn't even notice.

"Ian," Michael said, as his brother came out of the house. His tone seemed to indicate he really didn't care if he ever saw Ian again.

"Michael, I'm sure you remember your niece, Megan," Ian said just as coldly as he steered his daughter away from Michael without giving her the chance to greet him. Wordlessly, Rick joined them on the far side of the table as Michael called loudly for a scotch and water. After a couple of false starts, Nana managed to get a stilted conversation going.

Over the next couple of hours, Megan tried to get to know her uncle and her cousin. Of the two, she definitely preferred to talk to Rick – when Rick talked, that is – since Michael made her skin crawl for some reason. Rick stayed quietly in the background for the most part, answering questions in short, one-syllable answers whenever possible. He startled her once, by gently brushing her hair back as an errant breeze blew it across her face. In that single touch, Megan could actually feel him trembling with anger.

She was wondering what she could have possibly done to him to make him so mad, when she saw him starring daggers at his father. Unaware Megan was watching him so intently, Rick drew a deep, shuddering breath and wrenched his gaze away from his dad. Turning, he stared out at the farm until he was under better control. Unfortunately, he was so tense and restless he couldn't sit still. More than once he got up to pace the length of the veranda, and, as well as Nana maintained the house, the wooden veranda would squeak as he paced.

Rick wondered about his cousin. Megan, he figured, was little Miss Prim and Proper. Totally different from him. He was sure she was used to getting her way and figured being an only child would make you that way. And yet, there was something about her which called to Rick's protective nature. Something that made him want to shelter her from everything, just as he tried to protect Jordan. And that included the Knights. *What's wrong with me?* he wondered angrily as he leaned against the rail and looked at his family.

As he brooded, Nana turned to ask Megan a question and frowned when she saw what Rick was wearing. It was as if she had just noticed the jacket and bandana, but something in Nana's suddenly steely eyes told Rick she had noticed them right away and had chosen to ignore them until that moment.

"Today, of all days, you had to be with those awful boys?" Nana demanded.

"Look, Nana, we've gone over this a million times. The Knights're my friends, alright? And I wasn't with them today," Rick sighed harshly.

Nana didn't say anything. She just continued to stare at her grandson. After a moment's hesitation, he reached up and jerked the bandana off, shoving it into his jacket pocket and running his fingers through his thick hair to comb it.

Still, Nana continued to stare until Rick was shifting from foot to foot. Finally, he shrugged off the leather jacket and tossed it over the back of his chair. *Here we go again,* he thought in frustration, turning his back to her. *Why can't she leave me alone?* He stood at the rail, angry and hurt.

"What's wrong with his friends, Nana?" Megan asked curiously. *He's definitely better looking without that silly bandana on,* she thought as she looked at Rick.

"They're thugs. I've tried to get Rick away from them repeatedly, but, as you can see, he just doesn't listen to me. Of course, if his father would be a father, this wouldn't've happened. Michael, can't you do something about your son?" Nana pleaded.

"Since when do I care 'bout him, Mother? You know that," Michael said, dismissing Rick and his friends with a shrug. Rick winced inwardly at Michael's casual dismissal, while Megan gasped out loud. Nana frowned, but before they could get into an argument about it, Frank dashed up.

"Sorry to interrupt, Mrs. Attison, but I need Miss Megan and Mr. Ian. Rick, too, if he can come. Mystique, Cherokee and Thunder got outta the paddock and cut up their legs on those unfinished barbed wired fences in the north pasture," Frank gasped out, trying to catch his breath.

Megan and Ian quickly stood up, while Rick looked up in surprise. Even though he hadn't been over to ride his black stallion in a long time, Cherokee was still his horse and his responsibility. Ian moved swiftly down the stairs, but, for some odd reason, Michael moved in front of Megan, blocking her.

"Deal with it yourself, fool. You're the hired help. That's what you get paid for, dummy. Can't you see there's company here, or are you blind? Sit down, girl," he snapped, slurring his words slightly and pushed Megan back towards her chair. Startled, she was thrown off balance and stumbled, almost falling over a chair. Rick grabbed her, the desire to protect her almost overwhelming. It reminded him of how he felt about a slender young girl living on the next farm over.

Once he had her steady, Rick turned to his father and snarled, "Leave her alone, old man. Mystique's her horse and her responsibility. C'mon, cuz." The two teens dashed down the stairs. They could still hear Nana's ringing tones halfway to the barn.

"Thanks, Rick," Megan began as they caught up to Ian and Frank at the barn.

"Don't thank me yet, cuz, 'cause you don't know squat about me. But I don't let my dad push me around and I'm not about to let him start on you," Rick interrupted harshly. He moved quickly towards the barn where he could see Cherokee fighting with the hands, leaving Megan standing, stunned, in the pathway.

Chapter 4

A couple of hours later, Rick, Megan and Ian returned to the back porch, tired and dirty, but satisfied their horses were going to be fine. Martha had the rest of the supper on the table while Frank was standing at the barbeque, cooking the steaks.

"Rick, your grandmother wanted me to remind you there'd be a change of clothes at the guest house. She thought you'd probably wanna clean up," Martha said. Rick nodded sharply and headed towards the only place he considered home. It'd also give him some time to re-establish his control. Otherwise, he was going to flatten his dad by the end of the night.

Megan and Ian were quicker to return to the porch after changing than Rick, but then, they had a shorter distance to walk. All three had just sat down at the table with refreshed drinks when Nana and Michael came out of the house, arguing loudly.

"Michael, I don't understand where your money goes. You work hard. Your company, I'm told, is quite successful, yet this is the third time in three months you've asked *me* for money. What's going on? Where's it going?" Nana scolded as if Michael was a child instead of a grown man.

Michael frowned. "Don't worry about it, Mom. Just gimme the money and leave me alone, 'kay? You don't need to know." Turning away from his mother, Michael sat down, called to Frank to bring him a steak, medium-rare, and for Martha to bring him another scotch and water. *How many's that now?* Rick wondered sourly as he waited to be served. Michael's coat was hanging on his chair and Rick, very slowly and carefully, reached into his dad's pocket and grabbed the other set of car keys, all the while keeping an eye on his dad. He'd drive home.

Stunned, Nana sat down slowly at the table. Supper was strained and quiet, to say the least. Rick kept his head down, ate quickly, grabbed another pop from the ice bucket and stood at the rail, staring at the farm as the others finished. He could hear the strained murmur of conversation behind him, but just ignored it and continued to brood. He knew why his dad needed the money, but he wasn't about to endure any abuse from Michael just to get some kind of petty revenge, no matter how tempting it was.

Sighing, Rick let his thoughts wander as he wished for a break from the miserable home life he had. As he stared out at the beauty around him, he wondered if he could talk Nana into letting him stay the night. He didn't want to go home with his dad. By the time they got home, Michael would either be passed out in the passenger seat or wound up and ready to fight. Neither prospect was appealing to Rick. *I really wish I could just stay here,* Rick thought as he leaned on the rail.

"Rick?" Nana called from the table. When Rick didn't answer right away, Nana called again and then a third time, each time a little louder until Rick looked up, startled. Megan giggled. Rick glared at her until she lowered her head in fear. The angry look in his eyes made her shiver. Raising her head, she smiled in apology and Rick nodded slightly. *Message delivered and received,* he thought proudly.

"Sorry, Nana," Rick said as he sauntered back to the table.

"That's okay, lad. I could see you were thinking hard. Perhaps I just didn't call loud enough the first time," Nana said as she smiled.

"Anyway, Rick, would you help Megan get around the school for the first couple of days?" Nana asked with a smile for Megan.

While waiting for Rick to answer, Ian caught his brother's eye and walked into the house. Scowling, Michael followed Ian to the library. It was far enough away no one on the veranda would be able to hear the two brothers arguing. And Ian knew they were going to argue.

On the veranda, Rick's eyes narrowed as he considered Nana's request. "Aw, c'mon, Nana, no one likes to baby-sit someone," he started to complain.

Megan sat up sharply and glared at her cousin. Rick couldn't help but smile at her indignation. "Gottcha! Relax, cuz, I didn't mean it. 'Course I'll take care of her, Nana, don't worry. I'll meet you inside the front door on the first day of school, near the pond in the student lounge, Megs. Trust me, you can't miss it," Rick said, chuckling. He decided he liked his cousin, no matter how prim and proper she seemed. *And Blade ain't gonna like it,* Rick thought sourly.

"You can introduce her to anyone in school, except those hoodlums in your gang," Nana said firmly. Rick nodded as he realized there were only two people he wanted to introduce Megan to and they'd take care of the rest. He grabbed pops for both him and Megan, and snagged a couple squares from the dessert tray before settling back in his chair to get to know Megan a little better.

"So, Megs, here's the thing. I don't know you. You and your dad had a place over in Clearsholme. So really – why move here?" Rick asked as he slumped down in his chair.

Megan hesitated, unsure of how much to say. After all, she'd just met this guy – *and they were cousins* – only a couple of hours ago. Nana smiled and moved away from the teens; she knew it was important for them to get to know each other on their own terms. It took a few minutes, but gradually, Megan allowed herself to tell him about her mom's accident. "So then Nana suggested we move here, just about a month ago. What 'bout you?" Megan asked. *We're cousins and he's a total stranger,* Megan realized. *That's so weird.*

Rick stiffened. But before he could form an answer that didn't involve snapping Megan's head off, Nana interrupted gently, having realized Ian and Michael were gone. "Lass, it's getting late. Go find your father and uncle. Michael and Rick might wanna think about going home soon." Megan nodded, brushed the crumbs off her jeans, rose gracefully, and went in search of the missing brothers.

Sighing in relief, Rick was glad Nana had stepped in. Rick leaned his head in his hands and tried to calm down. His life hadn't been easy, and Nana did her best to keep others, even family, from asking about it. Deep down inside, Rick knew this was what kept him in the gang. They didn't care about his past, just his presence.

His mom always called him "Ritchie," which led to being bullied in Grade 1. The other kids called him "Ritchie Rich," because of the family money and Rick hadn't taken the name-calling lightly. There had been some great fistfights in the first couple of years of school and Nana had bailed her grandson out more than once.

Unknown to everyone, his parents had been having marriage problems for some time. He and his older brother, Nelson, had come home about two months after Rick had started Grade 1 to find their mom gone and their dad, as usual, passed out on the living room couch. Nothing Rick could do would wake his father. When Michael finally came to, Rick told him Mommy wasn't home and he was hungry and Nelson wouldn't feed him. Michael was so angry he had backhanded Rick and told him it was his fault Mommy had left. Rick fled to his room, bawling. Nothing Nelson or Nana did or said could wipe away the angry and bitter words Michael had said that day.

Now, Rick lived with that shame every day. For ten long years, Rick had lived with his father's anger and apathy towards him. Nelson was lucky – he ran away when he was 15 and hadn't set foot in the house since. Rick didn't even try, since Nana had told him if he left, he would get nothing from her. It was the only thing Nana could use to keep Rick where she could keep an eye on him. Nelson she trusted on his own, Rick not so much.

Usually, Michael would just ignore his youngest son. Occasionally, especially if Michael had had problems with his drinking and gambling, he would taunt Rick, trying to goad his son into a violent rage. Unfortunately, it worked and now Rick had a bad reputation.

Rick soon learned to taunt his father just as well as Michael taunted him, especially about the number of different ladies Michael would bring home. It was a new one almost every week. Eventually, tired of being ignored, Rick's anger grew so much he was involved in more and more fights at school. It was the only way he could get his father's attention.

Nana did her best to keep Rick from getting into too much trouble by putting Rick in anger management sessions. They had worked until Rick was about 15 when Rick had somehow managed to get involved with the Knights. Rick had become more involved over the last year, especially in petty theft and vandalism. More often than not, the gang was given warnings, since Blade intimidated their victims into not pressing charges.

Rick always claimed the gang gave him the respect and attention he couldn't get from his father. Nana didn't believe Rick for a minute and knew the gang was going to get Rick into serious trouble one day. The day after Rick joined the Knights was the day Nana built the guesthouse for Rick and let him spend as much time there as possible. It got him away from his father, but more importantly, it got him away from the gang.

While Rick and Nana chatted on the porch, Megan headed into the house. She'd noticed Rick was relieved to not answer her about his family. Megan just smiled to herself. She was patient. She'd get the story out of Rick eventually, but when would really be up to him. *Oh well,* she shrugged philosophically, putting the entire conversation out of her mind as she searched for her father and her uncle. The first person she checked with was Martha.

"They're in the library, Miss Megan," Martha said with a frown. "There was some awful yelling a little while ago."

Megan nodded her thanks and went to the library. The door was slightly ajar, as if the last person in thought they had closed it, but even if it had been closed completely, Megan was sure she would have heard her father and uncle.

"What do you think you are? My keeper?" Michael yelled.

"No, but I *am* Mother's heir, despite being younger than you, and I *will* protect her even from her own son. I wanna know what you're doing demanding money from Mother. What's going on that you need $30,000 three times in three months!?" Ian shouted back.

"None of your damned business! I can demand money if I want and I don't have to explain it to anyone, especially you!" Michael roared. Megan froze at the anger and hatred in her uncle's voice. Whatever they were arguing about wasn't good. Although Megan was scared to interrupt, she knocked loudly on the door. Instantly, the two voices fell silent.

"Daddy?" Megan called tentatively, tapping at the door again.

"What, lass?" Ian replied roughly as he jerked the door open. His face was flushed with anger and Megan could see he was struggling not to yell at her for the interruption.

"Is everything okay, Daddy?" Megan asked softly. Her father took a deep breath and nodded sharply. Taking that as a sign not to ask questions, Megan raised her voice so Michael could hear her. "Nana says it's getting late and she'd like you both to return to the veranda."

Ian ran a hand through his hair in frustration. "Alright, lass. Tell Nana we'll be right there," he said gravely. Megan hesitated, not wanting to leave. Ian smiled and gave her shoulder a quick squeeze, then firmly closed the door behind him and turned back to his brother.

"I don't know what game you're playing, Michael, but I won't let this go," Ian said softly and menacingly, his Scottish accent thick. "And leave Mother alone."

Seething, Michael stormed past Ian, out of the library, and back to the veranda. His good-byes were abrupt and he left, dragging Rick behind him, and somehow managed to grab a set of keys away from his son.

Rick called out a good-bye and assured Megan he'd meet her on the first day of school. His voice faded as they rounded the house. Megan could hear the car doors slamming and the tires flinging up gravel as Michael tore out of Glencrest.

"Holy Christ, Dad, slow down! You're gonna get us both killed!" Rick snapped as Michael swerved down the highway, dodging vehicles and taking the corners so fast the car seemed as if it had gone up on two wheels.

"Do I look like I give a rip, boy?" Michael snapped back.

Rick sighed. This wasn't good. He knew he should've asked Nana if she would let him stay at the farm. His dad was impossible and it was only going to end with one of them in the hospital if he let his dad come home. "C'mon, Dad, head to East Side's. You can drown your sorrows there," Rick advised.

Michael didn't even slow down. He raced through town until he screeched to a stop in front of his favourite watering hole and staggered into the bar. Rick followed more slowly. He took a look around and thought he spotted an unmarked police car in the parking lot. *I'm taking a hell of a chance*, Rick muttered to himself as he followed his dad into the bar. It didn't take long to spot the undercover cop sitting at the bar, nursing a drink.

"Out, Moneyman," the bartender said immediately, pointing to the door.

"Chill, Greg, I'm not here to drink. Just lemme get the old man set up and then I'm outta here," Rick said as he stared into the smoky room looking for Michael. Greg hesitated, then nodded to Rick to follow him. Michael was already slumped over a dark table, but he bolted upright when Greg put the drink down in front of him. He didn't even look at Rick as he downed the scotch and water and snarled for another.

"How long before he's out cold?" Greg asked quietly.

Shrugging, Rick reached into his dad's jacket and pulled out his wallet. Greg whistled at the wad of cash Rick pulled out. The teen peeled a few bills off and gave them to the bartender. "Is that enough to give him a few more drinks and a room upstairs? I don't wanna wait around until he passes out. He's mean enough at home when he's not drunk and he's too heavy to carry," Rick replied.

Greg took the money and nodded. "You coming back to pick him up in the morning?"

"Hell, no. He's on his own. I'll leave him enough so he can get some food and a cab, but I ain't babysitting him," Rick said shortly. "You gotta pen and some paper? I'll leave him a note so he doesn't think someone robbed him."

Rick scribbled a note to his dad on the paper Greg brought him, letting Michael know he had the money and it would be put in its usual place. Then Rick just left his dad there to drink himself into oblivion. He tossed another bill on the bar for Greg's help and nodded at the cop as he walked out.

As Rick drove home, he wondered about his cousin. What was it about her that made him so protective? Was it the sadness in her eyes when she talked about her mother? Was it because she seemed so frail and helpless, although he knew very well she had to be strong enough to control a wilful mare like Mystique? What was it? Rick pulled his thoughts away from Megan as he drove past the front of the house and noticed Brain's Camaro sitting in the front driveway, and Blade pounding on the door.

Rick continued around to the back. He reached into his coat pocket and pulled out his garage opener. Punching in his private code, he watched the door slide slowly and quietly up. Easing the car into its spot and shutting it off, Rick wondered what the hell was going on now. Blade had known Rick had been at the farm, so he couldn't have been there to bitch about Rick not being around. He got out of the car, hid the money in the safe Michael had in the garage, locked everything up tight and slid silently out of the garage. He eased up beside the Camaro, and leaned carefully against the black car, being very careful not to set off Brain's sensitive alarm.

"Open up, Moneyman! I know yer home! Open up or I'll hun'cha down!" Blade shouted as he pounded on the door.

Rick said nothing as he stared at the two boys on his deck. He noticed Brain's jeans were ripped and he was holding one arm funny. Blade was cut and beaten up, but otherwise it was the way they usually looked after a Saturday night on the town. *Wonder who they've been fightin'? Didn't hear nuthin' 'bout a rumble,* Rick wondered as Blade continued to pound on the door.

Just as Blade was winding up to break the door down, Brain spotted Rick leaning against the car. "Blade, hold up. He's over there," Brain groaned softly.

"Where the hell've ya been?!" Blade shouted, as Rick sauntered up onto the porch. Rick hadn't seen Blade this angry in a long time and knew he was in trouble, but he didn't care.

"At Glencrest, like I told ya. Y'knew fer the last week. Wasn't like I cut outta rumble just to piss ya off by havin' supper with my gran. What happened?" Rick demanded as he grabbed a swaying Brain and eased him down onto the porch swing.

"Slayers," Brain gasped as Rick probed the other boy's arm, where he thought he felt a small break.

"Jumped us, just after Crank and Pup left," Blade groused as he paced. "We were headin' to Brain's when Crank's dad's freaked, put his foot down and made Crank stay home and my old lady had Social Services over about Pup. Why the hell weren't'cha here?" Blade grabbed Rick and shoved him against the house.

"Look, Blade, I've had enough. As much as I love bein' with the Knights, y'all just don't have several million dollars with my name on it and she does. So if Gran tells me to jump, I don't ask 'how high.' I just do it. Yer damn lucky she didn't haul my ass out to Glencrest after the fight with the Slayers last month. And since I know both Brain and Crank have summer jobs, don't give me that crap about me being the only one not around. Now back off and lemme look at Brain," Rick said and shoved Blade away.

He knelt down in front of Brain and was reaching for his arm when Blade's fist cracked across the back of his head. Stars exploded behind Rick's eyes and he went down in a heap.

Chapter 5

Rick awoke in Emergency with Nana standing over him, talking to the doctor as he finished stitching several cuts. Rick groaned softly as he shifted on the bed, trying to get away from the bright lights being shone in his eyes. *What the hell just happened?* he wondered, dazed. *How did I get to the hospital?*

"Lad, what happened?" Nana demanded when she saw Rick was awake.

"Nothing you can fix, Nana, and don't bother calling the cops. I won't press charges," Rick said shakily. What the teen couldn't figure out was what he had done wrong this time. Blade had never attacked him like this.

"In other words, those good-for-nothing boys you hang out with did this and you're too scared to press charges," Nana said hotly. Rick gasped as the doctor jerked another stitch through a cut on his arm as if he was just as angry as Nana.

"Take it easy, doc. No, Nana, not too scared – too smart. You think this is bad? If I press charges, Blade'll carve me up and nothing'll be left. Now drop it, please. Dad's probably passed out at East Side's anyway, and I just wanna go home," Rick said defensively. Nana pressed her lips together, but dropped the subject. Rick struggled to sit up as the doctor finished the last set of stitches in his arm. With a firm hand, the doctor pushed him back onto the bed.

"Sorry, kid, but you were out for at least an hour. You're just lucky one of your neighbours heard the commotion, saw you get hit and called the ambulance. Otherwise you'd still be lying there, out cold. You're staying overnight, at least, until I know you haven't suffered anything more than a mild concussion," the doctor said firmly and motioned for the nurse to take Rick up to a private room. Rick groaned.

Once he was settled, Nana sat down beside him. "Look, Rick, I know you don't wanna press charges, but they attacked you, for no reason. How could it get worse than that?" she asked, trying to make her grandson see reason.

"Chill, Nana. Blade was just mad I wasn't around to help out with a fight. They got jumped by another gang and it was five-on-two. That's all. He took his anger at the other gang out on me. Trust me. They really do care about me," Rick said sleepily. His whole body, especially his head, hurt like crazy, but he didn't want to ask for anything for the pain. He would take his punishment like a man. He fell into a deep and, thankfully, dreamless sleep.

After Rick was released the next morning, Nana made good on her threat; Rick spent the rest of the summer at Glencrest. And when Blade complained, Rick merely said it was Blade's own fault. "If ya hadn't jumped me that night, I wouldn't be in this mess, so no good yelling at me, man. This is all yer fault," Rick replied hotly. He missed being with the boys, but Nana kept a close eye on her grandson and no visitors were allowed, not even Jordan.

"Tell me, Moneyman, is Granny worth it? Wha'cha willin' ta lose fer the Knights?" Blade asked ominously and slammed down the phone.

Rick blanched as he slowly hung up the phone. If Blade was willing to take on Nana for Rick, was Rick willing to fight to save her life? *What about Megs? Jor? What was he willing to lose?* It was a question for which he never came up with an answer, and he spent many a sleepless night wondering.

Nana finally let Rick go home a couple of days before the end of the summer. "Remember, lad, you go see Dr. Jim at the clinic tomorrow to get the rest of your stitches out. And if I hear of one more fight with those boys of yours, you'll be living with me. Permanently," Nana warned as she dropped Rick off at home.

"Promise, Nana?" Rick smiled as he eased his way up the stairs and into the cold, silent house.

Michael hadn't come home from work yet and Rick wasn't about to give his dad something else to yell at him about, so he grabbed some food and dragged himself up to his bedroom. Turning on his television, he threw on a movie. He was just getting settled when Brain and Blade sauntered into his room.

"What the hell?" Rick demanded as he sat up.

"Moneyman. Yer back," Blade said as he dropped into a chair.

"No kidding. Wha'cha want?" Rick asked, leery of Blade. He was being too nice.

"Came to apologize, man. I was so pissed Ricardo got the drop on me, I took it out on ya. How bad?" Blade asked.

You could have knocked Rick over with a feather. Blade seemed sincere, but Rick knew something had to be up. Blade never apologized for anything he did, even to his boys. You just learned not to annoy him.

"It's nothing, man. I'm good," Rick assured him.

"Good, let's go. I wanna teach Ricardo and the Slayers a lesson they won't soon ferget," Blade said immediately and stood up.

I knew it, Rick thought angrily. *Nana's right. He doesn't care about me. He just wants another fighter.* But it was for honour and it didn't take long for Rick to gear up. "Let's get 'em, Blade."

It was a short and nasty fight, one the Knights won easily. The whole thing left a bad taste in Rick's mouth. The Knights blindsided Ricardo and left him for someone else to find, instead of taking on all of the Slayers. Rick didn't throw a single punch. This fight was just for Brain and Blade. The others were there as lookouts only. All in all, if Ricardo recovered, he'd probably never lead the Slayers again, which was what Blade wanted.

Rick arrived at the clinic shortly after ten the next morning, tired and sore and was led to an exam room to wait for Dr. Jim. Rick liked the doctor and loved how he ran a tight clinic. Nana's name wasn't on the outside, but everyone in town knew it had been Nana's generosity which had managed to get this badly-needed clinic built. The nurse told him Dr. Jim would be with him shortly. Indeed, Rick only had to wait a couple of minutes before the doctor walked into the room.

Dr. Jim Mason was a 53-year-old Texan who had wanted an opportunity to work in a small community. When he was offered the chance to come up north to help build and run a family clinic in a small town, he and his wife jumped at the chance. Everyone loved Dr. Jim's rich Texas accent and tanned skin. His brownish-grey eyes were always full of compassion as well as life. He had a ready smile and a quick wit, which were used to make his patients feel at ease.

Dr. Jim eased Rick's shirt up over the cuts to examine them quickly. "Okay, son, strip down. I wanna take a good look at every wound today," he drawled.

As Rick sat, half-naked, on the exam table, Jim probed each cut gently before removing the stitches. As the final piece of thread hit the tray beside Rick, Jim pulled back and looked at the troubled teen in front of him. "Lemme just say this, Richard. You're one lucky young man. Any one of those stab wounds could've killed you if that knife had just been pushed a little bit further. As it is, you're probably gonna have some trouble breathing for another couple of weeks. Is this gang of yours really worth all this trouble?" the doctor wondered as he finished completing Rick's file.

Rick sighed. *Geez, I wonder who told him. Thanks, Nana,* Rick thought sourly. "Not you too, Doc. Why can't everyone understand I like being with the Knights? They're my friends. No, more importantly, they're my family. I got no one else, Doc," Rick protested, but even to his ears the protest sounded weak.

"They aren't family!" Jim snapped. "Nana's your family. What about that nice cousin of yours who just moved here that Nana's told me about? She's not family? And don't think I don't know about Jordan O'Reilly. Take some advice I'm sure you've heard before, son. Get away from the Knights before you get killed." With that, Jim got up and left the room, shutting the door firmly behind him. Rick sat in stunned silence for a couple of moments, then slowly dressed. *Killed? Did they really think Blade would kill one of his own?*

In another exam room, Megan waited nervously as Dr. Jim filled out her personal information in her file. The doctor listened to her heart and lungs, checked her ears, nose, throat and eyes, and weighed and measured her. He made a lot of notes in her file and mysterious sounds resonated from his desk as Megan fidgeted on the exam table. Finally, she couldn't take the suspense any more.

"Dr. Jim, is everything okay? Is something wrong?" Megan finally whispered.

Dr. Jim looked up and sighed. His eyes never left Megan's as he got up from the desk and walked over to her. Putting his hand on her knee, he said, "I'm sorry, Megan, but I'm afraid I have some bad news."

"Bad news?" she repeated, stunned. *Am I sick?* she wondered frantically. *What's Daddy gonna say? He'll be shattered if he loses me, too.* She was so upset she almost missed Dr. Jim's next words.

"Yes, my dear." He sighed again as if trying to decide how to tell her. "I'm afraid you'll just have to go to school on Monday and wow them all with your pretty looks. I'm sure they'll be just as smitten with you as I am!" He laughed out loud at the look of surprise on Megan's face.

She laughed shakily as Dr. Jim pronounced her healthy enough to live to be 100. He had a nurse draw some blood for a routine check and then escorted Megan to the waiting room where Ian was talking with Rick. Both laughed when the doctor told them what he had done to the young girl. She had the grace to blush a rosy pink as she and her father thanked Dr. Jim and left the clinic. Rick stood in the front door watching them, wishing, and not for the first time, he had a dad like Ian.

The weekend raced by. Megan was so excited to begin another school year she could hardly sleep. She had always done well in school and she was determined to continue to do well, new school or not. She had her school bag packed and her clothes laid out, ready for the next morning.

As Megan puttered around her room, she thought about her cousin. Rick's attitude during the barbeque had bothered her. He seemed so proud to be in his gang, but Megan wondered what part of the gang really called to him. Somehow, through the anger and hatred she sensed in him, Megan knew Rick would be loyal to anyone he chose to. Megan also knew, deep down inside, she could trust Rick, maybe with her very life.

Unlike his father. There was something in Michael's voice that just made Megan shiver. She didn't think Michael cared about anyone but himself and she included Rick. She shivered again as she recalled the anger and hatred in Michael's voice as he argued with his older brother at the barbeque. She fell asleep, wondering if Nana should have been told about it. As sleep overcame Megan completely, she was no closer to an answer than before. She just knew, however, that fight was going to come back and haunt her.

Chapter 6

Monday morning, Megan was too excited and nervous to eat breakfast, and so, unfed, Ian drove her to school. As they pulled up to the door, Megan noticed the school was a combination of old world and new technology. Colonial High sprawled over the grounds, its two floors filled with windows. The red brick seemed oddly out of place when Megan noticed at least two satellite dishes on the roof. She was eager to find Rick and start the school year.

"Come to Hollyhock's after school, lass. Have Rick show you the way. Tell him I asked him to do it," Ian said as he waved good-bye.

Megan nodded and turned towards the school. She felt naked as everyone around her greeted old friends, and she had no one. Shyly, Megan joined the throng heading towards the main entrance. The double doors led into a wide-open student lounge area. There were chairs, couches, benches, tables, vending machines and even a student-run canteen. Megan noticed a trickling sound over top of the cacophony of student voices and turned to her right to see a small waterfall and an indoor meditation garden. Signs hung everywhere telling the students not to feed the fish or to damage the plants. Megan smiled as she realized where she would be spending as much of her free time as she could. It would be very relaxing to study there.

Somehow, over the rest of the students' voices, Megan heard her name called. She turned back to her left and saw Rick waving to her. He was standing with four other boys, talking quietly, as the sea of humanity gave them an extremely wide berth. As Megan approached, Rick told the other four he'd meet them later at assembly. The oldest one nodded and turned away abruptly. As he turned, he looked Megan up and down, nodded with a slight sneer on his face, and then left. Megan shivered.

"Rick, who was that?" she asked as her cousin guided her down the hall to the left of the student lounge.

"The Black Knights, cuz," he said proudly. *The boys Nana didn't want me to meet,* Megan remembered. She noticed Rick was wearing the same outfit he had been wearing at Nana's, and, while Megan admitted to herself Rick looked good in the outfit, she also noticed the other students were giving both of them a wide berth and several actually cringed when Rick swaggered by.

"Rick, why?" she asked curiously, trying to ignore the glares from the students as Rick's arm went out to steady her in a thick crowd that parted immediately.

"You'd never understand, Megs," Rick said roughly, dismissing the question with a shrug. He led Megan in to the main office and introduced her to the secretary, vice-principal and the principal, Mr. Delaney. While the secretary helped Megan complete her registration, and gave her a school map, the principal pulled Rick aside.

"Let's keep the visits down to a bare minimum this year, okay, Richard?" Delaney said firmly. Rolling his eyes, Rick nodded and went to turn back to Megan. The principal's eyes narrowed. Rick wasn't taking his warning seriously enough, and he'd had enough already. He seized Rick by the arm and swung him back to face him.

"Look, Richard, I've just 'bout had enough of your little gang. Step out of line too often, and I'll make sure you don't come back. Period. Do you understand me now, 'Moneyman'?" Delaney snapped, his patience gone.

"Loud and clear, Delaney," Rick said icily and jerked his arm out of the principal's grasp. *Why doesn't he ever give these damn lectures to Blade?* he fumed. *Blade's just as much trouble as he thinks I am, yet he never says* anything *to him. He only picks on me.* He joined Megan at the desk where the secretary reminded him of his Homeroom assignment and that he'd get his schedule there. Since they had the same Homeroom, Rick led the way to their class.

"Good morning, Richard," the teacher, Mrs. Salisbury, said dryly. "I see we're getting off to a fine start this year. It's only the first day, and already you're late for Homeroom. Don't make it a habit," she warned, as she indicated the two remaining seats. Conveniently, they were right in front of the teacher's desk.

"Sorry, Mrs. Salisbury, but I was helping my cousin here, Megan Attison, get her schedule and stuff at the office and it took longer than I expected. She's new to Colonial," Rick said politely as he and Megan slipped into their seats.

Mrs. Salisbury turned to gaze at Megan. Megan returned her gaze without flinching. *Wow, has she ever got intense eyes*, Megan thought. When Mrs. Salisbury smiled, though, her eyes softened and she didn't seem so intimidating. "Sorry, Richard, I didn't realize that. Here's your schedule. See you in second period for CALM," she said as she handed Rick a piece of paper he just shoved into his pocket without looking at it. She returned to the rest of the class and finished taking her attendance and handing out the schedules.

The bell sounded and Mrs. Salisbury directed everyone to the gym for the first assembly of the year. As Megan and Rick walked together, Rick pointed out the computer lab, cafeteria and library. There was a home economics room, metal and wood shops, art studio and a choir and band room. The walls were all painted a soothing light yellow and the doors and all the trim were painted white. The gym Rick led her to was quite large and he showed Megan the divider which made the larger gym into two smaller ones. Megan was so excited to think of everything she could do at this school.

Rick quickly scanned the crowd and pulled Megan along towards the same four boys she'd seen him with earlier. "Come on, cuz. I want you to meet them," Rick urged. *I don't wanna meet them*, Megan wanted to say, but let Rick pull her along without uttering a word.

Rick introduced the gang with pride. The youngest, Mark, was only fourteen and the leader's cousin. Rick called him Pup. "It's 'cause he's always following us around like a lost puppy," Rick chuckled as Pup glared and tried to shove the larger boy. The others just laughed as Rick didn't move an inch.

The second one was a 16-year-old stocky kid with grease under his fingernails. Rick introduced him as Eric, "but we call him Crank. He's real good with cars," Rick explained. *I'll bet,* Megan thought sarcastically. *Real good at stealing them.*

Brian was also 16, and Megan noticed a distinct difference in his clothes, compared to the others. Like Rick's, they were of much better quality and fit him better. *He comes from a good family*, Megan realized. *What's he doing in a gang?* The others called him Brain, "'cause he's so smart. Give him a problem and he'll give you an answer," Rick boasted as Brain nodded.

As Rick prepared to introduce the leader, Megan noticed how the rest were standing. The other three were arranged behind their leader, facing Rick, but not challenging him. They were just watching the rest of the students very carefully. They were looking for trouble, and guarding their leader. Megan shivered.

The leader was a real piece of work, in Megan's estimate. He was wiry, with short-cropped black hair. His dark brown eyes never stopped moving as Rick was doing the introductions, but when they finally rested on Megan, she was pinned with a single piercing look. She couldn't've moved if she'd wanted to, and she really wanted to. He was the one who had leered at Megan first thing that morning and Megan's opinion changed rapidly. At first, she had thought he was just a kid who was playing at this gang thing. Now she understood he lived, breathed and survived for the gang and only the gang. Megan was sure he was in school only because it was a great place to have some fun.

"This, Meg, is Johnny, or Blade, as we call him. He's the best thing that ever happened to me. Before I met him, I didn't know what loyalty and family meant. These guys have shown me that," Rick said softly as he watched Blade hold Megan tightly without laying a single finger on her. He prayed silently Megan understood. If she didn't, he didn't think he could keep Blade away from her. Rick could see Blade thought Megan would be fun to play with.

Before Rick could say anything else, Megan held up her hand. "I understand Rick, really I do," she said, tearing her eyes away from Blade's intense stare. *He's like a wolf,* she thought. He scared her. There was something about those eyes that bothered her and she wanted to get as far away as possible. Rick paused as he heard the fear in Megan's voice, and he frowned. This was a complication he didn't need.

"C'mon, Moneyman, ditch the chick and we'll blow 'til lunch," Blade drawled lazily as his eyes roved the stands quickly.

"Wait outside, Blade," Rick said quickly. "She's my cuz and I can't just ditch her. Gran'll freak if I did. Gimme a sec." Blade's eyes narrowed at Megan again but he nodded sharply when Brain nudged him. The four sauntered out of the gym just as a large group of students were coming in.

Rick scanned the crowd again, looking for someone else. "C'mon, cuz," he said suddenly and pulled her towards a couple of teens standing off to one side of the gym. Both had red hair and green eyes, so Megan assumed they were brother and sister, if not twins. The boy was taller than Megan, muscular and athletic-looking. The girl was slender, like Megan, almost frail looking, but Megan could see the strength in her shoulders.

Both were in blue jeans and cowboy boots, but the boy wore a tee shirt, while the girl had on a blouse. *They're farm kids,* Megan decided with certainty. As the boy turned to talk to the girl beside him, Megan was caught by the intense green of his eyes. She was staring, she knew, but she couldn't help it. He was very handsome and she wondered who he was.

"Mick?" Rick called out to the boy over the noise. The red-haired boy turned at his name, and Megan was caught again by his face. He cocked his head to the side as he glanced at Megan and Rick, and then nudged the girl beside him. Her face lit up when she saw Rick.

"Hey, Rick, have a good summer?" Mick said, politely. A shiver ran down Megan's back at the slight Irish brogue in his deep voice.

"Same old story, Mick. Hey, listen, man, I wanna introduce you and Jor to my cousin Megan. She just arrived at Glencrest a month ago. Megs, these're the O'Reilly twins, Mickey and his sister, Siobhan, but everyone calls her by her middle name, Jordan, since no one else around here can pronounce her first name. You'll have most of your classes with them, I'm sure," Rick said as he returned Jordan's smile. He slipped up beside her, and quickly gave her hand a gentle squeeze, knowing no one else would see. He bent closer to Jordan to whisper in her ear. She sighed, but nodded.

Megan smiled at the twins. "I'm pleased to meet you," she said shyly. *I was right,* she thought. *He'll be great to get to know. I love his accent. Daddy'll be pleased I know someone from the Island.*

"Hello, Megan. I'm sure my brother'll remember his manners in a moment," Jordan chuckled as she looked around. Rick had used their distraction to his advantage and disappeared. *Oh well,* she thought. *I'll see him at lunch.*

Mickey flushed slightly. Like Megan, he was stunned. *I've never seen eyes as pretty as hers,* he thought. "Hi, Megan. Would you and Rick like to sit with us?" he began as he glanced around for Rick. Mickey sighed as he realized Rick had slipped away. *When's that boy gonna learn?* Mickey thought with disgust. *He's got the best thing in the world with my little sis and he still blows her off for the Knights.*

"Come on, ladies, let's sit," Mickey decided quickly and escorted his sister and Megan to an empty bleacher seat. He sat between the two girls and tried not to look too smug. There may have been lots of pretty girls at Colonial High, but Mickey O'Reilly was sitting with the two prettiest. Even if one was his sister.

The principal walked onto the stage, got the students' attention and welcomed everyone to the new school year. He began to outline the school rules for the new students but Megan paid him scant attention. She was too busy thinking about Rick and his gang. Blade really scared her, but she thought Rick got her message. At least she hoped so. She didn't relish the thought of trying to protect herself from Blade. As strong as she was in some ways, she knew she'd never be strong enough against Blade if he really wanted to hurt her. Those thoughts quickly faded, however, and turned to the young man sitting next to her.

She couldn't believe how strong her initial reaction to Mickey was. She wanted to spend the rest of the day just talking to him, and his sister of course, but mainly to Mickey. Megan was very conscious of Mickey's leg pressed against hers. *Granted,* she thought grudgingly, *there's not a lot of room left on these bleachers, but he doesn't seem inclined to move over.* If anything, Mickey had shifted closer, after throwing his arm across his sister's shoulders to give them all more room.

As the principal droned on, Megan kept sneaking looks at Mickey. His hair was cut sort of short, yet a bit shaggy so it could be brushed back by running his hand through it. Megan noticed he did that fairly often, almost as if he was agitated. His face was the kind any photographer would kill for in a model, and unlike his sister, there weren't a lot of freckles on it. Megan could see the muscles in his shoulders and wondered how strong he was. Yet, she could also see how gently he held his sister. They really cared about each other, and it showed. She noticed right away he smelled just like her father, a combination of horse and cologne. She liked it.

Mickey turned suddenly as if he could feel someone staring at him, saw Megan looking at up him and smiled softly. Megan blushed and ducked her head, as he chuckled low in his throat.

Finishing his speech, the principal dismissed the students to their various classes and reminded them that each of the rest of their classes would be shortened by about five minutes to make up for the assembly. Mickey was startled. He didn't think he had heard anything Mr. Delaney had said. He had been too busy thinking about Megan.

"What's your first class, Megan?" Jordan asked as the three of them stood up. Megan was bumped and jostled, and Mickey put a hand on her arm to steady her. She dazzled him with a smile as she pulled out her schedule from her back pocket. Mickey was thrilled to see Megan didn't remove her arm from his hand. Jordan just shook her head. *Good grief. You'd think he's never seen a pretty girl before*, she muttered disgustedly to herself.

"History with Mrs. Salisbury in Room 208," Megan said finally.

"Us, too," Mickey said with delight. By the time they arrived at their first class, they discovered they had History and English in the morning, a spare right after lunch and then Chemistry as their last class of the day. Megan was thrilled to be in all of her classes with the O'Reillys. Even in the short time they had been together in assembly, she felt like she had known them forever.

Mrs. Salisbury strode in. She reminded Megan of a little fire hydrant – squat and full of energy. "Good morning, ladies and gentlemen. Welcome to History 11 and to those of you who are new to my class, welcome as well. We're going to cover a lot of ground this year. I expect great things from this class. I know most of you from History 10 and I remember the fabulous discussions we had. I hope we'll be able to continue those this year." Mrs. Salisbury paced at the front of the room. "I also want to introduce you to a couple of new concepts this year – Thinking for Yourself, and Writing to Defend a Point of View. These are critical ideas you'll learn over the course of the year, especially since I do not like reading essays which are just a simple rehashing of my notes to you. I want you to think about what you are writing and learn to defend your thoughts.

"History is more than just names, dates and places, people. It's about the people and what they thought at that point. I have an old professor who has promised to cut off my fingers with a sharpened clamshell if I ever allowed my lessons to become boring. Trust me, folks, he was serious. I've seen the clamshell. Shall we begin?" Megan giggled with the rest of the class while Mrs. Salisbury turned to the white board to outline what the class would study that year.

By the time the bell rang for English, Megan liked Mrs. Salisbury. She never raised her voice, nor changed the pitch very much, but she conveyed an enthusiasm for her subject that Megan matched, although few did. Mickey and Jordan were just as animated, and the three new friends talked all the way to their English class.

English was another of Megan's favourite classes. Megan loved to read, especially Shakespeare and other classics. In fact, authors many found dry, Megan found challenging. She was thrilled when the distinguished Mr. Robson told the class they were going to be studying two different Shakespearian plays and a novel by Ernest Hemmingway. The lunch bell interrupted a lively discussion about who really wrote Shakespeare's plays.

The three teens joined the rest of the student body in the cafeteria. They got their lunch and quickly sat down. Jordan saved room for Rick, just in case he decided to join them. Megan hesitated for a couple of minutes while everyone settled, and then began to speak. "Mickey, what do you know about that gang Rick hangs around with?" she finally asked.

Mickey chewed his hamburger thoughtfully as he glanced at his sister. Jordan just shrugged. *Go ahead*, her eyes told her brother. *How much should I tell her?* he wondered. "The other four boys have been together for a long time. Rick just joined in the last couple of years or so. I'm not even sure what they see in him, since he's really nothing like them. All five have been in more trouble in the last couple of years than everyone else in the school combined. They skip class, and fight with anyone. Just wait. I'll be they'll be here for lunch and end up in a fight. They always do. They're vicious at times, and a lot of people're scared of them.

"They've been caught vandalizing lockers and classrooms," he continued quietly, as Megan sat, stunned, "but no one's willing to press charges. They've even been accused of stealing from the canteen, but no one can prove anything. Apparently, they smoke on school grounds and I've heard one or two of them may do drugs. But those're just rumours," Mickey hastily assured Megan. *Idiot,* he fumed at the shock in Megan's eyes.

If Rick was doing anything like that, and Nana found out about it, that would be the end of any inheritance Rick would get. Megan was about to ask Mickey for more details when a commotion erupted at the door of the cafeteria. Rick and the gang followed Blade into the room, all the while pushing around a couple of smaller boys. The teacher in charge of the cafeteria managed to break up the teens and ordered Blade and the others to leave the boys alone. Laughing at the teacher, the gang joined the lunch line, jostling others out of their way until they were at the front.

Rick snagged a sandwich from the ready-to-eat section, and spying Megan and the twins, started walking towards them. He hadn't paid for his sandwich, but a sharp look of disapproval from Jordan made him flush, turn back and pay. Rick would do anything for Jordan. Their relationship had solidified over the past couple of years, despite the efforts of both her father and brother to keep them apart. In private, they were a couple, but Rick didn't dare make his feelings for her too public, or Blade would crucify him and her. Jordan was one of the few people left in the school who actually trusted Rick. Unfortunately, she just didn't understand what he saw in the Black Knights, and Rick could never explain it to her satisfaction.

Rick sat down quickly in the space Jordan had saved while Jordan smiled at him. Softly she said, "Thank you." Rick smiled back at the young Irish girl. *Man, I keep forgetting how her eyes shine when she smiles,* Rick thought, stunned again at Jordan's simple beauty. He wondered when he would be able to sneak off to a movie with her again. It had been well over a month since he had been able to spend any time with his girl and he missed her.

"You're welcome, Jor," Rick replied just as softly. They quickly squeezed hands under the table where Rick hoped Blade wouldn't notice, even though Rick knew he would pay the price later on just for sitting with her. *Maybe I can convince him I had to spend time with Megs,* Rick thought as he took a swig of his pop.

"Hey, Megs, how's your first day going?" Rick asked his cousin, slipping his hand out of Jordan's and grabbing up his sandwich, hoping beyond hope Blade hadn't seen anything.

It was too late. While the rest of the gang had moved off to one side and were talking with a few of Blade's other friends, Blade noticed the exchange and glared at Jordan. She seemed to shrink down as if trying to hide from him.

"Jordan, what's wrong, sis?" Mickey asked immediately.

She nodded towards Blade and lowered her head. Mickey turned around, and Blade had no trouble reading the challenge in Mickey's eyes. The leader of the Knights just grinned viciously as Crank and Brain both stepped up to back their leader. With an almost silent growl, Mickey broke eye contact first. He understood their message.

Rick sighed in frustration. "Mick, don't push him, okay?" Rick said wearily. "I'll deal with Blade. I'll convince him to leave her alone, I promise. It's not Jor he's after, it's me, alright? Just leave it with me," Rick said, trying to keep the anger out of his voice. He slipped his hand into Jordan's and winced as she held onto it tight enough to make his hand crack. *Bloody hell, Blade, just leave her alone. I can still be a Knight and love her too,* Rick fumed.

Not believing the other boy for a minute, Mickey just nodded and returned to his lunch. Rick again asked Megan how her day was going. She answered and the four teens spent the lunch hour chatting happily as they ate. By the end of the hour, Rick had shifted close enough to Jordan to show she was under his protection. Blade had turned away long before to talk to Crank and Brain, but Pup was watching Rick's group intently. It was Pup who noticed the subtle shifting on Rick's part and it was Pup who noticed Rick leaning over to whisper in Jordan's ear and she smiling in response to him. It was Pup who noticed Rick was paying more attention to Jordan than he really should be.

Pup's eyes narrowed as he watched the couple. At 14, he was the youngest of the Knights and he was only in because he was Blade's cousin. He understood and accepted it. He had come to live with Blade after his parents died in a house fire caused by a dropped cigarette. Blade was Pup's idol and Blade used that every chance he got.

Pup was Blade's eyes and ears. It was Pup who would rat on the other members of the gang. Blade had only one ironclad rule and that was no girlfriends. Nothing that would distract you from the gang was ever allowed. Pup had often noticed Rick's concern was more for Jordan than for the gang, and for that reason alone, Pup didn't trust Rick. Rick just never seemed as committed to the Black Knights as the rest.

Pup watched Rick and Jordan for a couple of more minutes then nudged his cousin. Blade's eyes narrowed at how close Rick was sitting to Jordan and Pup could've sworn he saw steam coming out of Blade's ears. *Man, he's pissed*, the younger boy chuckled with glee. *Moneyman's in fer it this time.*

Blade continued to steam as he noticed the pair holding hands under the table again. *Probably thought I wouldn't see*, Blade thought angrily. *We'll just break up that little party.* It didn't take long for Blade to spot the same two small boys the gang had harassed on their way into the cafeteria. Walking with them this time were two older boys, obviously jocks, and judging by the resemblance, brothers as well. *This'll be fun*, Blade thought.

"Let's go, boys," Blade snapped. Laughing, the four boys blocked the path of the jocks who shoved the two smaller boys behind them. Blade and the oldest jock traded a couple of insults, then a shove or two and finally the jock swung for Blade's head. The fight was on. Pup gave a sharp, short whistle that sliced through the general rumble of voices in the cafeteria. Rick's head shot up and he saw the fight.

"Rick, don't! Please?" Jordan begged with her hand on his arm. All three friends were shocked at the change in Rick. His eyes glittered and he was actually grinning as he shook off Jordan's hand and darted in to join the fight. It took only a couple of minutes for the teachers in the cafeteria to come and break up the fight, but by then, Blade was ready to back off. He'd managed to get his boy away from the girl, and that's all that mattered to him. Rick looked up, startled, at the teacher who had pulled him off of one of the jocks.

"You five," the teacher snapped, pointing at the Knights. "Office. Now!" The teacher glared at the Knights until they began to saunter away. The two jocks and their brothers were picked up off the floor and pulled away by a couple of other teachers to get their side of the fight. Meanwhile, the gang was buoyed by the fight and left the cafeteria high-fiving each other, thoroughly enjoying their first fight the year. As the gang left the cafeteria, Rick looked back at Jordan and grinned. The grin faded quickly and he hung his head when she turned away. "I'm sorry, Jor," Rick whispered quietly.

Chapter 7

As Rick slowly followed the others to the office, he thought about the fight. He couldn't understand any of it, especially why Blade had started it. *Those boys weren't disrespectin' us. They weren't wearin' our colours, and they sure as hell weren't a rival gang. Hell, there was no reason fer Blade to start fightin',* Rick realized suddenly. Then it dawned on him. *If there was no reason fer Blade to start the fight, why the hell did I join in? Is this what Nana's talkin' 'bout?* Rick wondered miserably. No wonder Jordan was so mad at him. As he walked, he could hear her pleas and see the look of disgust she gave him when he grinned at her afterwards.

Rick continued to brood while the other four kept rehashing it, over and over, in more and more vivid detail. It didn't get any better the more times Rick heard it. *I'm a friggin' idiot,* he snarled to himself as he shuffled along. It didn't take long for the others to notice how quiet Rick was. This time, it was Brain who nudged Blade, who nodded back at his second.

"Whassup, Moneyman?" Brain asked quietly as he dropped back.

"Nuthin', man," Rick replied even quieter, keeping his head down. He didn't want anyone, especially Blade, to see how revolted he was with himself. Blade would only see it as a sign of weakness. "Just thinkin' 'bout the fight."

"What 'bout it? Man, it was great, so what's eatin' ya?" Brain pressed. *Yer pushin' it, boy,* Brain thought ruefully. *Blade'll put up with this crap fer only so long and then he's gonna pound ya.*

"Why'd Blade start it, man?" Rick finally asked. He wasn't sure he would like the answer, but he needed to hear it.

"Fer you, idiot. Obviously," Brain answered, with a shrug. The two of them had stopped, and Rick just stared at his friend, more puzzled than ever. *For me? What's Brain talkin' 'bout now?* Rick wondered, as he shifted from foot to foot.

"Ditch the chick, and Blade'll leave ya alone," Crank pointed out, dropping back to stand beside Rick, on the other side. Rick turned, went to step away, and ran smack into Blade.

Rick saw the anger smouldering in his leader's eyes. *Oh crap, he's pissed,* Rick thought as his heart fell to somewhere near his feet. *I'm so dead.* "Whassup, Blade?" he asked, already knowing the answer. He tried to act casual, but his stomach was in knots and his hands hurt from being clenched.

Blade stood in front of Rick, while the rest of the boys surrounded them. It was Rick against the gang, and he knew he didn't stand a chance. Blade got right in Rick's face and whispered, his voice devoid of any emotion but anger. "Yer in fer life. Don't let a pretty face make ya ferget, Moneyman, or I'll just have to chat with her. Alone."

Blade turned away and, nodding to the rest of the Knights, continued down the hall to the office. Rick slumped weakly against the wall, all of the tension running away quickly and feeling as if Blade had just punched him square in the stomach. Rick was sick at Blade's not-so-subtle message. Jordan was now fair game and Rick had better shape up. Period.

Rick sighed and pushed away from the wall, knowing he'd better get to the office before Delaney sent someone looking for him. Sickened as he thought about the fight, Rick thought hard about what was happening. He knew the other Knights had enjoyed the fight way too much, but there was just no reason for it. Nana's question from earlier that summer kept running around Rick's head. What *was* he willing to give up for the Knights? Jordan's respect? Her love? Her *life*? With a start, Rick finally realized what his dreams at the beginning of the summer were about.

Nana's right, Rick decided as he walked along. *These guys're trouble. More trouble than I can handle, especially by myself. There was no reason for Blade to start that fight except to get me away from Jordan, and now she's gonna be in trouble.* "Great. O'Reilly's gonna kill me," Rick muttered to himself as he arrived at the office. He could hear the principal yelling at the other four as he pushed open the door.

"Wait there, Richard," the secretary said and motioned to the row of chairs against the wall. "Mr. Delaney wanted to talk to you after he deals with the others. Alone."

Terrific, Rick snarled silently, flinging himself into a chair. *Just friggin' great. What the hell else can get screwed up today?* he wondered, as he tried to keep his legs from jumping with renewed tension. Ten long minutes later, the Black Knights walked out of the office. Rick could hear Mr. Delaney giving them one final warning that Pup wasn't to be seen hanging with them, even if Pup and Blade were cousins. Crank, Brain and Blade just laughed, but Pup looked miserable.

"Chill, Pup, yer stayin'," Blade reassured his cousin who brightened immediately. Blade planned on ignoring Delaney's warning. *Typical,* Rick thought, suddenly annoyed at his leader. *Does he ever listen?* Blade sauntered over to Rick when he saw him sitting by the wall.

"Say nuthin', Moneyman, " Blade hissed as the Knights swaggered on by. Rick had no idea what Blade thought he'd say, but he just nodded anyway.

"Richard! Get in here!" Mr. Delaney shouted. Rick winced as he stood up.

"Well, let's see. I think this is a new record for you, Richard," Mr. Delaney said harshly. Rick stood motionless in front of the desk, scowling, his arms folded.

"I seem to recall saying to you this morning – you do remember that far back, don't you?" Delaney asked sarcastically. At Rick's sharp nod, Delaney continued. "I seem to recall telling you I'd make sure you'd never come back if you stepped out of line. Now here you are only a half a day in and already you've been in a fight! What do you think I should do, Richard?" Delaney rose from his chair and leaned heavily on his desk. His face was flushed with anger. *Can't you understand what I'm trying to do for you, son?* the principal raged to himself. *I'm trying to save your life! Johnny's gonna kill you one of these days!*

"Look, Delaney, either kick me out or lemme get to class. And lay off me. Hell, I never hear you giving these lectures to Blade, or Brain, or Crank. Just me. And I've had enough. Do whatever you want, just get the hell off my back. You don't want me here? Fine. I'll leave. And, for the last friggin' time, the name's Rick," Rick growled and turned to the door. As he flung it open, he heard Megan and Jordan begging to speak to the principal on Rick's behalf. Rick was floored. *Does she really care that much?* he wondered in amazement.

"Rick, close the door. Please," Mr. Delaney said softly. He looked at Rick and, for a very brief instant, saw a scared kid who was into something he didn't know how to get out of. It was only a fleeting moment, and then 'Moneyman' dropped back into place. "Rick, please?" Mr. Delaney asked again. Rick hesitated a moment, then closed the door softly and stood again in front the desk. Silence filled the room as both tried to figure out how to deal with a situation way out of control.

"Rick, I realize you have a lot of problems at home. But this gang of Johnny's isn't the answer, and deep down, I think you know that. What do you really get from it? Some different coloured clothes and a group of bullies who'll beat the crap out of anyone who looks at you wrong? What kind of friends're those?" Mr. Delaney asked, sitting back down.

Rick lowered himself into a chair. "You'd never understand, Delaney. The Black Knights're more than just guys that'll fight for me. They're my family. They're the only family I've got, the only ones who give a damn about me," Rick said a bit more defensively than he really wanted. He looked down at his hands. They were clenched into white-knuckled fists. *They're my family*, he thought angrily.

Delaney was bewildered. "The only family you've got? Don't think so, son. What about your grandmother? Megan? Jordan even? They care about you, don't they? Take my advice, son, and get away from Johnny before he gets you into more trouble than you can escape.

"Get to class now. You have detention. Every afternoon, here in my office for the next week. Don't miss it or I'll tell Nana. I've given Johnny and the others detention, but I doubt they'll go. Now, no more fighting or you'll be suspended, period." Mr. Delaney dismissed Rick with a wave and he marched from the principal's office with a heavy heart.

"Rick?" Jordan and Megan were still in the office waiting for him. Jordan reached for Rick, but recoiled when Rick turned his anger-filled eyes towards them.

"What?" he hissed. Jordan was startled. Rick could see how much his anger hurt her, but right then, he didn't really care. He was being punished for something he didn't start and he was taking it out on the first person who crossed his path.

Megan, however, laid into her cousin. "Y'know, I though you had better sense than this. You're the stupidest boy I've ever met. Halfway through the first day of school and already in trouble. Did he suspend you? No? Too bad. I'd've loved to hear you explain that to Nana! As for us, I guess we're too blind to see how a spoiled brat like you could care about anyone but himself! We were concerned enough to wait for you and, if it took long enough, we were gonna miss our next class just to help you. Our mistake. Go back to your...your homeboys, I believe the term is. I don't want anything to do with you ever again!" Megan snapped, her Scottish accent suddenly so thick, it was almost impossible for Rick to understand what she was saying.

Rick was stunned, but only for a moment. "Look, cuz, you're not my mom," he replied heatedly, once he had figured out what she had said.

"You're right and I'm glad. I'd be too embarrassed to be your mother," Megan snapped back and stormed from the room. Jordan followed more slowly. What was hardest for Rick to take was Jordan, the one person who supported him no matter what, didn't say anything to him. She just stared at him with a mixture of pity and anger in her green eyes, then turned and walked slowly away. Rick thought he heard a soft sob escape from her, but by then she was too far away for him to say anything.

Rick could only stare out the door at Jordan's retreating back. *What the hell was that?* he wondered in shock. He jumped when Mr. Delaney's hand came down on his shoulder. "Think about it, Rick. Are the Knights *really* worth it?" the principal said softly.

Rick angrily shrugged the principal's hand away and stomped out of the office. No one understood how he felt about the Knights. The other boys cared about him in a way no one else did or ever would. They gave him friendship without question. They protected him. They were always there for him. The gang *was* his life and his family. They were loyal and he didn't have to ask for it. Most important to Rick was the Black Knights didn't make him prove himself to them, day after day. Being accepted into the gang meant he had already proven himself. He liked how the other students feared him and always made room for him. It was a powerful drug, and Rick was addicted to it.

And yet...there was Jordan. Rick remembered how her green eyes smiled at him when he told her a joke. He loved how she would snuggle against him in the movie theatre, content just to be with him, not really doing anything special. He could still smell her perfume from lunch, and feel her holding his hand under the table. Even worse, he could still recall the hurt in her eyes when he snapped at her in the office. Rick would do anything she asked, absolutely anything.

Deep in his heart, Rick finally admitted Jordan meant something special to him, and had for several years. They'd met in third grade and had been an unofficial couple since eighth grade. Rick wondered if she meant more to him than the gang, and if she did, what he was gonna do about the Knights and Blade. Rick knew his leader wouldn't give him up without a fight.

Rick brooded for the rest of the day. He got in trouble from his last teacher for not paying attention in class. Rick didn't even care. He just reported to Mr. Delaney's office, no closer to an answer than when he had left after lunch.

Rick's detention was an essay on gang life. Mr. Delaney needed Rick to explain why the gang was so important to him and what he saw in the Black Knights he thought he couldn't get anywhere else. As Rick worked at a desk in the corner of the office under Mr. Delaney's watchful eye, the teen kept thinking about Jordan and Megan, not Blade and the other boys.

Rick struggled for the next hour and sighed silently. He would start writing, tear the paper out of his binder, crumple it and throw it on the floor, only to start all over again. The principal hoped this week of detention would help Rick see he was on a collision course with a jail cell.

Or a coffin.

At the end of the hour, Rick stood up, stretched and gathered up his work so he could leave. "Leave your essay, Rick. You'll be working on it all week. I want you to go home now and think about what you're writing. Good night," Mr. Delaney said, holding his hand out for the essay. Rick hesitated for a moment, then shrugged and handed it over. *What do I care if he reads it?* Rick thought with another shrug.

The Knights had already left. Rick was sure they hadn't bothered to go to detention and wondered why he did, except if he hadn't, he knew Delaney would call Nana, just like he'd threatened, who would then call her grandson and tear into him. Rick knew the Knights would be at Crank's house working on Blade's Harley Davidson bike or working on the car Crank would get once he got his license in a couple of months. Brain would be working on some new scheme of Blade's and Pup would be running for food and drinks.

Eventually, they'd take off in Brain's car and go looking for trouble, and probably wouldn't even call Rick to join them. If Rick didn't come with them right after school, they never thought to come and get the fifth member of the gang. Yet he was always expected to be part of the gang. And for the first time since joining the Knights, Rick really and truly questioned what he was doing with them.

Rick grabbed a snack and headed up to his room, thankful Michael wasn't home yet and he could have a few minutes of peace and quiet. He cranked on his stereo and flung himself across the bed, only half-listening to his favourite rock band. *We don't like the same movies, music or anything. I hate working on cars and they live for it. I don't like hanging around the pool hall all day long, even if I play a wicked game and can kick everyone's ass. So what am I doing with these guys?* Rick wondered again as he stared at his reflection in the dresser mirror. The face staring back at him all night didn't give him any answers.

What's he doing with those guys? Megan wondered to herself as she and Jordan finished their spare in the library with Mickey. Their last class of the day was Chemistry, which was enough of a challenge Megan spent little time worrying about Rick and his friends. By the end of the period, though, Megan began to worry.

"What's wrong, Megan?" Mickey asked as the three new friends threw their books in their lockers and grabbed their coats.

"Daddy wanted me to meet him at Hollyhock's and Rick was supposed to show me the way. I don't know my way around town yet," she said softly, lowering her head in embarrassment. Mickey looked at Jordan, who nodded.

"Nothing easier, Megan. We pass Hollyhock's every night heading home. We'll drop you off," Mickey nodded as he guided Megan out of the school. His knees went weak as Megan smiled gratefully at him. He tried to cover his shyness while leading the two girls to his truck.

What's wrong with me? Mickey wondered as Jordan settled beside Megan in the truck. *I know lots of pretty girls.* Megan slid over into the middle, right next to Mickey, and while there wasn't quite enough room for all three to be totally comfortable, no one would be really squished. Mickey walked around the truck, and threw all three backpacks in the jockey box in the back, still struggling to figure out what was going on with himself. All he knew was from the moment he had laid eyes on Megan, he would do anything for this slender little Scottish girl.

Mickey climbed into the driver's seat and, once buckled in, backed the truck out of the parking lot. The three chatted as Mickey drove the short distance to the store. Megan noticed nothing seemed to be very far apart in Collingwood and realized she could have easily walked to Hollyhock's from the school. She had to admit, though, this was much nicer. Due to the slightly crowded conditions in the cab, Mickey had put his arm across the back of the seat around Megan, pulling her just a little bit closer to him. They were almost at Hollyhock's when Jordan noticed where Mickey's arm was and snickered. Megan giggled, too.

"What's so funny, sis?" Mickey asked, a bit distractedly, as he pulled into Hollyhock's parking lot.

"Nothing, bro, nothing at all," Jordan replied, fighting hard not to laugh out loud.

Yeah, right, sis, Mickey thought sarcastically as he shifted even closer to Megan, if that was even possible. All of a sudden, he realized what Jordan was laughing at. He had been just a little too obvious in putting Megan beside him and now his arm was wrapped around her shoulders. *If this is what she does to me after less than a day,* Mickey thought, a little dazed, *what's gonna happen when I really get to know her?* Despite his embarrassment, Mickey couldn't help but chuckle at the situation. Still laughing, Mickey smiled down at Megan, gave her shoulder a quick squeeze, but didn't move his arm until Jordan got out of the truck.

Once outside, Mickey pulled his sister aside. "Did she object?" he asked anxiously.

Jordan shook her head. "Not that I could tell. In fact, I'm pretty sure she'd like to get to know you better, bro. Take it slow, though. Something tells me she can be shy at times. She's not like the other girls you've dated before. You don't know how she'll react," Jordan cautioned as she responded to Megan's call to hurry up. Mickey nodded, and strode ahead. He got to the door first, and held it open for the girls.

"C'mon, you two. I want you to meet my dad," Megan said. She was disappointed to discover that Ian already knew the O'Reilly twins, by reputation at least.

"How's your dad, Mickey?" Ian asked as the three teens helped in the store for a while. The girls began putting out some clothing and Mickey helped Ian refill some bulk food on the shelves. Hollyhock's sold just about anything and everything a farmer might need for his farm – except the animals.

"Doing great, sir. He and Tony gotta new police community group going," Mickey replied with a grunt as he hefted a bag of minerals up on to the pile they were stacking.

"What're they up to now? Doesn't Seamus have enough to do, running the station and the farm and keeping up to you two?" Ian chuckled.

Mickey grinned. "Guess not, sir. Anyway, it's a youth counselling group called The Youth Justice League. Tony suggested it 'cause he got tired of arresting the same kids all the time and no one else wanted to do anything about it. He hopes if kids have someone to talk to, maybe they can get out of the trouble they're in. Like Rick, I guess. Where do you want these bags of salt, Mr. Attison?" Mickey asked, changing the subject quickly. The last person Mickey really wanted to talk about was Jordan's 'boyfriend'.

"Mickey, if you're gonna be friends with my daughter, and I think Megan would like that, you can call me Ian," Ian smiled as Mickey nodded.

Ian helped the teen pile the salt on the stack near the door, but couldn't help noticing Mickey's eyes were constantly seeking out Megan and watching her for a moment. His 'Daddy' radar went off. Mickey, despite having only met Megan today, had a crush on Ian's little girl, and Ian planned on using that. There was something going on in Collingwood Ian couldn't quite put his finger on, and he wanted his daughter protected.

After half an hour or so, Ian called a halt to the work. "The staff can finish," he said as he led the kids back to the office for a quick snack. They sat in Ian's roomy office, eating and chatting.

"Lass, where's Rick?" Ian asked suddenly. "He was supposed to walk you here."

"He got into a fight at lunch, Daddy. I, um…" Megan hesitated, unsure how to tell her father what she had done.

"Megan told him off, but good, Mr. Attison," Jordan snickered. "Right in the office and in front of the principal." Megan hung her head as she blushed and then told her father exactly what she had said to her cousin.

"It's Ian, please, Jordan," Ian said after Megan finished. He shook his head at Rick's behaviour. "Did he get suspended? Nana won't like it if he did."

"From what I could tell, I don't think so, Daddy, but since I don't have any class but Homeroom with him, I don't see him after lunch," Megan replied, thoughtfully.

"What's that boy thinking of?" Ian asked rhetorically, exasperated with his nephew's behaviour. He finally understood the kind of trouble Nana said Rick was in.

"Can we do anything, Ian?" Mickey asked politely.

Ian shook his head. "Unfortunately, until Rick learns to help himself, nothing we do or say'll get through to him. He has to realize there are other people who care about him, other than that gang. Like Megan, despite what she may have said, or Jordan even," Ian chuckled.

Jordan hung her head as she blushed. She knew her dad and Mickey didn't approve of how she felt about Rick. *It's not like I planned to fall in love with a gang member,* Jordan thought bitterly. *I can't help how I feel.* Mickey gave her a quick hug. He swore to himself he'd learn to like Rick, if only to make Jordan happy.

"Don't worry about it for now, kids," Ian said. "Mickey, can I ask you a favour?"

"Sure, Ian," Mickey replied. He stood up and threw out the garbage from their snacks, then stood behind Megan's chair, his hands resting on her shoulders. He didn't even realize he had done it. Ian smiled to himself. *Yep, he's already in love with my lass. Good,* Ian thought with a chuckle.

"Would you mind picking Megan up for school in the mornings? I know you live on the next farm over and I really don't want her taking the bus. It's too long of a drive with all the detours the bus has to take to pick up kids. And I'm not always gonna be coming in to town first thing in the morning," Ian explained with a hidden smile at the way his daughter's eyes lit up.

Megan smiled. "I'd like that, Daddy. That is, if Mickey and Jordan don't mind," she added hastily.

"What do you think, Jordan? Can we stand to pick up this poor lost lamb every morning?" Mickey teased Megan gently as she turned to smile up at him over her shoulder. *Can I really stand to be that close to you every morning?* Mickey wondered, drowning in Megan's eyes. Jordan nodded enthusiastically.

"Done, then, Ian. We'll be there 'bout quarter to eight," Mickey said. His knees weakened again at Megan's smile. *Gosh, she's pretty*, Mickey thought again, stunned. Jordan just snickered at him.

"Thanks, Mickey. Now, I have another couple of hours work here yet. Why don't you three head home?" Ian said, standing.

As the girls left the office, Ian held Mickey back. "Thanks again, Mickey, for keeping an eye on her." Ian didn't say anything more. He didn't need to. Mickey nodded tersely; as young as he was, he got Ian's message. Sometimes it paid to be a cop's kid. He knew Ian wanted his little girl watched without knowing it. Mickey silently vowed nothing would happen.

To either girl.

Chapter 8

By the time he got home on the second day, Rick really didn't know what to think. Mr. Delaney's little essay managed to get Rick thinking and he was confused. *I suppose that's the point,* he mused as he got himself a snack and climbed the stairs slowly up to his room. What *did* he want? Did he wanna be a Knight or did he wanna be Jordan's boyfriend? The gang gave him a sense of family. Even Pup, who bugged Rick to no end at times, was more like an annoying little brother than anything else. Every time Pup got under Rick's skin, Rick said a silent thank-you to Nelson, *his* wandering brother. But the Knights were just like Nelson had been before he left – always there to protect him and help him, so they weren't just friends.

Michael hadn't really cared about Rick, even when Rick's mom was around. But Blade and the others had accepted Rick as soon as Rick shrugged that leather jacket on for the first time. Sure, they'd rough people up or damage property, but no one ever *really* got hurt, at least not at first. Rick knew it cost to replace car windows or fix the dents and scratches, and maybe Blade and the others went a little too far in their fights sometimes, leading to stitches or the occasional broken bone, but Blade always said they deserved it and fighting made the weak ones stronger.

Problem was, no matter how Rick tried to justify things lately, every time he looked in the mirror, all he saw was a rich little brat who didn't care about nobody or nothing. *Just like my old man*, Rick thought bitterly. *Just throw money at a problem and it'll go away.*

Blade had blown a fuse one day when Rick refused to break one of his dad's car windows, so Blade did it for him. But Blade didn't stop at one window. He broke them all and then dared Rick to tell his dad. Rick had paid for the windows himself and managed to avoid telling Michael what had really happened. He hadn't dared to defy Blade ever again.

The other problem Rick had always had with Blade was the fights. If Blade was in a real foul mood, he wouldn't hold back and he expected his boys to follow suit. He didn't care if there were broken bones, or if someone got badly hurt. He just didn't care. Blade would use fists, knives, bottles, bats, rocks; whatever was handy. Crank, Pup and Brain were always willing to help, but Rick held back. He just couldn't be that brutal; he knew what it was like to get beaten, having been on the receiving end of beatings once or twice himself and not just by Blade either.

It made him sick, usually physically, to watch the fights and see how much the Knights enjoyed them. And Blade would always come up with the thinnest of excuses for fighting. The kid could be too smart, too dumb, too ugly, a pretty boy, a nerd or a jock. The kid could just be walking down the hall and look at Blade so as to not run into him. The worst beating in Rick's memory with the gang was a slender boy who had arrived at the school in May of last year. The beating took place in the first week of June and had led to Rick's nightmares of late, he was sure.

The kid in question had unknowingly come to school wearing a black and silver leather jacket, white tee-shirt and black jeans. Not a good idea when Blade's gang wore those colours. Blade had made it clear anyone caught wearing the Knight's colours deserved a beating. The poor kid had been caught outside the library on his way there for his next class. Blade and Brain were the only two who laid a hand on the younger boy, while the rest kept his class at bay, but those two were more than enough. Rick watched as Brain pinned the kid to the windows that looked into the library, with his arm firmly pressed into the kid's throat. The kid couldn't even cry out for help.

Blade and Brain each held a solid piece of oak in their hands and threatened to beat him with them. Terrified, the boy struggled to escape and had managed to push past the two taller boys, although Rick realized later Blade had let him think he could escape. Just as the boy thought he was free, the two grabbed him and threw him back against the windows, causing them to shake dangerously.

Laughing at the terror on the kid's face, they both swung their fists at the same time and connected solidly with the kid's head. With a cry, the boy grabbed his head as if he could end the pain Rick could only imagine was shooting through his skull. Laughing even harder, Brain swung again and his fist slammed into the kid's jaw, dropping him like a stone. Rick could see him twitching slightly as he lay on the ground. Three punches was all they threw, but Rick knew the kid had been seriously hurt. He quickly swallowed a few times, trying to keep from throwing up.

Brain pulled the jacket off the unconscious kid and slung it over his shoulder, laughing. Pup was grinning like a maniac and Rick was sick to his stomach. The rest of the Knights continued to howl with laughter as the teacher finally ran into the hall and screamed at someone to call an ambulance. The gang had sauntered off, leaving the boy on the floor, surrounded by panicking teachers and students.

Blade and Brain had been arrested, but since the kid, wisely in Rick's opinion, had refused to testify or press charges and no one else present wanted to get on Blade's bad side, the charges were reluctantly dropped. The judge did strongly suggest Blade and Brain get some anger management counselling, but they just laughed in his face. They returned to school where their reputations for brutality grew.

The kid had returned to school in September. With careful questioning of the secretary, Rick had found out the young teen had suffered, at the very least, a severe concussion and was now subject to blinding headaches and panic attacks. He was somehow dealing with both, but Rick felt responsible since he had done nothing to stop Blade and Brain. Blade had made it very clear that day no one was safe from him.

Thanks to a conversation Rick had had with Blade after the fight, Rick got the message loud and clear. That meant the gang, too, or maybe especially the gang. Blade didn't say anything to

Rick until later, but when they finally "chatted" about the fight, Blade made it very clear to Rick if he didn't shape up, and quick, he'd be next.

"Look, man, the kid was new," Rick pleaded. "He didn't know. Yeah sure, everyone else knows, but no one warned him. I don't care what you say, Blade, he didn't deserve that." Rick had defended the kid and had paid the price. He had come away from that day with a cracked rib and a black eye. But he had made his point with Blade.

Now Rick had a big problem. Every time he thought about that fight, and some of the other things he had done with the gang, he was almost physically sick. He slowly began to realize he wasn't like the other Knights. He didn't enjoy beating someone up just for the fun of it. If they'd disrespected the gang, that was different. Then Rick was fighting for gang honour. Otherwise, what was the point?

And then there was Jordan, the one person Rick admitted he cared about. Jordan's eyes haunted Rick. He saw them in his sleep. He saw them when he looked in a mirror. Sometimes he could almost see her standing behind him, looking at him with that look of disapproval in those pretty green eyes. He thought about having her beside him, walking down the hall in school, holding hands and not having someone else shy away from him in fear. Rick knew Jordan didn't want him in the gang. They had argued about it more than once when they had managed to sneak off to a movie. He just couldn't explain the attraction of the gang to her, and eventually, he stopped trying.

Rick had always been closer to Jordan than Mickey, from the day they met on the first day of school in third grade. He knew and understood Mickey and Seamus tolerated him, Mickey barely and Seamus not at all, around Jordan only because they loved her. Although lately, it seemed like Seamus was doing everything he could to keep Jordan away from Rick. What did Jordan really mean to him? Did he love her enough to leave the gang? Did he love her enough to leave his "family"?

Rick hardly slept that week. When he wasn't thinking about his essay, he kept having the same nightmare about the gang he had had at the start of the summer. Every night it would be the same face Rick would see at the end and, since he had the dream two or three times a night, Rick wasn't getting much sleep. Every night, Rick would see Jordan lying on the ground before him, beaten and still, her red hair fanned out around her battered face. When Rick had the same dream for the third time on the fourth night, he just sat up and stared out the window.

His detentions weren't helping, either. Rick spent more and more time thinking about his life, and the more he thought about it, the more he realized, that despite everything he felt the Knights meant to him, he wanted out and now. Rick knew he wanted to spend more time with Jordan, not with Blade. He had come to realize, while he loved the feeling of power the gang gave him, the fear and hatred in the other students' eyes just wasn't worth it. Not any more. That was what he finally wrote about in his essay on Thursday, choosing his words carefully. He knew he would have to do this slowly and cautiously. Blade was not going to give up without a fight.

By Friday, Mr. Delaney was ready to talk to Rick. "Well, Rick, I must admit this was very interesting reading last night," the principal began as Rick came in for his final detention.

"You wanted me to do some thinking, man, and that's what I thought 'bout. You asked me last year what I was willing to lose for the gang. Nothing's worth the gang, for me, at least not any more. Over the summer, a couple of things happened. I don't like what I've become, and I think I finally woke up. I've started to realize that maybe, just maybe, they're what you said they were. Trouble. Big trouble. I'm seriously thinking 'bout getting out. For Jor, if nothing else," Rick said with a shrug. *Am I doing the right thing?* Rick wondered for probably the hundredth time.

"That's why I chose this essay, son. It helped you see you're not like Johnny and the others, didn't it? You don't like it when they intend to hurt someone. Like that boy last June. I know you pulled away from that fight, because the teachers and some of the other students told me you were throwing up later in the bathroom. The whole thing disgusted you, what Johnny did, and don't think I don't know who gave you the cracked rib and black eye afterwards, either. You don't like those kinds of fights. Problem is, Rick, you don't stop the fights either and kids could get killed.

"You have a lot of built-up anger and you enjoy destroying things, if only to get rid of your anger. You need to get some counselling, Rick, anger management especially, before you hurt someone and trust me, son, you're not that far away. You need to make some big changes in your life, Rick, and you can start by breaking away from the Knights," Mr. Delaney urged. *Before your Nana's scraping you up from the street with Johnny's bloody knife in you,* the principal thought, worried his message wasn't getting through.

"It ain't that easy, Delaney. I'm not as scared of Blade as some of other guys are, but I can't just walk up to him and say I'm out. He'd kill me. He's stronger than I am. I've always known that. Whatever he didn't finish off, the others would. As soon as Blade figures out I'm gone for good, Jor's gonna be fair game, too, but I...I gotta try," Rick said softly. He stared off into space for a few moments, then stood up to go.

Mr. Delaney didn't say anything further. Taking the principal's silence to mean he was dismissed, Rick left the office and ran into Megan and the twins as they were passing the office on their way home. Rick smiled at them, a smile that quickly faded as all three turned away. "Wait! Please?" Rick begged, wanting to reach out and grab Jordan.

Only Jordan turned back. "Yes, Rick?" she said softly. He couldn't see it in her face, yet Rick was positive she still cared about him.

Rick hesitated for a long moment. *What've I gotta lose?* Rick wondered. *Everything,* he immediately answered himself, *including Jor, when Blade finds out.* He decided to go for it anyway. "I'm sorry, guys. For everything. Delaney's made me take a good, hard, long look at myself," Rick began slowly.

"And?" Megan said sarcastically over her shoulder.

Rick winced at her tone, but knew he deserved it. He also noticed Mickey had shifted to Megan's side, arm wrapped around her slender waist, yet Rick knew if he tried to get at Megan, Mickey'd be in front of her before Rick could take a single step. Someone asked Mickey to be the girls' protector, whether they knew it or not. Rick wondered if it had been Ian, Seamus or if Mickey just decided to do it on his own. Either way, Rick knew who the men felt the girls needed protection from.

"And I don't like myself, 'kay? I don't like what I've become. I've done some stupid things. Made some bad choices, like joining the Knights. And I've never tried to stop Blade from doing anything. Remember that kid in June? *I* should've stopped them, but I didn't," Rick said, miserably. Megan and Mickey had finally turned to face him, but it wasn't Megan Rick was concerned about right now.

He stepped closer to Jordan. Out of the corner of his eye, Rick saw Mickey tense, but Rick ignored him. It was Jordan Rick needed to convince. He took her hands in his and looked into her eyes. Rick saw those eyes were no longer hiding her feelings for him. "Jor, babe, listen to me. I'm not proud of what I've become. I finally get what you and Nana've been saying for so long. Nothing's worth the gang, especially not you or your love. All I'm asking for now's a chance," Rick begged softly. *Please gimme a chance*, he begged her silently. She nodded slightly, almost as if she had heard him.

"A chance for what, Rick?" Megan asked. Rick cringed at the thinly-veiled anger in her voice. He turned to face his cousin, but didn't drop Jordan's hand.

"A chance to change, Megs. To work myself away from the Knights. To earn your respect and friendship. To love Jor. To prove to y'all I can change. To prove to myself I'm not like the others. A chance, Megs. That's all I want," Rick said quietly. Silence filled the hallway. Unknown to the four teens, Mr. Delaney stood in the office, just inside the door, listening to it all. *Keep going, Rick*, he encouraged silently.

- 87 -

Megan didn't say anything right away. She leaned over to Mickey and asked quietly, "Does he have a chance?"

Mickey shook his head, but didn't lower his voice when he replied. "Not bloody likely, baby. I've heard stories about Blade. He doesn't like it when someone tries to leave. Apparently, just after the Knights formed up, Crank wanted out. He didn't wanna be in a gang, he just wanted to hang with Blade and be friends. Blade didn't like that and beat the crap out of Crank. Ever since then, the two have been best mates," Mickey replied, never taking his eyes off of Rick. Rick nodded.

Megan stood there, digesting what she had heard from both boys. *He's not telling us everything*, Megan realized suddenly. *He's scared of something and doesn't want us to know what it is. Why?*

"What aren't you telling us, Rick? There's something else you're worried about," Megan said suddenly.

Rick nodded solemnly. "Once Blade realizes I'm trying to get out, he won't come after me directly. He doesn't work that way." Rick paused, looking at both girls. He held onto Jordan for a moment, then pulled back to stare into her face. *How do I tell her I've just put her in danger?* Rick worried.

"He'll come after you two," Rick said ominously, pointing at Megan and Jordan.

Chapter 9

After that day, Megan and Mickey at least *tried* to be friends with Rick, but Megan didn't even really *know* him yet, and Mickey hadn't trusted Rick from the moment they had met. But from that day on, Rick and Jordan were openly a couple, even though her father, Seamus, had thrown a huge fit when Jordan told him.

Rick warned the other three his break from the gang wasn't going to be obvious, at least not right away, and he prayed Blade wouldn't notice Moneyman wasn't hanging with the gang. What Rick was really hoping for was that Blade didn't notice who Rick had started to hang around with.

Blade noticed immediately, however, and he wasn't happy with Moneyman. Rick hadn't shown up Monday morning when the rest of the gang skipped their second class, as usual, to go play pool. All week long, Rick refused to join in with the gang, no matter what they did. Blade started two different fights, both in the cafeteria, but Rick pointedly ignored him, even going so far as to turn his back, literally, on the gang. Each time he did, he felt a little stronger and a little more liberated. Jordan would always smile that soft smile of hers when Rick chose her over the gang. Finally, Blade decided to leave Rick alone for a couple of weeks and see what developed.

It wasn't as if the gang was idle. Far from it. They took their pleasure at making sure they did as much damage as they could every single day. Lockers were broken into. Graffiti was sprayed on the walls of the gym, both inside and out. They were loud and disruptive in class, a couple of which Blade and Crank had with Rick, who would just shake his head, disgusted at their antics. Fights were normal for the gang at some point during the day.

Yet, oddly enough, all four Knights managed not to be expelled or suspended. Their marks, while not the greatest, were just good enough to keep them from failing and they attended enough classes to keep from being truant. It also helped their teachers were so scared of them nothing was usually mentioned. Fear was a great tool and Blade used it every chance he got.

Towards the end of September, though, Blade had had enough of Rick's little rebellion and he decided to end it. After class on Thursday, on his way to meet Megan and the twins in the parking lot, Rick wasn't paying attention as much as he usually did and found himself surrounded by the Black Knights just outside the cafeteria.

"Moneyman. Long time no talk," Blade drawled as he leaned against the far wall. The leader of the Knights stood with his arms folded and a sneer plastered across his face.

"Hey, Blade, what's up, man?" Rick asked idly, as if he didn't have a care in the world. Inside, he was tense and worried. He knew exactly what was up, and he wasn't sure he'd be able to talk his way out of this. As Rick stood there, he noticed some movement to his left and turned to see Pup standing there. When Rick turned his head back towards Blade, he could see Brain out of the corner of his eye on the right and without looking behind, Rick knew Crank was right there. *Great*, Rick snarled to himself. *I'm toast.*

"Where ya been, boy?" Blade drawled again, but didn't move. Rick growled softly at the one word Blade knew he hated to hear. Still, Rick found himself feeling caught even tighter by the other three. No one had laid a hand on him, yet Rick felt like he'd been punched in the stomach.

"Hell, Blade, Gran put her foot down. Do better in class or get shipped out. I've been studying, man," Rick said quickly. *Nice bit of truth, too*, Rick congratulated himself.

"Hmph. Right," Blade said sarcastically. "What's yer old man gotta say?"

"Since when does my old man care?" Rick snapped angrily, flushing at the insult. "Y'know he doesn't give a rip about me.

Gran has all the dough, man, and if she says study, I study. I don't wanna lose my inheritance. That's a good chunk of change, man," Rick protested. His heart sunk like a stone when Blade slowly shook his head and grinned slyly at Rick.

"Strike out, Moneyman. I know yer hangin' with that pretty little Irish thing. Is she really that good?" Blade leered. The rest of the Knights chuckled nastily.

Rick stiffened. *Crap, he's caught me*, Rick panicked. *He knows about Jor.* "Alright, Blade, what do you want?" Rick demanded harshly. He abandoned all pretence of being the student, although he refused to use the gang speak he had in the past. Now he had to be 'Moneyman.'

Suddenly, Blade moved swiftly across the hall. Rick tried to dodge him, but Crank grabbed his arms and Rick couldn't escape the stronger boy. Now he knew why Crank was behind him, and not to one side. Rick didn't flinch when Blade stopped less than a finger's width away from his face. He could see the veins pulsing in Blade's neck.

"Yer mine, Moneyman. Yer in fer life," Blade hissed softly. He nodded to the other boys; Crank and Brain grabbed Rick and dragged him down the hall, Rick struggling and fighting every step of the way, to the computer room where the computer club was just finishing up their meeting for the night. There was only one kid left, and with a sinking heart, Rick recognized who it was.

It was the same kid who had mistakenly worn the black and silver leather jacket. Rick knew the kid was still having headaches and problems with his eyes from the concussion Blade and Brain had given him. As the gang stopped in the only door, the boy looked up and realized he was alone and in deep trouble. Rick could see the panic in his eyes.

Blade nudged Rick into the room. The gang leader was grinning viciously. Rick knew what Blade wanted, but the very thought made Rick sick to his stomach. *What now?* Rick wondered. *If I don't beat this kid up, Blade'll pummel him and then me. If I hit him even once, I could kill him.* It was at that moment Rick told Blade he was out.

"No," Rick said softly, but intensely.

Blade just laughed, as if he had expected the response. "Then I will." He sauntered into the room. Rick tried to follow, but Crank tightened his grip, almost bruising in his strength. Blade eased further into the classroom and approached the now-terrified boy trapped there. Smiling, Pup closed the door and stood with his back to it. Rick struggled harder against Crank's iron grip while Brain and Pup just laughed.

"Hey, Tomboy. Feelin' better?" Blade sneered as he moved closer and chuckled nastily. Tom begged Blade to leave him alone, but Blade just laughed harder. He cuffed Tom hard across the side of his head, driving Tom to his knees, clutching his head in pain. As Tom continued to beg to be left alone, Rick cringed at the panic he could hear in the smaller boy as he struggled even harder against Crank's grip and felt it slip ever so slightly. Before Crank could adjust, Rick gave a violent wrench and broke free. He dashed into the computer room, praying he got to Blade before he could strike again.

Rick caught Blade's hand as it was descending. "Enough, Johnny! Your fight's with me!" Rick growled and threw Blade's hand back at him.

"Are ya challenging' *me*, Moneyman?" Blade asked, amazed. "C'mon, *boy,* let's see who's better," Blade snarled as he ignored Tom.

Rick shook his head, and backed away with his hands up, as if surrendering. "No way, man. You'd kill me, Johnny. I've always known you're stronger. But I won't stand by and let you kill this kid," Rick said staunchly. He pushed Tom behind him.

"Too bad," Blade said lazily and suddenly lashed out at Rick. Rick ducked and pushed back at Blade. Tom didn't need Rick to tell him to run. The boy fled, somehow shoving past Crank and Brain and rushed to the office.

Rick and Blade circled each other, but Rick planned on letting Blade take the first shot, even if it put Rick flat on his back. Blade suddenly struck out, connecting with Rick's head, causing him to see stars for a moment. Rick struck back, hitting Blade in the mouth. Rick had put everything he had into that shot but Blade didn't even blink. Grinning even more broadly, Blade pulled his arm back and Rick knew if that blow landed, it would knock him into next week.

"**STOP!**" a voice thundered from the door. Blade was distracted enough Rick managed to avoid the punch by dropping to his knees. He stayed down, breathing hard. He thanked his lucky stars that shout had come when it did.

Mr. Delaney stormed into the room. "Johnny, my office. Right now!" the principal snapped. "Mr. Robson, please escort Johnny so he doesn't get lost." The sarcasm in Delaney's voice made Blade growl low in his throat as Mr. Robson grabbed his arm and led the youth from the room. Rick looked up and noticed Crank, Brain and Pup had all disappeared before Mr. Delaney could send them to the office, too.

Mr. Delaney waited until Blade and Mr. Robson had left. Then he turned to Rick who had picked himself up off the floor and was sitting on top of a desk, still trying to catch his breath. "What happened?" the principal asked pointedly.

Rick didn't wanna be a snitch, but Mr. Delaney didn't seem to care. He folded his arms across his chest and stood there, staring at Rick. "Richard, I'm waiting. What happened?"

Rick looked away from Mr. Delaney and took several deep breaths. "Is that kid, Tom, okay?" he asked instead of answering Mr. Delaney's questions.

"I'm fine. Thank you," Tom said shyly as he came in the door. He appeared calm, but Rick saw how pale and shaky the younger boy was.

"Richard," Mr. Delaney said intensely.

Rick took another deep breath and began to tell the principal what had happened. Occasionally, Tom would throw in some information as well. "I'm trying, Delaney, I really am. Johnny just doesn't like someone leaving the gang," Rick finished miserably.

Mr. Delaney nodded. "It's not gonna be easy, Rick, nothing worth doing ever is. I have a problem here, though. Even though you were defending Tom, you were still fighting and I'll have to suspend you. Come back on Monday. That's a one day suspension," Mr. Delaney said sadly. He had hoped not to have to do this, since Rick really was making an effort to get away from the Knights, but people would talk if he didn't punish Rick somehow.

Rick sighed. "I understand," he said as he stood up and moved towards the door. "What's gonna happen to Johnny, sir?" Rick asked without turning around.

"I'm gonna give him a lecture, not that he'll listen to it, and also suspend him for a day. Neither one'll work, I know, but I have to do something," Mr. Delaney said, frustrated.

"Kick him out, Mr. Delaney," Tom said fervently.

"I could, Tom, but problem is, he'd just come back into the school and cause even more trouble. I'd rather keep him here and try to keep an eye on him," the principal replied as all three walked towards the door. He didn't say anything else until they were by the exit doors. Then, he turned again to Rick.

"Rick, I want you to talk to someone at the Youth Justice League. Get some counselling. There's more to this gang thing of yours than meets the eye and I think if you understand more about why you think you need the gang, the easier it may be for you to get out of it," Mr. Delaney added.

Rick nodded abruptly. He left the school and to his amazement, Megan and the twins were still waiting for him at Mickey's truck. "What happened, Rick? Where've you been?" Mickey asked as Rick walked up and gave Jordan a hug. He held on to her for a long moment. *What've I dragged her into?* he thought, furious at himself. He couldn't speak for a long time, knowing how easily it could've been Jordan in that room instead of Tom.

Rick told the other three what had happened. He was more worried than he had let on to the principal. "Johnny's gonna come after you, I know it," Rick said softly, looking at Jordan. "I'm sorry, babe," he whispered again.

Jordan didn't remove her arms from around Rick's waist. She just held on even tighter. "Don't worry about me, love. I'll be okay," she assured Rick.

After a couple more minutes of talking, the four friends split up. Mickey got the girls settled in the truck for the ride home. Jordan turned and waved at Rick out the window and called to him to call her later that night. Mickey gave Megan's hand a quick squeeze as they settled into their seats. By now, Megan knew Mickey well enough she felt confident in asking for a favour.

"Mickey?" Megan began as she settled into the crook of his arm with a soft sigh. Nothing had differed from that first trip home. Megan always sat beside Mickey and Mickey's arm always went on the seat behind her.

"Yes, lass?" he smiled down at Megan, using her father's pet name for her. Megan felt a shiver run down her spine at his smile and soft accent.

"Do you think your dad could help Rick?" Megan asked, smiling shyly back.

Mickey's knees quivered again. *Man, she does that to me every time*, Mickey thought, dazed. He wondered again how this sweet little Scottish lass had been able to get so deep into his heart after only a month. Mickey had picked New Year's Eve to ask Megan to be his girl. He just wondered if he could wait that long.

"Yo, bro, Meg asked you a question," Jordan pointed out, hiding a smile at the two of them. *They are so lucky*, she thought sadly. *At least they get to be together.*

Mickey jerked his thoughts back to Megan's question. "I don't know, lass. Dad really doesn't like Rick. The Knights've caused a lot of trouble over the last couple of years and Dad doesn't like what he can't control. He's always been like that, I guess. He's not real crazy about Jordan being Rick's girl, either. Now he's really gonna worry when we tell him about the threats," Mickey said soberly.

"Daidí should be able to do something, though, Mickey. If nothing else, maybe Tony can get Rick in to see a counsellor at the

League. Isn't that why it was set up, to help people like him?" Jordan asked, pleading for her boyfriend. "We've gotta help him, now that he's making an effort."

"Hey, sis, we're not in the old country. Don't call him Daidí," Mickey corrected his sister gently as she flushed. Embarrassed, Jordan nodded.

"That's all I'm asking for, Jordan. We agreed to give him a chance, but maybe we need to help him a bit, too. Could you ask your dad tonight?" Megan asked as Mickey pulled into Glencrest. A quick kiss on Megan's cheek and Jordan's assurances she'd talk to her dad that night was their good-bye. Megan watched her best friends drive away then turned and walked into the main house.

"Nana? Daddy? I'm home! Hi, Martha," Megan called as she passed the kitchen. She decided to stop in and grab a light snack before dinner.

"Afternoon, Miss Megan. Your grandmother's down at the barn," Martha said, tossing Megan an apple. Megan thanked the housekeeper and dashed up to her room to change. Once in her working jeans and shirt, Megan pulled on her cowboy boots and headed to the barn.

Nana was just inside the door talking to Frank. "Hi Nana, Frank," Megan said as she walked to Mystique's stall. She didn't want to interrupt them.

Her horse was fidgeting in the stall when Megan went to get her. "Come, Mystique. Stand," Megan commanded. Even with no lead rope on her, Megan's horse stood idly outside the stall while Megan took a quick look around.

"Nana, who locked Mystique's door?" Megan called as she unlocked it.

"I must've brushed it closed when I was in there earlier. Sorry, girl," Nana said with a caress for the mare. Mystique just snickered.

"Come, Mystique," Megan commanded and walked outside. "Stand." Megan gave her horse a quick once over and then began to give the young mare a thorough grooming, which

Mystique leaned into shamelessly. Nana watched the two of them for a couple of minutes then spoke quietly.

"How was school, Megan?" she asked.

"Okay, I guess," Megan replied. She began to tell Nana about Rick's troubles at school that day and the end result. "So because he saved that boy from a beating, Rick was suspended. I only hope that awful Blade got something as well," Megan finished as she threw the curry comb into the grooming kit and picked up a different comb to use on Mystique's mane.

Nana nodded sombrely. "We can only hope, but even if he did, I doubt it'll be more than a couple of days. No one actually saw him hit the other boy except his friends and Rick, and if either one says anything, the gang'll go after the boy again, this time making sure they finish what they started," Nana said philosophically.

"Stand, Mystique," Megan commanded again as the horse began to fidget. "Nana, I asked Mickey and Jordan to talk to their dad and see if he could get Rick some help. Do you think I should've? Rick's always saying I meddle too much, especially in his life," Megan worried aloud.

"No, lass. You didn't meddle. You only made a suggestion. Nothing may come of it. C'mon now. Let Mystique loose in the pasture and we'll have some supper," Nana said with a smile. Megan didn't say anything. She just led Mystique over to the pasture gate and with a couple of more gentle caresses, turned the mare loose. The two watched the horses frolic for a couple of minutes then walked back to the main house.

"Hurry and change, lass. Martha's already laying supper out," Nana said.

"I'll be back in a couple of minutes," Megan assured her grandmother. The teen dashed up to her room and quickly got out of her horse clothes. After a quick bird bath in her adjoining bathroom, she slipped into a pair of comfortable sweat pants and a tee-shirt two sizes too big for her. She liked to be comfortable after supper so she could concentrate on her homework. After brushing her hair out of its long braid, she tied it into a bun at the nape of her neck. Ready for supper, and a quiet evening of homework, she dashed back down to the dining room. Once there, Megan noticed only two places were set.

"Where's Daddy, Nana?" she asked quietly.

"He's gone out of town, lass. I've got a couple of horses in a show jumping competition this weekend and your father's there with a couple of prospective buyers. He's also looking at a couple of older horses getting ready to retire for breeding new rodeo horses. If they look good, your father's gonna buy them for me," Nana said, unconcerned, as she helped herself to the roast Martha had just placed on the table.

"Oh," was all that Megan could say. She missed her father suddenly. It was at supper where they talked about Megan's day at school and what she'd learned. It was a ten-year-old habit that had never been broken. Until today. She sighed.

"Don't worry, Megan, he's only gone for the weekend. He'll be back Sunday night," Nana said, misunderstanding Megan's sigh. Megan didn't say anything else. She was sure Nana just wouldn't understand.

Chapter 10

"Look, just place it! I'll get you the bloody money!" Michael snarled and slammed down the phone. He began banging around in the kitchen, making himself a drink.

Must be his bookie, Rick thought sourly as he ran a hand through his hair in frustration. *I'll bet he's behind on his payments again. When's he gonna learn?* Rick shook his head in disgust. *My old man can invest someone else's money and make them thousands of dollars and he can't even keep his own books straight. What a waste,* Rick thought as he continued to struggle to concentrate on his homework. It wasn't easy.

The noise from the kitchen got louder and louder.

"Dad, can the noise, will ya? I'm trying to study!" Rick finally shouted down the stairs, more than a bit irritated. He sighed when silence reigned downstairs and he returned to his room to continue struggling with his homework, only just managing to not slam the door.

"Since when do you give a rat's ass about school, Richard?" Michael sneered as he stood in Rick's doorway.

"Since being threatened with a suspension, like you give a damn. I didn't think Nana'd be too crazy 'bout that," Rick snapped back, instantly angry. He clenched his pencil so tight he felt it snap. *Why is it just the sound of his voice can piss me off?* Rick wondered.

"Thought all you cared 'bout was your boys," Michael drawled and took a long pull at the drink in his hand. "Something change your mind? Or someone?"

Rick kept quiet. The last thing Michael needed to know about was how Rick really felt about Jordan, although Rick was positive Michael already knew. Michael made a few more sarcastic comments about Rick studying and then fell silent. Rick could feel his dad staring at the back of his head.

"Anything else, *Dad*?" Rick asked sarcastically, gritting his teeth and trying to keep his anger in check.

"I'm outta here. Don't wait up," Michael said finally, turning away. Stomping down the stairs, he slammed the door behind him.

"As if I would. Maybe now I can get something done," Rick muttered under his breath. He ran another hand through his hair and bent back to work as he heard his dad tear out of the driveway. Because Rick had been such an indifferent student for the last couple of years, homework was hard for him. He really didn't have the proper foundations for some stuff and at times, eleventh grade was almost impossible. Rick was too proud to ask for help, though. *Oh well*, he thought as he struggled. *I got no one to blame but me.*

An hour later, Rick decided to take a break and get himself a snack. He grabbed a pop from the fridge, cooked a small frozen pizza in the microwave and sat out on the front porch so he could get some fresh air. The night was still fairly nice which was rare this late in September. It was dark enough the lights from inside the house shone on the porch and gave Rick plenty of shadows to hide in, just like he liked. He sat in the swing and watched the world go by.

It wasn't long before Rick noticed the four figures walking down his street towards the neighbourhood playground. The four were laughing loudly, almost too loudly, like they wanted to be heard and Rick could see at least a couple of smokes glowing in the darkening night. He knew who they were just from their voices, and the arrogant swagger they all had, but what the Knights were doing in his neighbourhood was a mystery, of sorts, to Rick.

"What're you up to now, Johnny?" Rick wondered out loud. He jumped up and sped back into the house. He grabbed his jacket and house keys, then followed his old gang to the park. Long before he got there, Rick could hear the sounds of breaking equipment and their raucous laughter. He just shook his head. Blade obviously wanted to make a statement of some kind. Rick wondered if it was a message to him or someone else. As he continued to the park, he could almost see Crank and Brain pounding on the equipment, trying to do as much damage as they could in as little time as possible. Pup, he knew, would be in charge of the graffiti. If nothing else, the kid could handle a spray can.

When Rick came around the corner, he could already hear the sirens in the distance, but he knew they could be for anything. Walking up to Pup, Rick jerked the paint can out of his startled hands and threw it up on the roof of a nearby car park. The roof was level enough the spray can wouldn't be easy to retrieve, unless you were willing to climb the ivy and risk the owner's unpredictable Rottweiler. He ignored Pup's wordless sound of protest and stalked towards Blade and the others.

"Knock it down, Crank," Blade ordered, in his lazy drawl. Laughing, Crank hefted a large sledge hammer and began to whack at the nearest leg of the swing set.

Rick grabbed Blade by the arm and spun him around. "What the hell're ya doing, man?" he demanded hotly. Rick knew his face was flushed and he was shaking with anger. It was bad enough Blade went after kids who could barely defend themselves, like Tom, but now he was going after the places kids went to play, to get away from all of their problems.

"Choose, Moneyman. Us or the playground. Keep swingin', Crank." Blade laughed at the struggle obvious on Rick's face.

"Grow up, Johnny! Your problem's with me, not the neighbourhood kids," Rick snapped back.

"Y'know, Moneyman, yer right. My prob *is* with ya and yer the only one who can solve it. Ya come back and the guys stop. Choose, Moneyman. Yer in for life, man. Why fight it?" Blade said smoothly and turned his back on Rick.

Rick couldn't believe what he had just heard. Either he came back to the Knights or the Knights were gonna destroy the park. *Some choice, Johnny* Rick thought as he darted around to where Brain was starting to tear apart a wooden play house. Just as Rick grabbed the hammer away from Brain, Blade yelled, "Cops! Move!"

All four Knights vanished into the darkness just as the park was lit up with the headlights of about a half a dozen police cruisers. Rick snarled in frustration when he realized Blade had planned this very well. Rick was the only one in sight and had been left holding the hammer. Literally.

Disgusted with himself and how easily he had been set up, Rick dropped the hammer at his feet, backed up and raised his hands over his head, all without having the police say a word. He was quickly arrested, read his rights and hauled to the station. He was charged, photographed, fingerprinted and led into an interrogation room before he really knew what was happening.

"Hey, can I make a call before I start talking?" Rick asked one of the officers who had led him to the room.

The officer hesitated, then nodded. "I'll bring a phone, but keep it short," he cautioned.

"Yes, sir," Rick replied. The officer placed the phone on the table, and Rick quickly dialled Nana's number. He knew there was no point in calling Michael. *Not like he'd care anyway,* Rick thought philosophically.

"Nana?" Rick asked when she picked up.

Seeing the number on her call display, Nana sighed explosively. "When will you learn, boy?" she snapped harshly and instantly regretted it. "I'm sorry, lad. I'll send Owen as soon as I get in touch with him. Don't say a word until you talk to him," she cautioned needlessly.

"Thanks, Nana," Rick said quietly. After hanging up, Rick got up and began to pace, thinking about what had happened. *I shoulda known he'd do something,* Rick fumed silently. *He's been too quiet, even with the attack on Tom. Dammit, why didn't I see this coming?* Rick continued to pace, waiting.

Nana hung up with a muttered oath and quickly dialled her lawyer. After apologizing for disturbing him, Nana relayed what had happened. "I know it's not your usual case for me, but he could really use your help, Owen," Nana said. "You're the best lawyer I've worked with in a long time, and I feel like we're both gonna need you before long."

"I'll head right over, Nana. Don't worry," Owen reassured her. Fifteen minutes later, Owen St. James walked into the station and asked to see his client. The young lawyer was led to the interrogation room where Constable Tony Whitefish had just begun to get Rick's personal information for the case file.

"Evening, Counsellor," Tony said as Owen was shown in. "Not your usual haunt, is it?"

"Evening, Constable, and no, it's not," Owen agreed as he took an unoccupied chair. Owen was young, only 35, but already was considered a gifted lawyer. He handled all of Nana's private legal matters and had made quite a name for himself in a couple of previous criminal trials before joining Nana's legal team. Now it appeared as if he had a new client, thanks to Nana. *Ready or not, here we go*, Owen thought as he gave the officer a look Tony had no trouble interpreting.

"I'll leave you two to talk for a few minutes," Tony said, leaving the room.

"All right, Rick, tell me what happened, and don't leave anything out." Owen said, getting right down to business, after introducing himself to his newest client. Rick detailed what had been happening at school and then what had happened that night. Owen listened and took lots of notes. He sat quietly for a couple of minutes after Rick had finished.

"Okay, son. It's not great but it's not hopeless either. Tell the judge the truth, of course. That goes without saying, but I always feel the need to tell people that. Is this your first arrest?" Owen asked as he continued to make notes.

"Yeah. I've been stopped a couple of times and given warnings, but I've never been arrested before," Rick assured his lawyer. *Not that Seamus hasn't tried,* Rick thought dryly.

"Believe it or not, that may make a difference with the judge. We'll be seeing a juvenile judge in the morning, hopefully the new one who likes to hear the cases right away and then

- 103 -

make a decision. It's a controversial way of doing things, but it generally works in small cases like this," Owen explained, then fell silent.

Owen finished making some notes on his legal pad, stood up from the table, walked over to the window and stood, thinking. Rick just sat in his chair and stared at his hands. The lawyer knew Rick was a gang member, and that was going to look bad on him, no matter how many times Rick said he was getting out. *It never matters what he's doing now, it's what he's done in the past*, Owen thought. But the more they talked, the more Owen realized there was something about the kid which called to him. *This kid's in way over his head*, Owen thought grimly. *He has no idea what to do and frankly, neither do I!*

"We're ready to talk now, Constable," Owen nodded to Tony as he came back into the room.

"Okay, Richard or do you prefer Rick?" Tony asked, noticing right away Rick stiffened when he was called by that hated first name.

"Rick," the teen said, more sharply than he really intended.

"Okay, Rick, tell me what happened tonight," Tony said as he set out a tape recorder.

Once again, Rick recounted his tale. Several times Tony stopped him and asked for clarification on some point or other, especially how the Knights reacted to, well, anything. Owen continued to take his own notes as Rick talked, and occasionally would ask his own clarifying questions, although Tony wasn't supposed to allow that. Once Rick was done, Tony leaned back in his chair and stared at Rick for a long time. The officer was silent for so long Rick began to fidget in his chair. *What did I say wrong?* Rick wondered.

"Hard to believe, kiddo," Tony said finally. He held up his hand as Rick began to protest. "I'm not saying I don't believe you, I'm just saying it's a hard story to believe. Think 'bout it, Rick. You were the only one in the playground when we showed up. You were found, holding a hammer and the play house had been

- 104 -

damaged with that hammer. There's graffiti everywhere and the only spray can we found has your prints on it. Sure, it's all circumstantial, but it's pretty damning, too.

"The judge'll probably hold you until trial," Tony continued as Rick stared at the officer in stunned disbelief, "and if you're found guilty, the worst you'll get's maybe a year in juvenile hall, but it's probably more like a few months. Trial could be as far away as five or six weeks, unless we get that new judge who likes to hear juvenile cases right away and make a decision on them then. Now, having said all of this, can you *prove* any of your accusations against the Knights?" Tony finally asked.

Rick shrugged. "Not unless Johnny speaks up," Rick admitted. *Gang loyalty my ass,* Rick muttered to himself. *He's loyal only to himself. He's not gonna take the rap for this and he's sure as hell not gonna let one of the other Knights take the blame. He's hangin' me out to dry! All 'cause I wanted some time with my girl!* Rick fumed. Tony just watched, saying nothing.

Owen spoke up. "You'll talk to the other gang members, right, Constable?" the lawyer demanded.

"Based on what? The fact Rick's accusing them of being there? There's *nothing* that points to them, except your client's accusations and since when has any criminal ever admitted to something without trying to put the blame on someone else first? I've seen it hundreds of times, especially with juveniles, Mr. St. James, and I can tell you there's no reason for us to look at someone else," Tony said gruffly, staring pointedly at Rick. Rick just stared right back, defiantly. Then the officer sighed.

"However, knowing what this gang is like, having been the investigating officer in a brutal assault they were involved in last year, I've my own reasons for keeping an eye on the Knights. So yes, Owen, I'll be contacting the rest of them and seeing if they have alibis for tonight. I doubt I'll get to any of them before morning and I'll let you know what I find out. Will that satisfy you, Counsellor?" Tony asked quietly. Owen nodded. It would have to.

"This gang's gonna be a big stumbling block for Rick, I can tell you right now," Tony continued. "Most of the judges're getting tired of the kids acting like they own the town and Blade's gang's the worst. Trouble is, no one's willing to press charges, and until someone stands up to him, he's gonna continue to terrorize this town," Tony said as he continued to stare at Rick. Rick got the message. It would probably be up to him to be the first person willing to stand up to Blade. *If only it didn't put everyone else in danger*, Rick thought wryly.

"Okay, kiddo, I've enough for now and you look like you've had it, too. You'll see the judge in the morning, first thing. Tell the judge the same story you just told me and Owen and we'll just go from there, 'kay? You'll spend the night here in a holding cell and we'll take you to the judge at eight. Okay, Counsellor?" Tony asked as he stood up. Owen nodded and told Rick he'd see him in the morning at the courthouse.

Rick nodded glumly as he watched his lawyer leave. *Man, am I ever in trouble*, Rick realized, his heart sinking to somewhere near his feet. "Can I get something to eat, Officer? Supper got interrupted," he explained dryly as Tony led him to the holding cell. The officer opened the door and guided Rick through.

"Sure thing, Rick. And don't worry 'bout a roommate tonight. You're a juvenile and we never put anyone in with a juvenile, not even another kid," Tony assured the teen. Rick jumped as Tony shut the door with a clang and called out to one of the other officers to see what they could find for a hungry prisoner. As Tony walked away, Rick looked around the cell and shuddered. He didn't like what he saw.

The cell was a monochromatic grey. There was a toilet and a sink, both metal. There was a set of metal bunk beds made up with a thin sheet and grey wool blanket, but that was it. He settled down on the bottom bunk to wait for morning. He didn't think he could sleep, especially with all the noise coming from the officers working at their desks. Rick lay back on the bunk and threw his arm over his eyes.

He was mad. Mad at himself, mainly, for falling for Blade's trick. But Rick was really furious at Blade for going after the kids when he was really after Rick. *If he hates me so much, why won't he just fight me?* Rick wondered. He jumped again as the cell door clanged open.

"It isn't much, but it'll keep you full until breakfast," the officer apologized, handing Rick a tray. On it was a couple of plastic-wrapped sandwiches and a couple of pops. The officer had also managed to find an apple and a bag of chips as well. Rick grabbed everything from the tray and settled back on the bunk to eat.

"That's okay. It's better than what I was gonna have at home," Rick assured the officer, who nodded and left. Rick finished the sandwiches and one of the pops, leaving the rest for later.

Settling back down on the bed, Rick tried to get some sleep. He tossed and turned for the first couple of hours, until, finally, miserable and unable to sleep, he got up and paced in his cell. He finished the apple and the chips, then laid down again. His mind refused to settle down at first, but eventually Rick managed to fall into an exhausted sleep.

Inspector Seamus O'Reilly himself woke Rick the next morning. Seamus was a large, burly Irishman with a shock of fiery red hair and a temper to match. He had been born and raised in Belfast, and was proud of his Irish heritage. Growing up with a military father, and living with the constant fighting in Northern Ireland, Seamus chose to become a police officer instead of joining the military.

It was in Belfast where he met and married his wife, Colleen. She knew what it meant to be married to a police officer – as did her mother and her older sister. Thankfully, Colleen's dad had retired after nearly 30 years on the force, unlike her brother-in-law who had been killed in the line of duty. Shortly after the birth of the twins, the O'Reillys left Ireland, and moved to Collingwood where Seamus joined the local police force. It had taken Seamus ten years to work his way up the ranks to Inspector and for the last six years, shortly after the death of his wife, Seamus had run the detachment with firmness and fairness.

Unfortunately, in the last couple of years, Seamus felt like he was losing control of his quiet town. Blade's gang caused more trouble than anyone else had in Seamus' more than sixteen years of law enforcement. Knowing Jordan had feelings for the gang member sleeping in his jail cell scared the hell out of Seamus. Rick was knowingly exposing Jordan to a danger Seamus couldn't protect her from. And the more he tried to keep her from Rick, the faster she ran to him, deliberately putting *herself* in danger. Seamus knew Blade didn't suffer distractions lightly and girlfriends were a distraction.

When did I lose control of me town? Seamus wondered as he stared at Rick's back. Between the gang and the shady activities of a bookie named Carlos Mendez, Seamus had more than enough balls in the air to juggle. That included trying to protect his children from everything. *Me problem is someone greased the balls when I wasn't looking and now I'm gonna drop somethin',* Seamus thought disgustedly. Yet, despite all the challenges he was facing, Seamus thought he managed to keep his feelings about Rick well hidden. Seamus didn't like Rick. Not at all. Seamus worried Rick was deliberately playing with his baby girl's affections and her loyalty to her father. So, Seamus tended to be just a little abrupt when it came to dealing with Rick.

"Are ye awake, boy?" Seamus called through the bars of the cell door, his Irish accent softly present. When Rick didn't respond right away, Seamus rattled the door loudly. Rick jumped and rolled out of bed, very disoriented and almost falling in his confusion.

Seamus chuckled nastily, not a bit sorry. "Breakfast's on its way, boy. Ye gotta date with the judge in an hour," the inspector said and stomped towards his office. He called out greetings to his officers, some who were just coming in for their shift and the night crew who were just leaving. *Why does she even like him?* the inspector wondered as he stood by Tony's desk, staring at the cell and only half listening to Tony as he detailed the night's work.

Rick stretched and rubbed the sleep out of his eyes. He splashed cold water on his face, hoping it would wake him up some. Another constable brought Rick some toast, a muffin and both apple juice and milk. He finished everything under the watchful eye of the officer and then handed the tray back. He sat back down on the bed and waited for someone to take him to court.

"Didn't turn out how ye wanted, did it, boy?" Seamus asked, as he came back to Rick's cell. He stood leaning against the cell with his arms folded over his barrel chest, glaring at the teen in the cell.

Rick looked up at a visibly angry Seamus O'Reilly. "In case no one told you, sir," Rick said sarcastically, "my name's Rick, not boy."

"Answer me question, boy," Seamus growled as if he hadn't heard Rick.

"Look, you don't like me dating Jor? Fine. Did it ever occur to you to ask your daughter how *she* feels?" Rick asked harshly. He vowed he wouldn't lose his temper, not now.

"Yer right, boy. I don't like ye. I don't like ye dating me daughter. Stay away from her," the inspector threatened quietly.

"Only if Jor tells me to," Rick replied shortly as he laid back on his bunk.

Seamus wanted to harass Rick some more but a couple of officers arrived to take Rick to face the judge. "Up, boy," Seamus barked. "Time to see the judge."

Rick nodded and stood up slowly. He kept his hands in front of him and made no sudden moves. He didn't want to provoke anyone, especially not Seamus. He was cuffed and led to the courthouse located right beside the station. Once there, Rick met up with Owen and went over the lawyer's plan again.

"Morning, Rick," the young lawyer said as he sat down.

"Morning, Mr. St. James, " Rick said as plopped into a chair across from his lawyer.

"Call me Owen, Rick, 'kay? Rough night?"

"Mmm," Rick said, stretching.

"You're gonna plead 'not guilty', 'kay?"

Rick nodded. "What're my chances?"

"Honestly? Depends on the judge, Rick. If it's the one I want, he'll hear all the evidence against you today. He'll ask you some questions and he'll question the arresting officer. If the prosecution has no objections, the judge could make his decision today. If the prosecution wants to go for a trial, it'll be put off until a later date, but I doubt that'll happen, since this is a minor case of vandalism. Now, once the judge has heard all the evidence, he'll make his decision. He could find you 'not guilty' and let you go. The other option's to find you 'guilty'.

"If so, I think there's enough coincidences in the evidence to sentence you to community service or counselling and probably not see the inside of the juvenile detention centre at all. It could be a combination of community service and jail time. It's all up to the judge. Tell your story and make sure it doesn't deviate from the one you told Tony and me last night, then leave it up to the judge," Owen finished.

The pair waited in the hallway with other young offenders and their lawyers. When Rick's case was finally called, Owen led the teen into the court room. Nana, Megan, and the twins were there to give their support. At least everyone but Mickey was. Mickey, Rick knew, was there to protect the girls. Still, Rick felt better to see some friendly faces.

"It's the judge I wanted, Rick," Owen said softly as they settled down at the defendant's table. The prosecutor pulled out his information and the case of the Crown vs. Richard Donald Attison began.

Rick pleaded "Not Guilty" when requested by the judge. The judge then asked the prosecution to present their case. The arresting officer was called to give his statement, and the crime scene tech explained the evidence they found and managed to process overnight. Minutes later, it was Rick's turn to tell his side of the story. He never deviated from the tale he told the police the night before, nor did the prosecution have any questions for him. In all, the testimony in the case took no more than 20 minutes. The judge sat for a few minutes to consider his verdict.

"Richard, while the evidence *is* circumstantial, it's overwhelming. My commendation to the Crime Scene Unit for getting the evidence processed overnight. Impressive, although quite unusual. Anyway, Richard, you were the only one found in the park. The hammer you were carrying was the one used to damage the play house. The spray paint can found had your fingerprints on it. While I realize no one actually saw you do anything, based on the evidence found, I'm gonna find you guilty of Destruction of Private Property."

Rick was not surprised. "Yes, your honour." He hung his head and waited for the axe to fall. When it did, he was surprised.

"You're hereby ordered to perform 100 hours of community service, specifically fix up that playground. If there're any hours remaining after that's done, your probation officer will direct you to another activity. You're also hereby ordered to remove yourself from the gang affiliation you have. Make no mistake about it, son, I understand getting out of a gang's a lot harder than getting into one. Lastly, you're ordered to undergo counselling. I'm putting you in the Youth Justice League program. It's one of the best counselling programs for juveniles I've seen in a long time. This counselling will start at the first available date, which is Monday," he said. "Their offices're in the Youth Centre downtown. Know where that is?"

Rick nodded.

"Good. Your counsellor there'll determine the exact number of sessions per week, based on their workload, but it won't be less than twice a week. Do I make myself clear, son? If you complete all of these conditions, and avoid any more trouble in the next two years, or until your eighteenth birthday, which ever's longer, I'll order your juvenile record sealed. Any questions? Do you understand the conditions of this verdict?" the judge asked sternly. He stared at Rick.

Rick raised his head. "Yes, your honour," Rick said softly, but clearly.

"Case closed. Next!" the judge called out, banging his gavel.

Rick turned to Owen. "Thanks, Owen. I kinda figured I wouldn't get off just the way you and Tony were talking, but I'm sure the sentence's a lot lighter compared to what I could've got. Hey, Nana," Rick said, smiling at her.

"How're you, lad?" Nana asked, giving him a hug.

"Okay, I guess. I could use a good meal, though. You don't get much in jail," Rick said lightly as Jordan came up beside him.

He stood beside Jordan with his arm around her waist. She had slipped her arm around Rick and she stood with him, facing Mickey, almost daring her brother to say something. Biting his tongue, Mickey sighed and just stared beyond Rick, shrugging his shoulders resignedly. Turning his head slightly, Rick could see Seamus O'Reilly glaring at him. He shifted around to stand behind Jordan and wrapped his arms completely around her. The two just stared defiantly back at Seamus. The elder O'Reilly frowned but finally dropped his eyes. *I won't leave her alone,* Rick thought in Seamus' direction. *Not now. Johnny'll kill her, I just know it.*

"Jor, what's it gonna take to convince your dad *I* won't hurt you?" Rick finally snarled, frustrated and willing to show it.

"I don't know, love. I'll try to explain it to him again, but don't hold your breath. I'm his baby," Jordan replied softly. She pulled herself out of Rick's embrace, but didn't drop Rick's hand. It was almost as if she was daring her father to do something.

"Owen, am I done?" Rick asked, turning back to his lawyer. Owen nodded and handed him a copy of the judge's order. "Thanks," the teen said weakly as his lawyer just laughed. Owen understood.

"Thanks for your help, Owen," Nana said, shaking her lawyer's hand. "C'mon, lad. You can stay with us this weekend. For some reason I couldn't get a hold of your father, " Nana said blandly. She motioned for Rick and Megan to proceed her out of the courtroom. Mickey and Jordan, after saying good-bye to their friends, went over to their dad. Rick could see Jordan speaking with her dad, but Rick didn't think Seamus was listening, or if he was, he didn't care.

The weekend passed quickly. Rick spent his time quietly in his house, struggling with his homework and coming to the main house for meals only. He needed a lot of time alone to think. He spent time thinking about what had happened, how it happened and what he should've done differently. Mainly he thought about Jordan and the danger he'd probably just put her in. *How'm I gonna fix any of this?* Rick thought miserably. *I care about Jor, but have I made her a target?* Every night Rick fell asleep, searching for answers and finding none. Needless to say, he was beginning to get very short on sleep.

By Sunday, when Ian came home, Rick was no closer to an answer than when he had arrived on Friday. He was short-tempered and really felt the desire to hit something. He kept wishing Blade was around to take his anger out on. Finally, realizing he was too tightly wound up to safely have supper with his family, Rick called the main house and begged Nana to be excused. Hearing the tension in her grandson's voice, Nana understood and excused him. Ian didn't. He came down and pounded on the door. Rick answered it reluctantly, knowing his uncle was going to insist Rick come up for dinner.

"Get your butt up to the house for supper! Now!" Ian barked.

"Uncle Ian, I really don't want to," Rick snapped back, frustrated. "I don't think it's a good idea. Besides, I'm not hungry."

Ian stormed into Rick's house and stood, steaming, in the living room. "Your grandmother built this house for you. Helps you when you really should be in jail. Loves you. Cares for you. Provides for you. The least you can do is drag your sorry butt up to the house and eat with her! Now move!" Ian growled and grabbed Rick by the back of his shirt.

The next thing Ian knew he was lying on his back, his head pounding and the hand he had grabbed Rick with was throbbing. Standing over him was his nephew. The look on his face was priceless, at least to Ian. It was a comical mix of fear, anger and, surprisingly, disgust. Ian began to laugh weakly.

"What're you laughing at?" Rick snarled, breathing heavily.

"You. Me. Us," Ian gasped as he levered himself into a sitting position. "I'm sorry, Rick. Here I am trying to force you to do something you clearly don't wanna do and when I can clearly see you're wound tighter than...well, I can't think of something appropriate, but you're angry enough. So what should I've expected you to do? Hit me, of course," Ian laughed weakly again and pulled himself completely up. He winced as his one hand explored a rapidly developing bruise on his cheek while he flexed the other one to check for broken bones.

Rick was horrified as he realized what he had done to his uncle, yet, oddly enough, he felt rather good. His anger and frustrations were suddenly gone. Just like Blade had taught him, he had defended himself. On the other hand, he had let his anger control him. Again. *Is this what Delaney's trying to get me to see with that essay? What's wrong with me?* Rick agonized yet again.

"I'm sorry, Uncle Ian, I really didn't mean...," Rick began hesitantly.

"Yes, you did," Ian interrupted softly. He fixed Rick with a sober gaze, until Rick dropped his eyes in shame. "The next time'll be worse. You really do have the potential to kill someone, in case no one's ever told you. You've been conditioned to react that way, Rick and it's dangerous," Ian warned. He could tell his warning wasn't sinking in, and he silently wondered what it was going to take for Rick to understand.

"No way, Uncle Ian. Not gonna happen. I know what to look for now," Rick reassured his uncle. Ian wasn't so sure Rick understood what he was talking about, but let the matter drop. He left his nephew sitting at the kitchen table waiting to eat a frozen dinner warming in the microwave.

Returning to the main house, Ian braced himself for Nana's reaction to his developing bruises. Nana didn't even blink, having seen Rick's anger first hand before. What shocked Ian was Megan's reaction. She was furious with her cousin and was on the verge of going down to the guest house to tell Rick off when Nana stopped her.

"Enough, lass," was all Nana had to say, putting her hand on Megan's arm, restraining the young teen gently.

"Mother's right, Megan. Enough. Anger's what got Rick into this mess and more anger won't get him out of it," Ian said firmly. That was the last mention made of the whole situation that night, even though Megan thought about it quite a bit as she did her homework and got ready for bed.

The next morning, Ian drove Rick and Megan to school on his way to Hollyhock's. As they drove, Megan remembered her dad's advice the night before and promised Rick she'd be a better friend. She discovered right away it was easier to say than do. She was a little wary of her cousin. Although Rick didn't say anything, Megan could see he was encouraged by the fact she was even willing to try.

As the two got out at the front door, Ian called to Rick. "Nana said to remind you about your counselling today. It's at 3:30 at the Youth Centre downtown, right after school. She also wanted to remind you Thanksgiving's in a couple of weeks. Supper'll be on the Monday at six. Tell your dad, okay?"

"Sure thing, Uncle Ian. Thanks for the lift," Rick said as he and Megan walked into the school. They caught up to Mickey and Jordan just inside the door. They also caught up with Blade and Crank.

"Yo, Moneyman, whassup, man? Didn't hear from ya all weekend," Blade drawled as he blocked Rick's way. Crank grinned viciously as Rick shifted in front of Jordan, and Mickey eased up beside Megan.

"Move it, Johnny," was all Rick had to say to the larger boy, trying to keep the anger out of his voice. *It's not like you don't know where I was all weekend, you piece of scum,* Rick snarled to himself. He could feel his hands clench and his shoulders tense as he waited for something to snap inside. He could feel the anger surging through him and he just knew he wouldn't be able to stop himself if Blade swung.

"Or ya'll what, Moneyman?" Blade asked softly, menacingly. His eyes narrowed as he tried to stare Rick down.

Rick just stared right back, unflinching. *You don't scare me, not any more,* Rick thought at Blade. *You just make me angry.* He felt someone stand beside him. To his surprise, Mickey was there, silently lending his support. But the young Irishman wasn't silent long.

"Or I'll just have to tell my dad who spray painted all the cop cars last summer. How about someone finally testifying as to who the hell beat the crap out of Tom? Say, I'd bet they'd all like to know who smashed the front windows of Dingle's Convenience store. You guys gotta learn not to brag so much, especially near a cop's kids. We tend to hear a lot," Mickey said blandly.

Crank stood right in Mickey's face. "Do it, Mickey Mouse, and see how pretty yer face'll look afterwards," the huskier boy growled. Blade snapped his fingers and he and Crank sauntered off to their Homeroom. The four friends could hear their laughter all the way down the hall. Mickey stood beside Rick, wondering if he had completely lost his marbles.

"Y'know something, Mickey, you're a bloody idiot," Mickey muttered out loud, shaking his head in amazement at what he had just done.

"I agree," Megan snapped. Mickey chuckled at her vehemence. She was standing next to Jordan with her hands on her hips and her eyes blazing.

"Thanks for speaking up, Mick," Rick said, slipping an arm around Jordan. "Appreciate it, man."

"I did it for Jordan, not for you. Face it, Rick. Dad and I don't trust you. But, unlike Dad, I'm willing to give you a chance. For her sake." With that, Mickey and his sister went to their Homeroom as Rick followed Megan to theirs.

By the end of the day, Rick was tired. Tired of dodging the Knights, of school, of the teachers, of trying to learn and trying to be someone he wasn't. By the time the final bell sounded, Rick only wanted to go home and collapse on his bed. He was halfway there when he remembered the counselling session. With an audible groan, he turned towards downtown and his date with his counsellor.

Chapter 11

Rick arrived at the youth centre with five minutes to spare. He gave his name to the secretary at the front desk who directed him to a group of offices in the back, where he gave his name to another receptionist who told him curtly to sit down and wait. His counsellor would be along shortly, she said without changing her tone. Sitting gingerly in a flimsy plastic chair, Rick waited for someone to arrive. He didn't have to wait long.

A tap on his shoulder brought Rick face to face with the last person he expected – his arresting officer, Constable Tony Whitefish. Shocked into silence, Rick just followed Tony into an empty office, sat in the chair Tony indicated and waited, watching the young cop warily, his attitude telling Tony more than anyone would've learned from talking to the teen.

Tony Whitefish was over six feet tall, slender, yet very muscular. His brown eyes seemed far wiser than his 26 years. His Cree heritage was clearly visible in his light brown skin and jet black hair braided in two braids that fell over his shoulders. Rick noticed the braids were tied off with what looked like two thin strips of leather.

This cop's traditional, Rick realized suddenly. He continued to study the man on the other side of the desk. Tony's uniform fit snugly across the muscular shoulders; Rick knew the cop would be very strong if pushed. If Rick had bothered to ask, he would have found out Tony was a well-respected dancer on his reserve. He was always chosen for the most complicated dances, such as the Hoop Dance so many people loved to see.

Tony was proud of his heritage, despite having to fight tooth and nail to be respected for who he was, not what he was. Tony made a point of going home to the reserve every couple of months to re-connect with his family and his roots. The last couple of visits had been spent with several elders and the medicine man, learning more about becoming an elder. But somehow Tony knew the kid sitting across from him would be a far harder fight than anything the cop had ever faced, including being native.

Tony sat quietly in his chair, pretending to read Rick's file. In reality, the cop was watching Rick. The teen was slumped in his chair, his arms folded over his chest and attitude written all over his face. It was an attitude Tony had seen far too many times. He had spent many frustrating days on his reserve in his youth watching family and friends fall victim to crime, drugs and alcohol and seeing that same look on their face with they were arrested. It was an attitude which screamed, *"You're wrong; I haven't done anything!"*

It was these years of frustration which had naturally led Tony to a life of fighting crime instead of committing it. It was the irritation of arresting the same kids over and over again which had, in turn, led Tony to approach Seamus O'Reilly with the idea of the Youth Justice League program. So far, Tony thought it was working. Only now, Tony knew, the League was about to face its biggest challenge, and he wasn't sure if the League would survive if everything went wrong. *Here goes nothing*, Tony thought with a small grin. *Or everything*.

"Okay, Rick. In case you don't remember me, I'm Constable Tony Whitefish. You can call me Tony."

"Back off, Officer. I ain't done nuttin' wrong," Rick said defensively, automatically falling back into the street lingo of the gang. "I just got told t' c'mere fer counsellin'."

"I know that, Rick and I'm your counsellor. Since I set up the League, I figured it was only right for me to take some of the cases that come our way, usually only one each school year. We've found, or at least *I've* found, sometimes it's better for certain types of kids to talk to a cop than to a shrink. Usually, my cases're someone like you. A basically good kid at heart who's just made some mistakes along the way and is now so mixed up he doesn't know what to do or how to fix it. And Rick, I know you can speak better than you just did," Tony chided gently, leaning back in his chair and watching Rick with his dark eyes to see how he reacted.

"Whatever, man. Is this better?" Rick asked sullenly, speaking clearly. *I don't need this*, Rick fumed. *Not now. Not with Johnny on the prowl.* The more he thought about his counsellor, the angrier he got.

"Thanks. Now we talk. My schedule often changes so we probably won't be able to meet here all the time. I've arranged with Mr. Delaney to meet you at the school at lunch, no matter what. The sessions're only supposed to be an hour long anyway and by meeting at school, I'm forced to keep it to an hour. Meeting here, we may end up going over time," Tony began. *Not that going over time with you would be a bad idea,* Tony mused, *if how you just reacted to having your speech corrected is any indication.* "If I can't make it, I'll call you. I'm assuming you have your own cell? Good. And, Rick, I expect the same courtesy. Don't leave me hanging, 'kay? Now, you're required to have two sessions a week. After today, I'll decide if that's enough. Deal?"

Rick still didn't say anything. He was too busy panicking over Blade's reaction. *This cop's gonna be my counsellor*, Rick ranted. *Jor's as good as dead!*

Tony sighed gustily. He knew these weren't going to be easy sessions, but he hadn't expected the dead silence. He knew Rick's reputation for violence and anger, so he decided to push a bit to see what happened. "Rick, these sessions are for you to talk to me so I can help you. Trust me, lecturing you won't do you a damn bit of good. So that means you have to open your mouth and say something," Tony said, exasperated.

"Having you as my counsellor's as good as handing Jor to Johnny along with a loaded gun and saying, 'Here, shoot her now!'" Rick snapped, his face flushed with anger he could barely contain. He stood up, stalked to the door and yanked it open. Without warning, Tony shot around the desk and slammed the door closed in Rick's face. Rick was stunned. And impressed. The cop didn't lend the impression of being that quick.

Tony roughly guided Rick back to his chair and snapped, "SIT!"

"I'm not your damn dog!" Rick snapped back. He yanked his arm out of Tony's iron grip. "You can't make me stay!"

Tony took a deep breath to calm himself down. "Sorry. And you're right, Rick, I can't. But understand this. This counselling's part of your sentence. If you don't do the counselling, you go straight to juvy. Don't pass go and don't collect any money. Your choice, man – counselling or juvy. Which is it gonna be?" Tony glared at Rick.

"The judge never said that!" Rick protested loudly, his face paling.

"Not specifically, but the type of sentence you received is essentially probation, since you weren't given any jail time. Your lawyer should've made sure you knew that. Along with fixing that playground, you have to come to these sessions and, in exchange, I tell the court everything's cool. Violate it or refuse to complete any part of your sentence and you go to jail. Period," Tony said emphatically, sitting on the edge of his desk with his arms folded. He almost felt sorry for Rick, but the cop knew if he didn't get this through Rick's head now, these sessions would be a trial for both of them.

"Great. Some choice. Either I sit here twice a week and listen to you lecture me or I go to jail," Rick said bitterly as he slumped in his chair again.

Tony moved away from his desk to sit beside Rick. *How am I gonna get through to you, kid?* he wondered, hesitating for a couple of moments. "Lecturing wouldn't do you any good," Tony finally repeated. "It'll just go in one ear and out the other, and you'll resent me for trying. I'm not here to lecture, but I *am* here to listen. Basically, I wanna know what is it about the Black Knights that calls to you and I'm here to help you change, if you really want to. What has Mr. Delaney been trying to make you see with that essay?" Tony asked suddenly. On Tony's desk was a file that contained, aside from Rick's personal information, a copy of Rick's detention essay which Delaney had provided when Tony had asked him for Rick's school record. Like Delaney, Tony had found it very interesting.

"To get me to realize what a dead end the gang is. Tony, I get that. Now. The problem's Johnny. The more I try to get away from the gang, the more danger I put everyone in, especially Jor. You know damn well I didn't wreck that playground – it's not my style. Yet I'm the one who's been arrested, charged, found guilty and has the criminal record. Johnny gets nothing. I bet you didn't even talk to them about it. They get *nothing*. That's the part I don't get," Rick snarled. He slammed his fist down on the arm of the chair and didn't even notice the pain. Tony just shook his head in amazement. *Where does this kid store all that anger?* he thought, amazed.

"Y'know, Rick, I understand your frustration. But look at it from our point of view for a moment. You were found at the scene of a crime holding the weapon which had caused the damage. Why should we look any further just on your say-so?" Tony reasoned. "And yes, I did talk to the Knights, but they all had someone to alibi them. Brain's little sister said they were home with her all night." *Not that I really believe her*, Tony thought with a shrug, *but it's an alibi and we can't go any further with it.*

Rick didn't speak for a moment. Tony could see the struggle going on in Rick's head. "Rick, c'mon, kiddo. I can't help you if you won't talk. Tell me about this gang and why you got into it in the first place," Tony said quietly. *That's as good a place as any to start*, Tony reasoned. *This kid's gonna be a challenge.*

"Why did I join? Man, that's tough. It's been so long I just don't know anymore, Tony," Rick shook his head. *Why does everyone wanna know that?* Rick wondered.

"Okay...what about your home life, Rick? Does your mom know what's going on?" Tony asked curiously.

He wasn't prepared for the violence of Rick's reaction, going from pretty calm to uncontrollable rage in less than a heartbeat. He jumped up from his chair so fast he knocked it flying. His face was flushed with anger and his fists were clenched so tight Tony figured his fingernails would leave dents his palms.

"Leave my mom out of this!" Rick shouted and suddenly swung wildly at Tony, who had jumped up at the same time, wondering what he had just said that was so wrong.

Ducking the wild punch, Tony kicked the other chair out from under his feet and towards the desk. The office was big enough to allow the pair room to manoeuvre but small enough to contain the fight. *Providing I don't let Rick get to the door*, Tony thought grimily, as he ducked a second wild punch. With that firmly in mind, Tony allowed Rick to manoeuvre him around so the cop's back was against the door and then just let Rick swing away. Rick's anger had blinded him and made most of his punches go well wide of their mark, but the ones that connected were solid and made Tony grunt with each impact.

For ten long minutes, Tony let Rick wear himself out. Then, when one of Rick's weaker punches was approaching his head, Tony grabbed Rick's arm, twisted it up behind him and shoved Rick into the wall. The cop could still feel Rick quivering with anger as the teen struggled to get free.

"Enough, Rick," Tony grated in Rick's ear, hoping he could reach Rick. "Stop fighting me, dammit!"

For a couple of minutes, Tony thought he hadn't succeeded. Rick continued to fight weakly. Then, he shook his head as if trying to clear it. Rick was honestly shocked to find himself pinned to the wall by Tony with no idea of how it had happened. He shook his head again, groaning as the world spun dangerously.

Slumping with sudden exhaustion, Rick allowed himself to be led back to his chair, which Tony picked up and set right. Rick couldn't understand why he was so upset. His hands were sore and he could feel his legs shaking. His breathing was ragged and he could feel a massive headache developing.

"What hap...what happened?" Rick asked fuzzily as he swayed slightly in his chair. Suddenly, whatever anger had been left ran away, leaving Rick drained and feeling like a wet wash cloth. He rubbed his left temple where he felt the headache the worst and wished silently for something to drink to ease the nausea he felt beginning.

"You don't remember?" Tony replied, amazed. The cop reached into a little fridge by his desk and tossed Rick a bottle of ginger ale, as if he knew what Rick was feeling. After Rick had taken a couple of gulps and shook his head, Tony continued quietly. "I asked about your mom and you just...blew." Tony was impressed at the strength he had felt in Rick and, given how quickly the kid had exploded over a simple question, knew he was about to start dealing with what he could only call a walking time bomb, one he was sure he would have to defuse many times. *Oh well, I asked for this,* Tony thought philosophically. *I could've picked a dozen different kids and I asked for Rick Attison.*

Rick nodded, tiredly. "It happens sometimes. I just go into a blind rage if someone even mentions my mom. Life ain't been too kind, y'know?" Rick's voice trailed off as he thought about his mom. *Where are you, Mom?* a desperate little boy cried. He could still see the empty house except for his dad lying on the couch and he could hear himself calling for his mom. Even worse, he could hear his dad yelling at him that it was his fault. It hurt all over again.

Tony didn't say anything for a moment. When he finally spoke again, his voice was quiet, but commanding.

"Tell me."

For the next couple of hours, Rick talked and talked, mainly about his family life, or what there was of it. Tony learned about Rick's parents' problems, at least as much as Rick knew, and about that horrible nickname in elementary school. The first of many scars a too-young boy had been given. Tony even learned about Michael's attitude towards his own sons and how Rick's brother, Nelson, had managed to escape.

"Nana wouldn't let me leave, though. She thought I needed to stay here," Rick said softly before continuing on about his fights in school and with Seamus. And Jordan. Every other sentence seemed to be about his girlfriend.

Everything Tony learned that afternoon told him exactly why Rick had joined the Knights, even if Rick didn't know it himself. Nothing in his home life gave him the level of comfort, security and respect the gang did. Blade would've seen that at once and would've played on it. Rick fell for it, hook, line and sinker, and Tony knew he had to get Rick off that hook before he died a slow death. Or a quick one, depending on the gang.

"Okay, Rick," Tony said after more than two hours. He was exhausted from the session, and he could see how tired Rick was, sitting slumped in his chair. "You've got some serious issues that need to be dealt with, son. Let's meet three times a week at school. I know you think it's dangerous, especially for Jor, but maybe seeing you with a cop constantly'll give Blade something to think about." *Other than you or her*, Tony thought grimly. *I hope so, or these kids're gonna end up dead.*

Rick nodded, exhausted, and agreed to meet Tony on Wednesday at lunch. "I'll wait for you at the office. I'm sure Delaney'll give us someplace to talk," Rick said as he stood and stretched. His shoulders and lower back both cracked loudly in the small room. Tony laughed at the look of relief on Rick's face.

"Sounds good, kiddo. Oh, one more thing, Rick," Tony said idly, as he sat back at his desk to make his notes on their meeting.

Rick turned away from the door. "Yeah? What?"

"Start leaving the colours at home. If Blade sees you without them, he may get the message sooner," Tony reasoned, looking at the teen. It wouldn't be easy, Tony knew, to help Rick overcome his reliance on the Knights, *but*, Tony thought as he scribbled down his notes, *some things're worth fighting for and, the Creator help me, I believe he's one of them.*

"I'll try," Rick stated flatly, as he slipped out of the office and went home.

By Wednesday, Rick felt a little more confident his plan to leave the gang was going to work. Taking Tony's advice, he'd left the jacket at home, although he still wore the black jeans, white tee and his cowboy boots, since that was all the clothes he owned and were comfortable. He had been successful in avoiding the

Knights all day Tuesday and Wednesday morning, but at his locker right before lunch, Rick's luck finally ran out.

Out of the corner of his eye, Rick caught a flash of black and silver right before he was slammed into his locker. He grunted with the impact. He could feel his face being ground into the rough metal. "Blade wants t' chat wi'cha, Moneyman," Brain hissed in Rick's ear. Blade's second-in-command yanked Rick around, catching his arm on the locker and slicing it open. Rick just ignored the blood dripping down his arm.

"Now!" Crank snapped and shoved Rick along down the hall and into the now-deserted auto shop. Blade was inside, pacing agitatedly and Pup was standing lookout in the hall. The smallest of the gang just grinned viciously as he saw Rick being almost dragged in by the other two boys. Blade stopped pacing and leaned against the workbench as the trio entered. He glared at Rick.

"What do you want now, Johnny?" Rick asked gruffly. *I won't be a part of this anymore,* Rick vowed silently. *I can't.*

Blade's eyes pierced Rick's. "Moneyman needs a lesson, boys. His brain's a little fuzzy. Gots no respect," Blade hissed softly.

Crank wrenched Rick's already-cut arm up behind his back and shoved him into a steel door, being careful to not get any of the dripping blood on his boots or clothes. "What's the name, punk?" Crank growled low in his ear.

"Break my arm, Eric, if you want, man, but either way I'm out," Rick gasped as Crank pushed him further into the door. Rick was suddenly whipped around, scraping his face against the door. He could feel the cuts bleeding and wondered how he would explain them to Tony.

"Moneyman, ya need t' understand the deal here," Blade hissed, just inches from Rick's face. "See, when ya join, it's fer life. No one leaves unless I say they can. And I never say that." Rick didn't flinch at the anger and hatred he heard in Blade's voice. If he really admitted it to himself, Rick felt the same anger and hatred towards Blade, too.

"Finish what you have to do, Johnny, and lemme go. I've gotta be somewhere, and I'm late," Rick said defiantly, standing proud against his former mates.

Pup came into the room carrying a bag and tossed it to Blade. Reaching in, Blade pulled out Rick's leather jacket and a black bandana. Rick blanched. He had only one jacket and he had left it in his room. Blade had broken into Rick's house and got his stuff to prove a point. He could get Rick any time he wanted to. *Great,* Rick thought sourly, *now he'll be in there all the time. Dad's gonna kill me.*

"Ya fergot these when ya got dressed. So Pup and I got 'em fer ya. Put 'em on, Moneyman," Blade sneered. Rick hesitated long enough Crank wrenched his arm up behind his back again, making Rick cry out.

Shaking in anger, Rick complied, shrugging on the leather jacket and tying on the bandana with some effort. He tried not to think about what his bleeding arm was doing to the butter-soft leather. "Happy, Johnny?" Rick asked sarcastically.

Crank cuffed Rick across the back of the head. "Blade, Moneyman. Blade," the larger boy snapped.

Glaring at Crank, Rick snapped, "Right, Eric. Can I go now, *Blade*?" Rick asked sarcastically and turned away. A knife whistled past his head and sunk into the wall. Dropping to his knees by sheer reaction, Rick knew just how lucky he was. Blade never missed a target he aimed at. He had meant to come that close to Rick's head.

"Remember" was Blade's parting shot.

The four went out the door, grabbing Blade's knife on their way out. They left Rick, stunned, on his knees, his face and arm bleeding. Finally, still shaking, Rick dragged himself to his feet and found the nearest bathroom to wash up. He swore under his breath at the cuts on his face and, after washing as much of the blood away as he could, went to meet Tony at the office. He was ten minutes late and Tony was unimpressed, especially when he saw Rick in the colours.

Tony didn't say anything about Rick's obvious injuries as he led the teen into a small conference room Mr. Delaney had agreed to let Tony use. "I thought we'd agreed you'd stop wearing that stuff," Tony pointed out. He tossed Rick a handkerchief he had in his pocket. Rick pressed it to his still-bleeding cheek. He grimaced at the blood he saw when he pulled the piece of cloth away. He shrugged the jacket off and wiped at the blood on his arm.

Tony didn't say anything as he dug through the cabinets looking for something. Finally, he stuck his head out the door and asked the secretary for a first aid kit. When it was passed to him, he knelt beside Rick and set to work bandaging the cut on the teen's arm. Rick only answered once the cop had sat down in front of him again.

"Yeah, well, Johnny had other ideas. He decided to break into my house. He grabbed my gear to remind me of who he thought I was supposed to be," Rick said, slumping in his chair. He was still shaking and thinking about how close he had come to having Blade's knife in his back. His face was sore and his arm throbbed. All in all, it was going to be a thoroughly miserable afternoon, Rick just knew.

"Tony, this ain't gonna work," Rick protested finally. "Seriously, man, Johnny's not gonna let me go. I mean, look what he did to me in just a couple of minutes. He hates me too much, and now he's taking this personally."

"What makes you say that?" Tony asked. Rick hesitated for a long time, then finally explained why he was late and what Blade had done. And almost done. The two talked for nearly an hour, in between bites of lunch.

Finally, Tony looked at his watch and stood. "Okay, that's enough for today. We'll meet Friday at the centre instead of here, and Rick? No one said this would be easy," the cop said as he opened the door. He motioned for Rick to lead the way.

"Nothing worth doing's ever easy, kiddo," Tony finished as they stepped into the hall. Standing there, waiting for them, were Mickey, Megan, and Jordan. Rick smiled at Jordan and gave her a quick hug. She reached up to touch his cheek and Rick just shook his head at her questioning glance.

"Tony, this is Mickey and Jordan O'Reilly and my cousin, Megan Attison," Rick said. "Guys, Constable Tony Whitefish, my counsellor."

"Hi, Megan, nice to meet you," Tony said softly, shaking Megan's hand once, as was the native way. Smiling, he nodded at Mickey and Jordan. "These other two trouble makers I already know. Don't be late Friday, Rick," Tony said, waving good-bye. Walking to his car, Tony decided to check out Rick's house. *At least I can make sure there's nothing else stolen,* Tony thought as he started his patrol car and drove away.

"How do you know Tony, Mick?" Rick asked as the four headed to class.

"We've known him ever since he joined the detachment, 'bout four, maybe five years ago, hey sis? Dad really likes him. Says he's a good cop," Mickey shrugged as Jordan nodded.

"He's not a bad counsellor, either," Rick admitted. He split from the group to head to his math class while Megan and the twins headed to the library for their spare. He stopped at the end of the hall to look back at Jordan. *"Nothing worth doing's ever easy,"* Tony's voice echoed in Rick's head.

How right you are Tony, Rick sighed as he headed to class.

Chapter 12

The next couple of weeks were almost a blur for Rick. He was harassed daily by Blade and Crank, especially in class. The teachers did nothing because they were too scared of Blade, which Rick totally understood and respected. Each day Rick had new bruises and cuts, some of which required stitches. He didn't mind putting his life on the line for everyone else; it was the least he could do after everything he had done. After Rick showed up at the centre for the second time needing stitches, though, Tony insisted he file charges against the Knights.

"Yeah, right, and get myself killed," Rick said sarcastically as he gingerly sat down in his chair after the pair had returned from the hospital.

"Look, Rick, either way this is gonna get worse. A lot worse. If you don't push back, and soon, Johnny's gonna think you're weak. Then he'll really come after you," Tony pointed out as he sat on his favourite corner of the desk.

Rick sat quietly, thinking. This time, Blade had somehow managed to slice Rick's ribs bad enough to need fifteen stitches, mainly because Rick refused to fight with his knife. But Rick didn't really want to press charges against Blade. The only witnesses were the rest of the Knights, and both Rick and Tony knew they wouldn't rat Blade out.

As Rick stewed, Tony watched. He could see the struggle Rick was facing and wondered if Rick realized just how close he'd come to dying already. Blade's knife was cutting deeper and deeper, the doctor at the hospital told Tony while Rick had been getting dressed. Blade wasn't going to stop until someone got really hurt, and his sudden physical attacks on Rick made Tony wonder who was next.

"Okay, kiddo, I won't push you right now. But I want you to understand something. Are you listening?" Tony asked and continued when Rick raised his eyes and nodded. "Johnny's trying to make a point – he can get you any time, any place. Now he may raise the stakes," Tony warned and waited for Rick to make the connection.

Rick already had. "He's gonna come after Jor." It was a statement, not a question. Nodding, Tony saw Rick was beginning to get angry, and maybe a little frightened at what he had started.

"I said this wouldn't be easy, Rick. You knew there was a distinct possibility Johnny'd do this," Tony pointed out logically.

"I know, dammit!" Rick snapped back heatedly, clenching his hands into white-knuckled fists. Tony didn't move until Rick had calmed somewhat. Then, and only then, when Tony was reasonably sure Rick wouldn't explode, did the cop move to sit beside Rick.

"I realize you know what's at stake here, Rick. Now you have to figure out how to keep her safe," Tony said quietly. Rick sat, saying nothing and staring at the floor between his still-clenched fists. "Promise me you'll keep me informed about everything, and don't do anything reckless. Just go home and take it easy for a couple of days."

Rick stood silently, nodded, and left.

Tony sat down to write his notes, but for the longest time he just sat, staring at Rick's chair. Tony knew he was getting close to a breakthrough with Rick, thanks to Blade's attacks, and when the breakthrough came, it would probably be violent and drawn-out. For that reason alone, he had arranged to be on the night shift with his partner right now. He had, somehow, made Seamus understand he would have to be able to spend several hours with Rick when the breaking point came.

Seamus hadn't liked putting one of his best teams on the night shift, but understood that if this new program was going to work, especially with kids like Rick, then some sacrifices would have to be made.

"Only 'til the beginning of November, though, Tony," Seamus had said. "After that, yer back on yer regular shift and we'll just have to work around these little sessions with the boy. I need ye on day shift." Tony wondered if that would be long enough. As he finished writing his notes, an idle thought made him sit up sharply.

"I wonder what my shaman would suggest," Tony muttered to himself. "He's dealt with kids like Rick on the reserve." Now that Tony had a plan, he'd just have to wait until he could go home to the reserve to put it into action.

The Friday before the Thanksgiving long weekend was a very busy day for Rick. He was still dodging Blade and the Knights with varying degrees of success. His marks were slowly improving and so was his rapport with his teachers. Just before lunch, Mr. Delaney called him into the office to get an update and was impressed by the progress Rick seemed to have made.

By the end of the day, Rick was actually felling pretty good. Delaney let him know how much he had improved in his classes and how happy he was Rick had stopped getting into so much trouble with his teachers. The teen still had a tendency to let his mouth run away with itself, but through hard work and determination, his marks had improved and the teachers weren't terrified of him anymore. Mr. Robson had even told him if Rick continued to work this hard, the teacher was going to recommend Rick be moved into the mainstream English program in Grade 12 instead of the secondary one he was currently in. Rick was proud of himself and what he'd already managed to accomplish.

The other plus in these last two weeks had been the small improvement in his relationship with Mickey. Jordan's brother didn't seem to hate him quite so much, and Rick was thankful. It made it easier to spend time with Jordan since the only one he looked over his shoulder for now was Blade.

Rick had his head lowered as he was thinking about Jordan and not really paying attention to where he was going when he suddenly found his path blocked. Snarling in frustration, since he was already late for his session with Tony, Rick tried to sidestep a couple of times, but whatever was in the way just kept moving with him. Rick finally looked up and sighed inwardly. There, in front of him, was Crank. Pup was on one side and Brain was on the other. Rick didn't have to look behind him to know where Blade was. Just the thought of Blade being behind him made Rick break out in a cold sweat.

"Hey, Moneyman. Inna hurry?" Blade drawled lazily. Rick didn't dare take his eyes off of Crank. He had a look in his eyes which said the larger boy was spoiling for a fight and Blade was about to give it to him. *I'm toast*, Rick thought, resigned to his fate.

"Johnny," Rick said without turning around. Blade whacked the back of Rick's head hard enough to drive him to his knees. *What the hell did he hit me with? A board?* Rick wondered as he tried to clear the stars from his eyes. Rick was desperate to get to his feet. He wasn't gonna be gutted like an animal.

"Looks like he's still gots that memory problem, Blade," Brain drawled. Rick could hear the other two laughing as he struggled to clear his head.

"Fix it fer him," Blade commanded. Rick could hear the anger in Blade's voice and knew if he didn't push back as Tony said, this could be the last chance he would have against the older boy.

"Dammit, hold on," Rick demanded as he finally managed to struggle to his feet. "Face me yourself, Johnny. You or Brian. One-on-one. Gimme a fair fight for once in your damn life, man," Rick demanded again, labouring to control his temper.

After a moment, Blade nodded and pointed to Brain. Rick and Brain circled, each looking for an opening. Rick was more confident facing Brain than he would've been facing Blade. At least with Brain he wouldn't face a knife, even though Brain carried one just like Rick and Blade did. Blade would pull his when his opponent wasn't looking. Rick was taller and had a longer reach than Brain, but Brain was stronger. Rick's only hope was to attack – and quickly. Brain wasn't expecting the sudden rush and Rick managed to land a couple of punches to Brain's stomach, then finished up with a pair to the head. The second punch knocked Brain down and he didn't get up.

"Finish it!" Brain gasped as Rick stood over him, breathing heavily and still mad as hell.

"No," Rick growled. "Now leave me alone."

Rick walked away, his anger at Blade smouldering all the way to the youth center. Waiting for Rick at the front desk, wanting to see for himself why the teen was late this time, Tony sighed as he couldn't help but notice the anger on Rick's flushed face. Without a word, he led the teen to the gym. Set up in one corner was a boxing ring where Rick could see several schoolmates going through various routines. Tony left Rick to stew while he went to find the boxing instructor. As Rick waited, he paced restlessly.

Returning, Tony said, "Rick, this is Bob Summers. He's the boxing coach here at the center. Your counselling session starts right here today. You're too angry to talk coherently. For a change, take it out on the bag, not me. See you in an hour in my office. Make him sweat, Bob," Tony commanded and nodded to Bob as he walked away.

Rick fumed as he wasn't given any choice about the training, but he silently followed the older man to the locker room to change. *Now we'll see what you're really made of, Rick,* Tony thought as he stopped at the door to watch Bob put Rick through the most exhausting workout Rick had ever had.

The trainer, a middle-aged stocky man, started Rick on the speed bag to warm his stiffening muscles and then got the stressed teen to stretch out. Rick returned to the speed bag where Bob gave him a specific sequence of punches to learn. The pattern was designed to improve Rick's hand-eye coordination, but, Bob also knew the rhythm would work to soothe Rick when he was agitated. Rick then spent time on the free weights, while Bob explained how the boxing would do no good if Rick didn't have the strength to back it up. Rick agreed silently as he worked out and finally returned to the speed bag to finish the session. As Rick moved through the regimen, Bob privately thought Rick was a natural boxer. By the end of the hour, Rick was dripping with sweat and he had no anger left.

"You gotta place to hang a speed bag?" Bob asked as he set Rick to do his cool-down stretches.

"Yeah. I can hang it in my room. Dad won't care," Rick said as he stretched out his shoulders. *Dad don't care about anything but himself*, Rick thought.

Bob handed Rick a new bag and explained how to hang it. "Now, do you remember the pattern I taught you today?" Rick nodded. "Good. That's what I want you to do every chance you get. You're a natural, Rick. You've got some good moves, son, but you're too angry right now. That's stopping you from getting the most outta your counselling sessions. By doing this at home, that's gonna help. How often're you here?" he asked, standing with his hands in his jacket pockets.

"Three times a week, but sometimes Tony likes to meet at the school," Rick said as the two walked towards Tony's office. Rick occasionally rubbed his hands or shook his arms to relieve some lingering soreness and tension. He was still trying to absorb what Bob talked about when he called him a "natural."

"Okay. I'll arrange it with Tony. Even if you meet at school, I still want you to come here after school, every day, if you can manage it. I want you in that gym as often as possible, but especially before you talk to Tony. It'll do you good," Bob said as he left Rick at Tony's door.

Rick knocked and entered when Tony called for him. They spent a while talking, especially about Blade's attacks. Rick still struggled to convince the Knights he was out and, because of that, he knew he was putting Jordan in danger. They couldn't reach a consensus by the end of the session, but Rick felt like he was making progress. They set up their next session at the school on Tuesday, since Monday was a holiday, and Tony knew the centre would be a madhouse in the afternoon. As they wrapped up for the weekend, Rick told Tony what Bob said about Rick continuing to box, and Tony agreed to talk to the coach about Rick's training.

The weekend passed quickly. Rick hung his speed bag and used it several times over the long weekend. By Monday, Rick was eager to see Nana and Megan again.

"Let's go, boy," Michael snapped, tossing the keys to the Corvette to his son. Rick was stunned, but only for a minute. Grinning slightly, Rick led the way to the garage. Michael hardly ever let him drive, even though Rick got his license when he turned 16. *He must've had more than a couple already*, Rick mused as they climbed into the silver car.

The drive to Glencrest was quick and silent. Rick pulled into the driveway and parked the car, taking care to park away from everyone else. Michael stomped into the house, leaving Rick to trail in afterwards. Martha directed them into the den where Michael immediately poured himself another stiff drink. Seeing this, Nana immediately limited further access to the booze by locking up everything hard and having Ian play bartender. Michael fumed, but he didn't argue as hard as he usually did.

"Supper will be in an hour, Mrs. Attison," Martha announced as she brought more snacks into the den.

"Thank you, Martha," Nana replied as Ian handed her a glass of wine. The adults remained near the bar while Rick searched for Megan.

"Hey, Megs, how're you?" Rick asked, spying his cousin at the one end of the den. He grabbed a couple of pops and carried them over to where she sat by the fire.

"Not bad, Rick, thanks. I heard you're in counselling. How's that going?" she asked as she opened her pop.

"Okay, I guess. Tony's suggested boxing training, too. Something about needing a way to get rid of the anger. Hopefully, it's gonna help. Can I ask you something?" he asked as he stood with his back to the fireplace.

"Sure," she replied.

"How come you never talk about your mom? Not that I do either, but I never hear you even mention her," Rick said softly.

"It's too hard, Rick. I keep expecting her to walk in the door any minute. I miss her lots, and I just can't talk about her,"

Megan replied quietly, blinking away the tears that had gathered in her eyes.

"Sorry, Megs, I guess I never realized that. Y'know, you may wanna talk to Tony about this, or one of the other counsellors at the youth centre. I don't think it's something you should keep inside," Rick said sagely.

"Like you ever talk about your mom," Megan said dryly. "And Rick, don't push, please. But...thanks for the idea."

Rick smiled softly. Just like the day they met, Rick felt the overwhelming desire to shelter her. "You're welcome, cuz. Anytime," was all he said, understanding her hesitation.

Rick settled on the arm of Megan's chair so that they could talk. They talked about school and friends for the most part, then shifted to Rick's counselling. Eventually Rick asked Megan what she thought Jordan might like for Christmas, and they began to make plans for the holidays. Their conversation was rudely interrupted by a loud argument at the other end of the den, where Michael was yelling at Nana.

"Great. Dad's asked for money. Again," Rick groaned quietly. Megan just looked at her cousin, but didn't reply. Rick ran his hand through his thick hair and sighed in frustration. *Why now, Dad?* he fumed silently. He'd finally just started to relax. Now, thanks to his dad, he was all tensed up again.

"C'mon, Mom, just give me the money," Michael growled.

"Not until you tell me where it's going. That's another $30,000, Michael! What's going on?" Nana demanded sharply. "You think I make my money just so you can throw it away? I don't think so, young man. Now, where's it all going?" Nana demanded again.

"I got behind on a couple of bills. Just give me the bloody money," Michael growled, slamming his hand down on the bar counter. Megan jumped at the loud noise in the silent room.

"Michael, you have a successful business and I know you've invested wisely over the years. Where's all your money gone?" Ian asked, puzzled.

"Do you know, Rick?" Megan whispered. She had squished herself into the chair to avoid being noticed. Rick knew how she felt. He wanted to leave, but the adults were now standing by the door and any movement would swing the attention towards the kids.

"Yeah, but it's not my business to say," Rick said shortly. He glared at his dad as Michael continued to argue with Nana.

Michael got right in his mother's face. "Give me the money!" he yelled, shaking his fist. Nana paled slightly at the implied threat Michael issued. She slumped, as if defeated.

"Very well, Michael," Nana acquiesced and moved to her desk. There, she wrote a cheque and handed it to her son. Michael just smirked. That smile was wiped from his face with his mother's next words.

"This is the last money you'll ever get from me, Michael," Nana said firmly. She remained seated behind the desk with her hand on the chequebook.

Michael was stunned. "What do you mean, Mom?" he asked weakly.

"This bank's closed, Michael. Whatever your problem is, I'll no longer bail you out. I'm tired of it," Nana said, as she dismissed Michael and his problems.

Michael stared at his mother. "What am I gonna do now?" he stammered. He was pale and shaking.

"I don't care. Solve this problem yourself," Nana said indifferently as she put the chequebook away, locked the drawer, and stared coldly at her son.

Striding around the desk, Michael shouted, "Now look here, you old..."

Pouncing on his brother, Ian grabbed Michael by the back of the shirt and dragged him towards the door.

"Get out! You're not welcome here anymore," Ian snapped.

Michael wrenched out of Ian's grasp, glared as his mother and brother, and stormed out of Glencrest. Rick was stunned at his father's sudden eviction. Now, unless Ian drove him home, he'd have to stay the night. *Not that I wouldn't mind staying here permanently,* Rick thought sadly.

No one said anything for a long time after Michael had left. The tension was thick and made Rick even more edgy. He couldn't stop his legs from jumping and he knew he was clenching his fists. Megan sat back up in her chair and softly asked Rick to get her another pop. Rick moved quietly around the room, trying to avoid being noticed. Ian and Nana were talking, but Rick wasn't curious enough to ask what they were talking about. He knew it had to do with his father. Everyone was visibly relieved when Martha announced that supper was served.

The four filed into the dining room and sat down. Silence hung over the room as they filled their plates and began to eat. Rick kept his head down, too embarrassed by his father's reaction to Nana's ultimatum to look at anyone. The more Rick thought about it, the more he wanted to stay at Glencrest, since he knew Michael's temper would be unbearable by now. If he was at home, Michael'd be drunk and passed out on the couch downstairs and if Rick made any noise and woke him, Michael'd become violent. Rick knew his father's habits far too well and he really didn't feel like ducking flying objects while trying to get upstairs. *Some days, I really hate my life,* Rick sighed.

"Megan, Rick, I'm sorry you were caught in the middle tonight. I saw both of you trying not to be noticed in the den," Nana said suddenly, making both teens jump. Her voice sounded loud after the dominating silence in the room.

"Nana, can I stay tonight? I really don't feel like going home. Dad'll be impossible by now," Rick begged. He could hear the tension in his own voice and it bothered him. He didn't even care he'd have to stop by his house first thing in the morning to get his books.

Nana looked surprised at Rick's request. "Of course, Rick. That house is for you whenever you feel like it. You know you don't need to ask," Nana assured him. He smiled gratefully and somehow managed to relax.

The rest of the evening passed in lively activity. The adults challenged the teens to a trivia game, which the adults won after a long struggle. There was a movie on everyone wanted to watch, so Martha served tea and snacks in the family room. Eventually, everyone retired to their rooms, while Rick went to what he was now calling his house, not the guest house any more. As he settled into his bed, he realized he was more relaxed than he had been in weeks. *Maybe I'll ask Nana if I can move in*, Rick thought as he fell asleep. For the first time in a long time, Rick didn't dream.

Chapter 13

The next morning, Ian drove Megan and Rick to school. Although breakfast had been lively, everyone was still tense about the night before, especially Rick. After all, he was the one who had to go home after school and deal with Michael. Ian noticed Rick's nervousness as he pulled into Colonial High's parking lot after stopping at Rick's house to get his book bag. Fortunately, Michael hadn't been home.

"Rick, if your dad gives you any trouble about last night, call me. I'll come and get you, no matter what time it is," Ian said firmly. Rick nodded absent-mindedly and climbed out of the SUV.

"I mean it, Rick," Ian insisted again.

"I will, Uncle Ian. I promise," Rick said. Megan said good-bye to her father and followed Rick into the school. They greeted their friends, and went to Homeroom, after agreeing to meet the O'Reilly's for lunch at the cafeteria.

The morning went by quickly. Megan beat Rick and the twins to the cafeteria. Jordan had told Megan to go ahead, since she needed to stop by the office for a minute, and Mickey had disappeared. Megan waited out in the hallway, calling out greetings to other friends. Rick arrived next, followed closely by Jordan.

Rick gave Jordan a hug and then moved between the girls. His back was turned away from the hallway, as he was trying to guide his cousin and his girlfriend into the cafeteria. He couldn't see anything coming up from behind him, but he was relying on his gang reflexes to warn him if something was going to happen. They always had in the past. His eyes searched automatically for the Knights while he urged the girls into the lunchroom.

"Mickey had to talk to Mr. Robson for a minute, then go to his locker. He said not to wait, he'd find us," Jordan explained as Megan looked for her boyfriend.

The three continued towards the cafeteria door but had to wait for a large group of students to enter before them. Without any warning, Rick felt a large hand come down hard on his shoulder. From behind him a deep voice growled, "Hey, Moneyman." Rick froze, but only for a moment. Then he moved like lightning.

Acting on pure instinct, Rick shoved Megan roughly to the floor, where she landed with a strangled gasp. Rick then quickly pulled Jordan down as he spun around, ready to fight. Jordan, like Megan, landed hard and her breath rushed out of her lungs. Rick's eyes never stopped moving, as he hunted for Blade, all the while waiting for Crank and Brain to come up behind him and the girls.

"That's why you need to get out," the deep voice said softly.

It took Rick a couple of seconds to identify the speaker. His anger drained away as he realized Tony, not Blade, had been the one who had come up behind him. Only partially relieved, Rick straightened, glared at Tony, then turned to help the girls up.

"What the hell happened, Rick?" Mickey demanded harshly, reaching to help Megan stand up. She was shaking as she realized what could've happened. Rick held tightly to Jordan. She was being the strong one while Rick was trying very hard to control his temper. *Damn you, Tony*, Rick thought angrily. *That wasn't fair*. It was several long moments before he could let Jordan go.

"Tony scared the crap out of Rick and he was only trying to protect us," Jordan laughed shakily.

"By shoving you to the ground?" Mickey asked sarcastically.

"Relax, kids. I was just trying to prove a point to Rick. My fault. Enjoy your lunch. Rick, let's go have a talk," Tony said as he gently placed his hand on Rick's shoulder. Rick backed away and continued to glare at his counsellor.

Rick had started to calm down, but his anger was slowly starting to grow again as he thought about Tony's prank. It bothered him Tony could trick him like that. He assured himself Megan and Jordan were truly okay and then stomped off to the office. He didn't speak to Tony again until they were alone in the conference room.

Unfortunately, Tony didn't come into the room right away. He left Rick alone to steam while he stopped off to talk to the principal and get Rick excused from his classes for the rest of the day. Tony could see the anger building and hoped this was going to be the breakthrough session he had been waiting for. By the time Tony entered the conference room, Rick had worked himself into a rage.

"What the hell was that stupid stunt, Tony?" Rick shouted. He was right in Tony's face and Tony could see the veins pulsing in Rick's neck. Rick was struggling with his emotions and forcing himself not to take a swing. Tony just hoped Rick realized if he swung at Tony again, this time Tony would have to arrest him.

Tony didn't blink as he faced Rick's anger, even though he knew Rick could put him down with one punch or break his arm and not even realize it. "Think," Tony demanded harshly, trying to get through the red haze of Rick's anger. "What did you do when someone came up behind you?"

"I don't care about that! I could've hurt Megs..." Rick's voice died as he realized what Tony was getting at. *My God, what did I do?* he panicked as he held onto the table, his legs suddenly weak.

"And Jor," Tony finished with a short, sharp nod.

Rick's anger melted away. His face paled and his knees finally gave out as he staggered to a nearby chair. Tony just sat on the edge of the table as Rick finally realized what was going on inside himself. The teen stared straight ahead. He could see what Tony meant. He could see Jordan and Megan lying on the ground, not moving, and knew in his heart he had done it.

"That's right, Rick. You react by instinct. Johnny's trained you very well. I've *never* seen you leave your back that exposed before, even in the short time we've known each other. You either have someone behind you or you walk with your head half turned. It's almost like you have a sixth sense, and for some reason, it failed you miserably today. You're like a snake; strike first and ask questions later. If you don't change right now, you'll hurt the people you care about the most. Meg and Jor are the most obvious targets," Tony said soberly. He was desperate to make Rick see the danger in which he was putting everyone.

Rick sat in stunned silence, his head in his hands. For the next hour and a half, Tony talked and Rick just listened. He was anxious to prevent the situation from happening again. He thought he could prevent an uncontrolled reaction now that he knew what to look for.

"No way, Rick," Tony said, shaking his head when Rick suggested that. "That kind of vigilance isn't possible, not for the long haul. You'll relax after a while, and Johnny'll pounce. Problem is, you *know* he won't come after you. Johnny doesn't operate like that, which is kinda strange for a gang leader. Jor'll be his most likely target, then Meg and maybe Mick. Only after the gang has eliminated those three will he come after you," Tony cautioned. Rick nodded glumly. He had to admit Tony had a point. Blade wasn't coming after him any time soon.

Tony even managed to convince Rick the gang wasn't the family he believed them to be. He pointed out the differences between the gang and Rick, differences Rick already knew. Tony finally got Rick to admit there wasn't anything he had in common with the rest of the Knights. Toward the end of their session, Rick even admitted something he'd been keeping from his counsellor. He wasn't doing anything with the gang, but he hadn't dumped his gang colours either.

"It's like a security blanket, I guess. I don't know...maybe I'm not ready to leave yet. If I leave the Knights, I won't have anybody. The gang's the one place where I can be myself. I don't have to prove myself to them, ever," Rick explained.

Tony nodded. "I understand, Rick. I do. I'm First Nations. I've always had to prove myself to the 'white man.' I had to be better than everyone else to be believed, and even then, sometimes no one would trust me. Think about something, though. You say the gang's all you have? I disagree, wholeheartedly. I think Meg and Jor might have something to say about that, despite this afternoon. They care, don't they? How about Nana and your uncle? Granted, Mick isn't real fond of you, but he'll come around. Eventually," Tony said with a small grin.

Shifting in his chair, Rick thought about what Tony said. He *did* have others who cared about him. Now that he had left the gang, other classmates were becoming friendlier. Rick knew he couldn't hide these new friendships from Blade and Crank. If he did, the Knights would find out and go after Rick's new friends anyway. There was one exception. Rick had one friend he kept hidden from everyone, including Tony.

The day he returned from his suspension, the boy he had saved, Tom Shelley, had sought Rick out and thanked him again. The two boys, as unlikely as it seemed, had become friends. Rick felt that same instinct to protect Tom as he did Megan and Jordan, and Rick couldn't understand where this instinct was coming from. At Rick's instance, Tom was learning some defensive tactics from him so Blade couldn't blindside him again, but Rick knew it wasn't enough. The teen planned to introduce Tom to Bob at the youth centre so the smaller boy could learn more.

By the end of the afternoon, Rick made up his mind to sever all ties to the gang. Period. No excuses. The gang had to go. He finally realized by keeping his gang wear, he had sent himself a subtle message he wasn't really leaving the gang. Rick decided to throw all of the clothes out that night.

"I'm keeping my knife, though, Tony. I just don't trust Johnny. Delaney knows I have it, and now you do. But you're right. I have to tell Johnny I'm out for good," Rick said. His voice shook and he could hear the fear in his voice. Tony heard it, too, and tried to deflect it.

"You're scared and I can understand that, Rick. Johnny's dangerous, extremely unpredictable. He's also got a problem with anyone who won't accept his authority, especially you. You know he's gonna come after you somehow, probably by coming after the girls. You need to be ready for that," Tony warned. Both he and Rick stood and stretched. They had been in the conference room for over three hours and both were stiff.

"C'mon, Rick. I'll buy you some supper and drive you home since I didn't let you have lunch," Tony laughed as they left the conference room.

"I'm supposed to go and see Bob this afternoon, even though we met here at school, but I'm too tired to box anyone's ears. Even yours, Tony," Rick said, with an answering grin.

Tony chuckled. "Don't worry, kiddo. I'll talk to Bob and get you begged off today. But tomorrow, before our regular session, you spend your hour with him, okay?" Tony said, throwing a friendly arm around Rick's shoulders. The cop could feel the teen stiffen, then relax. It was then Tony realized Rick's dad had never done anything like that.

Outside the office, the pair ran into Tom. "Are we on for tonight, Rick?" he asked, as he took a quick look around. Like Rick, he kept their friendship as quiet as possible.

Tony stood in the background, trying not to smile. To see the victim of gang violence being a friend to one of the gang who nearly killed him was encouraging, to say the least. *Now if only they can keep Johnny from finding out,* Tony thought darkly. *I'd give Tom a snowball's chance in hell of surviving a second attack from Johnny.*

"Sorry, man. Just had a killer session with Tony and I'm beat. Can we do it tomorrow?" Rick asked quietly. Tom just looked at Rick and then shrugged.

"Sure. I can practice at home," Tom said, unconcerned.

"Actually, Tom, meet me at the youth center after school tomorrow. I have someone I want you to meet who'll teach you more than I ever could," Rick called out as Tom moved down the hall. The younger boy waved in acknowledgement as he rounded the corner.

Tony led Rick out to the parking lot to meet up with Megan and the twins. Rick walked up to Jordan and gave her a hug. His girl held on, knowing, somehow, he needed her strength for a little while. Then, catching Mickey and Megan's eyes, Rick took a deep breath and spoke softly. He could see the tension in Mickey's stance and knew his little 'protection' job in the cafeteria had done nothing to make him more likable to Jordan's brother.

"Guys, I'm sorry about what happened at lunch. This thing with the Knights makes me kinda tense. Tony says it's gonna take some time for me to learn not to send you guys flying when I get startled. I'm gonna need you guys to be patient." Rick explained, looking around.

All three nodded, Mickey a little more hesitantly than the others, and Rick continued, ignoring a sudden dead feeling in his stomach. "I've also decided Johnny has to be told I'm outta the gang. I'm getting rid of my gang stuff and I'm out," Rick finished. His voice had dropped into a harsh whisper.

Tony looked at the other three teens. "Unfortunately, Johnny's really gonna flip when he finally admits Rick wants out. No gang leader likes it when someone quits. Most leaders go after the person who wants out, but not Johnny. He seems to go after the people who mean the most to someone. That means you three are targets. Yes, even you, Mick. Keep an eye out for anything unusual. Mick, Jor, make sure you tell your dad if you think something's wrong. Tell the principal. Tell the teachers. Most importantly, trust your instincts, okay?" Tony said. All four nodded. Only much later would Tony come to regret saying those few innocent words.

Mickey got Jordan and Megan into the truck. He walked up to Rick, looked him straight in the eyes, and very quietly spoke.

"You get my sister or my girl hurt and I promise Blade won't be your only problem."

Rick only nodded. He understood where Mickey was coming from.

Tony and Rick left the school, grabbed a burger and fries each, and talked all the way to Rick's house. Tony wanted to get to know who Rick was and Rick was willing to answer his questions. When Rick realized Michael wasn't home yet, he sighed with relief. If his luck held, he'd be able to finish supper and retreat to his room before his dad barrelled into the house, most likely drunk as a skunk. As Rick climbed the steps to the front door after watching Tony pull away, a sound on the porch made Rick snap his head around. Hiding in the shadows and sitting on the porch swing was Blade.

"Moneyman." Blade's voice came out of the dark like a knife.

Rick scanned the yard quickly. He put his back to the door, knowing he could be inside before Blade could blink if he needed to. Rick also knew where Blade was, the others weren't far away.

Blade swung lazily. "We gots some unfinished business, man."

"I'm out, Johnny, out for good," Rick said, pointedly. "I'm done with being a machine, man. I'm not like that, never was, and you know it. You and the others wrecked that play-ground, but I gotta fix it up and everything. You never came forward, man. Where's the loyalty in that? You're always preaching gang loyalty and where was it? I was loyal to you for a long time, man, until you started becoming something I'm not.

"Christ, I loved being with the Knights," Rick continued to rant while Blade just sat in the swing. "but now, man, you're too violent, Johnny, too vicious and way too mean. What was the point in attacking Tom? Either time? Just 'cause he wore a black and silver jacket you had to nearly kill the kid? That's not what I signed up for, man. I am *out*," Rick said defiantly as he scanned the yard for Crank and Brain. Pup, he knew, would be the lookout, watching for the cops and Michael. He turned back to Blade as the older boy abruptly stopped the swing.

"Moneyman, yer not out unless I say yer out. Guess I need to be clearer," Blade sneered as he stood and pulled his knife. He balanced himself on the balls of his feet and held his knife loose in his hand as he waited for Rick to respond. "C'mon, Moneyman, I've been waitin' fer this fer a long time," Blade growled. "Let's go," he taunted.

Rick reached for his knife, then stopped and shook his head. "Skin-on-skin, Johnny, or no go," Rick stated firmly. He held his breath while Blade decided if he wanted to knife Rick or punch him.

Blade nodded and returned his knife to its sheath. He approached slowly and swung at Rick's head. Rick easily ducked the punch and was suddenly grateful for Bob's boxing lesson. Blade missed punch after punch, and was soon gasping for air. Rick's punches connected time after time, and Blade's lip began to bleed. One eye had already started to swell shut. Seeing this, Rick suddenly grasped Blade's arm and threw him off the front porch.

"Get outta here, Johnny, and leave me the hell alone," Rick snarled as he worked at catching his breath. He still had his fists clenched as if waiting for Blade to get back on the porch.

"Good fight, Moneyman," Blade gasped, sprawled on the ground. "Yer better. Ya gonna fight like that fer yer girl?"

Rick froze. "You leave Jor alone. While you're at it, leave Megs alone too," Rick warned softly. The threat didn't even faze Blade, who grinned, breathing heavily.

"When yer back and not until. We're family, Moneyman. We're more family than that jackass who calls hisself yer dad. Besides, I'm sure Jor and I can have all kinds of fun," Blade smirked as he hauled himself to his feet.

Rick stood defiantly in the porch light. "No, Johnny. I'm out. For good. Now get outta here." Blade sauntered out of the yard, his laughter floating back to Rick on the night air.

Rick slammed his way into the house, shaking with anger and fear. He knew he had just put both Megan and Jordan in danger. Rick climbed the stairs to his room and spent almost fifteen minutes taking his frustrations out on the speed bag, pretending it was Blade. He couldn't stop thinking about what he had just done.

It doesn't matter, Rick decided as he towelled off. *They've all been warned. I can't do anything else to protect her. If her father can't, I won't be able to either.*

Remembering his promise to Tony, Rick moved around his room and quickly gathered up his bandanas and his leather jacket. He looked at them, wondering if he could really get rid of them. They represented a portion of his life which had meant a lot to him, not to mention a fair chunk of money. Then, recalling Blade's threats, he scowled and grabbed a garbage bag. He stuffed his expensive leather jacket in without another thought. He turned to his dresser and pulled out his jeans and tee-shirts. Rick got rid of just about every piece he had. He only kept a couple of pairs of jeans, enough to last until he could go shopping. He'd beg Nana to help him replace his stuff. He knew Michael wouldn't help.

Rick took the bag out to the garbage cans in the alley behind his house. Tossing the bag in made Rick feel free for the first time in ages. He was free of the gang life. As he returned to the house to study, Rick neither heard nor noticed the shadowy figure who grabbed the bag he had just thrown out. Ghostly laughter drifted on the night air once more as the figure moved down the dark alley.

Chapter 14

The next morning, Rick woke up feeling strangely liberated. Thinking about the fight, he suddenly realized he was stronger than Blade, maybe not physically, but definitely mentally. Blade's threats weren't subtle, though, and Rick knew he had to warn the twins and Megan again. *Maybe I should warn Nana, too,* Rick thought as he lounged in bed, not really wanting to get up quite yet. *I know Uncle Ian can handle himself, but Nana's not gonna be able to. If Seamus can't protect himself, well, hell, that's his own friggin' prob.*

Climbing out of bed and seeing himself in the mirror, Rick noticed a black eye developing. *Looks like Johnny gotta couple good shots in, too,* he chuckled dryly. After showering and dressing, Rick grabbed his book bag and thundered down the stairs for breakfast. He stopped in the kitchen door and stared at his dad, shocked for the first time in a very long time.

Michael's eyes were bloodshot and it appeared he hadn't slept. His hair and clothes looked like they were in a contest to see which could be messier, and Rick was positive an open sewer smelled better than his dad did this morning. Michael didn't even turn his head as Rick walked in the room, snickering.

"Can't you be quiet, boy?" Michael snarled, holding his head in his hands. *Can't anyone remember my name?* Rick wondered idly as he sauntered through the kitchen. He made no effort to be quiet as he grabbed some cereal, a bowl, and the milk, then sat down at the table, making sure to drop everything on the table. Determined to get a couple of shots in on his dad, Rick chuckled mercilessly, trying to keep his laughter from erupting.

"Don't know when to quit, do you, Dad?" Rick sneered.

"Richard!...ohhh..." Michael winced.

"Alright, Dad. I'll be nice to your poor aching head," Rick whispered. He poured his breakfast and began to eat. Inside, he was howling with laughter.

"Don't lecture me, boy. You ain't my mother," Michael said, standing up gingerly. He swayed on his feet and caught himself on the table. "Just sit quiet. I'm going to sleep. I already called the office and told them I'm not coming in. Lock up behind you."

Michael burped and staggered from the kitchen.

Hearing his father stumble around upstairs and collapse on his bed, Rick muttered, "I'm *glad* I'm not your mother. Hell, I don't even wanna be your *kid*." He finished up quickly, dumped his dishes in the dishwasher and left the house. The walk to school always took fifteen minutes. He managed to arrive at the opposite side of the parking lot just as Mickey was helping the girls out of the truck.

Rick caught up with them just as they got to the front door. He gave Jordan a quick kiss and hug. "Morning, cuz. Hey, Mick," Rick said with his face lowered. Jordan just smiled and shook her head. She gently touched his black eye and wasn't surprised when Rick flinched.

"Nice shiner. Where'd you get that?" Mickey asked, as they stood by the pond.

Quietly, Rick told the other three about his fight the night before and Blade's threats. "I figured you should know," Rick said. He knew what Seamus would say if Jordan told him and most of it would revolve around getting Jordan to drop Rick like a hot potato.

"Don't worry, love. I'll be okay. Mick's always around so I'm rarely alone," Jordan reassured her boyfriend.

"Megs, warn Uncle Ian, okay? Johnny'll come after you, too," Rick cautioned. Megan nodded soberly. She was scared, but she tried not to show it.

Standing behind the four friends, hidden in the shadows, were another four friends. The Black Knights listened quietly as Rick detailed Blade's threats, all the while grinning at each other.

As Rick, Megan and the twins went to Homeroom, the Knights had a quick conference, then went their separate ways. Brain had to move quickly to be in place in time, but he wasn't delayed as the other students easily melted out of his way.

After Homeroom, Megan led Jordan and Mickey to History. As she passed by a group of boys, she felt someone shove her hard from behind. Her books went flying and she fell to the floor with a muffled oath. Mickey helped her up while Jordan gathered Megan's books in the crowded hallway, protesting loudly when a couple of older girls laughed and kicked the books all over the hall.

Mickey frowned as he noticed how pale Megan was and how hard she was shaking. "Megan, you okay, lass?" he asked.

She nodded as she stood up shakily. "I *thought* I felt someone push me, but now I'm not sure. Maybe I just tripped," Megan replied sheepishly, and blushed in shame. The group of boys she remembered being by the lockers as she passed were long gone. No one else was around, and yet she distinctly remembered a shove in the back. *I must be losing it,* she thought.

Jordan handed her friend her book bag. "You sure you're okay?" she asked.

"Yeah, I'm all right. Let's get to class," Megan said, determined to put the matter out of her mind.

Unfortunately, Lady Luck wasn't smiling on the trio that day. They arrived late for class, much to Mrs. Salisbury's annoyance. She stood by her desk with her hands on her hips. "Megan. Jordan. Mickey. Why're you late? Do you have a note?" she demanded, frowning.

"Sorry, Mrs. Salisbury, it's my fault," Megan said softly in the sudden silence that fell over the room. The three friends quickly took their seats. "I tripped in the hall and sent my stuff flying everywhere. Mickey and Jordan stayed behind to help me."

Mrs. Salisbury didn't say anything more as she began the lesson, but Megan could hear a couple of students in the back of the room snickering. She knew she wasn't overly popular, partly because of her family's money, but mainly because of who her cousin was. Until now, she hadn't realized how much some of the others disliked her and wanted her to fail. She didn't participate in class discussions, despite Mrs. Salisbury's attempts. The teacher frowned at the snickering students but they didn't stop. Megan was embarrassed and almost in tears. If there was one thing Megan hated more than anything, it was being laughed at, and now the whole class was doing it. She just kept her head down and prayed for the suddenly-long class to end.

When the bell finally rang, Megan stood quickly. She wanted to get out of the room before Mickey could see her crying, even though it was already too late. Mickey understood Megan's hurt and embarrassment at the first snicker. No one as confident as his lass would like to be laughed at. As the classroom emptied and Mickey's attention was on Megan, Jordan stumbled and fell over a desk. Mickey whipped around at the sound and saw Jordan lying, sprawled, on the floor.

"Jordan!" Mickey cried, reaching for his sister.

"Are you okay, Jordan?" Mrs. Salisbury asked, just as concerned as Mickey.

Jordan nodded, picked herself up and dusted her pants off. Her books, like Megan's, had scattered at the front of the room and Mrs. Salisbury bent to pick them up. Jordan finished dusting her jeans off and took her books back from her teacher. Unlike Megan, though, Jordan stood straight and tall by her brother while Megan seemed to shrink into herself.

Mrs. Salisbury was shocked. "What's going on, girls? You two're the least clumsy people I know!"

"In the hallway, I was positive someone had shoved me, but when I looked up, there was no one around but Mickey and Jordan," Megan said shyly. *And I know neither of them did it,* Megan didn't have to add.

"I thought the same thing, but with Meg and Mick in front of me, and everyone else gone, I'm not so sure now," Jordan said, puzzled, as she looked around.

"We'd better hurry or we'll be late for English," Mickey said as he escorted the girls out.

In the hall, Megan could hear a couple of the more popular seniors talking. They were taking History 11 this semester, despite being in Grade 12. "Hey, Miss Klutz. Have a nice trip, Meggie?" one of the girls snickered while the rest of her friends roared with laughter.

Ashamed, Megan felt tears well up in her eyes again and she stumbled along to her English class, the girls' laughter echoing in her ears. Mickey and Jordan hurried after her, calling Megan's name all down the hall. Megan didn't stop. She didn't want Mickey to see her crying like a baby. After all, she'd only stumbled in the hall. *Why should that upset me?* Megan wondered as she suddenly found herself outside of English.

"Megan, lass, wait, please," Mickey begged, catching her arm. She kept her head averted, but Mickey could see her shoulders shaking. Jordan shared a quick glance with her brother as he gathered Megan into his arms. She nodded once and strode into class. Quietly, she explained to Mr. Robson what had happened in History and then took her seat.

"Where are they?" Mr. Robson asked firmly. He didn't like having his routine disrupted, and, no matter how much he liked Megan, the English teacher wasn't impressed with his best student's hysterics.

"Just outside, sir," Jordan said softly.

Mr. Robson gave the class the assignment, then moved to the door and stuck his head outside, prepared to order the pair into the classroom. When he saw Megan still crying, he sighed and slipped outside. "Mickey?" he asked, touching the boy on the shoulder. *Why her?* Mr. Robson wondered sourly. *Just when she was beginning to really fit in, why this? Why now?*

"Sorry sir, I know this is a pain, but can we be excused? I just can't get her to calm down," Mickey said, frustrated. Mr. Robson nodded in sympathy.

"Jordan told me what happened. I'll mark this as an excused absence. Take her to the library or some place quiet and calm her down. Here's a couple of hall passes and today's assignment. Due tomorrow," Mr. Robson said shortly, handing

Mickey a couple of sheets of paper. Mickey nodded and slipped them into his notebook.

"Sir, could you escort my sister to the library after class? We're having...trouble with some boys," Mickey said dryly as he led Megan towards the library. Mr. Robson agreed as he re-entered his classroom. "Must be the Knights," he muttered. "I knew it. I just knew it."

Once in the library, Mickey sat Megan down in a secluded corner and tried get her to talk to him. "Megan, please, baby, look at me," Mickey begged. He kept trying to catch her eye, but she refused. Megan struggled to pull her hands out of Mickey's strong grip, but, he refused to let go. Even though she acted so confident all the time, she hated to be laughed at, and when it happened, she was so embarrassed she tended to curl into herself. She continued to sob silently and refused to look at Mickey.

Mickey finally reached under her chin and gently forced her head up. He stared into her green eyes and tried to express how he felt. "Megan, listen. I know you don't want me to see you cry and I understand. Y'know I can't stand to see you upset. But, please, don't shut me out, lass. Talk to me, please," Mickey begged softly. As he waited, he wondered once again, how he had come to love someone so deeply when he'd only known Megan for a couple of months. If he had the strength to tell her how he really felt, Mickey was sure Megan would trust him enough to confide in him.

"Don't worry, lad. It's nothing, really. I just can't stand to be laughed at, that's all," Megan sniffled, wiping her eyes. She smiled at him wanly.

"No one does, lass. We'll just have to be more careful. Rick warned us this may happen, but honestly, I didn't think it would start so soon," Mickey said bitterly. *Rick, what the hell've you dragged us into?* he fumed. With a deep sigh, Mickey handed Megan her copy of the English homework. He flashed her a small grin and kept his thoughts to himself. Megan was upset enough already. "Feel like doing some English?" Megan smiled back and bent her head to the task at hand.

The rest of the week was a living nightmare for Megan and Jordan. Not a moment went by between classes where one or the other was tripped, they stumbled or were outright shoved. No one was ever seen, and there was always a whole lot of witnesses who reported seeing a whole lot of nothing. Megan's fragile self-esteem crumbled with every attack, especially when her classmates laughed at her. It was all Mickey could do to not snarl at those who laughed at his girlfriend.

Lunchtime seemed to be the only respite, but even then Megan noticed she was often shoved in line. She ended up ruining a couple of very nice and expensive outfits when she spilled food on them, so she took to bringing a change of clothes with her, just in case. The attacks would continue right up until Rick showed up, then mysteriously stopped. Megan never mentioned her suspicions to anyone, but she had begun to wonder what kind of game Rick was playing with her. *Why's he doing this?* Megan wondered miserably. *I thought I could trust him.* She tried not to look afraid of her cousin, but she wasn't sure how much longer she could hide it.

It didn't take Rick more than a day to notice the change in his cousin. In fact, he would've been blind not to see it because Rick was certain Mickey didn't. Megan watched him warily; the fear she thought she hid was always in her eyes and it made Rick tense when he saw it directed at him. Since Rick didn't have classes with Megan or the twins, he never saw the attacks or heard about them, but the change in Megan was evident. Rick decided not to wait for Megan to come to him and tell him what was wrong.

"Megs, what's wrong? You've been staring at me at lunch for the last three days straight, and now you look like you think I might hit you," Rick finally asked bluntly Wednesday at lunch. Subtlety was never Rick's strong point.

Megan flinched at the harshness in Rick's voice. "N-n-nothing, Rick. I'm just not feeling good and I seem to have a bad case of the stares. S-s-sorry," Megan stammered. Rick snorted in derision as Megan lowered her head to pick at her lunch. *I don't believe it*, he thought sarcastically, but left her alone. He didn't flinch when Mickey turned and glared at him. *Obviously, Mick thinks this is all* my *fault.*

By Friday, Megan was a bundle of nerves. Her teachers had even noticed the difference. When the term had started, you couldn't keep Megan out of the in-class discussions. Now? Megan stopped answering questions and refused to participate in discussions. Her eyes were constantly red and her head was always lowered. Mickey was frustrated since he couldn't protect his girlfriend, but didn't know what else he could do. He tried to boost Megan's self-esteem, but nothing was working. Although Megan seemed to be the main target, Jordan had also gained the reputation for being clumsy, but unlike Megan, Jordan held her head high. She was, after all, the daughter of a cop.

At the end of the day on Friday, Rick met Jordan and Megan at the front of the school and walked out to the parking lot to meet Mickey. Megan stayed a safe distance away from Rick who sighed loudly and with a considerable amount of frustration. Nothing he had done all week had made Megan open up to him. Rick couldn't stand it, but he knew if he said anything, Megan would just deny it. The trio walked to the parking lot in strained silence.

Mickey, on the other hand, had been called to the office just before the end of Chemistry to pick up some papers for his dad, and since he finished at the office just as the last bell rang, he decided to wait for the others at the truck. When he arrived, he stunned to see tons of random scratches on the paint job which had just been finished the week before. Everything was completely destroyed. He began swearing in Gaelic, just as the other three arrived.

Megan stared at the truck. She tried not to blame anyone, but after everything else that had been happening this week, she couldn't help but blame one person. From the way Mickey was reacting, he was blaming the same person, since they all heard Rick's name quite often during Mickey's tirade, although no one but Jordan understood Gaelic. She blanched once or twice at the language her normally calm brother was using.

Both girls were stunned at the vast amount of damage. The truck was a Chevy short-bed pickup Mickey and his dad had bought when Mickey was 15. They had spent the last two years completely rebuilding the engine and doing a lot of body work. The dark blue and white paint scheme had been designed by Mickey and the actual paint job had been Mickey's birthday present from his dad. On the tail gate was a stylized Irish flag. The colours didn't really match, but Mickey had insisted on having the flag of his homeland on his truck. He had been handed the keys the day he passed his driving test and Mickey was proud of that truck. Everyone knew it. Now it was ruined.

Megan and Jordan both tried to calm Mickey down, while Rick stood back, trying to keep out of Mickey's sight. Somehow, after just glimpsing the damage to the truck, Rick knew who was going to be blamed. *Whatever happened*, Rick told himself, *don't lose control. You didn't do it.*

When Mickey finally saw Rick, he charged at him, spun Rick around and pinned him against the damaged truck. "What the hell do you think you're doing, 'Moneyman?' You have any idea how much it's gonna cost me to fix this?" Mickey shouted, his face flushed. He was so angry Rick could feel the young Irishman shaking.

"What're ya talking about, Mick? I didn't do anything!" Rick demanded as he struggled free. He stood breathing heavily and sternly reminded himself to remain calm.

Mickey pointed mockingly at the truck. Rick didn't move, but the girls looked closer. Most of the scratches were random, but Megan realized there were several sets of stylized MM's mixed in as well. Megan tried to deny what she saw, but in her head she knew who those M's belonged to. She had received a couple of short notes from her cousin with those very letters as the signature. Rick was rocked back on his heels when Megan glared at him.

"Rick, how could you?" Megan demanded harshly. Even Jordan looked faintly disappointed, although she wasn't openly condemning her boyfriend. Not yet, at least. Jordan was positive there had to be a rational explanation, even thought she couldn't think of one right now.

Rick paled. "What do you mean, cuz? I didn't do anything," he protested again. Mickey pointed once more at the damage. Rick leaned in and paled even more when he saw the two M's everyone, especially the Knights, knew was his gang sign. Rick flushed as quickly as he paled when he realized what the others were thinking.

"C'mon, man. Gimme one damn good reason why I'd do this, Mick! I know how much this truck means to you, and I know exactly how much it's gonna cost to fix this," Rick snapped harshly. Recovering from her initial shock, Jordan now agreed with her boyfriend and stood defiantly by his side.

Mickey shoved Rick away. "Get the hell away from me, you little punk! I'd better not catch you around my sister, either! You understand me, 'Moneyman?'" Mickey snarled. Jordan made a wordless sound of protest while Rick growled low in his throat. He knew the fragile harmony he had had with Mickey was now gone, probably for good.

"That's for Jor to decide, not you, Mick," Rick snapped at the teenage boy, who was struggling to grab his sister away from Rick.

"Definitely," Jordan agreed immediately, pulling her arm out of her brother's death grip.

"Jor, you believe me, don't you?" Rick asked softly, slipping his arms around her.

Jordan didn't hesitate. "Of course I believe you. This isn't like you, love. Go home. Mick'll cool down and I'll talk to him later. I'll get him to admit he was wrong," she said, confidently. Rick hugged her gratefully and gave her a gentle kiss good-bye. She let Rick go as Mickey steamed behind them.

"Get in, Jordan," Mickey commanded bluntly. She was hurt by her brother's condemnation, but climbed silently into her seat.

- 160 -

Megan was already sitting in the middle, her face set in anger. Jordan sighed. *Innocent until proven guilty*, she thought bitterly. *For everyone but Rick.*

"I just don't understand why he did this," Megan complained to Jordan as they waited for Mickey to climb in.

"Why's it everyone but Rick's innocent until proven guilty?" Jordan said bitterly to the one person she had considered her best friend.

Megan didn't respond as Mickey climbed onto the seat and slammed the door hard enough to make the truck shake. "Mickey, please drop me at Hollyhock's. I'm going out for supper with Daddy and Nana," Megan explained with a sigh. *Not like I really feel like going out tonight*, she thought bitterly.

Mickey slipped his arm around her shoulders, nodded tersely and pulled out of the parking lot. Megan didn't say anything. She could feel him shaking with anger and wondered how he was able to drive. She put her hand on Mickey's knee in silent support. *He's tried to help me all week. The least I can do is be here for him*, Megan thought.

Mickey smiled down at her. *What would I do without her?* he wondered.

"Mickey?" Jordan began tentatively. She could feel the tension.

"Leave it, Jordan. I'm in no mood to talk about your stupid infatuation right now," Mickey said sharply. Jordan was stung. Tears fell silently as she sat as far over as the small cab would allow. Her brother had never talked to her like that before and Jordan was surprised at how much it hurt.

"Mickey," Megan hissed, horrified. "Don't be mad at Jordan. She didn't do anything. Look, call your dad, report the damage, and press charges if you're really that upset. Just don't fight with your sister!"

"You're right, lass," Mickey whispered back. Raising his voice, Mickey apologized to Jordan. "Look sis, I'm sorry. I'm not mad at you. I'm just mad at that...that stupid idiot. He's caused a lot of damage I can't afford to fix right now," Mickey said angrily.

"Innocent until proven guilty, bro and you can't prove anything," Jordan said bitterly. She wiped some tears from her eyes as she continued to defend Rick. "How do you know the gang didn't do this to frame Rick?"

"The M's, Jordan," Mickey said patiently as he turned a corner. "Everyone knows they're Rick's gang sign, his calling card if you will." He fell silent as he navigated through some heavier traffic. Thanks to Megan's support, he was beginning to calm down slightly.

"That's right, Jordan. I received a couple of notes from him before he left the Knights and they were signed with those M's," Megan said with sadness in her voice. *Why did you do this, Rick?* she wondered.

Jordan lifted her head defiantly. "Exactly! *Everyone* knows about those M's! *Anyone* could have scratched your precious truck and put Rick's calling card, as you put it, on the damage. *Anyone*. And until you have clear proof Rick did it, I'll stand by him," Jordan said with finality. Mickey looked like he wanted to continue to argue, but Megan squeezed his leg as if to say "Enough." With a sigh, Mickey dropped the discussion, and an uncomfortable silence filled the cab for the remainder of the trip.

The three pulled into Hollyhock's a couple of minutes later. Jordan refused to get out or even talk to Megan and Mickey. She kept her head down and brooded about Rick until a knock her window startled her. It was her dad.

"Daddy, what're you doing here?" Jordan asked after she opened the window.

"Helping Ian with some counterfeit money, Jordan. What's wrong, honey? Why're ye fighting with yer brother? Everything okay at school?" Seamus O'Reilly asked softly. He looked down at the living picture of his now-dead wife and marvelled again at how much his daughter reminded him of Colleen.

Jordan wanted to tell her dad what had happened, but she hesitated. She knew how her father really felt about Rick. Before she could say anything, though, Mickey came up behind his dad and pointed out the damage, and when her brother firmly placed the blame on Rick, Jordan immediately spoke up in her boyfriend's defence. "You have no proof, Mickey O'Reilly! Stop saying he did it!" Jordan said, shrilly.

Seamus looked at his daughter and could see how upset she was by her brother's accusations. He sighed as he tried to figure out how to mend the fences between his children. "Jordan, look at it from me point of view. Mickey's told me about the problems ye and Megan've been having at school. Now, don't get upset," he warned as Jordan began to protest. "I asked him how things were going a couple of days ago, and he flat out told me. Admit it, Jordan. Nothing ever seems to happen when that boy's around. Yes, I agree it's all circumstantial evidence, but it's pretty strong evidence, don't ye agree? No, I can see ye don't. Doesn't he have a session today with Tony?" Seamus asked, abruptly changing the subject. Jordan nodded hesitantly. She wondered where her dad was going with his questions.

"Here's what we're gonna do. I'm filing a vandalism report, son. I'll call Tony and have him talk to the boy. We'll get both sides of the story, and when I've enough evidence, I'll charge the punk." Before Jordan could say anything, Seamus picked up his cell phone and called Tony. Jordan slumped. She was tired of defending Rick, since it seemed that her father had already tried and convicted Rick, with or without the evidence. *Why can't they trust him, just once?* she fumed as she and Mickey headed home.

After Mickey had taken off, Rick stood steaming in the parking lot for several long minutes. He just stared at the back of Mickey's truck as it faded in the distance. Finally, he remembered his counselling session with Tony at the youth centre. Still angry at Mickey's false accusation and his unwillingness to listen, Rick started walking downtown. He was looking straight ahead, but didn't seem to see anything. That was why he jumped when Brain stepped out in front of him. The two boys just stared at each other for a long time until Rick broke the tense silence.

"What now, Brian?" Rick snarled. He was in no mood to deal with Blade or his flunkies.

"Gotta message fer ya," Brain drawled lazily. *Sounds just like Blade*, Rick thought sourly.

"Like I don't know what that is," Rick said wearily. "Come back or Jor's next. Right?" *Why can't Johnny just come after me?* Rick wondered as he stared at Brain. *Why drag the rest of them into this?*

"Shame about Mickey Mouse's truck, isn't it, Moneyman? And those two pretty things being so damn clumsy all week? Shame really. Wonder what's next?" Brain shook his head, grinning at Rick. Rick froze and then silently cursed his inattention. Now he knew what had been bugging Megan all week. He was being blamed for her "clumsiness." He should've known.

"Look, Brian, tell Johnny to grow up. If he wants me that bad, then tell him to be a man and come after me. Leave them alone!" Rick snapped. His patience with Blade was finally gone. He stood stewing and waited for Brain's next move.

"Don't worry, Moneyman, we will. In the meantime," Brain chuckled and lashed out suddenly. He caught Rick unprepared and knocked him flat on his back. Before Rick could recover, Brain was all over him, connecting solidly. With every punch, Brain grunted "Remember." Rick finally managed to get his hands free and land a couple of solid punches himself. Brain backed off at that point. Rick was bleeding from a cut lip and his ribs were sore. Brain looked like he hadn't been in a fight at all.

"What's the matter, Brian? Too scared to finish it? Or am I the better fighter?" Rick gasped. He struggled to catch his breath.

"Nope. Message delivered," Brain said, grinning viciously and sauntered off to his car. He climbed in, and, with his music blaring, drove off with a squeal of rubber. Rick just laid on the sidewalk, wishing the past week away.

Chapter 15

After a couple of minutes laying on the ground, trying to catch his breath, Rick finally dragged himself to his feet and staggered to the youth center. He was fifteen minutes late and Tony was furious, especially when he saw evidence of another fight. The cop grabbed Rick by the arm and hauled him to the office, ignoring Rick's protests the entire way.

"Sit down, close your mouth and listen good, boy!" Tony yelled. Instantly the cop regretted it. He had promised himself that was the one thing he would *never* call Rick. It made Tony sound just like Seamus and that wasn't what Rick needed. He could see his anger had been transferred to Rick, who clenched his fists so hard Tony swore he heard a bone crack. *I'm not supposed to lose control like that*, Tony fumed to himself. *I'm better than that.* Rick stumbled blindly to his chair, falling heavily into it.

"After everything I've tried to do for you, after everything we've talked about, and after supporting you, no matter what, imagine my surprise when I get a call from O'Reilly saying Mickey's filing a vandalism report against you! Do you have any idea what this means, you...you blockhead? You're on a direct route to prison if the judge gets that report! What the hell were you thinking?" Tony snapped heatedly.

"I DIDN'T DO ANYTHING!" Rick shouted back. He stood up so fast he knocked his chair over. Before Tony could stop him, Rick fled from the office and headed straight for the boxing gym.

Bob didn't say anything about Rick's sudden appearance. He had already heard about Tony hauling the kid into the office, and several others had reported hearing the two yelling at each other. The boxing coach could see the uncontrolled rage in Rick's eyes, something he hadn't seen before, but he didn't say a word.

He knew better. He just made Rick change and then taped up Rick's hands and let him go at the speed bag. But when Bob saw how hard Rick was hitting the bag, he stopped him after only a couple of minutes.

"Come over here to the heavy bag, Rick. You'll break the speed bag at the rate you're going. Just remember, keep your wrist locked," Bob cautioned as he got some gloves on Rick. The coach could feel Rick trembling with absolute raw emotion. Before he let Rick go, Bob demonstrated how to hit the bag right, and just like with the speed bag, gave Rick a specific pattern of punches, then just let the angry boy go.

Tony came into the gym about an hour later. Bob walked over to the cop, concerned. "He's been going at that bag for over an hour, Tony. He's not getting any weaker and he's not calming down. Tony, this isn't good. I'm really getting worried. I've never seen him this angry. If he doesn't collapse from exhaustion soon, he's gonna break his hands, but I don't dare make him stop," Bob said, frowning.

Tony walked over to Rick. He could see what Bob was talking about. Rick was pounding on the bag, hard, and the longer Tony stood there, the harder Tony swore he was punching. Coach was right. This wasn't good.

"Rick? Rick, listen to me," Tony said, pitching his voice to be heard over the sound of Rick's hands hitting the bag. Little did he know that the entire boxing team had stopped their workouts, and were watching this latest Rick-Tony drama unfold.

"Rick? C'mon, kiddo. Please stop for a minute and let's talk, 'kay?" Tony pressed again. He reached out and tapped Rick on the shoulder. Nothing. Tony's hand came down a little firmer on Rick's shoulder, gripping it to turn Rick around. That got a reaction alright, but not one Tony was expecting.

Without warning, Rick spun and swung. Tony had no chance to avoid the punch that landed square on his chin, stunning him. He flew backwards and landed hard, knocking over a bench nearby. Rick didn't even watch Tony land. He just turned back to the bag and kept on throwing punches. If anything, they were harder and faster.

"Dumb move, Tony," Bob said, frowning as he extended a hand to help Tony up.

"Man, he's strong," Tony groaned as he struggled to his feet. "What've you been teaching him, dammit?" Tony gasped as his hand explored his tender ribs.

"Lemme look at that," Bob demanded instantly. He lifted Tony's arm and probed the suspect area.

"I think I cracked a rib – OW! – or two when I fell over that bench," Tony winced as he turned back to watch Rick. The sweat was pouring off the teen's face. *Or was it tears,* Tony wondered. His jaw was clenched so tight Tony wouldn't be surprised to find out Rick had cracked a couple of teeth. The cop could also see Rick's eyes wide open, but clearly unfocused.

"Tony, what the hell's wrong with him today?" Bob demanded. "He's gonna hurt himself if he keeps this up," Bob fumed again as he watched one of the best natural boxers he'd ever seen battle the strongest opponent he'd ever face – himself.

"He's been accused of scratching the crap out of Mickey O'Reilly's truck. I think he got into a fight with one of the Knights, and was late for our session. I was choked when O'Reilly called and I made the mistake of blaming Rick without getting his side of the story. Now look at him," Tony said grimly.

Some counsellor I am, Tony cursed himself. *I've done more harm in one session than the Knights ever did. If I wanna be an elder, I've gotta learn how to listen better. I gotta listen first, ask questions later.* Some of the other boys had gathered around when they saw their favourite cop get flattened. Tony could feel a couple standing behind him, muttering angrily and he didn't want to get them involved. He prayed they would calm down. The last thing he needed was for the boys to get into a fight with Rick. He was positive Rick would win, even two or three on one.

"How about going a couple of rounds with him, Tony?" one suggested finally.

"Yeah. If he's that pissed at you, let him hit you in the ring," another chimed in.

"Bob, what do you think? Would it help?" Tony asked. He grimaced again when a shaft of pain shot through his ribs, but he didn't care. If it helped Rick, he'd gladly take more pain.

The boxing coach stared at Rick for a couple of seconds, then shook his head. "Won't help him, Tony, not right now. You're not the right guy. I've been listening to him as he's been swinging. It's like he's seeing faces on that bag. I've never seen anyone, including *any* of my best fighters, place punches so precisely. He hasn't moved from two areas and I'm gonna have to fix the bag, he's been pounding on it so hard. He's been muttering names, too. The names of choice seem to be Crank, Brain, Pup...," Bob began.

"And Blade," Tony interrupted with a sinking heart. *Man, this kid's really screwed up,* Tony thought glumly. *I'm way outta my league here.*

"Bob, realistically, how much longer can he go?" Tony asked quietly. The cop knew he needed some help and he had one counsellor at the centre in mind. He just prayed she could and would help. Rick wasn't exactly popular with the other counsellors. Most firmly believed the former gang member should be in jail and weren't hesitant to let Tony know their opinion. Some of the counsellors had clients who had been terrorized by the Knights, and disliked Rick for that alone, even if he hadn't been the one who had attacked the kid in question.

Bob gazed at Rick again. One of the other boys was holding the bag for Rick, and, despite being taller and more muscular, was getting pushed all over the place.

"Providing he doesn't break anything, I'd say anywhere from another half an hour to 45 minutes before he collapses from sheer exhaustion," Bob replied thoughtfully.

"Good. That gives me some time. Keep your eyes on him, but let him go as long as he needs to," Tony said as he dashed off.

He interrupted the counsellor in the middle of a session. He apologized to her client, but when he briefly described what had been happening with Rick, the counsellor immediately rescheduled her client and invited Tony to sit down. The advice she gave to Tony, she felt, would help Rick immensely, even though she didn't like Rick.

True to Bob's prediction, about 45 minutes after levelling Tony, Rick's punches grew weaker and weaker. He finally collapsed on the floor, breathing raggedly. The boy helping Rick had orders to let Bob know when Rick finally buckled. He gave a sharp whistle towards the ring and caught Bob's eye.

"Here, Rick, just rest for a couple of minutes. You've been going at that bag pretty hard. Easy, I'm just gonna help you get the gloves off, that's all," the boy said gently as Rick jerked back at first. Rick finally nodded, too exhausted to fight. The boy quickly stripped off the gloves and tape and then handed Rick a towel and a bottle of water. Rick guzzled half of the water down before the boy could stop him.

Bob finished his training in the ring and walked over to the two. He watched Rick for a couple of moments to make sure the water wasn't about to come spewing back up, then motioned to the other boy. "Carl, help me get him over to the bench there," Bob said softly.

Between the two, they got Rick to his feet and over to the bench. Rick's legs gave out again as he reached the bench and he fell heavily onto it. Bob sat down and began to massage Rick's left shoulder and arm. "Just trying to keep you from cramping as you cool down," Bob assured Rick as the boy looked at his trainer oddly. "I'll get you to do your stretches in a couple of minutes." *Providing you don't go ballistic on me again*, Bob thought grimly.

He had moved from Rick's left arm to his right when Tony returned to the gym. Bob could immediately feel Rick tense back up as the teen watched the cop cross the gym with narrowed eyes. Bob moved far enough away to let the two have some privacy, but close enough to keep an eye on Rick. Something told Bob this wasn't done yet. The rage hadn't left the boy's eyes. Usually an hour of hard hitting and the anger was gone. Not today. Bob waved to Carl and three of the larger boys who trained at the gym to come and back him up.

"Feel better?" Tony asked softly, as he stopped in front of Rick.

"Nope," Rick replied shortly. He shifted his weight slightly as if he was going to get up, and Tony stepped back, startled. He knew he had to start using the advice the other counsellor had given to him.

"He has to know you believe him and believe *in* him, Tony," the counsellor's final words came back. "Make him believe you trust him." *I hope you know what you're talking about, Doc, or this kid's gonna kill me,* Tony thought, worriedly.

"Look Rick, I'm sorry I yelled at you. I'm your counsellor here, not a cop. I should've listened to your side before saying a word. I was wrong. When no one else believes you, I have to. You need to have one person believe in you no matter what. That's me. Period. Listen to me, Rick. I believe you. I'm sorry," Tony said again. His heart sunk when he realized not one word had made it through the anger. If anything, he had only made it worse. *I'm over six feet tall and I'm scared of this kid*, Tony thought in a panic.

"No, you're not!" Rick yelled as the anger rebuilt. This time Rick managed to get his legs to obey his commands and he pushed himself up from the bench. Tony took another step backwards, as Rick stood there on wobbly legs. "You're not sorry! You'd like to see me in jail! Everyone wants me in jail! O'Reilly does! No one cares that I DIDN'T scratch Mickey's truck! I was in a gang so I'm guilty! I DIDN'T DO ANYTHING!" Rick screamed. He tried to shove past Tony but, somehow, Tony stopped him.

"Rick, listen to me. I believe you. If you say you didn't scratch Mickey's truck, then you didn't scratch Mickey's truck. Rick, please. Listen to me. I believe you. Nana believes you. Jordan believes you. You didn't do anything. Rick, please, listen," Tony begged, struggling to hold the angry teen.

It was no good. Rick had been worked back up. Blindly, he swung wildly at Tony, who easily ducked out of the way. Rick used the momentary distraction to shove his way past both the cop and his boxing coach. Everyone in the silent gym heard the sound of crunching wood and plaster as Rick slammed out of the gym door.

"Holy crap! He's heading outside, Tony! C'mon!" Bob grated as he dragged the cop along. Tony winced as they dashed out the broken door. Rick had hit it so hard it was imbedded in the wall behind it.

They caught up to Rick in the parking lot. He had stopped running and stood, ironically, by Tony's car, muttering under his breath. His hands were clenched so hard the knuckles were white. The rage shone in his eyes, and Tony knew Rick wasn't going to be easy to contain, never mind calm down.

"Bob, spread your boys out around him. We can't let him get outta this parking lot or I'll be in *deep* trouble," Tony ordered quietly. He never took his eyes off Rick, whose eyes narrowed when Bob and his boys moved around the car. Tony could see Rick was tensing to run again. No matter what it took, Tony couldn't let Rick get out of the parking lot. If someone else got in Rick's way while he was in this blind rage, Tony was sure he would be looking for a murderer.

"Rick, look at me," Tony commanded in a low voice. Rick slowly turned his hate-filled eyes towards Tony. The cop shivered. *I'm terrified of this kid*, Tony thought again. *I'm supposed to be able to deal with anything a crook can throw at you, and I* am *terrified of one kid. What's wrong with me?*

"Rick, I know you're mad at me for not believing you, and you have every right to be. I should've listened to you. But, Rick, c'mon, son, please don't do this. Please? *Do not* make me take you down. *Do not* force me to be a cop. You don't need that right now. I don't wanna be a cop – I wanna be your friend. You need me to be a friend," Tony said intently. He reached slowly towards his gun belt, since he was still, technically, in uniform. His gun, and extra clips, were safely locked away in his desk at the centre, but his belt held a couple of other surprises, including a taser he really didn't want to use. Tony thought he could reach his mace if it truly became necessary, but the cop was praying he wouldn't need it.

"Go away, Tony. You're just like my dad. You don't give a damn about me. You'd rather see me in jail. Just like Seamus," Rick grunted harshly. Suddenly, he pushed away from the car and lunged towards Tony.

It was so sudden Tony didn't get a chance to grab for anything to defend himself. The enraged teen swung at Tony again, and as before, Tony easily ducked the punch. Rick kept swinging and somehow managed to manoeuvre Tony up against his car. *Great,* Tony thought grimly. *Now what? If he hits me again, I* have *to arrest him.*

Tony stood, seemingly helpless, against the car, as Rick stepped back slightly to throw another punch at the cop's unprotected head. Tony froze for only a moment, then dropped to his knees. There was just enough room between the cop and the teen for the move to work. When Tony heard the sound of shattering glass, he covered his head to protect himself from the pieces raining down. Tony quickly bounced back to his feet, just in time to dodge another punch. This time, Rick put a fist-sized dent in the side of Tony's car.

Tony didn't wait for Rick to pull back a third time. He immediately grabbed Rick, spun him around and tried to pin the boy's arms to his sides. Rick struggled hard against Tony, his head thrashing back and forth as he fought to get loose. Tony grunted as Rick's head suddenly slammed back into his. He could feel his grip loosening, as his vision swam and his knees buckled.

"We've got him, Tony. Let go," Bob growled as his four boys held onto Rick. Rick fought and struggled, all the while shouting he'd make them pay and he'd kill them all. Tony collapsed in a heap, his nose bleeding from the impact of Rick's head, as Bob and his boys continued to fight with Rick. Bob had no idea who "they" were, but if "they" got Rick this angry, Bob didn't want to meet them. Tony looked up through bleary eyes to see Bob and the boys struggle to contain the angry teen. Even through his swimming vision, Tony could see Carl and his friends were about to lose the battle.

"Coach, I can't hold him much longer. He's too strong and I'm getting tired," Carl grunted as Rick almost slipped away.

"Take him down," Tony groused from where he lay on the ground. The cop could feel the glass cutting into his cheek and hands as he fought to push himself up without cutting the hell out of himself. Carl nodded at Tony's suggestion and threw all of his weight into a punch that landed squarely on Rick's jaw. The punch was hard enough to daze the over-wrought teen and Rick finally slumped to his knees, Carl and his buddies holding Rick's arms so he didn't collapse into the glass next to Tony.

"Tony, you okay?" Bob asked as he squatted next to the cop.

Tony nodded wearily. "Nothing broken, just some cuts from the glass and my nose's bleeding some. Thankfully, I have a hard head. God, what a mess," Tony said, shaking his head and instantly regretted it as the world spun like crazy. He closed his eyes until everything steadied again, then opened them to stare at the glass around him and Rick. Then he sighed. Rick's head lolled against his chest and Tony could see the glazed look in his eyes.

"At least he didn't slice his hands," Bob muttered as he examined Rick.

Tony nodded and stood up. *Now what?* he muttered to himself. *By rights, I should arrest him and haul his sorry butt off to jail.* "Bob, what the hell'm I gonna do?" Tony demanded roughly. What he should do and what was best for Rick were definitely two different things.

"Talk to him, Tony. Find out what set him off, I guess. Be a friend. Be a big brother. Hell, be the dad he's never had. But whatever you do, *do not* haul him off to jail, no matter what the law says you should do. That's the one thing he doesn't need right now. It'll break him for sure. Seamus'll lock him up and throw away the key," Bob warned as he steadied Tony.

"Coach, he's under control for now, but if he comes to any time soon, we won't be able to handle him. I'm beat," Carl said, wearily. The other three just nodded as they were too tired to talk. Bob nodded and looked at Tony. The cop knew this fight was gonna be the talk of the centre for days. Carl and his buddies were going to be heroes for taking on Moneyman.

"Take him to my office, boys. I'm gonna have to deal with this tonight. Bob, can you help?" Tony asked weakly. Carl and his buddies hefted Rick up and dragged him to Tony's office. Tony and Bob followed with Tony using Bob as a bit of a crutch since his legs felt like rubber. Rick was unceremoniously dumped into a chair by the four boys. With a grimace as he, too, fell into a chair, Tony thanked them and gave them some money to buy some burgers for helping.

The very sore cop then locked Bob and himself in the office with an unconscious Rick. *What a mess*, Tony thought again as the two men waited for Carl's punch to wear off. Tony sat stiffly behind the desk while Bob guarded the door. The two adults began to shift uneasily as the minutes ticked away, and Tony worried that Carl had hit Rick too hard. Another couple of minutes passed until Rick twitched suddenly and opened his eyes. It was clear from the confusion in those eyes Rick remembered little of the last couple of hours.

"Rick, you okay?" Tony asked softly. He kept his voice low. The cop shifted in his seat and winced at a sharp pain in his side. He wondered if he had been badly injured or if he was just getting too old to be fighting with kids like Rick.

"Tony, what's up, man?" Rick asked puzzled. He rubbed his aching hands. They were throbbing and starting to swell. He could feel his whole body shaking with exhaustion. *What the hell's going on?* Rick wondered wildly as he stared at Tony. *What happened? What've I done now?*

"Take it easy, son. Just take a couple of deep breaths and relax," Tony encouraged Rick as he noticed how scared the teen was. "Bob, we need some ice. He may have cracked some bones in those hands," Tony continued softly. At Bob's sharp look, Tony reassured him. "Go on. I'll be okay. He's over it now." *At least I think he is,* Tony thought wryly. *Besides, I need to talk to him alone first. I need to make him believe I trust him.*

Tony kept the desk between himself and Rick as he told the exhausted teen in low tones what had happened. Rick was stunned. All he remembered was arguing with Tony in the office the instant he walked into the centre, then nothing. But he couldn't ignore his throbbing hands and legs, so he knew Tony wasn't lying. Then Rick took a good look at Tony. He could see the swelling eye and split lip. There was some dried blood Tony didn't know about right under his nose, and more dried blood on his shirt. He knew Tony's ribs hurt, just by the cautious way his friend moved. After all, he'd had more than his fair share of cracked and broken ribs, thanks to the Knights.

"Tony, did I really do that?" Rick asked, crushed. *What's happening to me?* Rick panicked. *I could've killed my best friend.*

"You gotta right hook that'd drop a tree, kiddo," Bob said, grinning as he came back into the office with the ice. Without another word, Bob began to tend to Rick's swollen hands, and, once the ice was wrapped around his hands, began to massage Rick's legs to keep them from cramping up. From the first touch, Bob could tell Rick's anger was completely gone now. *Thankfully,* the coach thought ruefully as he only paid partial attention to what Rick and Tony were talking about. *No one's in any condition to take this kid on again, at least not today.*

Tony continued to talk Rick for another few minutes, trying to make sure Rick knew Tony believed him. "I know the evidence points to you, Rick, because of those stupid *M*'s. But, everyone's known for the last couple of years those're your gang sign. So anyone could've scratched the paint and placed the blame squarely on you. My biggest concern right now, though, is the rage you came in with. What happened before you got to the centre?" Tony asked. *Now we'll deal with what's going on,* Tony thought firmly. *Once he admits it, that is.*

For the next couple of hours, Tony and Rick talked about what had happened. Bob stayed quietly in the background, tending to Rick's injuries and massaging sore arms, shoulders and legs for both Rick and Tony. They talked about the fight with Mickey and all the accusations. Tony realized immediately when Megan and Mickey didn't give Rick a chance to defend himself, that was what had really set him off. They believed what they saw instead of listening to Rick, despite their promise to him. Rick also told Tony about the fight with Brain and what the other boy had said.

"Unfortunately, it's my word against his, and, since I already have a record, the cops're gonna believe him," Rick said glumly. He knew he was in deep trouble with Seamus and would probably never be trusted by his cousin again. He was so deep in thought he nearly missed Tony's next words.

"Some cops, maybe, but not this one. I don't trust the Knights. What's happening's just too damn convenient, but I'll worry about that later after I make some calls. I need to save you from Seamus. Do you have someone who can say for sure you were in class at the time of the supposed vandalism?" Tony asked. He shifted out of his chair and perched his aching body on the corner of the desk. Bob just smiled as Tony grimaced.

"English, with Mr. Robson. I sit right in front of his desk, so he can keep an eye on me," Rick chuckled weakly. "Call him. He'll confirm. He doesn't exactly like me, but I know he won't lie just to get me out of his class."

As Rick carefully unwrapped his now-numb hands, Tony called the English teacher at home and was pleased when Mr. Robson confirmed Rick had arrived on time for class and had never left. Tony even called Rick's teacher for the class before who also confirmed Rick had been on time for class and had not left for the entire period.

Tony felt better, since he could now prove to Seamus Rick wasn't the culprit. Rick had been in class all afternoon and with Megan and the twins at lunch. As far as Tony knew, Mickey had been to the truck at lunch and it was fine then, so the damage was done after that. Unless Rick had a twin somewhere in the school, Rick was cleared. *Maybe,* Tony thought wryly.

After the brutal session, Tony and Bob took Rick home. "Keep ice on the hands as much as you can tonight. Massage your legs some more, too. If you have a Jacuzzi or something like that, soak for a couple of hours in it and to hell with your dad. If the swelling hasn't gone down visibly by morning, go to the hospital," Bob cautioned Rick. Rick nodded as he eased himself out of Tony's car. He steadied himself on shaky legs as he listened to the advice of the two older men.

"And lay off the speed bag, too. Your hands won't be up to it for at least a couple of days," Tony cautioned. He escorted Rick to the front door only because the cop wanted to make sure Rick made it up his front steps. The teen was still shaking badly.

"What about that vandalism report O'Reilly has?" Rick worried as he tried to unlock the front door with shaky hands. Tony reached out and steadied Rick's hands; Rick smiled back gratefully.

"I'll explain what I found out to O'Reilly. Don't worry about our fight either. I'll explain it somehow, if anyone asks," Tony said as he and Bob left. "Oh, by the way, Happy Birthday, a day early," Tony called from the end of the sidewalk. With another small grin, Rick waved good-bye and closed the door.

He managed to climb the stairs to his room. He was too sore to want to eat anything, but he knew he'd regret it if he didn't. He grabbed a bag of chips and some pop on his way through the kitchen. After tossing his book bag and coat in the corner, he sank carefully down on his bed. He was sore and still upset, mainly at himself. He still couldn't believe what he had done. Why Tony hadn't hauled him down to the station, Rick didn't know, but he was grateful. And with everything else that had been going on, he'd forgotten his birthday was tomorrow.

Rick's phone rang. He groaned as he reached for it. "Hello?" he said, wincing as he rolled onto one of his sore hands.

"Rick, it's your uncle," Ian said blandly. Rick knew right away something was wrong but he couldn't figure out what. Ian was being far too polite.

"Hey, Uncle Ian, what's up?" Rick asked.

"Your grandmother wants to know if you're getting your dad to bring you out to the ranch for your birthday supper tomorrow," Ian continued neutrally, almost as if he hadn't heard Rick speak.

"Ouch," Rick hissed softly as he shifted and his legs throbbed in protest.

"What was that, Rick?" Ian asked more out of politeness than any real concern.

"Oh, nothing, Uncle Ian. I just rolled over on my wrist, that's all. I haven't seen Dad yet, so I don't know, but after Thanksgiving, I didn't think he was welcome at Glencrest," Rick replied.

"*He's* not, but he could still bring *you* out. Never mind. Meet me at Hollyhock's around 2 p.m. and I'll bring you. Bring a change of clothes so you can return home Monday after school. Bring your homework as well," Ian said, his voice still neutral.

"Okay, Uncle Ian. Thanks. See you tomorrow," Rick said. He hung up the phone and sat on his bed, wondering about the lack of emotion in his uncle's voice. *I'll bet anything he's heard about Mick's truck,* Rick realized suddenly. And *I'll bet he's not too happy about me being near Megs, either. What a mess,* he sighed.

Rick stayed in his room all night, keeping out of his dad's sight. He managed to get back down to the kitchen and get some ice for his aching hands, and something more substantial than a bag of chips to eat, but Michael's early arrival home prevented Rick from soaking in his dad's precious Jacuzzi. Instead, the battered boy settled for a long hot soak in the regular tub. He managed to drag his aching body back to his bed where he just fell across it. He pulled the bedspread over himself as he fell into an exhausted, and fortunately, dreamless sleep. He just couldn't wait to see what the next day would bring.

Chapter 16

Michael had stayed downstairs drinking all night and left long before Rick awoke the next morning. A sarcastic note on the kitchen table wished Rick a Happy Birthday; a cheque was attached to the note, and Rick chuckled when he saw it had been drawn on the business account, not Michael's personal one.

"Managed to scrape enough together, eh, Dad?" Rick muttered. "Oh well, at least he remembered this year." There'd been far too many birthdays Michael hadn't remembered, and it bothered Rick just as much now as it had when he was little. Rick moved around the kitchen slowly, getting breakfast, while every muscle in his body protested. His hands didn't seem any less swollen, but they definitely weren't any *more* swollen, and, since he could move them a bit easier than he could the day before, he decided he didn't need to go get them checked out. Besides, he didn't want Dr. Jim to call Nana and tell her before he had a chance to explain.

He also decided to have another long soak in the Jacuzzi, just so he would feel half-way human at Nana's. For almost two hours he lounged in a very hot tub. The heat and massaging jets felt good, and he felt slightly better than he did when he first woke up. After a quick lunch, Rick cleaned up for supper at the farm and somehow Rick just knew his uncle wouldn't be happy about it. *Come to think of it, I'm not real crazy about being the main attraction at the zoo, either. I hate being stared at,* Rick thought sourly as he finished dressing. Before he left, though, he called to check up on Tony.

"Hey, kiddo, how do you feel? No more blackouts?" Tony asked.

"Naw. My hands aren't as bad today but I'm sure sore all over. I had a long soak last night in the tub and another this morning in Dad's Jacuzzi so I feel almost human. I'm going to Nana's for supper, but I wanted to know how you were doing," Rick said, still ashamed at what he had apparently done.

"Sore, like you, but, thankfully, no broken ribs, just slightly cracked. Man, you have a solid punch, kiddo. I really thought I broke something when I fell over that bloody bench," Tony chuckled dryly. He winced as his ribs protested.

"Tony, I'm … really sorry," Rick began hesitantly. He felt horrible as he replayed, yet again, what he knew had happened. He could hear the pain in Tony's voice.

"Monday, Rick," Tony interrupted firmly, yet gently. "We'll deal with this on Monday. I'll see you at noon for a brief session, and you'll come to the centre after school where you and Bob have a date with a punching bag before we talk again. And I don't mean me," Tony finished with a smile. By then, Tony hoped to have a better idea of how to deal with someone who could potentially kill him if he wasn't careful.

Rick hung up slowly and called a cab. His legs were just too sore to walk across town to Hollyhock's. The cab ride was short enough it didn't cost Rick too much, yet long enough he had time to do some hard thinking. Unfortunately, he didn't come up with any new answers to the questions running around in his head.

As the cab pulled up in front of Nana's store, Rick groaned. It just wasn't his day. Seamus O'Reilly was coming out of the store, followed closely by Mickey and Jordan. From the look on Jordan's face, she was being kept close by her father and she was definitely not happy about it. *No surprise there,* Rick thought with a grin. *That's my girl.*

Rick paid for his cab ride and got out. Jordan was the first to see him and started towards her boyfriend. Seamus grabbed her arm and spoke sharply to her. Rick was too far away to hear Seamus' comments, but he clearly heard Jordan's reply.

"I don't care what you think, Daddy. Tony proved Rick didn't do anything, even if you don't believe him. And I don't care if you don't like him – I love him. Now LET ME GO!" Jordan snapped, jerking her arm out of her father's grip. Seamus was so shocked he just stood with his mouth hanging open as his daughter went to be with the one boy he couldn't stand.

"Hey, sweets," Rick said, smiling as he gave her a soft kiss.

"Hey, Rick," Jordan said as she gave him a firm hug. Rick hissed with a sudden surge of pain.

"What's wrong, Rick? What did I do? What happened?" she asked, each question tumbling out faster than the one before. She stepped back and looked at Rick. She could see the swollen hands and the bruises on his battered face. She reached up and gently brushed his hair back from a wicked-looking black eye.

"Another fight with Tony, this time during a blackout. Look, call me tonight. I'm staying at Glencrest at my house there and I'll explain then," Rick said softly as Seamus and Mickey approached.

"Harm a hair on her head, boy, and I'll see ye rot in jail," Seamus growled. Jordan gave a wordless sound of protest her father ignored as usual.

"Look, Inspector, I'm sorry you don't like me. But how about we try to get along for Jor's sake?" Rick said, offering a handshake. Seamus glared at him in undisguised contempt and waved angrily at Jordan to follow him to the truck. Rick dropped his hand and stood in the parking lot like an errant schoolboy. *What'd I do to make him hate me so much?* Rick wondered. It wasn't the first time he'd asked himself that question, and he knew it wouldn't be the last.

Father and son escorted Jordan to Mickey's truck. As he waited for his uncle, Rick could see the vast amount of damage done to the paint. It wasn't going to be cheap to redo that special paint job of Mickey's. The Irish flag on the tailgate would be the easiest, but the rest was a special pattern of blue and white which only meant something to Mickey. *Maybe I should offer to help pay for the truck*, Rick thought. *That might make him believe I had nothing to do with it.* Ian stomped out of the store and over to Rick who didn't turn at his uncle's approach, although he would've been deaf to not heard Ian coming.

"Let's go, Richard," Ian said, keeping his voice neutral. Rick sighed gustily. It was going to be a very long night if Ian was already upset. *What do I have to do to convince everyone I didn't do anything?* Rick fumed silently.

"Look, Uncle Ian, despite what you saw and what you may believe, I didn't do anything to Mick's truck," Rick protested yet again. But he knew his protests fell on deaf ears. Ian was in no mood to listen.

"Right. Let's go. Your grandmother's waiting," Ian snapped. Rick didn't move.

"I was in English class with Mr. Robson, Uncle Ian. Tony even confirmed it with him," Rick continued to protest. He could feel his anger quickly rising and clenched his sore fists as tightly as he could to maintain some kind of control, even though it hurt like hell to do.

"Don't even get me started on Tony!" Ian snarled, whipping around so fast Rick stepped back, startled. "Seamus saw the bruising when Tony came in this morning and made Tony tell him what happened. He covered for you, boy, calling your attack a fight he provoked. He claimed he pushed you too far during a session and you were just defending yourself! Likely damn story! Get in, sit down, and shut up so we can get this miserable dinner over with!" Ian slammed his truck door so hard the vehicle shook.

Rick climbed in slowly. His anger continued to simmer, but he vowed to maintain control this time. "Why won't anyone believe I had nothing to do with any of this?" Rick demanded as he snapped his seat belt on.

"Process of elimination, boy. Nothing ever happens when you're around," Ian snapped back, then refused to talk anymore. The silence in the truck was thick and uncomfortable and the ride felt like it took forever.

As they pulled into Glencrest, Ian had one last thing to say. "One more thing, boy. After tonight, cousin or not, you stay the hell away from my daughter or I'll hunt you down myself! You hear me?" Ian hissed.

"Loud and clear, Uncle Ian. By the way, my name isn't *Boy*," Rick said wearily as he climbed out of the SUV. *Man, I'm getting tired of this*, Rick thought miserably.

Rick slowly walked up to the front door. It opened and Nana came out. It didn't take her long to size up the situation. "Ian, son, please take Rick's bag over to his house," Nana said softly, never taking her eyes off Rick. She guided her grandson over to a bench on the front porch, sat down and faced Rick, all of her love and compassion evident in her large, dark eyes. "Well, my lad, it hasn't been easy these past couple of months, has it?" she asked.

Rick shook his head. Tears suddenly gathered in his eyes. "I'm trying, Nana. I've asked for a chance and I thought they were gonna give me time, but they didn't. No one but Jor cares and no one believes me when I say I didn't do something. Even if someone backs me up," Rick cried. He couldn't believe how upset he was. All it had taken was someone to care about him again, and Rick was ready to bawl like a baby.

"I believe you, lad." With those four words, Rick's tenuous hold on his tears broke and he collapsed in Nana's arms. He sobbed like he hadn't since his mom had left. Ian came back up the front steps and watched Rick cry in his grandmother's arms. *Well, he's certainly got Mother firmly wrapped around his little finger*, Ian thought bitterly as he watched with his arms folded. *What a great actor.* Through his sobs, Rick didn't hear his uncle stomp by him and slam the door on his way into the house.

After a couple of minutes on the porch, Rick and Nana headed into the dining room for supper. Rick felt better for crying, but he wasn't really comfortable in the house. The meal was strained, to say the least. No one talked to Rick very much, and if they did, the questions required no more than short yes or no answers. As he ate, Rick knew he would have had a better birthday at home alone. Megan refused to have anything to do with Rick at all, and only said hello when Nana reminded her sharply of her manners. Martha brought Rick's birthday cake out at the end of the meal, but only Nana sang "Happy Birthday."

"Make a wish, lad," Nana urged.

I wish everyone would believe me, Rick wished silently and blew out the candles. He just sat staring at the smoke drifting away while Martha brought plates and a knife. In the stony silence, Rick cut the cake and handed out the pieces. Still no one, except Nana, talked to him. Once everyone was done their cake and Martha had cleared away the plates, Nana brought out the presents. The first one was from Ian. Inside was a set of boxing gloves. Rick was thrilled with the gift. He could leave them at the centre and wouldn't have to use ones someone else had. The gloves, Bob had told him, had to become part of his hands, moulded to the unique shape of Rick's fists in order to make him a better boxer.

Ian's comment, however, shattered Rick's momentary happiness. "They're for the next time you feel like flattening a cop," Ian said sarcastically. Rick flinched and hung his head.

"Ian," Nana said reprovingly. Ian just grunted and turned away.

Megan's gift was a new set of CD's by Aerosmith, Rick's favourite band. Rick was stunned at the gift. Every CD ever put out by the band, and at probably around $20 a pop, this wasn't a cheap gift. "Thanks, Megs. These're great," Rick said, trying to catch Megan's eye. She refused to look at him or to say anything. That was the last straw for Nana.

"Alright you two, that's enough. I've had it up to here with your attitudes, so I can just imagine what Rick's going through. You're behaving like a pair of spoiled brats," Nana snapped at her son and granddaughter. "If Rick said he didn't do it, why won't you believe him?"

"Because he's done this before, Mother. We know he has," Ian replied with some heat.

That's it, Rick fumed. *I've had it, too.*

He didn't stand up, but he faced his uncle, anger plain in every line of his body. "So I'm not allowed to change, is that it, Uncle Ian? Innocent until proven guilty – isn't that the *law*? Why am I *presumed* guilty? Just 'cause I made a mistake and joined a gang, I'm automatically guilty? Is that it? Are you telling me you've never made any mistakes?" Rick said angrily. He took several deep breaths and forced himself to calm down.

"Sure, I've made mistakes. Everyone has," Ian replied sarcastically. "What's that gotta do with you, boy?" He had partially risen to his feet when Rick began talking, as if he was planning on throwing Rick out of the house.

"Were you ever blamed for something 'cause of those past mistakes?" Rick asked quietly, finally back in control. He lowered his eyes as he waited for his uncle to reply, even though he was sure of the answer.

"Well...no," Ian replied after a minute of quiet thought. "What're you getting at?"

"If you've made mistakes in the past, but you didn't get blamed because of that, why can't I make mistakes? Why am I so damn different than everyone else in this flippin' room?" Rick said finally, raising his eyes to meet his uncle's blank stare.

Ian and Megan were stunned at the accusation. *He's right*, Megan realized, horrified. *We promised to give him a chance, and the very first time something goes wrong and Rick seems to be responsible, we automatically blamed him*. Ian sat down hard. His head was spinning at Rick's accusation. He hadn't even realized they had presumed Rick was guilty simply because of his gang history. And if there was one thing Ian prided himself on was being fair to everyone no matter what their history was.

"I'm sorry, Rick," Ian apologized. "I'm as bad as your father. I'm sorry I never listened." Ian was too embarrassed to look Rick in the eye, but Rick understood.

"Me, too, Rick. I'm sorry," Megan added in a soft voice.

Rick smiled at her to try and ease her embarrassment. "Accepted, cuz. Listen, do me a favour, 'kay? You're the only one Mick'll listen to. Call him and tell him," Rick begged. He shifted in his chair and hissed as his legs throbbed. He'd been sitting too long and he was stiff and sore.

"Now that everyone's come to their senses, I have *my* gift for Rick," Nana said, smiling. She handed Rick a small box. Inside, Rick was stunned to find a set of car keys lying on the bottom.

"Nana, what...?" Rick asked, puzzled. He didn't want to get his hopes up, but it sure looked like Nana had just bought him a car.

"Go to the garage and see, lad," Nana chuckled. She could see plans already forming in her grandson's head and she was sure most of them had to do with Jordan.

Rick hobbled outside and opened the garage door. Inside, beside Nana's truck, was a black and silver Firebird. With a wide grin, Rick opened the driver's door and saw the CD player, AM/FM stereo, automatic, leather interior and all the bells and whistles any 17-year-old could possibly want in a new car. Sliding behind the wheel, Rick was thrilled at the gift. *Wait 'til everyone sees this at school*, Rick giggled to himself.

"It's up to you now, lad, to keep it running, filled with gas, et cetera. That's gonna mean a job, at least in the summer, but during school, I'll help out. I'm sure I can find something for you to do at Hollyhock's. I've paid for the car and your first year of insurance and registration. Be careful with it. I'm sorry about the colour, though. It was all they had and I didn't have time to get it repainted," Nana apologized. She shivered, despite the warmth of the heated garage. *Those colours're gonna cause trouble – I can feel it in my bones,* she thought.

Rick didn't care about the colour. All he cared about was finally being free. He could get away from Michael any time he wanted and go anywhere the gas in the car could take him. He could take Jordan out on a real date and they wouldn't have to walk or rely on someone's generosity to drive them around. He could come and visit Nana or slip out to the farm and ride his horse any time he wanted. The Firebird was *freedom*. Rick struggled to his sore feet and hugged Nana.

"Thanks, Nana," he said softly. "This is the best birthday gift ever."

That night, in his house, Rick thought about his new car. He knew what his dad's reaction would be, but Rick didn't really care. Nana had insisted Rick get his licence right after he had turned 16 because of Michael's tendency to drink too much, and then climb behind the wheel. Not that he used Rick very often as a designated driver, but at least Nana felt better knowing Rick was available if Michael wanted. Rick spent an entire hour just staring at his license and realizing the freedom it truly meant.

After lunch the next day, Rick drove his new car home. He didn't speed, nor did he have his stereo too loud. He drove responsibly. He knew it wouldn't do to give Seamus another opportunity to lock him up and keep him away from Jordan. As Rick pulled up to his house, he grimaced at the thought of his father's reaction, and true to form, Michael didn't disappoint.

Michael was standing on the porch as Rick pulled up. "Where the hell've you been and where did you get that car? It's not hot, is it?" Michael demanded hotly as Rick got out.

Rick snorted as he climbed the stairs and stared defiantly at his dad. "Don't think so, Dad. Nana gave it to me last night at Glencrest. For my birthday."

"Give it back. My son doesn't need her charity," Michael said bitterly.

"One – no. Two – it's not charity. Three – it's my car, lock stock and barrel," Rick said as he pushed past Michael.

"Look, boy," Michael snarled and grabbed Rick's wrist. Rick cried out as pain shot up his arm but Michael refused to let go. "If you want a car so bad, I'll buy you one. You don't need her charity."

Rick worked his hand out of Michael's iron grip, trying not to hurt himself anymore. "Leave it, Dad. It's mine and I like it." Rick went up to his room and finished his homework, trying to ignore his father banging around downstairs.

Monday morning, Rick drove his new car into the school parking lot, just as Mickey pulled up. Megan and Jordan jumped out and came over while Mickey followed a little slower. The young Irishman looked like he had swallowed something that didn't agree with him.

"Hey, Rick," Jordan said with a soft kiss.

"Like the wheels, sweets?" Rick asked proudly, grinning from ear to ear. She giggled as he patted the car like a proud new dad.

Even Mickey liked the new car. He stood shifting from foot-to-foot before he apologized, grudgingly, to Rick for his accusations. "Megan reminded me of our pledge. We promised to give you a chance and I blew it. I should've listened, Rick. I'm sorry."

"Mick, don't worry about it. I accept," Rick said firmly as everyone went to their Homerooms. *Please just let me get through today*, Rick thought miserably as he sat down. *I hurt too much to deal with anything else.*

Chapter 17

The rest of the morning was quiet. No one bothered Rick or the girls. Everyone was getting ready for mid-terms and concentrating on school. But the sign someone was still after Megan and Jordan came with a renewed series of slips, trips and falls which began right after lunch. Only now Rick was being seen in the vicinity of the attacks and the focus had shifted more to Jordan than Megan. Despite Mickey's assurances only that morning he'd give Rick another chance, Jordan's brother immediately began to keep Rick from seeing Jordan.

"I'm trying to protect you, dammit," Mickey growled at her after Jordan loudly protested as Mickey hustled her away after school. Nothing she said even began to dent Mickey's stubbornness.

Mr. Delaney called Rick into his office after the second day. Megan had bruised both of her knees badly on the sidewalk outside the front doors that morning, and Jordan had mildly sprained her wrist when she was knocked awkwardly against the lockers. Neither girl saw Rick push them, but someone immediately yelled at "Rick" to leave them alone. That was enough for the principal.

"Look, Rick, I could understand you going after Johnny after all he's done to you in the last couple of months, but I just can't understand why you're hurting these two girls, especially Jordan. I thought you cared about her," Mr. Delaney said, puzzled. The principal sat behind his desk while Rick stood in front with his arms folded, silently fuming as he was, once again, accused of something he didn't do.

"Here we go again! Y'know something, Delaney? I'm getting damn sick and tired of defending myself. What's it gonna take for you, and everyone else, to believe me? I didn't do it!"

Rick snapped. "You're right about one thing – I love Jor. I wouldn't hurt her. Ever. Period. End of discussion."

"Now Rick, really, son, do you think I'd accuse you without something to back me up? Several people reported seeing you deliberately push Jordan into the lockers, walk away laughing and then show back up less than a minute later, all concerned that she'd been hurt," Mr. Delaney protested.

Rick steamed in silence until his quick mind came up with a question. "What was I was wearing?" he asked quietly, suddenly back in control.

"Black jeans, white tee-shirt, black and silver jacket and your bandana. In other words, young man, full gear. Although the witnesses did say your bandana was covering your face, instead of your hair," Delaney replied, puzzled by the question. He couldn't figure out where Rick was going with his question and was even more puzzled by Rick's answer.

"Mr. Delaney, think about it. Jor's pushed by 'me' in full gear. I walk away and then show back up less than a minute later all concerned that she's been hurt. Hardly enough time to completely change my clothes, don't you think?" Rick indicated his snug fitting stonewashed blue jeans and a black snap-front long sleeved shirt. It reminded Mr. Delaney of a cowboy shirt, and not normally something he thought Rick would wear. Oddly, it looked good on him. "Especially the shirt, since I can tell you for a fact it takes a while to do up all the snaps, but less than a second to rip them open." Rick opened the neck further to show he didn't have an undershirt or tee shirt on underneath, either.

The principal didn't know what to say. Rick had made a good point, and yet everyone had identified him as the one who had shoved Jordan. Delaney was at a loss. "Rick, you still in counselling?" he finally asked for lack of anything else.

"Yes, sir. I meet with Tony three times a week and I have boxing training every day after school. I can control my anger better. I punch a bag now, instead of people," Rick said proudly. It was the only thing he had done lately that he was proud of. Every night he would go to bed feeling guilty about what he had done, or almost done, to Tony, and the boxing was helping him to deal with the guilt.

"Alright Rick, I get it. Get outta here and go home," Mr. Delaney dismissed him with a sigh. *What a mess*, the principal thought as Rick strode confidently from the office.

Rick walked slowly to his car. When he finally arrived, he found a scrap of paper with the word "Remember" scrawled on it tucked under the windshield wiper. It was easy for Rick to figure out who had put it there. Blade's gang sign was at the bottom. *As if you'll ever let me forget, Johnny*, Rick though angrily as he crumpled the paper and threw it away. Everyone but the teachers had left for the weekend, including Jordan, without being able to say goodbye, thanks to Mickey.

Rick screamed out of the parking lot and headed to the youth centre. He was so angry at what was happening he was shaking and he could barely control his car. He needed to go a couple of rounds with Carl, if Coach would let him. Sometimes Bob wouldn't take the chance of Rick hurting the other fighters. Since the fight with Tony, Carl was the only one in the boxing program willing to step into the ring with Rick. Carl didn't care about the terrific right hook Rick had already developed in such a short time training with Bob. Carl just liked to box.

While Rick had been defending himself to Mr. Delaney, Mickey had hurried Megan and Jordan out to his truck. All the way, Jordan protested she wanted to say good-bye to Rick.

"No," Mickey said firmly. "I've already called Dad, sis, and he told me to keep you away from that boy," Mickey said, pulling her along, despite her struggles and protests. "I know we promised to give him a chance, Jordan, but I can't. I'm sorry, but I just don't trust him," Mickey continued.

"He didn't do anything," Jordan protested, as she stood by the truck and refused to get in. She knew by now her pleas were falling on deaf ears. Her father didn't like Rick at all and now it seemed her beloved brother was becoming just as unreasonable. *What am I gonna have to do to get them to trust Rick?* she thought sadly.

"Get in, sis or walk home, I don't care right now. But I'm done talking about that boy," Mickey snapped roughly. After a couple of seconds, Jordan slowly climbed into the truck, sat miserably beside Megan and didn't speak again.

Mickey dropped Megan off at Hollyhock's where the two spent a quiet moment in the parking lot saying their good-byes, oblivious to the pain they were causing Jordan. Jordan resented her best friend's luck. *At least she gets to kiss her boyfriend good-bye every day,* Jordan thought bitterly. *I'm not even allowed to look at Rick anymore.* The more she thought about her father's attitude towards Rick, the less she understood it.

Mickey climbed back into the truck and pulled out to head home. The silence grew thicker and tenser as Mickey guided his truck out of town. Once on the highway, Mickey sped up and set the cruise control. He was silent for a couple more minutes, as he studied his sister out of the corner of his eye. *She looks so miserable,* Mickey thought sadly. *Why doesn't she just dump Rick? Then Dad and I'll leave her alone.*

"Look, sis, I know you think I'm being unreasonable, but I'm worried about you," Mickey began quietly. "You're my baby sister and I love you..."

"If you love me so much, why can't you understand? I *know* Rick isn't doing this. He loves me and I love him. What's wrong with that?" Jordan interrupted quickly.

"He's a hood, Jordan. He's getting his kicks out of claiming he loves you and then he attacks you in plain sight. He's no good, sis," Mickey growled. *Why can't she see that?* he thought angrily. *How much more does he have to do to her to get her to see the truth?*

"Lemme make my own mistakes, Mickey. If it's my choice to love a hood, as you call him, then let me. Why can't you and Daddy just leave me alone?" Jordan's voice trailed off. She had half-turned in her seat to confront Mickey as they argued. Out of the corner of her eye she noticed a black sports car and a motorcycle coming up hard. The two looked like they were racing each other but, what had really caught Jordan's eye, was how they were sling-shotting past each other. Something about the way they were racing told Jordan they were trouble.

"Mickey, slow down!" Jordan cried. Mickey immediately hit the brakes. The bike stayed behind as the car pulled up beside the truck and began to edge the truck closer and closer to the ditch. Mickey had slowed down, but he knew he was still going too fast. If they hit the ditch, they'd probably flip. If he stopped completely, the vehicles behind the bike would cause a huge collision.

"Hold on, Jordan!" Mickey said firmly as the car finally forced the truck into the ditch, then shot out of sight, the bike following close behind.

The ditch, fortunately, was a gentle slope and not deep enough to flip the truck immediately. A couple of hard frosts after Thanksgiving had made the ground less boggy, but extremely slick. The truck bounced heavily over rocks and brush as Mickey fought to keep it upright. Despite their seatbelts, the twins were bounced around. Jordan hit her head twice off the window and Mickey wrenched one wrist as he fought with the truck. Suddenly, the truck slipped sideways on the frozen grass and headed straight for a barbed wire fence. Jordan screamed as the truck ploughed through the fence and finally shuddered to a stop.

The two sat in the truck, shaking. Jordan tried to stop the tears that had begun, but couldn't. After a minute of stunned silence, punctuated by Jordan's sobs, Mickey pulled out his cell phone, and, after a couple of false starts, finally managed to call his dad at the station to report the accident. He couldn't help the way his voice shook as he talked. Seamus roared up with two other cops and a tow truck a short time later. To Jordan, it felt like an hour. Despite how she felt about her dad's attitude towards Rick, Jordan was never so glad to see her dad as she was right then.

"Mickey, Jordan. Are ye okay, kids?" Seamus demanded as he pounded up to the truck. Mickey had climbed out and stood staring at the fresh damage.

"Jordan's pretty shook up, Dad, but mainly just some bumps and bruises, I think. I know I've twisted my wrist while fighting with the steering wheel and I think Jordan may've hit her head. It's nothing serious, I think. Man, my truck really needs to be fixed now," Mickey chuckled nervously. He ran his hand through his hair, unconsciously mimicking Rick, and Seamus could see how much his son's hands were shaking. Not that he blamed his son. That was one phone call he never wanted to get again.

"Don't worry, son. I've got the weekend off, so we'll take it over to Mac's. He's already set up to get it painted and fixed," Seamus assured his son.

Jordan finally climbed out of the truck. Her legs were shaking so much she could hardly walk to her family. Mickey caught her as she stumbled and almost fell. Seamus gathered both of them into an embrace while Jordan continued to sob. The full impact of what could have happened had finally sunk into her frozen brain.

"What happened, son?" Seamus demanded after he let go of his children. He had shifted Jordan slightly so he could also hold his son and be Dad for a few moments. Now he returned to being Inspector O'Reilly. He motioned to one of the cops to take their statements.

Mickey detailed what had happened, trying to be concise, like Seamus had taught them. "It was Rick, Dad. I recognized the car. It was black and silver and it had the same detailing. It was Rick," Mickey repeated stubbornly.

Jordan's tears stopped abruptly as she pushed herself away from her father. "There you go again, Mickey Liam O'Reilly. Accusing him without proof! Quit blaming Rick!" she shouted, enraged.

"Jordan, no one else we know has a black car like that!" Mickey protested. "It has to be him!"

"Gimme one good reason why Rick would do this!" Jordan shouted again.

"I don't know!" Mickey shouted back. The twins glared at each other and Seamus shook his head. It wasn't good for his kids to be fighting with each other.

"Enough, kids. Look, everyone's upset right now. Jordan, fer now, I'm trusting yer brother. Now, look, me girl, hear me out," Seamus said firmly, holding up his hand as Jordan opened her mouth to protest again.

"Until I hear from Rick, I'm considering him the prime suspect. Mickey's right. Can ye name one other person ye know who has a black and silver Firebird, Jordan? No? Didn't think so. So as of right now, Tony and his partner're gonna be at school at different times. I'm sorry, me girl, but after everything that's happened to ye this week, I just don't trust that boy," Seamus said in a voice that ended the discussion on the matter. He glanced at a nearby officer who had been standing back, trying not to listen.

"Take 'em home, Marshall. Jordan, we'll talk more later," Seamus said as he tried to catch his daughter's eye. Jordan, however, refused to look at her father as she grabbed her book bag out of the back of the truck and stormed over to Marshall's car. Mickey followed more slowly.

"Yes, sir, Seamus," Marshall replied blandly.

Jordan was quiet the entire – and mercifully short – trip home. When they arrived, she went directly to her room and refused to speak to her brother, despite Mickey's repeated attempts. When Seamus arrived an hour or so later and tried to talk to his daughter, Jordan gave him the silent treatment as well. Seamus decided to leaver her alone until she calmed down. She inhaled her supper then soaked in a hot bath for almost two hours. When she finally emerged, feeling more relaxed than she had all day, Mickey was waiting for her in her room, looking absolutely miserable.

"GET OUT!" Jordan demanded loudly, pointing to the door. Her green eyes snapped and her face was flushed.

"Talk to me, sis! Please?" Mickey pleaded. They had never fought before and it was tearing him apart.

"Get out!" Jordan yelled. "Leave me alone! I never wanna talk to you again!"

Mickey hadn't moved from his chair. "Why can't you understand I'm just trying to protect you, Jordan? He's bad news and he's gonna hurt you! Why're you so eager to defend him?" Mickey demanded.

"Why're you so eager to condemn him?" Jordan replied softly. Mickey sat, stunned, at her gentle words. She pointed to the door one more time, and after staring at his sister for a couple more moments, Mickey pulled his long frame out of the chair and left the room, closing the door quietly behind him. To Jordan, he might as well have slammed it. He tried to concentrate on his homework, but Jordan's words weighed too heavily on his mind.

Both twins fell into their respective beds later than they usually did, the fight and the accident uppermost in both of their minds. Neither one slept much, but for vastly different reasons. Mickey was worried about both Megan and Jordan, but more about his sister. He couldn't understand why she continued to protect someone like Rick and why she refused to see how Mickey was just trying to protect her. Jordan ended her day much as she had started it – thinking about Rick and why someone was so determined to come between her and the one she loved.

In fact, if Rick had known how much Jordan was thinking about him, he never would've done very well in the ring against Carl. Rick was easily distracted whenever he thought about Jordan, no matter what he was doing, so he forced her from his mind, although very reluctantly. Bob made Rick work hard in the ring, harder than most of his boys. Bob would always say it was because of Rick's anger and how Rick always needed to be physically exhausted when he talked to Tony. In reality, Bob worked Rick hard because Rick had caught onto boxing so quickly Bob needed to keep him challenged and that meant trying to stay at least two steps ahead of Rick.

Rick loved it. Bob was proud of all of his 'boys', but especially Rick. Rick had improved so much in the short time he'd been in the club Bob had approached Tony about entering Rick in tournaments. Tony, however, advised him to wait.

"Wait 'til we get him outta this mess with Seamus and Blade. He won't have enough control until then, not to mention the anger's still an issue," Tony advised as the two watched the match going on in the ring. Bob nodded absently as he watched Rick get a couple of good body shots in, making the other boxer grunt with the impact.

"Okay, Rick, Carl, enough. Good job, both of you," Bob called to end the match. The two dropped their hands and began to pace to avoid stiffening up as Bob delivered his assessment. "Carl, you need to work on your left side defence. Rick got in several good shots there. Don't gloat yet, Rick. You keep dropping your right hand when you go for a left hand shot," Bob said as he climbed into the ring to show them what he was talking about. After watching Bob demonstrate several times, both boys nodded. "We'll work on those areas on Monday, " Bob continued. "Go stretch it out completely and then hit the showers." With a wave, Bob dismissed his two best fighters.

Twenty minutes later, stretched, showered and changed, Rick emerged to find Tony and Seamus arguing with Bob. Rick sighed. O'Reilly could only be there for one thing – Rick and Bob's next words confirmed it.

"And I'm telling you that's impossible, Inspector. He's been here for the last two hours under my constant supervision," Bob protested hotly.

"Are ye quite sure? He never left yer sight for any length of time?" Seamus drawled. Tony stood behind his boss, looking like he wanted to be anywhere but right there.

"Rick couldn't've left this centre, drove to that highway, run your kids off the road at the time they said he did and then made it back here in time to have a two-hour workout which included a session on the weights and the heavy bag, which I spotted for, and an hour-long sparring session. Especially since I met him at the front door at 3:45 as usual. Check the sign-in log if you don't believe me. The trip there and back's almost an hour with lights and the traffic at this time of day. I'm telling you, Seamus, it's impossible," Bob protested again.

What the hell? Run O'Reilly's kids off the road? Rick thought as he listened to the argument. "Hey Tony, everything okay?" Rick asked politely as he approached the men.

"Rick, please tell me you know where your car is?" Tony begged. Rick immediately tensed. Tony never begged Rick for anything. It wasn't his way.

"What about my car?" Rick demanded roughly. "Tony, what's going on?"

"Mickey and Jordan were run off the road about an hour ago and Mickey swears you did it," Tony said after a moment's hesitation. He knew Rick would go ballistic if anything else happened to Jordan.

"Is Jor okay? What about Mick?" Rick asked quickly. He couldn't help but think about the O'Reillys being hurt. *If I get blamed, Seamus'll lock me up and throw away the key,* Rick thought grimly.

"Don't give me that innocent look, boy. I know ye did it. Let's go," Seamus grunted, reaching for his handcuffs. Rick stiffened and backed away from the older cop.

"I tell you, Seamus O'Reilly, Rick has been here for the last two hours," Bob protested again, standing in front of Rick. Tony cheered silently as Bob continued his vigorous support of Rick's innocence. It was good to hear someone else support the kid.

"Let's just go and see yer car then, boy, and when I prove ye did this, Jordan'll never see ye again." Seamus motioned sharply for Rick to lead the way. Rick hesitated for a moment, then walked straight to where he had parked his car, which just happened to be right beside Tony's. O'Reilly checked the car over several times but finally had to admit he couldn't find anything to prove Rick had run his kids off the road. There were no scratches or other damage.

"Alright, boy, I guess yer cleared. This time. But I've got me eye on ye, boy. Don't step outta line by so much as an inch, or so help me God, I'll slap ye in cuffs faster than ye can blink. Do ye understand me, boy?" Seamus growled. "Oh, and one more thing."

"Yes, sir?" Rick said, never taking his eyes off the larger cop. Tony he could handle, but Rick wasn't so sure about Seamus, especially if he was angry.

Seamus stepped closer to Rick until their faces were only an inch or two apart. His voice was deathly quiet as he spoke. "Stay the hell away from me daughter."

Rick just nodded. Nothing he'd say would ever get through Seamus' bias. Seamus turned without another word and gave Tony a funny look as he walked away. Rick stood by his car, lazily, as if he didn't have a care in the world and waited until Seamus was in his car. Then, shaking with anger and fear, he slumped against the car bumper as Seamus left with a squeal of rubber. Tony and Bob exchanged a look that spoke volumes, then Tony returned his gaze to Rick. The boy was sitting on the hood of his car, pale as the shirt he was wearing. Tony knew Rick was thinking, not about Seamus' accusations, but about Jordan.

"Tony, why am I always guilty?" Rick demanded suddenly. "Y'know what's happening, don't you?"

Tony shrugged philosophically. "Maybe, kiddo, but you still can't prove it," Tony replied honestly. Bob nodded.

"You can't prove it was me, either, but that doesn't stop O'Reilly. Why isn't Brian being questioned? You know he has a black Camaro and, at highway speeds, his car and mine look alike. Adding the pin stripping I have wouldn't take someone like Eric very long to do," Rick said sourly as he jumped down. Tony came over and put his hand on Rick's shoulder. He understood all too well what Rick was feeling. He may have only been Rick's counsellor for a short time, and yet he felt more like a big brother than a cop, especially at times like this.

"I don't know, Rick. I'm just as frustrated as you are. The inspector's focussed on you, for some reason. Must be because of Jor. For as long as I've known him, he's been protective of her," Tony said, distractedly.

There didn't seem to be anything else to say and there didn't seem to be any point in having a counselling session with Rick. They'd only hash over this latest incident and that was one thing Rick didn't need to do. He didn't need to be any more worried about Jordan than he already was. Tony brushed his braids back over his shoulders and walked back into the centre with Bob, talking quietly.

Rick climbed slowly into his car. Now he understood why Nana was so concerned about the colour of his car. Anyone with a black car, and talent, could paint on the silver strips and decals that accented Rick's car, just like he had suggested. Brain had probably done just that over the last week, with Crank's gear-head help. Unfortunately, it would cost too much to repaint the car, money Rick didn't have. Rick didn't want to be like his dad and ask Nana for the money, even though he was sure his grandmother would willingly give it to him.

All in all, it had been a rough day.

That night, as Rick watched a movie in his room, he tried calling Jordan to find out how she was doing. Seamus, however, was monitoring both the family line and Jordan's private number. Every time Rick dialled, Seamus would answer and refuse to let Jordan talk to Rick. By the end of the night, Rick was beyond frustrated. He couldn't imagine how Jordan was handling her father.

Rick spent a quiet weekend. Michael left early Saturday morning to visit his latest woman and Rick was left alone. He knew his dad would be gone until late Sunday night and he'd drag himself home, somehow, and probably be hung over and definitely grumpy. He'd pick a fight with his son and make Rick's night miserable. The more Rick thought about how his weekend would probably end, the more he thought seriously about asking Nana if he could move to Glencrest permanently. *After all, she built that house for me,* he reasoned, *so why shouldn't I stay there permanently?* Rick was getting as tired of being a target for Michael's anger as he was of defending himself after Blade's antics. Rick wanted some freedom and he wanted it now. Before he went bonkers.

Rick got through the weekend and somehow managed to avoid his father. He finished his homework early on Saturday and then spent a good deal of time working out on the speed bag. When he wasn't punishing the bag, he was pacing and worrying about Jordan. There'd been no point in trying to contact her after Friday night. Seamus wasn't going to allow it. Monday morning was the only chance Rick would have and he vowed to make the most of whatever opportunity he had.

Rick arrived well before Mickey and the girls on Monday morning. He waited for them in the student lounge just inside the main doors. The sounds of the mini-waterfall should've been soothing, and under any other circumstances they probably would've been, but, today, Rick was a bundle of nerves. When Mickey escorted the girls into the school, Rick stood up and walked slowly towards the trio.

Jordan's face was scratched and lightly bruised, with a small lump just visible on her temple from where she must've hit her head, and Rick memorized every single injury. He swore silently and vowed Blade would pay for every scratch he saw, and the ones he didn't. Her face lit up when she saw Rick, and she began to walk towards him. Quickly, Mickey grabbed her by the arm, and nearby students stopped to listen as their argument grew loud and heated.

"Let me go! You don't own me, Mickey Liam O'Reilly!" Rick heard Jordan yell shrilly as he got closer. *The whole school probably heard her*, Rick chuckled to himself. He had forgotten how piercing her voice could get when she was upset.

"Look, sis, you heard Dad this morning. You're to stay away from that...that person," Mickey said just as loudly and refused to let his sister go, despite how hard Jordan struggled.

"'That person' has a name and 'that person' is innocent until proven guilty, a simple fact you and your dad seem to have conveniently forgotten," Rick broke in gently as he came up to the group. "I also seem to recall saying it's Jor's choice who she dates.

Not your dad's and certainly not yours, Mick." He stopped right beside Mickey and just as gently as he was speaking, he pulled Mickey's hands off Jordan's arm.

"Stay out of this, punk!" Mickey's face flushed bright red as he struggled to keep his anger in check.

"Not a chance. Not when it's Jor's choice. Hey, man, here's a thought. How's about you take a swing and *try* to hit me?" Rick taunted, emphasizing the word 'try.' "Let's see if hitting me makes you feel any better. C'mon, boy, hit me!" Rick continued to taunt Mickey, calling him by his dad's favourite nickname for Rick as he just stood back and waited.

Finally, Mickey couldn't take it anymore. He swung hard and fast. Rick just stood as still as a rock while Mickey's fist rushed towards his seemingly unprotected face. At the last possible second, so close Jordan was certain her brother would flatten her boyfriend, Rick's hand shot up and deflected Mickey's fist away. But, instead of swinging back like he knew everyone was expecting, Rick just gave Mickey a look.

"If I really wanted to, Mick, I could've flattened you with one shot. I know how. But I won't. Know why?" Rick said softly. Everyone stood around waiting for the drama to play out. Mickey shook his head as he held onto Megan, still shaking with barely-controlled anger.

"Because of Jor," Rick said and dismissed Mickey with a flick of his hand. Taking Jordan by the hand, the pair moved away and spent a couple of minutes in quiet conversation. Rick made sure Jordan was okay, but he felt absolutely helpless as he left Jordan with her brother. As she walked away, Jordan looked like she would have been happier going anywhere with Rick instead of to Homeroom with Mickey.

"Richard, I wanna word with you," Megan called out as they, too, went to Homeroom. A third teen stopped and ducked into an alcove nearby to listen.

"Look, cuz, I gotta take that 'Richard' crap from my old man, but I don't have to take it from you," Rick hissed as he whipped around to confront his cousin.

"What has Jordan ever done to you, except love you? Mistakenly, I might add. Why won't you leave her alone?" Megan demanded loudly.

"Great! Here we go again. How many times do I have to tell you guys *I didn't do anything!*" Rick protested just as loudly. He clenched his fists in a desperate effort to control his anger. No matter what he did, no matter who he had to back him up, he just couldn't prove his innocence to Megan and Mickey.

"Don't give me that, Richard. Mickey called me Saturday and told me what happened. He described your car perfectly! Why're you trying to hurt her?" Megan's voice was getting more and more shrill and her accent thicker.

"Are you saying I'm the only guy with a black and silver sports car, cuz? Really? 'Cause I can name at least two other people in this school *alone* who have a black car and it wouldn't take much to add the same detailing that's on mine. Is anyone looking at that? No. Why not? 'Cause Seamus O'Reilly has already tried and convicted me and convinced you I'm guilty. After all, what Seamus says, goes, and who the hell cares what anyone else says, never mind what the truth is," Rick snapped roughly. He continued to clench his fists. Tony's words about Jordan and Megan becoming targets if he lost control at school were coming back to haunt him. *I won't lose control*, Rick vowed silently, *I can't afford to lose control!* Rick struggled so hard with his temper he almost missed Megan's next words.

"Well, all I know is even Nana's having a hard time believing you. All anyone wants is an explanation. Why Jordan? Why me? Why? Is that too much to ask for?" Megan demanded one last time.

Rick was stunned, his anger doused by the cold shock of Megan's words. Nana had been his one unwavering supporter, aside from Jordan. If she no longer believed in him, then Blade had already won and what was the point of resisting any longer? But, before Rick could fall completely into despair, he remembered the look of absolute trust on Tony's face after the night in the centre when Rick knocked the cop on his back. *Tony trusts me and Tony believes me. I can still beat this,* Rick thought determinedly.

"For the last time, Megan Louise Attison, I *did not* push or trip Jor. Ever. I *did not* push or trip you. I *did not* scratch Mick's truck. I *did not* run them off the road!" Rick walked into Homeroom just as the final bell went and slid into his seat, still shaking with anger.

Megan sighed. "Sure you didn't, Rick," she muttered sarcastically as she followed him into the room. She spoke just loud enough for the eavesdropper to hear.

Brain chuckled as he eased out of his hiding spot and glided down the hall. Instead of entering his homeroom, he turned down another hallway and turned a couple of more corners until he found Blade standing by his locker near the metal shop.

"Yo, Blade," Brain called out, nodding to a couple of other friends as they passed.

"Yo, Brain, whassup in the think tank, man?" Blade drawled lazily. The ever present Pup handed Brain a can of pop the older boy gulped down quickly. *If there's no one else around,* Brain thought sarcastically as he finished the drink, *this little punk will watch his cousin's back.* Some days, Brain couldn't understand why Pup hung around with the gang, but Blade wanted his cousin around, so the kid stayed. What Blade wanted, Blade got.

Dismissing Pup, Brain quickly detailed what he had seen between Rick and the other three. Especially interesting to Blade was Mickey taking a swing at Rick. Blade chuckled nastily at Brain's tale – it was just perfect. Crank had arrived while the two were talking, and now he and Pup stood watching everyone, making sure no one disturbed their leader and second-in-command.

"That's the key, Blade," Brain said quietly. "All we have to do is get the others to do our work for us. We get to them and they'll just blame him. Moneyman'll come crawling back when he's got no one left. He'll be back by Christmas," Brain said confidently.

Blade agreed. "Cool, man. Watch yer backs, all of ya. Since we can't get Moneyman to come back by bustin' 'im up, I'm green-lighting the chicks. Ya've got 'til Friday." The other three nodded and split up.

For the rest of the day, it seemed, Megan and Jordan were constantly harassed. Even with Mickey walking with the two girls, someone, somehow, always managed to get a hand on one or the other and send them flying, usually into lockers or a doorjamb. By lunch, both were sore and bruised and Mickey had a very short fuse. Anyone coming near the girls was sent scurrying away by a glowering Mickey O'Reilly. Friends or not, Mickey wasn't taking any chances. More than once he heard someone tell "Rick" to lay off.

Problem was Rick had someone to vouch for his whereabouts the whole morning. Someone even Mickey couldn't refute, no matter what. Constable Tony Whitefish.

Tony had shown up, on Seamus' orders, just after Homeroom only intending to check in with the kids, but, after talking to a very upset Jordan and an even angrier Mickey, had decided to stay at the school and shadow Rick. Even with someone they trusted being with Rick, when Tony finally caught up to Mickey and the girls right before lunch, after leaving Rick in the office under Delaney's eye, Mickey refused to accept the cop's word.

"Both girls were shoved into the lockers at least twice this morning. Shoved at the beginning or ending of every class, with Jordan just about cracking her head open on the desk. Megan's cut and Jordan's limping. I've asked four other people and they all swear it was Rick. They described his outfit perfectly, Tony – black jeans, white tee, and the jacket," Mickey protested loudly. "Why won't you do something about him?"

Tony shook his head and shoved his hands into his pockets. "Don't care what anyone said, Mick, it's not possible, son. First of all, Rick doesn't have any classes with you, so if they're getting attacked actually in class, it's not him. Second, that's not what Rick's wearing and, besides, I've been with Rick the whole morning, since just after Homeroom, which you know. You saw me meet up with him. He's never out of my sight, even in the bathroom. Rick's innocent," Tony said firmly, defending Rick for the umpteenth time. If pushed, though, Tony would've admitted he was getting tired of defending the boy. *What the hell's going on in this school?* the cop wondered. *What're they up to?*

"If he's so innocent, Tony, then perhaps you can explain this. I found it in my school bag this morning, just after History. The only time it's ever out of my sight's during Homeroom. Rick must've slipped it in then," Megan said quietly, handing Tony a note.

When Tony read the note, he was stunned. In it, 'Rick' asked how Megan was feeling. Did she hurt enough? If she didn't, he could change that. He'd take care of her. It was signed with those stylized *M*'s Tony was beginning to hate. *What's going on?* Tony wondered again. *First physical attacks, and now this. Is he trying to get locked up? If he's really doing this,* Tony amended quickly. He sighed and put the offending note in his shirt pocket. He stared at the trio and tried not to appear as frustrated as he felt.

"Since I wasn't here before Homeroom, I can't explain it. I do want you to think about something first. Since it's asking how you're feeling, I'm going to assume this was put in your bag after the attacks began and since you don't have any classes with Rick except Homeroom, I'd say someone else put this in your bag. And, unless you have a witness, a very reliable witness seeing him put the letter into your bag, it's all circumstantial. Rick's innocent until proven guilty, guys," Tony repeated.

Unhappy, Mickey and girls went off to lunch. They weren't happy with Tony's answers, but even Mickey had to admit he had a point. Without a witness, there was really no evidence against Rick, and they had to accept that. Tony returned to the office and walked into the conference room where Rick was pacing, a very worried look on his young face. The cop thanked Mr. Delaney for keeping an eye on Rick, quietly asked the principal if they could talk after his session with Rick, and then motioned abruptly for the teen to sit. Tony couldn't help but be furious about the note, now that he had had time to think about it and, truth be told, he didn't know how much longer he could defend Rick without having some evidence to the contrary.

After the silence had stretched on uncomfortably, Tony spoke, his voice barely loud enough to reach Rick, who sat less than three feet away. "What is it about you, Rick, that makes Blade want you back so bad?" Tony asked rhetorically. He continued quickly before Rick could say a word. "You don't like bullying like Blade. You're not a gear-head like Crank. You're not a thinker and planner like Brain. You're nothing like them and yet, through all of this, you're insisting it's the gang that's harassing the girls. All of this is an elaborate attempt to get you back into a gang, which, in reality, you don't fit into," Tony said harshly. *What's it gonna take to get through to you?* Tony wondered angrily as he jumped to his feet to take over the pacing where Rick had left off. *Your cousin beaten to a pulp? Jor dead?*

"I don't know, Tony. I've got no idea what Johnny's thinking, but this seems to be his plan," Rick agreed. He watched as Tony paced restlessly. The more the cop paced, the more nervous Rick became. *What's going on?* Rick wondered. *What happened? What's wrong?*

"And you *swear* to me you've never attacked the girls, including this morning? Now think carefully before you answer. Did you ever attack your cousin and your girlfriend?" Tony asked idly, as he stopped at the far end of the table and faced away from Rick. He knew what the kid must be thinking, and Tony really didn't like what he was about to do, but it was something that suddenly needed to be done and now, not later.

"Hey, what the hell is this, an interrogation?" Rick snapped. "Tony, unless you've gotta body double, you've been with me all morning, man. I've never been out of your sight," Rick protested harshly. Straightening his shoulders, Tony turned and stalked down the length of the table, and stopped right beside Rick, forcing the younger man to look up. Rick's face was flushed and Tony could see the tension building. Thankfully, there was no anger. Yet. But he knew that was going to change, quickly.

"Then how do you explain this?" Tony asked quietly, pulling the note out of his pocket and throwing it at Rick.

Puzzled, Rick opened up the folded piece of paper and read the note. Then he read it again. He read it for a third time. It didn't get any better the more times he read it. In fact, the more he read it, the sicker he became. "Where'd you get this?" Rick demanded, brandishing the note. He didn't need Tony to tell him he was in deep trouble.

"Y'know something, kid, this little innocent act of yours is beginning to wear a bit thin and is actually getting on my nerves. You know bloody well where I found that note. My question is why?" Tony demanded again. He finally sat down across from Rick, prudently out of the kid's reach.

"What do you mean? 'Course I don't know where you found it. Dammit, Tony, why won't anyone believe me?" Rick flared.

"Probably because you're the only one who's being 'seen' attacking these girls, Rick, and y'know something else, kid, I'm getting more than a little tired of defending you constantly, counsellor or not," Tony said disgustedly. Outside, Tony looked just as cool as Rick remembered him from the first time they had met at the police station. Inside, the cop's guts were churning and Tony figured he'd be sick later. He hated what he was doing, but he knew it had to be done, so he just sat back and waited.

Rick sat in his chair, completely stunned. *First Megs and Mick. Then Uncle Ian. Now Nana and Tony,* Rick though in a panic. *How many others're gonna bail on me? Jor?*

Tony just watched, impassively, his arms folded across his chest. He tried not to feel for the kid across from him, but he couldn't help it. He knew exactly how Rick was feeling and his heart went out to Rick, but counselling session or not, elder or not, Tony needed to be a cop right now and get something through Rick's stubborn head. Someone was going to get hurt. Badly. So, despite the panic Tony could clearly see on Rick's face,

Tony prepared to be extremely blunt. *I just pray it works,* Tony thought grimly.

"So now, Rick, we're gonna do the one thing you didn't want to do during these sessions. I'm gonna talk and you're gonna listen." To a very grim teen, Tony began to talk, quietly, intensely, passionately.

"This game has to stop and quickly, Rick. Otherwise, it's probably gonna blow up in your face and get someone badly hurt, if not killed. And we're both pretty sure it's not gonna be you. So, if these attacks don't stop and soon, Rick, Seamus isn't gonna wait for you to be proven guilty. You know that and I know that. He's gonna lock you up in the deepest, darkest jail cell he can find then wait about 10 or 12 years before he tells anyone he has you, let alone charge you. Either get me proof it's Johnny or start taking the blame like a man," Tony said bluntly.

"Like hell! I'm not taking the blame for anything I didn't do," Rick said with considerable heat. "No matter what you say, Tony, I swear to you I didn't do this!" Rick defended himself. Like Tony, though, he was getting very tired of having to.

Unable to think of anything else to say for the moment, Tony just sat across from Rick, thinking. No matter what Rick said, someone, namely Seamus, would somehow twist it around to make Rick look guilty, evidence or no evidence. *Now what do I do?* Tony wondered, not for the first time.

"I didn't do this, Tony," Rick said quietly. "You've gotta believe me."

"Right now, kiddo, I don't know what to believe. You can't give me anything that says you're not doing this and everyone else, unfortunately, is," Tony replied. He hesitated before continuing.

"Rick, there's something else you need to think of," Tony began, then hesitated again. *How far do I go?* Tony wondered. *How badly to I try and scare him?*

"Tony, as bad as my life's been lately, what the hell else do you really think can go wrong?" Rick grated.

"Actually a lot, Rick, an awful lot. If someone, say Mick or Seamus, convinces Meg or Jor to press charges, you'll be back in court and behind bars faster than you can say 'hello', with your probation most likely revoked," Tony pointed out. "Even worse, you'll be looking at a lot more than just the original charges and a hell of a lot more time. You'll lose more than just your girl, my friend. You'll lose your freedom."

"There's only one person who'll do that to me – Seamus O'Reilly," Rick growled. "Tony, you've told me I can trust you, so get this through *your* head. *I didn't do anything!*" Rick snapped. He stood up so fast his chair flew backwards. He resumed his pacing. Tony could see the tension quickly being replaced with anger, but, before he could do or say anything, Rick spun and slammed his fist against a cabinet door in the corner. Tony heard the wood crack sharply and he shot to his feet.

"Are you okay?" he demanded as he grabbed Rick's hand and tried to look at it. Rick just jerked his hand out of the cop's grip. He knew he hadn't broken it. It was just very sore. He rubbed absently as he stared at the young Cree cop. At this moment, he didn't really consider Tony a friend, let alone a counsellor.

"Don't get all concerned about me now, *Constable*. If you really cared, you'd believe me when I tell you I didn't do this. Nobody gives a damn about me!" Rick shouted hotly.

Tony had a queer feeling that he was transported back in time. *Didn't I run this course already at the youth center?* Tony wondered. "Enough, Rick, alright? You're right, son. I'm sorry. 'Kay? Just chill. Look, all I'm saying's I need something more than your word Blade's doing this," Tony tried to explain.

"Why? O'Reilly doesn't. He just takes everything at face value while *I* have to come up with enough evidence to clear the entire world first," Rick snapped.

Startled, Tony had no reply. Unfortunately, Rick was right. Tony was demanding Rick to provide him with some kind of proof the Knights were after the girls, yet everyone else was taking the unsubstantiated sightings by others to convict Rick.

Uncomfortable silence reigned in the conference room as Tony struggled to figure out what to do.

At the end of the hour, Rick left the room without saying good-bye to Tony and headed to his next class. On his way, he passed by Jordan and Megan heading to the library for their after-lunch spare. Mickey was nowhere to be seen, but Rick had no doubt the other boy wasn't very far away. Mickey wasn't about to let the girls out of his sight. Neither of the girls stopped to talk to Rick, although he stopped to let them pass.

Megan just glared at her cousin but the look Jordan gave him was one of longing. Megan just snorted and dragged Jordan into the library. He watched them wind their way to the back of the library and join Mickey at a table. He caught Jordan's eye again and just stared until Mickey saw him and quickly moved them to another table away from the windows. "I'm sorry, babe," Rick said softly as he pulled himself away.

Angry, Rick decided to skip his next class and hunt Blade down. At this time of day, if Blade decided to come back from the pool hall, he and Crank had metal shop. Usually the gang would stay around for lunch and then skip off to the pool hall or vice-versa, so Rick took a chance that today they'd stick around and be near the shop. As Rick turned the corner, Blade and Crank were just emerging from their class. Rick knew they had slipped out and were heading off to find Brain and Pup. *What idiots*, Rick thought, disgusted he had ever been part of that life.

"Hey, Blade, look who's come to visit, man," Crank drawled, nudging his leader.

Blade glared coldly over his shoulder at Rick. "Whassup, Moneyman?" Blade said softly as his hand shifted towards the small of his back.

Even over the sounds coming from the metal shop, Rick could hear the whisper of Blade's knife leaving its sheath and tensed immediately. He knew he was treading some very dangerous waters here if Blade was already reaching for his steel. It wasn't a very big knife, only eight and half inches long from end-to-end with a well worn handle and a very sharp blade. Brain had given it to Blade a couple of years earlier to match the one he had, and Rick had copied both of them as soon as he had joined the Knights. Only Crank and Pup didn't have one, since Pup was too young, in Blade's eyes, to carry one, and Crank usually had either a wrench or a screwdriver in his pocket.

Rick's knife, like Blade's, had served him well in a couple of fights, once he had mastered the art of knife fighting, thanks to Blade's teaching. In fact, the only one who was better than Rick at knife fighting was Blade. Unlike Blade, though, Rick couldn't throw his knife and hit the broadside of a barn. Blade didn't throw his knife often and never without a good reason, at least in his mind, but he always hit what he aimed for. That was how he'd earned his street name, and his vicious reputation. Everyone knew who you were talking about when you said "Blade", and everyone knew about that knife. No one ever turned their back on Blade during a fight unless they had a death wish.

Rick approached Blade cautiously as soon as he heard the whisper of that knife. "Eric, leave us," Rick ordered, never taking his eyes off his former leader. Blade was glaring right back at Rick. Hesitating for a couple of moments, Crank looked at Blade who nodded sharply, still glaring at Rick. Crank just shrugged and sauntered to the end of the hallway to wait. He may have been at the other end of the hall, but Rick knew he still had Blade's back. Rick would have to be very careful.

"Look, Johnny, what's up, man? Why're you hurting my girl and my cuz? You too damn chicken to face me?" Rick demanded finally, after he figured the mutual stare-down had gone on long enough. Blade's shoulders tensed immediately and Rick mentally cursed his clumsy tongue.

"Y'think *I'm* chicken, Moneyman?" Blade hissed. He whipped around quickly and shoved Rick into the lockers. The knife was now held dangerously close to his throat while Blade's other arm pinned Rick against the lockers. "Who's chicken now, Moneyman?" Blade growled quietly. The knife pressed against Rick's throat, and Rick never moved an inch. He wasn't scared, just very angry. He continued to stare into Blade's eyes and prayed this wouldn't go south in a hurry.

"What's your problem, Johnny? Why won't you let me go?" Rick demanded softly. He kept his voice low, and tried to keep the anger he felt in check.

"'Cause y'owe me, Moneyman. I took ya in. Gave ya everythin' yer old man wouldn't. Friendship. Security. Loyalty. Hell, I gave ya a family that would never, ever betray ya. And look at how yer repayin' me. I made ya and *you...owe...me*," Blade snarled back. Each word was punctuated with a small jab of the knife into Rick's throat. Rick tried not to wince, but he knew he would have something to show for this little confrontation.

"That's what this is about? Payback? Payback for what you gave me? Payback for what you made me into? What you made me into, Johnny, is a machine. A machine that reacts without thinking. You gave me a reputation I can't shake. There're still kids in this school who wince and shrink away from me when I walk down the hall, and I haven't worn the gear in over a month.

"You've wound me so tight I've attacked a cop at least twice and those're the ones I know of," Rick continued roughly. "I go into a blind rage if someone says the wrong thing at the wrong time. If I get angry enough, I have blackouts and I've damn near killed the best friend I'll ever have in this world. That's what you gave me. That's what you've made me. I can't stand to look at myself in the mirror, man. If that's what you want me to pay you back for, then kill me now. I won't come back to that life. Period," Rick said hotly.

Blade stared into Rick's eyes, the knife pressed firmly in place. Rick stared back without blinking, telling himself repeatedly not to show any fear, not that he was actually afraid of Blade anymore. He knew Blade would just laugh if he saw fear. Rick put all of his hatred and disgust at what Blade represented into that look. Blade just chuckled nastily.

"No way, Moneyman. Yer in fer life. I'm gonna break ya first and enjoy every second of it. Yer gonna beg me to take ya back, just to end *their* pain. Yer gonna be a broken, broken man 'fore I let ya go," Blade gloated. Suddenly, Blade pulled his knife away and Rick jerked his head back as he felt the knife slice across his throat. His hand shot up and came away bloody. Rick could only stare at his bloodied hand as Blade just laughed.

"Remember," Blade warned and, whistling for Crank, the leader of the Knights sauntered away with Crank falling in behind. Rick could hear Blade's laughter drifting back towards him, as he stood there, stunned.

That went real well, you idiot, Rick sneered to himself as he headed to the nearest washroom. He washed his neck and saw Blade's cut was really very small, compared to what Rick knew it could've been. It just bled a lot. Rick shook his head again at his stupidity and headed to his final class. But instead of paying attention to his teacher, Rick just kept replaying his confrontation with Blade. The more he did, the angrier he got at the Knights. He knew things were just beginning.

Chapter 18

It was a long, hard week for both Rick and the girls. Jordan and Megan were constantly pushed, shoved and tripped, and, while no one actually *saw* Rick do anything, he was somehow always blamed. As the week slowly progressed, though, Megan's attacks fell off to almost nothing and Jordan appeared to be the sole target. But no matter how much Mickey and Megan kept insisting Rick was behind the attacks, Jordan firmly believed Rick was innocent. She kept trying to point out to her brother the lack of physical evidence, but Mickey never listened. It was all Jordan could do to keep her brother from hunting Rick down and challenging him.

The week came to a crashing halt on Friday. Rick had spent the whole week dodging either Mickey or Blade and by Friday, he was thoroughly tired of the whole situation. He was tired of being falsely accused and defending himself. More importantly, he was tired of being unable to talk to Jordan. By the start of last period, Rick was bound and determined to talk to Jordan after school, Mickey or no Mickey.

Jordan was just as frustrated as her boyfriend. Every time she tried to slip away to find Rick and talk, Mickey somehow always managed to find her and drag her away. This over-protectiveness of Mickey's was leading to some fantastic fights, both at school and home. No one missed the closeness the twins had had more than Mickey, but he kept justifying what he was doing by telling himself he was only protecting his baby sister, even if Jordan didn't believe she needed it. Even worse, Jordan couldn't protest to her dad, since Seamus whole-heartedly approved. Jordan was frustrated beyond words.

Jordan wouldn't even sit with Mickey and Megan anymore, whether at lunch, in class or during their spare in the library. She sat at the opposite end from them at whatever table was chosen and sulked. Her marks were suffering because of all the troubles at school, which made her father less than happy with his wayward daughter. And after several thwarted attempts to see Rick, Jordan knew better than to try and slip away. Mickey would notice and the hunt would be on.

On this particular Friday, though, Jordan noticed neither Megan nor Mickey was watching her very carefully. They were too absorbed in an English project she was *supposed* to be helping with, but really didn't feel like doing. A quick glance at her watch made Jordan realize it was only a couple of minutes before the end of the spare and since the other two were distracted, Jordan decided to go and finally find Rick.

She quietly gathered up her books, slipped around a wall of bookshelves and headed for the door. Instead of walking past the wall of windows where she knew Mickey and Megan would clearly see her, she walked down to the back of the library and headed to Rick's math class. She sighed when she discovered the class had already been dismissed. Jordan scanned the crowded hallway, but she couldn't see Rick. Grinding her teeth in frustration and muttering a curse, Jordan headed to her final class of the day, no closer to seeing her boyfriend than she was when she started the day.

Adding to her frustrations was the fight which suddenly erupted and spread across the hallway, blocking her path. Looking around quickly, Jordan spied an escape route down a seldom used hallway. She darted through the kids who had stopped to watch the fight and strode purposefully down the dim corridor, her cowboy boots echoing sharply in the sudden silence. It didn't take long to outdistance the now-ended fight. She knew this hallway looped around the ceramic workshop, having used it once before when she was late. Students rarely used it unless they had electives, or, like Jordan, were late for class. So Jordan was surprised when she heard muffled talking coming from one of the classrooms. She dismissed the noise as her imagination until she walked by the open door and was grabbed roughly from behind.

"What the hell?!" she exclaimed at the rough treatment. A sudden backhand sent Jordan reeling into the teacher's desk with a thud, causing her to cry out in pain. Someone spun her around and punched her hard in the stomach. She fell to her knees, gasping, trying desperately to get enough air in her lungs to yell, but every time she thought she could, another punch or kick would land, driving the air from her once again.

"Good shot, Moneyman!" Jordan heard someone shout. "Hit her again! Harder!"

Rick's attacking me? Jordan thought wildly. *Impossible!* she babbled to herself as she struggled to catch her breath. Jordan's attacker suddenly yanked her to her feet, hit her once more hard enough to stun her momentarily, then wrapped his hands, gently, around her slender neck and squeezed. It took Jordan's battered brain a couple of precious seconds to realize what was happening, then she panicked. She batted wildly at the hands around her throat, yanking at them, trying to loosen them and, when that didn't work, began to claw at his face, as she struggled to breathe.

As darkness finally overtook her, Jordan scratched again at her attacker, catching his bandana hard enough to pull it off. Unfortunately, by then, Jordan's vision was so blurry she couldn't see who he was and her oxygen-starved brain shrieked it couldn't be Rick, no matter what she had heard. *He loves me*, Jordan thought sluggishly as her knees buckled. *I know he does.* The last thing Jordan heard was "It's okay, Jor. Rick'll take care of everything." Then she collapsed, battered and unconscious, as her attackers fled, laughing.

When Mickey and Megan couldn't find Jordan after spare, the couple just shrugged it off as Jordan going to class early to escape from Mickey's watchdog routine, and they'd see her there. When she didn't show up at the start of class, Mickey began to worry. Halfway through class, he was in a state and by the end, he was in a panic. The pair shoved their way out of Chemistry and sprinted for Mickey's truck, as Mickey frantically called his dad on his cell.

"Dad, Mick. Have you heard from Jordan? No? Crap. Something's wrong, Dad. I can feel it. No, she missed Chem. I don't know, Dad, she must've slipped away during spare. I'm sorry, alright? Are you sure? Okay. I'll find him. Thanks." Mickey snapped the phone closed as he pounded up to the truck.

Both teens could see Jordan wasn't there. She had her own key and would always wait in the truck if she was early, which was extremely rare since the attacks started. Megan's heart went out to her boyfriend. His eyes were wild as he tried to figure out what had happened to his baby sister and what he should do. Not even having a sibling, Megan couldn't begin to understand how Mickey was feeling with his twin missing.

"Dad hasn't heard from her. I thought she might've called him or something, knowing how mad she is at me right now, but he hasn't talked to her since we left the house this morning. Tony's here, so Dad said to get him searching. He's probably at the office, waiting. Let's go, lass," Mickey finished breathlessly and dashed off to the office without waiting for an answer. He knew Megan would follow without question. As they arrived, Tony was there, leaning on the counter, talking to the principal and waiting for Rick.

"Tony, Jordan's missing!" Megan cried when she caught sight of the cop.

"What?" Tony and Mr. Delaney chorused. Tony muttered a curse. *Run, Rick, run,* the cop thought quickly. *Seamus'll love this.*

"Jordan's missing!" Mickey cried again. "She slipped away during spare and she never arrived at Chem," Mickey panted, screeching to a halt in front of the men, out of breath.

"Now, kids, she's probably just at your truck, waiting for you, wanting a little space to herself. Go on, now, head home," Mr. Delaney soothed, trying to keep the panic he felt out of his voice.

"No, she's not! We just came from there," Mickey said frantically. The young boy's voice rose in panic, trying to get the two adults to understand Jordan *was missing*.

"Tony, have you seen Rick yet?" Megan asked quietly.

"No. He's late," Tony said blandly, knowing exactly what would happen when Mickey heard him.

Mickey paled and immediately jumped to the only conclusion his frantic brain would allow. "He's got my sister!" Mickey yelled and dashed from the office. Tony was right behind, followed by Megan and the principal.

Crank, meanwhile, had slipped into his last class of the day with Rick and passed Rick a note. *"Hey, Moneyman. The Irish sure put up a good fight."* Rick read. As he looked at Crank, puzzled, Crank grabbed the note back and chuckled evilly as he slowly tore up the note into tiny pieces and shoved them in a pocket.

What the hell does that mean? Rick wondered as he tried to, and failed miserably, to concentrate on English. He left class quickly before Crank could catch up and headed to the Chem lab where Jordan's last class was. Rick was determined to talk to her, now more than ever. Something in Crank's attitude told him he had better find his girl and quickly. Blade wasn't one to do anything halfway.

Rick was surprised to see Mickey and Megan tear out of the lab, Mickey babbling she had to be at the truck. Rick paid no attention to them and stood near the door waiting for Jordan to come out, thinking it was odd she hadn't been with Megan and Mickey. By the time the last student filed out, Rick realized who Mickey was talking about and what Crank's note had meant. Blade had Jordan. His heart sunk as he imagined what Blade would do to her. Tom's attack would look like a walk in the park compared to Jordan, Rick was positive.

He hurried away. He knew Blade would have chosen an out-of-the-way classroom and he decided the best place to start looking would be down by the shops, since that was the part of the school Blade knew best. Rick started at the metal shop, near Blade's locker and then moved to the wood shop area, searching quickly and quietly. By the time he got to the ceramics area, down that fateful hallway, Tony and the others had reached the metal shops to begin their own search.

The sight which greeted Rick as he stuck his head in the door of one of the seldom-used classrooms was one he wasn't likely to forget any time soon. Jordan lay sprawled on the floor, her red hair fanned out around her head like a halo. "Oh hell, Jor. Please be okay. C'mon, babe, wake up, please," Rick begged hoarsely as he ran to her side.

Jordan stirred slightly at the sound of Rick's voice and moaned in pain, but didn't wake. Just as Rick stopped and stood over her, Tony and Mickey stuck their heads in the door. After a second of stunned silence, Mickey shot through the door with a roar and launched himself at Rick. Tony just stood in the doorway, as if he couldn't believe what he was seeing.

"Mick, wait! Don't do this! I didn't hurt her!" Rick yelled as he easily avoided Mickey's first rush. Mickey didn't say anything as he rushed Rick again, forcing Rick to defend himself. While Mickey's punch missed by a mile, Rick's connected solidly, and it sent Mickey reeling back into a desk. The young Irishman was stunned for only a second before he was back up and ready to run at Rick again.

"Alright, enough, you two," Tony grunted as he grabbed Mickey by his collar. "You, over there, Mick, now," he snapped as he pointed toward the far side of the classroom. Mickey retreated, glaring at Rick. Tony slowly turned his gaze to Rick, wondering what was going on in his young friend's head.

Rick's face was flushed with anger, and he was trying to catch his breath. He knew exactly what was going to happen. Everyone was going to believe what they saw and not what Rick said. *No one believes me anyway*, Rick thought harshly as he stared defiantly back at Tony. *Not even Tony.* The cop was trying to keep his own temper under control. No matter what happened now, Tony doubted very much he'd be able to help Rick. *So much for being a friend and mentor*, Tony thought sadly, as he struggled to understand what he had seen. *I can't be either of those now.*

"Go ahead, man. Cuff me, *Constable*," Rick said, angry at Tony's immediate lack of support. "Yer gonna anyway. No one in this friggin' room's gonna believe me when I say *I didn't do anything*," Rick said bitterly. He turned and stuck his arms behind his back, unable to believe the one person who had promised to always trust him was doing anything but trusting Rick. It hurt Rick badly.

Tony hesitated for a long moment. The cop didn't really want to arrest Rick, but he knew he had no choice. Mickey and Seamus would freak if he didn't. Tony thought back to a session earlier in the week when he and Rick had talked about the way everyone treated him. Tony had called it "Guilty by Reputation." Rick had called it prejudice and a huge pain in the ass. Tony had laughed at the time as he had agreed with the teen. Now, Tony knew Mickey, at least, had already tried and convicted Rick without any evidence. No doubt Seamus would follow suit.

Sighing inwardly, his anger completely drained away, Tony silently snapped the cuffs loosely on Rick's wrists, turned the boy around and stared at him, trying to figure out what was going on behind those eyes. Rick returned the look, defiantly. *No one believes me anyway, so go ahead, I've nothing to lose anymore,* Rick said with those haunted eyes. Tony winced as he realized Rick had included Tony in that group. All of Tony's hard work over the past couple of months had been completely destroyed. Still glaring at Tony, Rick slumped down on a chair to wait for whatever was going to happen next.

Tony turned at the sound of Megan's shrill voice. "No kidding no one's gonna believe you, you…you….you monster. Look at this, Tony!" Megan cried, holding up a piece of black cloth, before Tony could tell her not to touch anything. Rick's heart sunk even further as he immediately recognized it, while Tony couldn't believe what his eyes told him.

"I've called an ambulance, and Seamus is sending another unit, Tony," Mr. Delaney said from the doorway. "Richard, why?" the principal asked sadly. "What did she do to deserve this?" He turned his head away to talk to someone just out of sight, telling them to wait for the ambulance at the front doors and guide them to the right room.

"I'm not saying a damn thing, Delaney. Not 'til I talk to my lawyer. Not like anyone's gonna believe me anyway," Rick said bitterly. He refused to look at anything or anyone. He knew he was in deep trouble, more trouble than he'd ever been in his life, but he wasn't about to screw up any chance he might have at getting out of this mess by talking out of turn.

"Hell, kid, I don't know if we're gonna get you out of this, Rick," Tony said for his ears only. *No kidding, Tony,* Rick thought sourly.

Another set of officers arrived, along with the Crime Scene Investigators who started to collect what evidence was there. Distracted by what was going on around him, Tony ordered the room sealed until further notice, but his mind was focussed on Rick. Mr. Delaney nodded. Jordan was taken away, followed by a silent Megan and extremely worried Mickey.

Once they were alone, Tony turned back to Rick and glared. "How could you, Rick? I thought you loved her!" Tony demanded.

"I do love her! Why does everyone think I'm trying to hurt Jor?" Rick shouted, surging to his feet. For once, he was glad his hands were cuffed, because he had an almost over-whelming desire to take a swing at the cop.

"Oh, jeez, I don't know, Rick. You standing over her unconscious body might have something to do with it," Tony replied sarcastically. "The bandana with your gang name on the floor beside her is another indication. But hey, why on earth shouldn't I think you're innocent? Dammit, Rick, this is what I've been warning you about. Someone's gonna get killed!" He sighed when he realized not one word had sunk into Rick's very thick, stubborn skull. The anger was too overpowering right now. He motioned for Rick to head out the door.

"Where're we going, *Constable*?" Rick sneered, just as sarcastically as Tony had been. *Like I don't know*, he thought bitterly. *Looks like you get your chance to lock me away, O'Reilly.*

"Richard Donald Attison, you're under arrest for assault. You have the right to remain silent," Tony began formally and a little sadly.

Tony had done everything he could to prevent this day from happening, but no one had listened to the cop, either. Oddly enough, Tony knew a little about how hurt and lonely Rick was feeling right now. The cop felt the same loss. Somehow, some way, Tony had to re-earn the trust which had been so quickly lost this afternoon between the two of them. If he didn't, Rick was going back to the Knights for good and nothing would ever get him back. Rick kept his head held high as Tony finished reading Rick his rights and then hauled the teen off to the station.

Rick's departure in handcuffs didn't go unnoticed. While most of the students were gone, four had remained. Chortling with glee, Pup raced back to Blade, who was waiting outside and told him what he had seen.

"I warned 'im," Blade said, shaking his head, as the four boys sauntered off. "This is just the beginning."

Chapter 19

All the way to the police station, Tony tried to get Rick to talk, to re-establish the trust they had had, but Rick remained stubbornly silent. Finally, Tony gave up. An uneasy silence fell in the car as both were lost to their thoughts. Rick was absolutely furious with himself. *Why the hell didn't I just go for help?* he wondered, but he had to admit he really didn't know how badly Jordan was hurt. As Rick sat in the back of the car, brooding, he realized Blade had made his point quite easily. He had just proven to Rick Jordan was a very easy target, no matter how well she thought she was protected.

Through the long, silent ride, Rick's thoughts danced between the sight of Jordan lying, sprawled, unconscious, on the classroom floor, her hair fanned out around her and what Rick would do to Blade if he ever got him alone in a room. Rick could see every bruise, every cut, every injury on Jordan as clearly as if she was still in front of him. *Johnny'll pay for every damn last one of them*, he vowed silently. He stared out the window as the car rolled on, and tears started to slide slowly down his cheeks as he could no longer avoid the one reality which would've prevented all of this. *Why'd I try to leave the Knights?* Rick wondered miserably.

Tony glanced in the rear view mirror as he thought he heard a soft sob and saw the tears falling. Tony sighed softly at the despair he could see on Rick's face. *Seamus'll throw the book at him,* Tony realized grimly. So when he saw the station ahead, he turned down a back alley instead of going through the front door. *Sorry, boss,* Tony thought as he navigated the alley, *but you can't have him yet. Not until I get my chance to talk to him first.*

Rick sat up abruptly when he realized Tony hadn't taken him to the regular prisoner entrance. "Whassup, *Constable*?

Giving the inspector a chance to get me alone 'fore I see my lawyer? Tryin' to beat a confession outta me?" Rick snapped.

He ruthlessly suppressed the sudden surge of guilt at his sarcastic comment. Tony might've been his best friend, but right now, there was no Rick Attison. It was all Moneyman, the cocky gang member. Tony didn't even blink. He knew Rick really didn't mean what he said. He was scared and trying to be brave.

"Give it a rest, Rick. I'm trying to get you inside and talk, *before* Seamus gets a hold of you. You know what his reaction's gonna be and I want your story before he *does* get to you," Tony replied shortly. He pulled up to the back door and stopped. Opening the back door, Tony helped Rick out of the car and guided him down a set of stairs to a dark room. Tony snapped on the switch and Rick blinked in the sudden light, startled.

As near as he could tell, they were in an old break room, one that clearly hadn't been used on a regular basis for several years. The couches were worn but looked comfortable and there were still a couple of vending machines filled with pop and junk food, with signs that said "Free". Silently, Tony removed Rick's cuffs and motioned to the nearest couch. Rubbing his wrists, Rick sat, wishing he could say something to Tony, now that they were at the station, but the words he wanted to say wouldn't come out, no matter how hard he tried. Somehow, he knew he was safe in this place, at least for a short time. Once again, he wondered how he'd managed to get into this mess. Finally, the teen couldn't stand the silence any longer.

"What is this place, Tony?" Rick finally asked, curious despite his anger.

"It's an old break room, mainly for beat patrollers," Tony smiled as he looked around. "I've a lot of good memories of this room from when I started on the force. It was where Seamus and I'd talk and he ended up teaching me some trade secrets. I've learned a lot from that stubborn Irishman. It isn't used anymore, since we did the renos upstairs and put in the really cushy break room. Still, every now and then, I like to come down here when I need some peace and quiet. I just never thought I'd have to use this room for something like this – I may never be able to come down here again without thinking of today. Anyway, there's a phone over there, so call Nana or Owen, but make it quick. If you get a hold of Owen, tell him to come to the alley, behind the station, just off Collins and I'll meet him there," Tony finished, standing and looking at Rick. The cop seemed to hesitate, as if he wanted to say more. Finally, he shrugged and left Rick alone for a few minutes.

Using the old, scratched up rotary phone, he dialled Owen's number with shaky fingers and when his lawyer answered, Rick quickly outlined what had happened. He begged Owen to come and help. Owen didn't like the desperation he heard in the teen's voice and quickly agreed to come.

"Come to the back door in the alley off Collins. Tony said he'd meet you there," Rick explained.

"I'll be there in about 15 minutes, Rick. Don't say anything and for heaven's sake, keep your temper. No matter who pushes your buttons," Owen warned and hung up. He sighed and apologized to his kids. The fort in the backyard would have to wait. Again.

Rick hung up and, after a moment's hesitation, dialled Nana's number. When Martha answered, Rick asked to talk to his grandmother. He winced at the coldness he could hear in the housekeeper's voice when she told Rick Nana wasn't home.

"She's not here right now. She's with Miss Megan at the hospital," Martha said stiffly.

"Does anyone know how Jor is?" Rick asked tentatively.

"Not like you care, Richard," Martha snapped and slammed down the phone. Rick slowly hung up and sat down at the table right by the phone. *Now what?* Rick wondered while he waited for Tony to return.

By the time the young cop came back with Owen in tow, Rick had begun to pace, trying to keep himself calm, unable to do anything else to ease his tension. The young lawyer gave Tony a look the cop had no trouble understanding. Owen didn't say anything as Tony left him and his client alone. He just pulled out

Rick's file and got himself organized. Only when he was ready did he look at his young client who'd finally sat back down.

"Well, Rick, in case you haven't figured it out by now, you, son, are in some very serious trouble. You've been charged with Aggravated Assault and Assault Causing Bodily Harm, well, you will be once Tony gets around to booking you properly. Consider your probation revoked, to say the least. What the hell happened?" Owen demanded quietly.

Rick thought quickly, his eyes restless and his legs bouncing with nervous energy. "Owen, do you believe me? I mean, really believe me? And are you willing to listen if I tell you what's been going on? Or do you just want me to plead guilty?" Rick asked quietly without looking at his lawyer. Owen was shocked. *What the hell's been going on?* he wondered. *Why would he even ask that?*

"Rick, look at me," Owen said. He leaned forward slightly to stare into Rick's troubled eyes now raised to face him. "Tell me the truth, son, always. I'm your lawyer and, well, even if you *were* guilty, I'd never say that to you. My job's to defend you the best I can against whatever evidence there is. It's up to the prosecutor to prove beyond a reasonable doubt you're guilty. I only have to convince a judge or jury of reasonable doubt. So, I have to believe you, end of story. If I truly believed you were guilty, I wouldn't come back and represent you. Besides, you've always given me the impression you'd tell me the truth, no matter how distasteful or how much the truth points to you. And no, Rick, I absolutely do *not* want you to plead guilty, ever. If you did, Seamus O'Reilly would send you as far away as possible for as long as possible," Owen replied, putting all of his conviction into his short speech.

Reassured someone was finally willing to listen to him, Rick quickly outlined what he'd been going through for the past couple of months. Owen wrote it all down, without interrupting, even though he was burning to ask the questions tumbling around in his head. When he was sure Owen had it all down, Rick then described what he had found in the classroom before Tony and Mickey had arrived, exactly what he found, saw and noticed.

Mostly nothing, but he still told his lawyer everything. Rick spoke for at least an hour and Owen was finally brave enough to interrupt to ask some questions.

After Rick finished, Owen jotted down a few extra notes and looked back up at his client. "Why didn't you tell anyone about this boy's threats?" Owen asked at the end.

"I told Tony every time something happened! Johnny seemed to wait until I had a counselling session and then he'd pounce! I'd always end up mad as hell so Tony made me talk about it! It wasn't like he didn't know!" Rick protested. He climbed back to his feet to take up pacing again. The tension was getting unbearable.

"Easy, Rick, it's only a question, but I needed to ask. Now, did Tony do anything?" Owen asked.

"No, Owen, I didn't. I couldn't. It was Rick's word against Johnny's and there's no evidence to support Rick's accusations against the Knights," Tony answered as he re-entered the room. *And every piece of friggin' evidence points right to Rick,* Tony didn't say. Both Owen and Rick jumped at the sound of Tony's return. Neither of them had heard the door open. Tony sat down across from Rick who settled back into his chair uneasily. He didn't like the way Tony was looking at him.

"Did you even try to find out if they had alibis for anything?" Owen demanded hotly.

"Every chance I could, Counsellor. Unfortunately, I have to do it carefully, very carefully. If Seamus ever found out I was doing investigating on my own time and doing my damnedest to try and clear that kid right there, I'd lose my job. I kind of like it, if you must know. There's a major problem, though," Tony snapped back. Rick hung his head at the thought of Tony losing his job over him.

"Only one?" Owen said dryly.

"Well, okay, two if you count Seamus. *I can't prove anything against the other boys,*" Tony said, emphatically. "They all have alibis, even if it's each other, but at least they have something and I'm sure they'll have alibis for this attack, too. Rick,

- 228 -

unfortunately, has no alibi or anything else for that matter, that anyone, especially Seamus, will accept. Seamus won't even accept *my* word Rick hasn't been attacking the two girls, and I've been right there watching Rick for over a week now. There're no fingerprints, fibre evidence, eyewitness testimony, nothing, which places the rest of the gang at any of the scenes.

"There is, unfortunately, plenty of evidence placing Rick at all of the crimes, including eyewitnesses who're very eager to give their testimony to get rid of "Moneyman." So you see my problem, Counsellor," Tony said, resignedly. Ignoring Owen for now, Tony turned back to Rick and stared at his young friend for a long time. *Part of me says you didn't do this, kiddo*, Tony thought. *The other part doesn't know what to think.*

All three sat in a growing tense silence as Tony just stared at Rick, who glared right back. Tony knew he was caught between a rock and a hard place. He knew what the evidence said and that was what the judge and prosecutor would believe. They didn't care that Tony had taken the time to get to know the kid sitting across from him. They definitely didn't care that Tony's gut said Rick didn't attack Jordan. All they wanted was proof someone did. *And everything's pointing right to you, dammit,* Tony thought.

"Well, Rick, I just talked to Mick, and Jor's basically okay. There's some bruising, cuts, a lot of damage to her throat from being strangled, one or two bruised or cracked ribs, and a possible concussion. Doc's gonna hold her at least overnight, possibly longer, just in case. She's a very lucky girl. It could've been much worse, I'm sure. However, she absolutely refuses to press charges. Seamus is fit to be tied and is apparently yelling at his daughter at the hospital, so you're still safe. For now," Tony said and continued to stare at Rick. The teen stared back defiantly, his blue eyes ice cold and stony. He knew he didn't attack his girl. No way was he taking the blame for something he didn't do.

"I'm not changing my story, Tony," Rick repeated firmly but quietly. "I didn't do this."

"Tell him what happened, Rick," Owen urged.

"Before O'Reilly comes back," Rick snorted. He took a deep breath and quickly outlined what happened before finding Jordan.

Tony shook his head in disbelief when Rick was finished. "Oh for crying out loud, Rick, you bloody well know Seamus ain't gonna buy that, neither will the judge. Everything *just happens* to happen? Not a chance. Too many coincidences, kiddo, and no one's gonna believe them," Tony scoffed and shook his head again.

He told himself to be as tough as nails on this investigation, even though he really wanted to tell Rick he believed him. Being as tough as nails was probably going to destroy their young friendship once and for all, Tony realized, even sadder than before. He couldn't believe what he was about to do, either.

Tony tossed a picture of Rick's gang bandana on the table. Off to the side, Rick winced as he could see Jordan's hair fanned out. "This piece of evidence really points to you, son. If you weren't there, how'd this get there?" Tony demanded roughly. *C'mon, Rick, gimme something, anything, to work with here or you're toast,* Tony prayed silently.

Rick looked sick. He stared at the bandana. Beside her hair, he could just see part of Jordan's hand in the picture. It looked cold and so still. *I'm sorry, sweets,* he thought sadly as he stared at the picture. He knew what he was about to say would sound really lame, but he had to tell the truth.

"I really don't know, Tony, but I have a theory, as lame as it is. Remember the day after Thanksgiving? The day you tricked me into pushing Megs and Jor?" Tony nodded thoughtfully, wondering where this was heading.

"That night, after you dropped me off, I had another go with Johnny. We fought on my front porch and, after I literally threw him off my porch, I threw out all of my gang stuff. The jacket, the bandanas, everything but my knife. Just like I promised you. Since the garbage wasn't collected for another day, anyone could have come along and grabbed that stuff, I guess. I don't know where Johnny and the rest went after we fought. I never even gave it a second thought," Rick shrugged. He paled when Tony laughed in disbelief.

"C'mon, Rick. What do you think I am? Some kind of idiot? This tale just keeps getting better and better. Not only are you telling me the Knights have been attacking Meg and Jor at school, now you're accusing Blade of stealing your stuff and planting evidence, trying to frame you," Tony scoffed again. *C'mon, kid,* Tony pleaded silently. *That's not good enough.*

Stubbornly , Rick repeated his tale again. And again. And again. Trying to keep the disgust at what he was doing out of his voice, Tony hammered at Rick for over an hour, but the teen never wavered. Finally, Owen called a halt. He could see Rick trying to control his temper and knew he was about to fail miserably. He was surprised Tony couldn't see the veins pulsing in Rick's forehead.

"Stop this, Tony. Enough's enough. Rick, please try to calm down while the constable and I talk. Outside," Owen said, as he motioned sharply to the door.

Tony nodded after a moment and stood up. He knew what was coming and how much he deserved the dressing down he was probably going to get, and yet he followed Owen out into the hall and closed the door softly behind them, leaning back against it for a moment with his eyes closed in pain. He absolutely hated what he was doing to his friend, no matter how necessary it might be. As the door closed behind Tony, Rick sighed heavily and went to the vending machines. He grabbed a pop and a bag of chips and flopped onto the couch. *What does Tony want from me?* Rick fumed as he munched. *What did I do to piss him off?*

Outside, Tony opened his eyes and faced a furious Owen St. James. "Just what in the hell're you trying to prove in there, Constable?" Owen demanded. Tony didn't back down from the lawyer's anger. He knew he was only getting what he deserved. He was pushing Rick hard and Owen was just protecting his client. He smiled grimly as he pushed himself away from the door and answered.

"Sorry 'bout that, Owen, but unlike my boss, I happen to believe Rick, no matter what I may've said in there. I've learned a great deal about that kid during our sessions and I know in my gut Rick wouldn't lay a finger on Jor. Mick, maybe, but never Jor," Tony said quietly. Owen calmed down a bit, but was still very puzzled and annoyed at Tony's actions.

"Then why the punishing questions? If you believe him, *tell him*. He needs to hear it, dammit!" Owen said. "Now more than ever, he needs to know you, of all people, believe him!"

Sadly, Tony shook his head and scrubbed at his face, exhausted already. "I can't, Owen. By the Creator, I am so sorry. More sorry than you can possibly believe, but I can't be his friend and counsellor right now. I *have* to be a cop. Believe me, I'd love to do nothing more than to go back in that room and tell that scared kid in there I believe him, but Seamus'll want a confession by the time he gets back. That's what I've been after. Personally, I'm sorry I've treated him like this, 'cause I know he didn't deserve it, but Jor didn't deserve to get the crap beat out of her, either. Seamus is outta luck, I'm afraid." Tony didn't know what Seamus' problem with Rick was, but it was just going to get a lot worse, now that Jordan had been attacked.

"Great. An inspector with a grudge against my client and who's gonna arrange to get what he wants no matter what," Owen sighed as if he had heard Tony's unspoken thoughts. *Maybe he did*, Tony thought as he nodded.

The two returned to the room to find Rick pacing. Tony could see how angry Rick was, but the cop knew he didn't have time to talk Rick through it. *One more thing to be sorry for today*, Tony thought as he approached. Tony gripped Rick's shoulder in silent apology, hoping Rick could one day forgive Tony for what he was about to do. Rick sighed and nodded. He just couldn't stay mad at his best friend, no matter how hard Tony had been pounding on him. He knew Tony hadn't really meant to be that hard on him.

"C'mon, son. Let's get you booked in and settled. I'm not sure when you'll see the judge but it may not be until Monday.

Think you can hold it 'til then?" Tony asked quietly. Rick shrugged and nodded as Tony re-cuffed him. *Not like I gotta choice*, Rick thought as he tried not to flinch at the cold steel on his wrists.

Tony led the way upstairs, and once again, Rick was fingerprinted, photographed and booked in. Tony disappeared during the process, and Rick figured he was answering questions about where he and Rick had been as it had been over two hours since Rick's arrest. He reappeared just as Rick was being led to the same holding cell as before. It took all of Rick's self-control to show no visible reaction as the door slammed behind him, even though he jumped about a foot inside. With a sigh, he settled in to wait for his date with the judge.

"Keep your chin up, Rick. We'll get you through this," Owen assured him. *Somehow,* the lawyer vowed silently.

"Yeah, right, Owen. Hey, do me a favour, 'kay? Get a hold of Nana, and let her know what's happened, please. I couldn't. Martha slammed the phone down in my ear," Rick said quietly. Owen nodded and left his client sitting on the bottom bunk, brooding and waiting for the appearance of Seamus O'Reilly. Fortunately, Rick was going to have a long wait. Seamus was still at the hospital trying to talk, or yell, some sense into his daughter.

Jordan's ambulance arrived at the hospital with Mickey and Megan trailing behind in Mickey's now-repaired and repainted truck. Jordan was wheeled into an examination room with Dr. Jim whipping the curtain closed right behind him to prevent anyone from following them in, and, with a low growl, Seamus led Mickey and Megan to an empty waiting room and closed the door firmly. His barrage of questions started right away. He was angry, Megan could tell. Angry and scared.

Mickey described their week and how Jordan kept trying to slip away. "She was determined to speak with him and I was just as determined not to let her, Dad. Today, she somehow managed to get by us and we didn't really notice until Chem. Sorry, Dad. I failed," Mickey said miserably. He hung his head, trying not to see his sister lying in that crumpled heap and trying just as hard not to cry in front of his dad.

Seamus reached out and forced his son to look at him. Gently, the inspector brushed away a tear which had slipped down Mickey's cheek. "Keep yer head up, son. Ye didn't fail. We just failed to realize how determined that boy was. He was bound and determined to hurt me girl, and, by God, he did it," Seamus said, slamming his fist into the arm of the chair where they had finally sat.

Megan hesitated. She really didn't want to point something out, but she felt compelled to, having calmed down enough on the ride from the school to think things through. "Mr. O'Reilly, are...are we really sure Rick did this? I mean, *really sure*? Yeah, I know we were there, but all we really saw was Rick standing over Jordan. We never *saw* him do anything to her. Shouldn't we at least talk to Jordan first to make sure *she* actually saw Rick?" Megan asked carefully. She winced at the force of Mickey's reaction.

"Whose side're you on, Megan?" Mickey demanded roughly, surging to his feet. He glared at his girlfriend. "After everything he's done to you two? What about the damage to my truck and the accident? Holy crap! You...you don't believe him, do you?" Mickey couldn't believe his girl, the one person he loved beyond all reason except Jordan, was taking the side of a maniac, even if he was her cousin.

Megan fell silent as she stood in front of the window, staring blankly out. Who did she believe? Was Rick really to blame? If he didn't do these things, then who did, and more importantly, why were they doing it? Megan didn't know what or who to believe anymore. She was so messed up. Her heart said she could still trust her cousin, but her head said he had attacked her and Jordan. Still, she hesitated as she thought back over the last couple of months.

She remembered how Rick protected her from his dad at the ranch and from Blade, especially the first day of school. She still shivered when she remembered how Blade had looked at her in the gym right before Rick introduced her to the O'Reillys. She was nothing more than a piece of meat to him. And even though other students had flinched away from Rick as they had walked the halls, Megan had felt incredibly safe, knowing no one would ever touch her. Yet, now Rick was being accused of beating up her best friend. Who was right – Rick or Inspector O'Reilly?

"I'm not sure what to believe anymore, Mickey. No – let me finish," she said, holding up a hand as Mickey began to protest. "I was there and saw what you did, and I know what I said to Rick, but I just don't know if I can now trust what I *saw*. I'm confused, I guess. On one hand, I feel as if I can trust Rick, but on the other, I know what he's been accused of. I still feel some of the bruises from all of my "falls". All I'm saying, Mr. O'Reilly, is we need more information from Jordan before we jump to any conclusions. After all, Rick's supposed to be innocent until proven guilty," Megan said. She turned away from the hurt in Mickey's eyes.

"Okay, Megan. We'll do it yer way and wait to talk to Jordan," Seamus agreed, albeit reluctantly.

Megan sat hesitantly beside Mickey. She knew he was mad at her for supporting Rick, but Megan had spoken nothing but the truth – she really didn't know what to believe anymore. After a couple of tense seconds, Mickey relaxed, smiled wanly at her and slipped his arm around her shoulder. She snuggled against his shoulder, safe, while they waited for word about Jordan.

The trio waited for about a half an hour before anyone came to find them, although it felt like much, much longer to Megan. Mickey and his dad were talking quietly while Megan flipped idly through some magazines. "Inspector?" a doctor asked, sticking his head in the door. Megan smiled when she saw Dr. Jim.

"How's me daughter, Jim?" Seamus demanded at once, jumping to his feet.

"She's resting right now. I have to admit, though, it could've been a lot worse, Seamus. Just remember that. She could've just as easily been killed, not just injured. She has a minor concussion, several cuts and scrapes, a black eye that's already a spectacular shade of purple and green and a couple of bruised ribs. The worst damage is to her throat when she was strangled. Her larynx's very swollen and bruised, so right now I'm not totally sure what kind of damage there is. The most important thing to remember, Seamus, is that nothing's permanently damaged, as near as I can see right now. Okay?" Jim finished firmly.

"Can we see her?" Megan asked while Seamus and Mickey stood, stunned.

Dr. Jim nodded and led the way to Jordan's room. She was tiny enough already and seemed even smaller in the white hospital bed. She was pale and lying so still Megan thought she had stopped breathing. Only by watching very closely did Megan notice Jordan's chest rose and fell. *She's so pale*, Megan worried as they gathered around her. *I can't believe how still she is.*

"Hey, sis," Mickey said softly, taking Jordan's slender limp hand in his. His hand seemed to dwarf hers, Megan noticed. Her eyes fluttered open and she smiled weakly.

"Hey, bro," she croaked back, clenching her brother's hand as if she'd never wanted to let go. She couldn't help but whimper as someone bumped the bed and made her aching body hurt even more.

"Careful, Dad. Hush now, sis. Dad's here. So's Megan," Mickey soothed. He brushed back a stray hair and smiled down at her, thankful she was alive.

"Hello, me girl," Seamus said softly, taking Jordan's unclaimed hand. Megan just smiled at her best friend, trying to ignore the bruising and bandages. The young Irish girl sighed as she settled into the bed with her family around her. Megan felt for her friend. She could tell Jordan hurt. *Damn you, Rick*, she thought angrily. *If not you, then who? And why Jordan?*

"I've some questions, honey. I'll try to make them yes or no questions. Explain only if ye have to," Seamus said in his official cop voice. No one said anything for a long moment, they were all so stunned.

"Come off it, Dad, can't this wait?" Mickey protested. Jordan seemed to wilt even further into the bed.

Seamus shook his head. "No, son, it can't. I need answers right now if I'm gonna throw the book at that boy," Seamus said firmly. His eyes were hard and Megan realized Seamus wasn't going to listen to anything she had asked, not an hour earlier. He'd already tried, and convicted Rick. Again. *Nothing's gonna save Rick this time, not even Tony,* Megan thought glumly.

At Seamus' unwarranted accusation, Jordan tried to sit up in order to better argue with her father. All that came out was an inarticulate groan, more of pain than anything. Mickey caught his sister in his arms and tried to push her back into the bed, while she struggled against his grip and tried to speak. Over the struggles and gasps, Megan could hear Jordan protesting Rick's innocence.

"No, Daddy! Not Rick! He loves me! I know he does! He didn't do this!" Jordan protested hoarsely. Her brother looked dubious and Seamus looked murderous.

"Jordan, do ye remember anything?" Seamus asked gruffly. As Jordan slowly recalled what happened, her voice low and halting in the room's deafening silence, Megan slipped from the room and went looking for Nana and her father.

Coming around the corner, Megan found her grandmother at the nurses' station. "Nana!" Megan called softly. Nana turned and smiled at the nurse who was helping her. Megan ran to her grandmother and held on tight as Nana murmured assurances. She felt safe once in Nana's arms and she clung to her grandmother for a long moment, before backing away.

"Where's Daddy?" Megan asked looking around for her father. She sighed when she realized he was nowhere to be found.

"Gone again, I'm afraid. Sorry, lass, but he'd already left by the time you called. How's Jordan?" Nana asked as she led Megan to an alcove to talk.

As best she could, Megan detailed Jordan's injuries and what she knew had happened at school. "I just don't know what or who to believe anymore, Nana. This whole mess stinks like last week's stalls. I'll try to explain. Something about Rick caught my attention when I met him the first time at the ranch. I felt, deep in my heart, Rick was definitely dangerous with all that pent up anger I saw in him, but I still believed I could trust him. Now, I'm not sure," Megan said glumly. *What can I believe?* the young girl agonized yet again. Her thoughts returned to her friend lying in the hospital and everything which had happened since Mickey's truck had been damaged. *That's when it really started*, Megan realized suddenly.

"What else is wrong, lass?" Nana asked shrewdly when Megan's silence stretched on for several moments.

"Well, it's Inspector O'Reilly, Nana. I mean, he started questioning Jordan right away, just as soon as she came to, trying to *force* her to blame Rick. He didn't look like he was gonna take no for an answer, either. I was there and I don't trust the evidence I saw. Nothing makes sense anymore. Y'know what's worse, Nana? I think Inspector O'Reilly doesn't like Rick," Megan said with a firm nod of her head.

Nana chuckled. "Now that's the understatement of the year, lass. No one really trusts the first boy who falls in love with their daughter. Heck, I even did it when your father brought your mother to meet me for the first time, and you know how much they loved each other. Yet, I didn't think anyone was good enough for my boy. I got over it. Seamus will too, but he's gonna take a bit longer, especially with Jordan's being hurt. Whether or not Rick actually did anything's immaterial to Seamus now. Until Rick's cleared and the attacks stop, Seamus isn't gonna trust Rick. Unfortunately, even then he may not trust my boy," Nana tried to explain.

As they walked down the hall, Nana put her arm around Megan's shoulder, hugging her close. As they got closer to Jordan's room, they could hear Seamus yelling at the top of his lungs. And they weren't the only ones. Megan could see a nurse talking urgently on the phone and the teen was pretty sure Dr. Jim wasn't going to be very happy when he finally showed up. Megan shoved the door open and hustled Nana into the room, before Seamus' voice could carry any more.

Jordan was sitting up, but she was a lot paler than when Megan had left. And despite her very bruised throat, Jordan was vigorously defending Rick for all she was worth. Megan could tell Seamus was not impressed by how stubborn Jordan was being, nor was Mickey. Unlike his father, though, Mickey wasn't openly accusing Rick, but Megan knew her boyfriend well enough by now to realize Mickey was just as angry at his sister as their dad was.

"No, Daddy, absolutely not. I don't care what you say or do to me! I won't press charges! You can't *prove* Rick did anything!" Jordan snapped hoarsely. She grabbed a glass of ice and popped a couple of pieces into her mouth in the hopes of soothing her battered throat. Nothing was going to soothe her temper, though, any more than her father. Seamus' face was bright red and he drew a deep breath to start again.

Megan quickly closed the door. She turned to Seamus and interrupted the elder cop before he could begin yelling again. "Really, Mr. O'Reilly, quiet! They can hear you yelling all the way down by the nurses' station! Stop yelling before someone calls security!" Megan hissed. Nana just glowered at Seamus. *What has happened to his good sense?* she wondered in amazement.

Seamus looked rebellious but lowered his voice as he continued to try to force Jordan to press charges. "Look, Jordan, sweetheart, be reasonable. That boy's a menace. Look at everything that's happened. He's tried to kill ye twice now, and what about yer brother? He's tried to kill him at least once," Seamus began yet again.

Jordan ground her teeth in frustration. *What's it gonna take to get through to him?* she fumed silently. She took a deep breath before continuing. "Daddy, I have had enough. *Until you bring me proof, I am not pressing charges!*" Jordan snapped. "And for the last time – 'that boy' has a name and it's Rick. If you refuse to call him by his name, I'm not talking anymore," Jordan whispered wearily. Megan could tell Jordan was tiring and quickly. Whatever energy she had had was long gone.

"Sis, please, just do what Dad wants and he'll leave you alone," Mickey finally put in his two cents worth. Jordan jerked her hand out of her brother's hand and glared at Mickey.

"Don't you start, Mickey O'Reilly. If I'd been allowed to talk to Rick like I wanted, this wouldn't have happened. I would've been with him instead of wandering down dark hallways by myself. No matter what you and Daddy believe, *I know* Rick would never hurt me," Jordan repeated firmly. She just sighed as her father and brother both continued to press her.

Dr. Jim burst through the door shortly after, fuming. "Seamus O'Reilly, what in the hell do you think you're doing? Since when do you conduct interrogations in my hospital? And at the top of your lungs?" the doctor demanded hotly. Jim was already tired and his night shift was just beginning. He didn't have time to be pulled out of Emergency to deal with Seamus O'Reilly.

"I needed some information and I couldn't wait," Seamus explained stiffly, flushing in embarrassment.

"Personally, I don't care if she has the winning lottery numbers or can prove who killed JFK. You don't yell at one of my patients. Ever. Now, get out and don't come back here until tomorrow night, Seamus. Let her rest! And when you do come back, you'd better be calm or I'll ban you from here, head police officer or not! Do I make myself clear, Inspector?" Jim said menacingly. Nodding abruptly, Seamus led everyone out of the room.

Seamus' frustration was such he slammed the door to his car so hard the driver's side window cracked. With a sharp glance to his son, Seamus tore out of the hospital parking lot and off to the station. Mickey could understand his dad's frustrations since he shared them. Mickey just couldn't understand why Jordan was being so stubborn. *Why won't she charge that punk?* Mickey wondered. *Everything would be fine if she'd just charge him.* Sighing, Mickey went to say good-bye to Megan and head home to an empty house.

"Join us for supper, lad. There's no point going home to an empty house. Seamus'll be at the station until late, I'm sure, and you need a good meal in you after today," Nana offered. Mickey agreed readily. As he turned and looked back up at Jordan's darkened room, he couldn't help but wish Jordan was coming home with him. He missed his sister already. They were rarely, if ever, apart. He climbed into his silent truck and followed Nana and Megan back to Glencrest.

Martha handed a message from Owen to Nana as soon as she walked into the dining room. "It's about your good-for-nothing grandson," Martha said disgustedly, as she brought supper in and set it firmly on the table. Megan kept silent. She still didn't know what to think. Did she trust her eyes or her heart? What did she believe? More importantly, who did she believe, Rick or Seamus?

"Martha," Nana warned. Martha sniffed in disdain and went to the kitchen to make tea and finish dessert.

Nana waited until after she was finished her supper and had settled the teens in the den with a movie before calling Owen at home. "My apologies if I've interrupted supper, Owen. I just got home. I assume you've seen Rick," Nana began, sitting down at her desk in the library where Martha had started a fire. She stared at the flickering flames absently.

"Yes, ma'am, I did. He's doing...okay, I guess. He's nervous, definitely tense and, Tony didn't help matters, but I'll let him tell you about that," Owen said. Nana could hear him flipping through a bunch of papers. "Ready? The story I got was he didn't do anything, and I believe him. No one could fake the anger and raw emotion I saw tonight, Nana, he was definitely mad. I'm just not sure who he was madder at – himself for going near Jordan when she was obviously injured or Johnny for attacking his girl.

"He won't get in to see the judge until Monday, however," Owen continued before Nana could ask any questions. "The docket was full by the time Rick was arrested and booked, so no one gets in until then. He's in a holding cell at the station when you wanna see him. Tony's on this weekend and promised to keep an eye on him," Owen finished.

"Thanks for helping out, Owen. What's his chances of getting off?" Nana asked as she made a couple of notes in her day timer.

"Depends on Jordan. If she presses charges, slim to none. If the prosecution tries without Jordan's testimony, it'll be touch and go, but it could still be done," Owen said truthfully. Nana sighed.

"Okay. So it's all up to Jordan and how fast her dad can push her into pressing charges," Nana stated.

"I guess it's more along the lines of *will* Seamus be able to push her into pressing charges," Owen said with a grin.

"That's true, Owen, and he won't have much luck with his daughter. Those two're a couple of peas in a pod – both incredibly stubborn. Thanks again for going, Owen. I'll make sure you get an extra bonus for this over and above everything you already bill me for. Have a good weekend," Nana said.

"You too, Nana. And don't worry about Rick. I'm on it," Owen said confidently and hung up. Nana sat in the library for a long time before returning to the den to finish watching the movie with her granddaughter. Mickey had left earlier, saying he was tired. Nana knew nothing could be done for her troubled grandson until Monday, and she would have to be prepared for anything.

Chapter 20

Rick spent a long, uncomfortable weekend in the holding cell. There was no opportunity to work out the way he was now used to, but he made the best of it, doing what he could to keep the tension and worry away. Rick was constantly under some cop's eye, usually Tony's. The young cop was busy fighting through the frustration of trying to prove Rick's guilt or innocence. Nothing Tony had found would clear Rick and the more he looked, the more evidence there was to convict the teen.

Tony's search didn't stop him from stopping to see Rick several times over the weekend, chatting when he could, usually at mealtimes. But Tony regretted the fact he had no time to spend really talking to Rick, like he did during their sessions. By Monday morning, Rick wanted nothing more than to be out of the cell before Seamus showed up. He knew he didn't want to face Jordan's father. Unfortunately, Rick's luck, bad or good or otherwise, had run out.

Seamus sauntered into the station at the stroke of seven Monday morning, calling out greetings to his men, pausing a couple of times to have longer conversations with one or two. He looked around the bullpen and saw Rick splashing some cold water on his face, trying to wake up. Seamus muttered a distracted answer to something one of his men said, then sauntered over to Rick's cell. The cop stood, leaning against the cell, staring at the teen, who just stared defiantly back. *Honestly, what does she see in him?* Seamus wondered, still furious Jordan wouldn't press charges.

"Well, well, well. What do we have here? Seems to me I'm not supposed to see ye in that cell for a couple of years, boy. What's it been? Two months? Gonna be very hard to get outta this one, boy," Seamus chuckled nastily.

It was hard, but Rick remained on his bunk, somehow managing to keep his temper. He clenched his fists so hard his hands were throbbing. He knew his face was as flushed as Seamus' and he could feel his legs shaking. Even though Rick knew it was wrong, he wanted to reach through the bars, grab Seamus and do...something. He didn't care what. Rick also knew, deep down, if he so much as breathed wrong, it would sink any chance of proving his innocence, at least to Seamus.

"What's the matter, boy? Can't stand facing someone who can fight back?" Seamus taunted. This time, the cop rattled the cell door lightly as if trying to get Rick's attention.

Rick clenched his fists even tighter while clamping his mouth tightly closed. He just knew he'd say the wrong thing if he allowed himself to speak. *Where the hell's Tony?* Rick wondered wildly. *I can't hold on much longer. C'mon, Tony,* Rick continued to beg his friend silently. *Help me!* Unable to stop himself, Rick shifted his feet as if he was going to get up. Startled, Seamus backed up a step before returning to the cell door.

"Look at me, boy!" Seamus thundered and shook the cell door again. Seamus' shout finally got Tony's attention. The young cop hurried over and managed to drag his boss away. Rick sighed with relief, and shook out his hands as he climbed to his feet. Pacing, trying to relax, he took several deep breaths and watched out of the corner of his eye as Tony continued to talk to Seamus. Unashamed of what he had just done, Seamus shrugged and went into his office, closing the door behind him.

Tony sighed and came over to the cell. "Rick?" he asked. He could see the anger on Rick's face and, truth be told, the cop was just as angry at Seamus as Rick was.

"I held my tongue and my temper, man, but it was close. Tony, I really need to hit something, preferably O'Reilly," Rick growled low in his throat. He could barely get his hands to unclench and his heart was pounding so hard he swore he could see it through his chest.

Tony looked at his watch and swore softly. "Aw, hell. Sorry, kiddo," Tony apologized, "but there's no time. I've gotta take you to meet with Owen." He opened the cell door and a visibly enraged Rick emerged. Tony could see Rick was shaking, but there was nothing they could do about it. There was no time to calm Rick down and no one was regretting it more than Tony. Silently, Tony just led the way to where Owen was waiting.

"Morning, Rick. Tony," Owen greeted the two of them. He sighed quietly as he realized just how angry his client was, and Tony wasn't able to do anything about it, simply because there was no time. *Seamus must've gotten to him this morning*, Owen muttered to himself. *Just great. Just friggin' great. Perfect timing, Chief*. Owen hoped and prayed Rick realized how much trouble he would be in if he didn't calm down and soon. There was no way Rick could go before the judge with this much pent-up anger inside of him.

"Morning, Counsellor. Ten minutes and then we'll head over," Tony said, leaving Rick alone with his lawyer. As Tony closed the door, he said a silent prayer to his totem animal, the bald eagle, asking for patience and guidance. He wondered if he'd ever receive either.

"Morning, Owen," Rick said sourly as he sat down hard. So hard, in fact, Owen swore he heard the chair crack. Rick was still shaking and he couldn't help but replay the scene in the jail cell over and over again, his anger growing by the moment.

Owen didn't bother to open his file or take notes. He looked at Rick and sighed softly. "Rick, I don't wanna know what happened this morning. Right now all I care about's getting you calmed down. If you go into that courtroom with any kind of visible anger, evidence or no evidence, the judge'll throw you in jail faster than you can blink," Owen pointed out quietly.

Scowling, Rick jumped to his feet and began to pace. "I can't help how I feel, Owen. If O'Reilly's allowed to deliberately do what he can to piss me off, then I'm allowed to be mad as hell about it," Rick snapped back.

Owen slowly stood. "On second thought, Rick, I think I *do* wanna know what happened," Owen said as he walked to his client, resting his hand on Rick's shoulder. The lawyer winced as he could feel how much Rick was trembling.

Rick took several deep breaths and quietly began to talk. The whole story only took a couple of minutes, but, by the end, Rick felt calmer and more in control, much like he did after a session with Tony. He could feel how sore his hands were and he knew he was still wound up. Yet Owen had listened to every word without any comment, just like Tony, and wrote down every word Rick said, just like Tony.

"Rick, I'm not gonna say anything about this yet. It's not gonna do you any good and probably'll do a lot of harm. I'm not sure what O'Reilly's problem is, but I'm not gonna add to it. Not right now," Owen said dryly.

Rick nodded as he sat down. Talking had helped, but he knew he was going to have to do a serious workout after he saw the judge, no matter what happened in that courtroom. *Control,* Rick muttered to himself. *I have to stay in control.*

"Alright, Owen, I'm ready. What's the plan for today?" Rick said as he firmly put the morning's incident out of his mind. With an encouraging smile, Owen sat back down across from Rick and opened the case file. *That's the ticket, Rick,* Owen thought. *Calm, cool and collected, no matter how hard you want to beat O'Reilly.*

They went over Rick's story once more, but nothing had changed from when they had talked the Friday before. Owen told Rick what he thought his chances were, and what he thought would happen. Rick was far more confident than Owen, but then again, Owen knew what could happen with scanty evidence and the right judge. Or the wrong judge in the wrong mood.

"Everything depends on Jor, then," Rick said hopefully. He couldn't see Jordan pressing charges, but her father could be very persuasive when he needed to be. Still, Rick knew Jordan. She trusted Rick, and Rick knew she wouldn't be easily "persuaded" to put her man in jail.

Owen nodded. "It'll be harder to convict without her testimony, but don't kid yourself, Rick, it can be done. I've seen it happen. A lot people've gone to jail with as little physical evidence as there is in this case and others have been convicted with no witnesses and every shred of evidence purely circumstantial," Owen warned with a raised hand. He didn't want Rick to assume he was going to get off if Jordan didn't testify.

"Alright, kiddo, time to go," Tony said, suddenly sticking his head in the door, causing Rick to jump. As Rick stood up, Tony was relieved to see his walking time bomb was ticking a lot slower.

Tony led the way over to the courthouse, running over his own testimony in his head as he walked. He left Rick and Owen waiting outside the juvenile courtroom for their case to be called. It wasn't long before Rick was brought before the same judge who had sentenced him after the playground incident. Rick wasn't too sure if this was good or bad. But with the judge's first words, Rick knew it wasn't going to be good. The judge, needless to say, was less than impressed to be seeing Rick so soon.

"Seems to me, Richard, you were ordered to stay out of trouble for two years," the judge stated, glowering at Rick from the high bench.

"Yes, sir," Rick replied shortly. He kept his head held high. He wanted to say he was staying out of trouble, but someone was doing his best to keep Rick in trouble. He decided the judge wasn't in the mood to hear him whine.

"How do you plead on the charges?" the judge asked formally.

"Not guilty, your honour," Rick replied firmly.

Of course, the judge thought critically. *Has anyone ever admitted they were guilty right away? Especially juveniles?* The judge ignored Rick and turned to Tony who stood right behind Rick. The judge noticed immediately how Tony had, perhaps unconsciously, perhaps not, given his support to Rick. *Very interesting. Need to keep an eye on that*, he thought as he made a couple of quick notes. *Something's going on that doesn't make a lot of sense. Yet.*

"Constable Whitefish, let's hear the evidence. I wanna decide today if we go to trial," the judge said. He frowned as Tony outlined the very limited evidence which had been gathered at the scene. Rick's heart soared as he realized there really wasn't that much, at least physically, against him.

The judge listened to all of it impassively. "Constable, what of the victim, Jordan O'Reilly? Does she intend to testify or press charges?" the judge inquired. *Seamus'll have her in here before she can blink,* the judge thought wryly. *I know him too well.*

"Not to my knowledge, your honour," Tony said truthfully. Rick sighed silently with relief. *That's my girl,* Rick gloated to himself. As quickly as his heart had soared, however, it sank just as fast with the judge's next words.

"Very well. Constable, I wanna see you back here on Friday at 10 a.m. If you don't have any further evidence or if the evidence isn't stronger, I will dismiss the charges," the judge said. "Take Mr. Attison to the juvenile facility. He's remanded into custody until his next court appearance. Next case," the judge called out, banging down his gavel.

Rick couldn't believe his ears. First the playground, and now he was going to jail for an assault he didn't do. He stood at the defendant's table, too stunned to move at first. *Dammit, Johnny, what'n the hell're you up to?* Rick fumed. He jumped when two strange cops grabbed him and snapped on the cuffs. He kept his head high as he was taken away to spend the week at juvy hall.

Tony shook his head as the trio began to move past him. "Don't worry, Rick. I'll come and see you as soon as I can. Hang in there, son," he said. Rick just nodded, struggling to keep from snapping. After all, it wasn't Tony's fault, was it?

Owen shook his head as he gathered his files and put everything away, struggling to organize his plans. First, report to Nana. He knew she wasn't going to be happy about what had just happened. Next, find out what Seamus had planned. He would freak if Tony didn't find enough evidence to put Rick behind bars permanently. As Owen marched from the courtroom, he was beginning to get a sinking feeling Seamus wasn't even looking for anyone else. After all, he had already tried, convicted and sentenced Owen's client before the judge did.

Blinking as he stepped into the sunlight from the dark halls of the courthouse, Owen watched from the top of the steps as Tony stood staring across at the park, trying to get up the courage to face his boss. Owen just shook his head as he finally realized how deeply the young cop was involved in Rick's case and wondered if Tony would ever be able to look at a young offender the same way again. *What a mess*, he thought and sighed as he watched Tony square his shoulders and head back to the station before climbing into his own car and heading out to Glencrest to bring Nana up to speed.

Once there, Tony immediately reported to Seamus' office for a meeting he wasn't really looking forward to. "What did the boy get?" Seamus asked, obviously assuming Rick had either pled guilty or he had been convicted.

"Nothing, sir. The judge says get more evidence by Friday or the charges'll be dismissed," Tony replied blandly and waited for the explosion. He didn't have to wait long.

"What do ye mean – get more evidence? Don't ye have enough?" Seamus shouted, his face purple with rage. He stood up and leaned over his desk, right in Tony's face. *What do I have to do to get rid of that boy?* Seamus wondered hotly.

Tony didn't flinch. "Look, Seamus, be reasonable. All we really have is Rick's bandana at the scene and Rick standing over Jordan. No one has ever come forward and actually claimed they saw him hit her – *ever* – let alone that day. There're so many fingerprints in that room it'll be *weeks* before we identify them all, if we can. Even if Rick's prints *are* there, we have no idea how long they've been in there. Rick remembers having classes in that room, but doesn't remember when, or for what or why. Trust me, Seamus, unless Jor agrees to testify and can clearly identify Rick as her attacker, we have nothing," Tony said reasonably. *Thank the Creator*, Tony didn't add.

"I don't care what ye do, Tony, get me the evidence to convict that boy!" Seamus snarled. He sat down so hard his chair groaned.

"Seamus, why do you hate Rick so much?" Tony asked quietly.

"None of yer business, Constable," Seamus snapped roughly. "Just get the damn evidence for Friday."

Tony looked at his boss. Seamus' face matched the shock of red hair on his head. It took Tony a couple of minutes to figure out what Seamus wanted and when he did, he was ready to spit. "Forget it, O'Reilly. I know what you're thinking, what you want me to do and I won't do it. Ever. No matter how badly you wanna conviction. I won't make up evidence. I don't operate like that and I thought you didn't either. You taught me better than that." Tony paused for a long moment. "Lemme talk to Jor and try to convince her to testify or we have to drop the charges," Tony said finally. He idly brushed his braids back over his shoulders, unconsciously drawing his heritage around him like a warm blanket. *I have my pride and I won't sacrifice any part of it to help Seamus convict my friend,* Tony swore.

Seamus glared at Tony. "Fine, Constable. Ye can talk to her today. She's been sent home to rest. Send a team back to the school. I want them to go over that classroom with a fine tooth comb. Tell them not to miss anything, do ye hear me, boy? Get me the necessary evidence, *Constable.*" He glared at Tony until the young cop nodded sharply and turned to leave.

Tony left the office, shaking his head and passed along Seamus' orders. The team grumbled as they headed back to an already processed classroom, hoping it hadn't been cleaned. Tony would've rather gone with them to the school instead of what he was going to do. His job was going to be much harder. *How do I convince Jor to testify against her boyfriend?*, Tony wondered as he grabbed his partner to visit Jordan at her farm. Mickey showed the partners into Jordan's room with a soft plea of "Don't tire her, please." Tony nodded as soon as he saw her white, pinched face. This wasn't going to be very nice.

"Hey, Tony," Jordan croaked. Her throat and larynx were both still swollen, making it hard for her to talk. She reached for some ice to soothe the pain those two little words had ignited. Tony sat on the edge of her bed while his partner sat in her desk chair, ready to take notes.

"Hey, kiddo. How're you feeling?" Tony asked, planting a fatherly kiss on her forehead.

Jordan giggled and gave him a hug. "Better, but not great. My throat's killing me," she whispered as she reached for the ice again.

"Jor, I hate to do this, but I *have* to go over the attack again. I'm sorry, but your dad's making me," Tony said quickly, seeing how her face fell. *Hang it all, Seamus*, Tony thought, furious with his boss. *She's been through enough, yet you force me to do this*. After this, Tony knew he would have to go home and spend a long time in his tepee, meditating, smudging with sage to cleanse himself. He felt dirty and worthless forcing Jordan to do this after how he had already treated Rick.

"How many times do I have to tell you I won't testify against Rick? I don't care what I thought I saw or heard! I know Rick didn't do this," Jordan sobbed, her voice breaking. "He didn't hurt me! He loves me! Tony, please, just go away and leave me alone." She turned away from the cop and sobbed even harder.

Tony gathered Jordan to him and held her as she cried. "Hush, Jordan, hush now. You're just hurting your throat. Here's the ice. Now, listen to me. I know you won't testify against Rick, no matter what your father does or says. And no matter what I saw in that classroom, I can't see Rick hitting you. He's too gentle with you. He's too gentle," Tony repeated softly. He stared off into space for a couple of minutes and tried to justify in his own mind what he was about to ask the young teen to do.

"And while I know you don't *want* to do this, I still need to go over the attack, just once more, to see if there's anything you remember, now that it's been a couple of days. That's all I want right now," Tony said gently but firmly.

Jordan sighed, but went over the attack, all the while making it very clear this would be the absolute last time she would. She described in as much detail what she could remember about how she was grabbed, beaten and then strangled. Tony listened without comment until she finished. His partner finished scribbling his notes in the sudden silence that descended in the room. While Jordan rested and soothed her throat with ice, Tony glanced at the notes and had a whispered conference with his partner.

"Okay, Jor. I need to clear up a couple of points and then I'll stop," Tony said quietly.

"You said someone spoke?" Tony asked as he looked at one point his partner had marked.

"Yes," Jordan replied softly.

"Was it the person hitting you?" Tony asked.

"Now that you mention it, Tony, no, it wasn't. He didn't say anything," Jordan said.

"The one who did talk. Did it sound like Rick?" Tony continued.

"Definitely not. It was too harsh. It sounded like someone who had been smoking for years. Rick's voice, even when he growls, is still smooth as melted chocolate," Jordan replied confidently.

"You said you scratched at the face of your attacker. Do you remember if you actually scratched his face?" Tony asked. *Keep it up, kid and your man's home free,* Tony gloated silently.

"I may not have at first, Tony, but I'm almost positive I scratched him bad enough to leave marks when I caught the bandana right before I blacked out," Jordan croaked. She reached for her ice again. Tony noticed her face was pinched and she seemed to be drooping quickly. He didn't know what drained the young girl more – the attack or the brutal way her father and brother were pushing her to blame Rick. Some days, Tony was torn between the job and the kids, especially since this whole stupid situation had began.

"We're almost done, Jor, I promise. So, as far as you remember, you did scratch your attacker deeply enough to leave marks? Do you know if anyone scraped under your nails for any skin that might have been there?" Tony asked gently. Inside, Tony was grinning. He'd have to double check, but he was almost 100% positive there were no scratches on Rick's face. *Strike out, Seamus*, Tony thought elated, although he was a little disappointed at Jordan's next words.

"Yes, I scratched deep enough to leave marks, but no, I don't think anyone checked and I know I've washed my hands and scrubbed them enough to get rid of anything. Sorry, Tony," the tired girl whispered.

Tony wanted to ask her a couple of more questions, but decided to bid the young teen good-bye. His heart went out to her as he saw her collapse into her bed with a sigh. No one should be going through what she was. Absently, he called Mickey to come and sit with her, since Tony didn't want her feeling like she was being left alone.

"Just don't try and push her into testifying against Rick, okay?" Tony warned Mickey as they met in the hall outside her door. "She'll deny it and argue with you, and that won't do her voice or her throat any good. Drop it for now." Mickey nodded.

Tony's mood was dark as he and his partner drove to the juvenile detention centre to talk to Rick again. When they were shown into the gym, Rick was working out on the heavy bag in a make-shift boxing area. Tony just watched with undisguised pride until Rick stepped back to listen to someone, nodded sharply and then went back to work.

Privately, Tony had to admit he was becoming too involved with Rick, too close. The cop in him knew he should back away, but the elder in him couldn't. Wouldn't. Rick was only one of a thousand troubled kids, many of whom Tony had arrested, but Tony knew no one was going to help Rick unless Tony did it himself. *Why me?* Tony asked himself. *Why not me?* his conscience replied, playing back memories that hurt.

Bob was there, working with Rick and Tony was grateful. Bob had taken a real interest in Rick, especially since the afternoon Rick had almost taken Tony down. Bob obviously saw something in the kid no one else did. *Especially Seamus*, Tony thought bitterly. *What is it about this kid that makes two different people want him in two different places so badly?* Tony continued to wonder as he watched Rick work out under Bob's sharp eyes. As he watched, Tony forced himself to focus on the investigation, going over everything he knew.

Tony knew from his sessions with Rick and talking to other students Blade wanted Rick back badly. He'd taken Rick's defection as personal. It was also obvious, at least to Tony, someone was trying to frame Rick, and Tony's money was on Blade. Unfortunately, all Tony had to go on was gut instinct, something Seamus wouldn't accept, since the evidence didn't point to the gang – it all pointed to Rick.

But even at his worst, which would've been last year, Rick hadn't been in this much trouble, while this would be considered an exceptionally good year for Blade. Delaney was beginning to worry about Rick's mental stability, since the few supporters Rick had were seemingly jumping ship faster than rats off the Titanic. And the more Tony talked with his young friend, the more Tony had to agree. Keeping Rick sane and stable was going to be a full time job. Between that and conducting this investigation, Tony knew he wasn't going to get enough sleep. Tony just hoped he was up to it.

The other problem Tony faced as he watched Rick, was this vendetta Seamus had against the boy. It didn't make sense to Tony. There was nothing in Rick's background, that Tony knew of at least, to suggest why Seamus hated Rick so much. If Seamus was truly angry about Rick's gang life, then Tony would've thought the boss would've been dancing now that Rick wanted out of the Knights, so that wasn't it. No, there was definitely something more to Seamus' attitude towards Rick than met the eye and Tony was determined to find out what it was. *No matter what it costs me,* Tony vowed.

"Hey, Tony," Bob said, coming to stand next to the cop. The boxing coach nodded a greeting to Tony's partner, who nodded back absently. He seemed focused on the boy punching at the bag.

"What're you doing here, Bob?" Tony asked curiously. He stood at ease leaning against one of the pillars in the room, with his arms folded across his chest, his uniform straining at the seams across his shoulders. He heard his partner chuckle softly and Tony just grinned back. He knew he needed to get a bigger shirt, he just hadn't taken the time to get one ordered.

"Rick asked me to come over here today. Seems O'Reilly got to him at the station this morning and he wanted some help to deal with his anger. Said you were busy and since he doesn't trust himself to go at it solo yet, I got a pass and came over, although this set-up's only temporary," Bob chuckled. Tony winced. He should have been here, not Bob.

"How's he doing?" Tony asked, putting his feelings aside.

"Doing good. Be ready for you in a couple," Bob said confidently as the three men continued to watch Rick work out. Tony immediately noticed the earlier anger was gone or at least greatly diminished. That alone made him feel better about not being available for his friend.

Rick finished his set and looked around for Bob. When he noticed his trainer standing with his friend and mentor, Rick strode over, confidence in every stride. He knew he hadn't done anything. Now he just had to wait for Tony to prove it. As he walked towards the three men, Tony made a note of Rick's face and nodded.

"Hey, Tony, what's up?" Rick asked, curious. He towelled off and took a long pull at his water bottle while he waited for Tony to answer.

Tony turned to his partner with a wink and a grin. "Hey, Marsh, do me a favour and forget what you're about to see, 'kay?" Tony requested.

Marshal shrugged and nodded. Tony had long ago earned Marshall's respect, first as his partner, second as a caring cop, especially with the troubled kids. He knew all too well what Tony was facing with this particular juvenile, and at what cost, with being this kid's counsellor. Tony would often use Marshall as a sounding board, especially after a particularly tough session, so looking away once in a while was a small thing to do for him.

"Care to try a couple of rounds, kiddo?" Tony asked and motioned to the ring.

Startled, Rick looked at Bob. "Go for it, son," Bob encouraged with a hidden smile. "Keep your temper under control and you'll be just fine."

What he didn't say was Bob felt Rick needed to do this. He knew Rick would prefer to be pounding on Seamus, but they couldn't arrange that. Tony was just going to have to be a sufficient substitute. Marshall helped Tony strip off his uniform, while Bob got the cop a padded helmet and mouthpiece, and then tied on his gloves. Then, while Tony warmed up, Bob got Rick ready.

The two met in the centre of the ring and, at Bob's sharp command, began trading shots. Tony remembered to pull his blows, as he didn't want to leave any bruises, nor did he want to lay Rick out, which he was sure he could still do, though for how much longer, Tony didn't know. Rick, on the other hand, didn't hold back and Tony winced several times when Rick's blows connected. After three minutes, Bob called a halt. Both Rick and Tony were drenched in sweat and Rick, especially, felt good. Most of Rick's frustrations at the system were gone. It didn't take long for Bob to strip the gloves off of Rick's hands so he could cool down.

As Rick stretched, Marshall helped Tony strip his gear off and get back into uniform. Tony towelled off and slammed back about a half of a litre of cool water. He was suitably impressed with Rick's skill and told him so. "Whatever Johnny taught you about fighting was good. No, really, I'm not kidding. You've got great reflexes and Bob can't teach you that," Tony assured Rick as the teen scoffed in protest.

"Keep stretching, kiddo, or you'll seize up," Tony encouraged. After a moment, Rick dropped his eyes and continued to stretch.

Bob agreed, knowing Rick needed a boost to his fragile self-esteem. "You've got speed in your hands and feet, son. Gimme another few months, especially without any more interruptions, and you'll be ready to step into the ring against any competitor in the country. Amateur, at least," Bob amended. Rick glowed at the praise.

Still high from his success in the ring, Rick returned to his room while Tony and Marshall returned to the station. After the sparring session, Tony decided not to spend any more time talking to Rick. The cop knew he'd seen everything he needed, especially since Marshall had taken a couple of discrete pictures of Rick's unscratched face. Marshall stayed at his desk to type up the interview with Jordan, while Tony checked in with the forensics team. He found most of them in their break room, arguing over the evidence, or lack thereof, they had found in the classroom.

"What's eating the Inspector, Tony?" one guy grumbled in disgust.

"Why? What's up?" Tony replied, sitting on the edge of the table.

"We went over that room on Friday. He made us go back again today. Twice. It was almost like he didn't think we did our job the first time," the tech complained. Several others nodded in agreement.

"Tell me you found something new," Tony begged.

"Nadda. Zip. Zilch. Nothing," the tech said mournfully. He sighed softly as he watched Tony hang his head. "Sorry, man." Everyone in the room knew Seamus wouldn't be happy, and none of them were happy Tony was the one who had to break the news to the boss. A whipping boy, Tony Whitefish was not.

Great, Tony sighed to himself as he left the break room. He checked in with a couple of officers who had been sent back to the school to see if they could find any witnesses who would place Rick in that classroom at the time of Jordan's attack. Not surprisingly, at least to Tony, the only ones who put Rick anywhere near that room were the Black Knights. Tony didn't believe a word of their stories. After everything else that had happened, of course the Knights would say Rick was in the room beating the crap out of Jordan.

"Problem is we also have Rick's teacher and classmates in that last period all claiming Rick was in class from the moment the bell rang to begin class, right up to the end when he tore out of it, and the teacher from the previous class said he never left. Now, her brother claims she never arrived in Chem, but with the teachers' stories, there's no way Attison left one class early or arrived late for the next. And since from what I understand, Mr. Robson, the English teacher, isn't exactly one of Rick's biggest fans, he definitely wouldn't lie to protect him. If Rick had been late to class, Mr. Robson would've said so," the cop agreed with Tony's silent assessment of the gang's statements.

"Gimme what you found, but keep those four 'statements' to yourself for a while. I'll take everything else to the Inspector and we'll go from there," Tony said dejectedly. Not surprisingly, Seamus ordered Tony and his team to go over everything again. As Tony sat at his desk, he stared at the file on Jordan's assault. There, glaring back at him, was Rick's picture at the time he was booked, completely scratch free. "Create the evidence you want, since I can't seem to find it, Seamus, or go with my gut?" Tony muttered as he stared back at the picture. It didn't give him an answer.

Chapter 21

Throughout the rest of the week, Tony gathered the information – what little there was of it – from the rest of the team and presented it to Seamus. Each day there was nothing new, nothing they didn't already know. Tony's team found no hairs or fibres or blood on Jordan's clothes or on anything else in the room. Not one single fingerprint in the room was Rick's. Absolutely nothing could be found to connect Rick to the brutal assault, but to Seamus it was always "Not good enough, Constable. Do it again," the inspector growled on Tuesday and Wednesday. Each time, Tony went back to the frustrated team and got them to go over the evidence yet again, struggling to find something that might've been missed, even though Tony knew in his heart they hadn't missed a single thing.

Thursday morning, Tony called everyone together one last time. "Talk to me, people. Tell me we have something new to take to O'Reilly. I'm really getting tired of getting my butt chewed on," Tony said flatly. He sat on the edge of the desk with his arms folded, scowling at his team.

To a man, the team shook their heads. "Tony, I'm not going over the interviews or evidence again," one cop protested firmly.

"It's pointless, man. There's nothing new, Fish," a second cop echoed, making Tony wince. Everyone grinned at Tony's nickname, relieving the tension somewhat. He had received it on his second day on the job, from the cop that had just spoken. And, with the exception of his partner, the cop was the only cop allowed to call him that. At least to Tony's face.

Tony smiled and nodded. "Thank you, Jonesy. Everything in those reports tells you what?" he asked no one in particular.

"Rick Attison did not attack Jordan O'Reilly. No matter how Inspector O'Reilly tries to twist the evidence, that same evidence still says the kid didn't do it." Tony didn't know who had spoken, but everyone seemed to agree.

Silence descended and stretched on as Tony struggled to figure out what he was going to do. Marshall looked at his partner with a sympathetic smile. He knew what kind of man Tony was, how strongly Tony believed in his heritage and his partner was going home, every night, and burning his sweet grass and other native herbs to help him, at the very least, relax.

It wasn't helping.

"Alright, then, boys. Back to your other cases. I'll go tell the Inspector," Tony said after a couple of minutes of strained silence and dismissed his team. Marshall was the last to leave. He walked by Tony and put his hand on his partner's shoulder in silent support. Then Tony was alone in the conference room.

Help me, Black Eagle, Tony prayed to his Spirit Guide as he gathered up the scant evidence. Outside, softly, distantly, he heard the cry of an eagle and he suddenly felt stronger. *It's not gonna be easy*, Tony realized with a sigh, *but Seamus has to be told there's nothing new. There hasn't been anything new since the first day.* He took a deep breath and, again asking Black Eagle to guide him, walked slowly down the hall and stopped outside Seamus' door. After another deep breath, Tony knocked.

"Come!" Seamus barked. Tony entered and stopped in front of the large oak desk which dominated the room.

"What do ye have for me today, Constable?" Seamus snarled.

Inwardly wincing at the lack of familiarity, Tony mourned the loss of camaraderie he and the inspector had once had. They had been friends once. Now they were nothing more than co-workers. Tony wondered if they were even *that* any more.

"Inspector, the team has gone over the evidence and the interviews three more times. The forensic team has gone over that room at least three times," Tony replied formally. Seamus wanted stiff formality, to remind Tony of his place, so the young native gave the old Irishman stiff formality. It would remain like this, Tony knew, until he could talk some sense into his boss.

"And?" Seamus growled. *Don't make him any madder than he already is,* Tony warned himself. Seamus had obviously had no luck, once again, in getting Jordan to press charges, so he was taking his frustrations out on Tony.

"Nothing new has been discovered since I first reported to you on Monday, Inspector. The team just met again this morning, right before I came to talk to you and we've all agreed spending any more man-hours on this investigation with its single-minded focus on Richard Attison would be a waste of those same hours and budget, and would not get us any closer to a conviction," Tony finished quietly. He stood at ease, his feet shoulder width apart with his hands clasped behind his back.

"Not good enough, Constable. Tell the team to go over it again and to keep going over it until *I* tell them to stop. Yer missin' somethin'," Seamus said bitterly. *Get me the evidence!* he wanted to shout at Tony. Yet deep in his heart, he knew Tony hadn't missed anything. Tony never missed anything. That was what made him such a good cop and a good leader in these investigations. It was just unfortunate the evidence Seamus wanted so badly wasn't there.

"With all due respect, sir, I agree with the team, and, furthermore, as their shift leader, I've sent them back to work on their other cases. There's nothing further to be learned. We've gone over all the evidence until we can recite it cold. Rick didn't attack your daughter. The only evidence putting him in that room is that bandana and the visual evidence of him standing over her. I've a sworn statement from Rick stating he threw out his gang clothes and, while it may be unlikely, it is also possible someone else could've picked them out of the garbage," Tony said tonelessly. *Put that in your war pipe and smoke it,* Tony groused to himself.

Seamus ground his teeth in frustration. "Why can't ye find the evidence I need to put this brat outta me daughter's life forever?" Seamus yelled, standing up half-way and leaning on his desk to get right in Tony's face.

"Why don't you just admit you hate Rick and you'd do anything to see him convicted, evidence or no evidence?" Tony yelled back, just as hotly. *Quit losing your temper, you idiot,* Tony swore at himself. *You're stronger than this.* Tony closed his eyes and took several deep breaths, trying to calm down. Once again, in the distance, he heard the soft cry of an eagle. *Give me strength,* he prayed yet again, wondering if anyone was really hearing him.

"What're ye sayin'?" Seamus growled after a moment of angered silence.

"Face it, Seamus. Jor's right. You've tried and convicted Rick without looking for another suspect. Take your kids' accident. Have you even tried to find out who really ran your kids off the road?" At Seamus' impatient head shake, Tony continued angrily.

"I didn't think so. I have. And you know something, boss? I've discovered there're three other black sports cars at the high school – one of which is driven by Brain, Blade's Second in the Knights. Rick's is the most obvious since it's black and silver. The paint job's damn easy to copy, and it really wouldn't take that long to do so. But since you seem to have a grudge against Rick, you haven't even told the investigating officers to look for other suspects. I know this because I've asked them. So why haven't you?" Tony snapped roughly. *What're you so afraid of, Seamus? What aren't you telling me?* Tony wondered. *How do I convince you this is illegal and immoral, Seamus? Right. How do I catch the wind?* Tony thought grimly.

"That boy has tried to kill me daughter! Twice!" Seamus continued to shout. His face was so red Tony feared his boss was on the verge of a heart attack.

"There's no evidence to prove it," Tony snapped back. He finally had his temper under a bit of control, even if Seamus didn't.

Seamus stopped, as if Tony had thrown a bucket of cold water on him. "Prove it?" he said, puzzled. "Prove what? That I hate him? That he's tried to kill me kids? I know he did!"

"There's no evidence to prove it, Inspector," Tony repeated, wanting to beg Seamus to talk to him, to get whatever the hell was bothering his boss off of his chest.

When Seamus didn't respond right away, Tony spoke again, this time softly. "What has Rick done to you to make you hate him so much?"

"That's none of yer business, Tony. I've already told ye that," Seamus said firmly, but distractedly. He idly reached for his sidearm, as if to reassure himself it was still there.

"I disagree, Seamus. Look, boss, you've done nothing but push us to find non-existent evidence against one suspect. Hell, you came damn close to asking me to fabricate it, all in an effort to convict Rick. If Internal Affairs ever found out, you'd face an inquiry or maybe even lose your command, or your job! Think about what that'd do to your kids. They'd never be able to hold their heads up at school again. And can you imagine what Mrs. Attison would say if *she* ever found out? And to top it all off, we might never find out what really happened to Jor now, thanks to your obsession with Rick," Tony said flatly as he finally sat down across from his boss.

Silence hung in the air as Seamus struggled to figure out what to do. "Do ye really wanna know, Tony? Does he mean that much to ye, already, that ye absolutely need to hear this?" the inspector finally asked quietly. Seamus had sat back down in his chair and leaned back to stare at the ceiling. *Do I really wanna tell him what happened?* Seamus thought.

"Personally, Seamus, I think *you* need to get this off your chest. It's eating away at you, clouding your judgement. But, yes, he means that much to me already. There's something about him that calls to me, I guess. Something which reminds me of the kids on the reserve. C'mon, boss, what is it about Rick you hate so much? It can't just be Jor," Tony reasoned.

"That's part of it." Seamus stared past Tony, not really seeing anything and when he spoke his voice was low, husky and full of suppressed anger. He talked like he wasn't sitting behind his desk, but like he was far away in another place and another time.

"It was just over a year ago now, I'd guess. Rick had known me kids since Grade 3, but now he was startin' to show teen-age infatuation with me Jordan. In case he's never told ye, Mickey's only reason fer hatin' Rick was Rick was separatin' Mickey from his twin. That's his only real reason. Mine's a little more, um … complicated. Anyway, Jordan responded to Rick's advances in kind. Y'know I've always been extra protective of her, especially since her mother died. I think if I had just let them be, none of this would be happening," Seamus sighed.

"What do you mean, Seamus?" Tony encouraged quietly. He knew he had to keep his boss talking or he'd just clam up again. *Just like a counselling session with Rick,* Tony mused, *only this is a much tougher nut to crack.*

"Rick had just turned 14 when he got really interested in Jordan. He kept callin' her, talkin' fer hours, even though they had just spent the entire day together and every time he was over at Glencrest they'd sneak off to meet, no matter how hard I tried to keep them apart and Jordan in the house. I found them in the barn, kissin' or walkin' through the woods, holdin' hands. Every time I found them, I'd lecture Jordan and growl at Rick. The kids just shrugged it off and went about their business, completely ignorin' what I'd just told them.

"On top of that, Rick was startin' to really get in trouble in school, gettin' in fights, talkin' trash to the teachers, y'know? I think it was more to get attention from his father after his mom left than anythin' else, but because of it, I really didn't want Jordan anywhere near the boy. I just didn't trust him. So, between the fights and his sneakin' around with Jordan, I was beginnin' to hate the boy. The fights were nothin', really, just a couple of swings here and there, but he always won. It was his attitude that got to me that day, more than anythin'. I don't even remember the date, but what he did's as clear now as when it happened.

"He picked a fight with Mickey's best friend at the time, Colin Falher. Nice kid, about as big as Rick, just not as strong or quick. Rick knocked the kid out and paraded around the school like he owned it, proud as could be. The teachers were already leery of angerin' Rick – he scared them with his strength and his anger. Unfortunately, Colin was never the same after that fight. Oh, Rick beat him, fair and square, but, Rick was already 5'8" tall and wiry strong. He has an instinct for fightin', as ye've no doubt discovered," Seamus said wryly. He sighed and fell silent. Tony could see his boss struggling with his memories. It was a good start, but Tony knew he had to keep Seamus talking.

Tony nodded thoughtfully. "C'mon, boss, don't stop. What happened?" Tony encouraged quietly.

Seamus didn't speak for several moments, trying to organize his thoughts. "Mickey called me right after the fight. He was cryin', like I've never heard him cry before, not even when his mom died, and he was there when she passed. The sound, Tony, it tore me heart, shredded it to pieces. Between his sobs and tryin' to help Colin, he managed to tell me what happened and somethin' inside me just snapped. I saw this as me chance to finally get rid of the boy. So I jumped in my cruiser and went lookin' for him. I found him saunterin' home like nothin' had happened. He really didn't care, good or bad, Tony, so long as Michael noticed. I pulled the car to a stop in front of him, got out and confronted the little punk.

"*He laughed*, Tony. Said Colin deserved it because Colin wouldn't leave his girl alone. He said he and Jordan were a couple, and Colin kept makin' passes at her, no matter how many times Rick told him to back off. This wasn't the first time Rick had taken Colin out either, but it was the worst. We started yellin' at each other; one thing led to another and I pushed him a couple of times. I could see him getting' angry, but I just kept pushin' him, tryin' to get him to admit he was wrong. That's all I really wanted, Tony. For that brat to admit he was wrong fer beatin' Colin up. He shouted somethin', I don't remember what, but what ever it was, it made me angry enough to take a swing at him.

"He ducked and let me take a few more wild swings at him, before he finally swung back. Hell, Tony, even then, untrained, he knocked me flat. Three punches," Seamus shook his head in disgust at the memory. Tony couldn't help but flash a knowing grin at his boss.

"Lemme guess. Ribs twice and an uppercut to finish you off?" Tony chuckled dryly.

"Yeah. He was almost as tall as me, but definitely not as strong as he is now. Now I wouldn't want to meet him in a lit alley, let alone a dark one, especially if he was really pissed at me. Trust me, I heard what the Knights did to the Slayers. Ricardo finally admitted it was Rick who put him in the hospital with a shattered knee and shoulder, but he wouldn't press charges. Too damn scared of Blade. And that was *before* he began to box. Still, I swear, though, if Rick hadn't caught me like he did, it may have been different." Three years later and it still made Seamus see red thinking about a kid getting the better of him.

"The next sound I heard as I lay on the ground gaspin', was the sound of a gun cockin'. I reached for me piece and found it in Rick's hands," Seamus growled.

"Seamus, how'd he get his hands on your gun?" Tony demanded, horrified at the implications. *If Rick had pulled that trigger*, Tony thought, shocked.

"Don't know, Tony. Pretty lousy job on me part, huh? Especially with all the gun safety I preach. But now ye know where that comes from. Anyway, he stood over me with that gun pointed at me head, hand steady as a rock and lookin' all the while like he'd love to squeeze the trigger," Seamus said seriously.

"But he didn't," Tony reminded Seamus.

"I know. It was because of Jordan. That's what he told me as he held me gun to me head. 'I could kill ya right now, O'Reilly,' he said softly. 'But I won't. Know why?' 'Why not, boy? Too scared?' I snapped back. 'Nope. 'Cause of Jor.' I think it was the first time I ever called him 'boy' and I've done it ever since. I just laid there, scared to death, Tony. He didn't move the gun from me head for at least a couple of minutes.

"Then he slid the round from the chamber, ejected the clip from the gun and tossed the clip to me. He's kept the single bullet, I think, but held the gun up for me to see. 'You'll get this back some day, O'Reilly, but not today.' He took off for home, whistlin' a tune and carryin' me empty gun in his coat pocket. It was more than 5 minutes before I had the strength to stand up and at least another five before I could stop shakin' long enough to drive home.

"When I got home and Mickey saw me injuries, he asked me what had happened and if Rick had done it. I lied to me son and told him, no, I hadn't found Rick, and someone else had attacked me. Tony, I lied to me son. Do you have any idea how hard that was for me? *I lied to me son!* And I hate meself for it every day. Every single day I live with that shame! No matter what else Rick Attison did, he made me lie to me son. For that alone, I hate that punk!

"I had to ask for a new piece the next day, and when pressed, I told them I had jammed me old one at home while I was cleanin' it and I needed one to use while I fixed me first one. Fortunately, they accepted me word, and have never asked for any other explanation or for the other piece back. I'm positive Blade was watchin' the whole thing. He hooked Rick into the gang the next day. I tried to press charges, but the prosecutor told me I had no case. The boy could plead self-defence because I had pushed him and swung first," Seamus finally finished. The silence stretched on uncomfortably.

"What about your gun?" Tony finally asked for lack of anything else to say.

Seamus reached into a desk drawer and dropped the gun on his desk. "I found it in me mailbox a week later. The clip's here, too. I pulled it from service and haven't fired it since," Seamus said absentmindedly.

He paused. "He made me look like a fool, Tony. No 15-year-old, snot-nosed, wet-behind-the-ears brat should *ever* make a cop look like a fool. I hate him fer it a little more every day. From then on, I've fought a losin' battle with Jordan to keep her away from him. It's not workin' and I hate him."

Seamus sat quietly waiting for Tony's reaction.

Well, I wanted to know, Tony thought to himself. The silence fell again and stretched on for several more minutes while Tony digested what Seamus had confessed. But the more he thought about it, the more Tony realized there was one glaring omission – not from Seamus but from Rick. A fight like this should've stood out in Rick's mind, especially if he had been hooked into the gang the next day. *Every gang member remembers his final initiation,* Tony realized with a start. *Yet Rick's never mentioned this fight to me in our sessions. I wonder why. I've gotta ask him about it next time.*

"I've always thought Rick was just the wrong boy at the wrong time. Now I understand. You really do hate him, don't you?" Tony inquired.

"Yeah, and if that wasn't bad enough, the boy's got bad blood from his father," Seamus continued harshly.

"But, Seamus, listen. I've seen him with Jor. Rick really loves your daughter and he wouldn't lay a finger on her, ever. Now, what's this about Rick's dad?" Tony asked curiously.

"We've had our eye on Michael fer some time regardin' a bookie named Carlos Mendez," Seamus said, still leaning back in the chair.

"Mendez?" Tony shook his head. "Michael doesn't choose his bookies wisely, does he?"

Carlos Mendez would always claim he was from South America, yet Tony knew for a fact he was from the Basque region of Spain. He was tall, dark and handsome, and the women were always falling for his good looks and sophisticated charm, even though he was happily married with several children living with him. He lived on the outskirts of town in a two-story modest-looking house, protected by guards (who were not usually visibly armed, but everyone knew they were) and trained attack dogs. Only a fool went to that house uninvited. What no one could understand was what this big-league bookie was doing in a minor-league town. There was nothing in Collingwood that should've attracted him to the city, yet here he was.

What really bothered Seamus was the feeling Mendez had somehow bought his way into the station and the inspector was mortally afraid one of his cops, one of his boys, was on the take. Mendez was known to rough up anyone who got even a dollar behind on their payments. But whenever the cops were ready to hit Mendez, he was never there and was always able to provide an airtight alibi. Seamus knew someone was tipping Mendez off, but he had no proof. What was worse was the cops could never prove it was Mendez who had ordered the assaults, nor did they ever find any evidence Mendez placed the bets for his clients. The bookie was good at covering his tracks. *How deep is Michael into Mendez?* Tony wondered idly.

"Don't worry about Mendez. I'll take care of him. And Michael. Just concentrate on the boy and get him the hell out of Jordan's life," Seamus growled, dismissing Tony with a wave.

Shaking his head, Tony left the office. Now that he knew what was going on with Seamus, he had to figure out what to do about it so it didn't cost Rick his freedom.

Chapter 22

Friday morning, Tony arrived at the court house at ten for Rick's court appearance. Nana was there, but Megan and the twins had been made to go to school, despite Jordan's protests she needed to be at court for Rick.

"Good morning, Mrs. Attison," Tony greeted Rick's grandmother.

"Morning, Tony. Call me Nana, like everyone else does, young man. Now, what's supposed to happen today?" Nana wanted to know.

"Yes, ma'am. I mean, Nana. As for what's gonna happen, well, that's really up to the judge, but personally, I think Rick'll be released," Tony said confidently.

Rick's case was called by the court clerk and the teen was led into the courtroom along with Owen St. James. Nana was glad to see Rick kept his head held high. He hadn't been broken, just bent a little in the wind. She smiled at her grandson and was rewarded with a tentative smile in return.

"Constable Whitefish, what further evidence did you find?" the judge asked with no preamble once everyone had settled into place.

Rick noticed Tony visibly steeled himself before he outlined what the investigation had turned up. Or didn't. Tony scored the winning point, at least to him, when he told the court about Jordan scratching her attacker's face. "Miss O'Reilly distinctly recalls scratching the face of the person who strangled her. As you can see, your honour, there are no such scratch marks on the defendant's face. While it has been more than a week since the attack and scratches could've healed by now, here's Rick's booking photo and, again, you can see there are no fresh scratches on his face. However, since we didn't know about that when Miss O'Reilly was admitted to the hospital, no scrapings from her fingers were taken and she had bathed several times before I could talk to her. Therefore we were unable to gain any possible DNA evidence to compare to the defendant," Tony finished with a shrug.

"What other suspects are there in this case, Constable?" the judge asked. It was a standard question, but Tony's answer was anything but.

"None, your honour," Tony replied and offered no further explanation. He planned on volunteering no information. If the judge really wanted to know, he'd have to ask the question.

"Why not, Constable?" the judge snapped, incensed. "Are you telling me there's no one else, not one single person who could remotely be considered a suspect in this case?"

"No, your honour, that's not what I'm saying. I'm certain there are others who could be considered suspects. However, we were ordered by Inspector O'Reilly to focus our attention solely on the defendant, your honour, to the exclusion of all others," Tony admitted, keeping his voice as neutral as possible. Now that it was out in the open, Tony hoped he'd be able to duck fast enough to keep his own career intact, let alone Seamus'. He knew from the gasp behind him that Nana was shocked. And incensed.

"Go back to school, Constable, you know better than that. You don't let the inspector or anyone else tell you who to look at – the evidence does. Better yet, tell Inspector O'Reilly I want to see him in my chambers at noon. Today, Constable," the judge snapped and dismissed him.

"Yes, your honour," Tony said quietly and left the courtroom. Outside, the cop sat in the park across from the courthouse, trying to figure out what to do. He was pretty sure something would end up in his personnel file, but he really didn't care right now. He also knew he should go back and give Seamus the message from the judge, but somehow he couldn't bring himself to move. It was too peaceful.

Somewhere overhead, Tony heard the scream of an eagle. Shading his eyes, Tony searched the skies but couldn't see anything. Sighing, the young cop stood up, and as he turned to leave the park, he heard the cry again, but this time, it felt like it was almost on top of him.

Suddenly, on a limb at eye level, there appeared a beautiful bald eagle. The bird chirped softly and showed no fear as Tony approached slowly. He smiled as he admired the bird. It was one Tony knew very well. He had first seen this eagle years earlier, sitting outside his shaman's tent after a vision quest. Tony had been trying to determine if he was really meant to be a cop. During his vision he saw an eagle perched on a police badge. The only thing Tony couldn't see clearly was his badge number. As he stumbled out of the tent, Tony heard the soft chirrup of a bird right in front of him. There was the eagle of his vision, right down to the slash of black over his left eye.

Tony had reached out that first day and received a wing feather from the eagle. His mother had beaded it and Tony kept it beside him all through his training. That feather now had a place of honour on his desk, held in a frame with an artist's drawing of the eagle Tony had named Black Eagle. Whenever Tony felt like he was in deep trouble, somehow his Spirit Guide would show up and give him support or comfort he needed.

Tony reached out carefully and stroked the soft feathers of Black Eagle's head. The eagle cocked his head over to the side as if to ask "Better now?" and gently nipped Tony's fingers. As always, that touch made Tony feel balanced and ready to face the world.

"Well, old boy, Rick may be in over his head, but I'll help him through it. Somehow. Just keep me from flying off at Seamus. That man's being a damned fool," Tony snorted softly. The eagle chirped again, ruffled his feathers, then launched himself into the air with a piercing scream that echoed forever.

"Thank you, my friend," Tony said as he watched the eagle disappear from view. Strengthened, Tony straightened his shoulders and strode purposefully back to the station to give Seamus the judge's message.

Meanwhile, inside the court house, the judge had been finishing up with Rick. "In light of the lack of any really hard evidence against you, Richard, I'm dropping the charges and ordering this part of your record cleared. Any objections, Mr. Blackstone? No? Good," the judge said to the Prosecutor. *What's that idiot cop doing?* the judge fumed silently. *I can't stop this from going in his file. He'll be lucky if he doesn't get I.A. after him. Both of them.*

"Thank you again, your honour," Rick said happily. He was thrilled to be cleared. His elation quickly evaporated at the judge's next words.

"However, until the police can figure out what's going on, I'm asking you to remove yourself from the school so the investigation can be continued. I realize I have no legal recourse to order you out of the school and you can rightly tell me to shove it. If you did that, though, I'd have to cite you for contempt of court and put you back in juvenile hall," the judge chuckled as Rick smiled weakly. "However, I think having you out of school will make it easier for Constable Whitefish to investigate this matter, at least for now. I also understand you've been accused of damaging a truck belonging to Mickey O'Reilly?" the judge asked. Something nagged at the back of the judge's memory, something about other vandalized vehicles, but it slipped away before he could get a grip on it. *Oh well*, he thought. *Must not be too important.*

"Yes, sir, but I've witnesses for when the damage was believed to have been done. My teacher, Mr. Robson, verified I was in class and had not left for the entire period," Rick stated flatly. *I have to leave school?* he thought angrily. *Who's gonna protect them now? Not Mick. Johnny won't stop until one of them is dead!*

The judge nodded thoughtfully. "Understood. Okay, Richard. I'm asking you to remove yourself from school, but even if you don't, you're to have no contact with Jordan or Mickey O'Reilly. Please continue with your counselling. I think it's doing you a world of good. Do you have some place you can be supervised?" the judge asked distractedly as he wrote out the court order.

Nana had been waiting for this. With a sigh, she stood up. "He'll be moving in with me, your honour," she said clearly.

"And you are?" the judge inquired politely, only glancing at her as he continued to write.

"Mrs. Megan Attison, Richard's grandmother. I own Glencrest and Hollyhock's here in town," Nana replied.

"Ah, yes, Mrs. Attison, sorry about that. I know you now. Thank you for taking him, but he does have parents, does he not?" the judge asked, puzzled.

Nana winced. *This'll break Rick's heart, but it's better he hears it now*, she thought sadly. "Yes, your honour. However, his mother has been gone since Richard was six and when I contacted his father about this hearing today, his response was Richard was no longer his responsibility. All parental rights have been signed over to me. I have a separate house Richard has used in the past and his belongings are now there," Nana finished, her grandson whipping around to stare at her in disbelief.

Rick barely heard her. He had his wish. He was moving to Glencrest, but he was still trying to wrap his head around the fact that Michael had disowned him. *First Mom. Then Nelson. Now Dad. Doesn't anyone want me?* he cried to himself. His only family now was Nana, Megan and Ian. And the last two weren't exactly in love with him. Rick struggled to pull his scattered thoughts back to the judge who continued to wrap up the proceedings.

"Very well. Thank you, Mrs. Attison. Richard, do you have any questions?" the judge asked, turning back to Rick.

"Do I continue my counselling at the youth centre or at the farm?" Rick asked finally.

"As long as you *swear* to me you won't attempt to contact the O'Reillys, it may remain at the youth centre. If I hear of even one attempt to contact them, Miss O'Reilly especially, your counselling will be done at the juvenile facility. Do you understand?" the judge warned again.

"Yes, your honour," Rick agreed quietly. *I'm sorry, Jor*, Rick sighed. *I can't be there to protect you. I just hope Mick can. God, could this be any more screwed up?*

"With those conditions then, case dismissed," the judge said, banging his gavel on his desk.

Nana hugged Rick while Owen packed up. "Welcome home, lad," she said smiling.

"Dad doesn't want me?" Rick asked quietly, returning her hug. Oddly enough, after the initial shock, it didn't bother him as much as he thought it would.

"Your father hasn't wanted you for years, lad. He's just made it official," Nana said with some acidity. "Now you can live somewhere where you *are* wanted, lad."

"Rick, do you understand what the judge asked you to do?" Owen asked as he snapped his briefcase closed and led the way out of the courtroom.

"Yeah. Leave school, even though he can't order me to. Leave Jor and Mick alone. Continue counselling," Rick said sourly. *Leave her unprotected*, Rick didn't add, but he didn't have to. Owen knew what the teen was feeling. *Johnny's gonna have a field day with her now that I'm out*, Rick fumed. *Dammit all to hell.* He took a couple of deep breaths and tried to calm down. There was nothing he could do about it right now and he had to accept it.

"Relax, lad. You'll get a tutor and work on school by correspondence. You can help Frank on the farm and spend some time with Cherokee. You get to continue your counselling since it's doing you a world of good and, my word, lad, have you been working out?" Nana asked surprised as she grasped Rick's upper arm. She could feel the power in that arm as he stood there, trembling with pent up emotion.

Rick nodded as he battled with his anger. After a moment he was back in control. "Yeah. Remember the early sessions with Tony? My anger was so bad he suggested I take it out on the punching bag instead of him," Rick chuckled. He didn't tell her about the one time he'd actually attacked Tony, but he figured Nana probably already knew.

"Hmph. Let's get you home, lad," Nana said and led the way to her truck. They stopped at the detention centre to get what few things Rick had left there then sign Rick out. They pulled into Glencrest a couple of hours later and Nana helped Rick get settled in his house. He was grateful to see his beloved Firebird parked out front. Nana, at least, wasn't going to make him stay at the farm all the time. She was going to allow him as much freedom as she could and Rick was grateful.

"I've got the phone and a satellite dish hooked up. I bought you a new TV and DVD player. Yours were pretty worn out. Michael sent everything over yesterday, including your speed bag, movies and c.d.'s. You have a session today?" Nana asked, standing at the door of Rick's bedroom as Rick unpacked the bags and boxes. He grimaced at the way his dad had packed some things. He was going to need a new frame for Jordan's picture, for one thing. *Oh well*, Rick shrugged philosophically. *I should've known he wouldn't give a damn about my stuff.*

Rick checked the clock quickly. "Yeah, at 3:30. I have at least an hour with Tony and a couple with my trainer, so I'll be home late," Rick said and turned back to his stuff.

Satisfied Rick had things well in hand, Nana left him alone. She returned to her office in the main house and put in a call to the police station. "Tony Whitefish, please," Nana said crisply when the desk sergeant answered. It didn't take long for Tony to pick up.

"Whitefish," Tony's smooth voice came over the phone. He grinned as he saw whose number it was. *Seamus is in for it now*, he chuckled to himself.

"What in the hell did you mean when you said no one else has been investigated?" Nana demanded harshly without saying hello. She was furious and Tony, unfortunately, got the brunt of that wrath first.

"Hey, don't blame me, Nana. I just do what Seamus tells me!" Tony defended himself quickly. Blindly following orders was no excuse, Tony knew, but it was the only one he had.

"Tell your boss I'm on my way and he'd better have a hell of a better reason than that for this harassment of my grandson!" Nana slammed down the phone. She sighed as she realized she was being far too hard on Tony but it couldn't be helped. She had called him instead of just going straight to Seamus only because she wanted to give Seamus a bit of a warning. This time, anyway. She called Owen at his office and arranged to meet him at the station, along with an informal complaint the lawyer had already begun drafting.

Nana and Owen arrived at the station after lunch and found Tony waiting for them at the front desk. He led them straight to Seamus' office without having the desk sergeant announce them. The inspector was still smarting from the dressing down he had received from the juvenile court judge and the formal reprimand which had been added to his personnel file when Nana arrived and started in on him the instant Tony closed the door behind them.

"Seamus O'Reilly, if I didn't know you better, I'd swear someone else had taken over this office. I was shocked to hear Jordan had been hurt. Now, imagine my surprise to hear you ordered – ordered! – your officers not to look for another suspect! Have you lost what few marbles you had? What're you thinking, boy?" Nana snapped, using O'Reilly's favourite insult for Rick. She stood over O'Reilly, pinning him to his chair with a piercing glare. Seamus was already squirming.

"Look, Megan," O'Reilly tried to placate Nana. She wasn't in the mood.

"Look yourself, Seamus. If anything like this happens again, and I don't believe it ever will, you'd better look for all suspects! Do you understand me? Have you even tried to find somebody other than Rick?" Nana demanded again. "Can you even tell me there are any other suspects?"

"Well, no, but…"

"Of course not. Why bother? It's far more convenient to blame my grandson who has fallen head over heels in love with your beautiful daughter. Get this straight, Seamus O'Reilly, and don't you ever forget it. I think Rick is very lucky to find someone like your daughter. Someone who's taught him about love. Something you bloody well know he never got at home. Don't make the same mistake his father has. Don't drive your daughter away with your hatred!"

With those parting words, Nana strode from the office, slamming the door hard enough to rattle the glass. Seamus and Tony were stunned at her anger. But she wasn't done yet.

Owen's voice was loud in the sudden silence. "Here's an informal complaint regarding your handling of this case. We decided not to mention anything to the investigating officers, as they were only doing their job. We haven't filed anything formally, Inspector, but remember, should anything like this happen again, we will," Owen said softly. He laid the papers on the inspector's desk, then the young lawyer turned and followed Nana out of the office, closing the door much softer than she did. It was several minutes before either cop spoke.

"Well, Tony, I guess I've been told," Seamus chuckled dryly. He picked up the complaint and read it quickly, his laughter fading. With a sinking heart, he realized his career would be sunk if Regimental Headquarters ever saw this informal complaint, much less a formal one. This one was for his eyes only, and Seamus knew it.

Tony glanced at his watch. He watched Seamus' face pale as he read. *It must be pretty bad,* Tony thought. *Just be more careful, boss, and you'll be okay.* "Yes, sir. Excuse me, Seamus. I've my counselling session with Rick in twenty minutes," Tony said, as he left O'Reilly's office. Seamus just sat behind his desk, trying to figure out when he'd lost control of everything and how he was going to get it back.

When Tony arrived at the youth centre, he spotted a black and silver Camaro parked next to Rick's Firebird. He stared at it for a long moment, noticing the silver paint on the Camaro was similar to the paint on Rick's Firebird. He also noticed the faint scratch marks on the Camaro. Too bad he didn't have more than a gut feeling about that car. He was sure he'd find flecks of blue paint which would most likely match Mickey's truck if he looked hard enough, but without probable cause, he couldn't even touch it. He noted the licence number to check on later.

No one was in either car, but Tony could hear a loud argument around the corner. He sighed gustily as he heard Rick's voice over the others. *When will it stop?* the cop wondered, his boots crunching in the gravel as he walked towards the corner. He was pretty sure who was with Rick and his fears were quickly realized as Rick's voice rose even louder.

"Leave me alone, Brian! I don't need the Knights or your life! Get the hell away from me!" Rick shouted. His voice died into an inarticulate groan which sent Tony flying around the corner, shouting for help.

Three of the Knights were busy thrashing Rick while Blade stood by, watching gleefully. Crank had Rick's arms pinned behind his back, while Brain and Pup took turns pummelling their ex-mate. Fortunately, Bob and Carl were just going into the centre and had heard Tony's shout. They thundered up as Tony pulled Crank off Rick's back. Carl managed to drag Pup off while Bob attempted to subdue Brain. Rick collapsed, gasping for air. Tony was torn between helping Rick and trying to hold onto a struggling Crank.

"Split, guys. Move," Blade snarled. Tony flinched silently at the hatred he heard there. No wonder anyone with any sense was scared of him. The glare directed at Tony was enough to make even the veteran cop pause. With violent wrenches, all three fled. Tony waved at Bob and Carl to just let them go as he knelt beside his friend. Rick's breathing was less ragged and Tony was glad to see there was little blood. The sound of squealing tires filled the air as Carl and Bob joined Tony at Rick's side.

"Thought you could fight better than that, kid. I know I've taught you better," Bob said helping Rick to his feet. Carl just grinned as he offered a hand up as well.

"One-on-one, no problem, Coach. When three jump you and only one's smaller than you, it's a little harder. Especially when they fight dirty," Rick said weakly. He straightened up slowly and gently probed a sore spot on his ribs. He smiled at Tony when he realized there was nothing broken, just bruised.

"You ready to talk, Champ?" Tony asked, throwing his arm around Rick's shoulders. At his nod, Tony led the way to their office, not talking. Silence was golden right then. Rick needed a friend, nothing more.

Rick slumped down in his usual chair and just rested. "Now do you believe me about Johnny?" Rick asked after a few moments of tense silence. He stretched out his legs as he felt the beginnings of a cramp. Rick could almost hear Seamus. "Once a Knight, always a Knight, boy." *I will get out*, Rick vowed silently.

Tony was surprised at the question. "I never doubted you, not about that. If I had doubts about other things, well, that should be understandable. But I never doubted anything you said about Johnny and the rest of the Knights. We just can't *prove* it. Yet. It really is your word against his and all the evidence conveniently points at you. I've seen his kind far too often, kiddo. They're mean and vicious. They care nothing about anyone, maybe not even themselves. They don't really even care about the guys in their gangs. It's all about power with them. If just one person can get away, they have no power. No good ever came of guys like Johnny. Now, what did you think about the hearing today, especially finally getting to stay at Glencrest with Nana?" Tony asked suddenly, settling on the edge of the desk and getting down to the business of counselling.

Rick was surprised Tony knew about the rest of the hearing, but realized Owen would've called and told Rick's counsellor, not the cop, what had happened. After some early hesitation, he talked for over an hour. All the slights and insults Michael had heaped on Rick over the years just came pouring out. For the first time, Tony learned about Rick's reaction to when his mom left and how Michael had treated him ever since. It didn't take Tony long to figure out what Blade saw in Rick, besides the raw fighting ability. When Tony explained it to Rick, the boy just laughed.

"I'm serious, Rick. Johnny sees something in you he never had and never will have. Despite how Michael treats you and everything he's ever done and said, you have, well had, a dad, not just a father. Johnny's never had one, from what you've told me, and believe it or not, he resents that. The others? They may have dads around, but all of them seem to resent the fact your dad paid attention to you. Good attention or bad, it doesn't matter," Tony said sadly.

"Now, I have something I want you to think about for a while. Well, two things really, but they're kind of the same. I want you to think about any reason, any fight, any insult you may have said or done, something, anything you can think of that would've made Seamus hate you this much. Can you do that?" Tony asked intently.

"Sure. It might take some time, but I'll try," Rick agreed as he stood up and stretched. Tony chuckled as Rick's shoulders popped and Rick sighed in relief at the sudden release of pressure.

"I'll bet that feels better, don't it? Now the other thing's kind of switching gears for a second, but not really. We've talked about your dad and how you feel about him. We've talked about Johnny and the Knights and we've definitely covered what happened to you while you were in the gang. Now, I've asked you to think about what you may've done to Seamus. Did I miss anything?" Tony asked with another chuckle. Rick didn't answer right away and Tony could see he was thinking hard, trying to fathom where Tony was going with this.

"I don't think so," Rick said as he continued to stretch. He could feel his shoulders tightening up after the fight and he knew he had to be loose before going to training or Bob would make him pay for it.

"What we really need to talk about is what got you into the gang in the first place," Tony said pleasantly. He hadn't moved from the corner and he just smiled as Rick looked up at him. Tony might have been talking about the weather for all the emotion he displayed.

"We've already talked about that, Tony. The way my dad treated me was the reason I joined," Rick protested. He wondered what Tony was getting at. His dad was the only reason Blade got him in the gang, plain and simple.

"That's the reason you stayed with the gang, Rick. But what got you *into* the gang? There had to be something that got Johnny to ask you to join. Some sort of initiation or final approval. Some 'thing' which said to Johnny this kid's good enough be a Knight. So off the top of your head, right now, can you think of anything?" Tony asked quietly. The cop gave no indication he knew about Rick's fight with Colin Falher. That was something Rick would have to think of himself and admit to it. It was the only way Rick would understand the importance of that one fight.

Rick shook his head immediately. "No, Tony. There was nothing. One day I was a free man and the next I was proudly wearing the black and silver of the Knights," Rick insisted.

"Take your time, kiddo. I want you to think back to the days leading up to when you joined the gang. There had to be something that finally convinced Blade. No gang leader just offers the life to someone, no matter how good of a fighter they are. Not without a final initiation. It's called "jumping in." Some gangs do it once someone's joined up. Others do it as the final act *before* asking someone to join. Chill, Rick. Just think about it for a couple of days. We'll talk again later," Tony said and dismissed Rick to the boxing ring. As he watched Rick leave, Tony thought about the fight outside for a couple of minutes, sighed and picked up the phone to call his partner.

"Andrews," Marshall's deep voice came back to Tony.

"Hey, Marsh, it's Fish. Look, I need a favour tomorrow. I need you to head over to the school and talk to the Knights. I got here today and found them beating the crap out of Rick and I want their 'statements'," Tony said blandly. In the background he could hear Seamus bellowing for his partner.

"Just a minute, Seamus," Marshall yelled back. "Is Rick pressing charges?" Marshall wanted to know.

"Only if he's lost what's left of his mind, especially after being blind-sided about his dad today in court. Trust me, he won't press charges. At least he never mentioned it in session today. I just want those four idiots to realize there're a couple of cops watching out for Rick and looking straight at them," Tony said grimly.

"Look, I've gotta go and see what Seamus needs before he comes over here and bellows in my ear. Leave it with me, Fish," Marshall grinned as he heard Tony snort. "Hey, you don't want the damn nickname, don't answer the phone with it, man. Later," Marshall laughed and hung up the phone.

"Idiot," Tony growled good naturedly. He hung up the phone and turned his attention to adding his notes from this session to Rick's file, including everything he had asked Rick to think about. It was up to Rick to remember what Tony already knew about the fight. It was only a matter of time before Tony got it out of the kid.

Rick left his counsellor and headed to the gym. Although he knew Rick was already sore, Bob put him through a gruelling workout. At the end of the session, Rick was dripping sweat, but feeling good. Bob made sure all of his top boys stretched out all the kinks, then sent them home. Rick left eagerly, ready to head to the only place he'd ever called home. He paused at the door and called out a greeting to Tom, who was there training as well. The smaller boy had blossomed under Bob's tutelage and Rick was pleased to know Blade wouldn't find Tom an easy target any more.

Rick arrived back at Glencrest with his music thumping and found an unfamiliar car in the driveway. He pulled up in front of his house and sighed. He clenched the wheel and lowered his head, vowing not to drive off in anger. He knew that wouldn't solve anything, but he was really getting tired of being treated like a criminal. With a soft growl, Rick lifted his head and stared out his window. Standing on the front porch of his house was a uniformed cop and Seamus O'Reilly. If the sour look on the uniformed cop's face was any indication, he wasn't exactly happy about this, either.

"What the hell did I do now, O'Reilly?" Rick growled low in his throat, knowing Seamus would hear him as he climbed out of his car. Nana was nowhere to be seen, but somehow Rick knew she was watching the whole thing.

"Nothing yet, boy and I intend to keep it that way. However, since yer grandmother can't always be here, I've decided ye need a guard. Don't try to ditch him, boy, or ye'll be in jail until ye rot," Seamus growled back.

The judge never ordered this, Rick realized quickly as he reviewed the court order in his head. *What's Seamus really up to?* he wondered. He studied the larger man for a long moment and realized no matter what he decided to do or how much he argued, Seamus was going to put a watch dog on him. Rick figured it was easier to just give in.

"Fine, O'Reilly, we'll do it your way. For now," Rick agreed resignedly. "Does he ride with me when I leave the farm?" Rick asked politely. He clenched his hands tightly and heard the knuckles crack softly. If this didn't end quickly, something was going to happen and the watch dog wasn't going to matter a bit. The uniformed officer tensed as if he could tell something was up.

"Don't get smart with me, boy. 'Course he rides," Seamus snapped. His eyes narrowed as he realized Rick had agreed to a spy way too easily. *What the hell're ye up to, boy?* he wondered.

"Okay, O'Reilly, chill. It was just a question. By the way, tell Jor I'm thinking about her and I'm sorry I wasn't there for her. And if Mick wants, I'll help pay for repainting his truck. Even though I didn't scratch it or run them off the road," Rick said quietly, coming up the stairs to stand right in front of O'Reilly.

Seamus' eyes narrowed as if trying to decide if Rick was serious. Rick stared back, unflinching. It was a game of chicken, and it told the other officer a lot when it was Seamus who dropped his eyes first and stomped down the stairs. He stopped at the bottom and looked back up at Rick. "Since I don't like ye, boy, I'll just ignore that."

As Seamus drove away, Rick just shook his head and went to introduce himself to his new roommate.

Marshall Andrews was as different from Tony as night and day. His hair was wheat blonde, whereas Tony's was midnight black. Marshall's violet blue eyes had deepened to almost black when Seamus had laid out the ground rules to him back at the station and what he was really expected to do. Marshall didn't like it and didn't have a clue as to what he should've done. In reality, he wasn't there to make sure Rick didn't run off – he was there to spy on the kid and find the evidence Tony hadn't. Seamus wanted the boy in jail, one way or the other, legal or not.

Marshall's quick call to Tony before driving out with Seamus had made Tony mad enough to spit nails. From their short conversation, Marshall knew the judge hadn't ordered anything like this and Tony was deathly afraid this could be the one thing which finally pitched Rick off the deep end. Once again, no one knew how to keep this off Seamus' record. One wrong word to the wrong person would land Seamus in jail for any number of reasons, and out of the force, not to mention what could happen to anyone caught in the cross-hairs, especially Rick or Marshall.

Rick examined Marshall even closer while they continued to talk. Marshall was slightly shorter and much stockier than Tony. Rick could see Marshall's muscles rippling under his uniform, whereas Tony's strength was much more subtle. Unknowingly, Marshall flexed and Rick nodded to himself. Seamus had chosen Marshall for one reason only. The cop was physically bigger and hopefully stronger than Rick. Seamus was assuming Marshall would be able to keep Rick under control if Rick ever gave him any trouble, and Rick knew it wasn't possible for anyone to contain him any longer without resorting to potentially lethal methods.

"So Marshall, what did you do to deserve this punishment?" Rick finally asked with a knowing grin.

Marshall laughed. "It's Marsh, Rick, and I'm Fish's – uh, I mean *Tony's* – partner. Inspector O'Reilly just has us looking at Jordan's assault in different ways," Marshall admitted cautiously. Rick's reaction would tell Marshall all he needed to know and Rick didn't disappoint.

Rick snorted. "You're a crappy liar, Marsh. You're a spy, plain and simple," Rick snapped sourly. *I should've known*, Rick fumed. *Seamus wouldn't trust the Pope to say I was innocent.*

"Alright, Rick. Fine. Yeah, I am. Look, I'm not really happy about this, either, but we've gotta make the best of it. Trust me, I don't like to spy on other people, but I figure if you at least knew the real reason I was here, you wouldn't go over the edge. I don't want a repeat of the day you took Fish out, alright? I'd never survive it, and you know it. We're both just gonna have to live with this. Okay? Friends?" Marshall anxiously extended his hand.

"Okay, Marsh. I know this isn't your fault, so I won't blame you for being a spy," Rick said finally, shaking Marshall's hand. Quietly, Marshall sighed with relief. He didn't know what he would've done if Rick hadn't agreed. Tony didn't give him any tips on controlling this kid.

Over the next few minutes, Rick learned about Marshall. He'd been born and raised in the Collingwood area where his father and grandfather had both been farmers. Marshall, despite being the oldest and raised to take over the family farm, didn't want it. It just wasn't in him. Instead, he left that to his younger brother, Zack. For Marshall, it was the justice system all the way. Marshall graduated from high school and then went on to earn a Criminology degree in three years, and was working towards his Master's degree in Advanced Criminology.

From there it was a natural progression for Marshall to become a cop, and he loved it. He had been a cop for nearly seven years and had worked hard to earn his upcoming promotion. He had become Tony's partner five years earlier after transferring in from another precinct and the two had meshed immediately. They seemed to know instinctively what the other was thinking and they were more successful than not, especially when it came to dealing with Collingwood's kids. Everything'd been going smoothly until this dust-up with the Knights. Marshall wondered where things would end. Nothing about this whole thing was making any sense, at least not to him.

Now the best team on the force had been split up and set on two different sides of the same investigation. Neither Tony nor Marshall liked what they were being forced to do, but one didn't question the orders of one's inspector, not if one wanted to keep one's job. He only hoped Rick didn't give him anything to report to Seamus.

As they talked, Rick had led Marshall on a quick tour of the house and had just returned to the kitchen when his phone rang. Glancing at the call display, he smiled. "Hi, Nana," he said, picking up the phone.

"Ready for supper, lad?" Nana asked. "Come on over and bring your 'friend'," Nana said sourly. Rick winced. Nana had definitely seen the confrontation with Seamus and had noticed the other cop hadn't left.

As the pair entered the main house, he introduced Marshall to Martha who directed them to the smaller dining room. While introducing Marshall to Nana and Megan, Rick noticed something wrong right away. Nowhere in the house could he hear Ian's strong gravelly voice, and that troubled him. If Blade knew how easy it was to get to Megan right now, he'd be after her in a heartbeat.

"Hey, cuz. Where's your dad?" Rick asked as he and Marshall sat down.

"Gone for the weekend," Megan said shortly. Nana frowned at Megan's less than impeccable manners around a guest.

"It's okay, Nana," Rick said quietly, glancing at Megan's haughty look. "I, uh… I understand. Let's just eat and then I'll leave." He could tell his cousin wasn't really comfortable with him in the house. She didn't trust him like she once had, and sadly, Rick had no idea how to get her trust back. It hurt almost as much as being disowned by his dad.

"Good idea, Richard," Megan said coldly as Martha served the first course.

Marshall kept his head down and ate quietly. He hated this. He wasn't a spy. This wasn't right.

Nana and Rick kept up a lively conversation with Megan grudgingly throwing in a monosyllabic answer every now and then. They even managed to get Marshall to comment occasionally. While they ate, Marshall noticed Rick wasn't the monster Seamus claimed he was. Nothing he saw during that one meal led Marshall to believe Rick was a troublemaker, and someone who would attack his own girlfriend.

Even though Rick had to know his cousin didn't like him or, for that matter, trust him, Marshall watched as the kid kept trying to talk to her and be friendly. *How could that be the face of a monster?* Marshall wondered as he watched Rick out of the corner of his eye. *What's* wrong *with this picture?*

With supper over, Rick led Marshall back to the guest house. "You might as well come in and be comfortable, man. I'm sure Seamus didn't mean for you to spend your time on the porch. It's cold out and it's just gonna get worse. And I'm pretty sure you're not gonna be pulled any time soon," Rick said sourly as Marshall made a move to stay on the porch. The cop left Rick watching TV as he settled in the spare room. A long conversation with Tony later, Marshall joined Rick, throwing himself on the couch to stretch out, but really didn't see what was on the TV screen.

Rick spent a quiet weekend, mainly with Marshall, who shed his uniform and stuck to worn-out jeans and tee-shirts in a desperate attempt to fit in with the rest of the ranch hands. He was visibly armed, however, as a not-so-subtle reminder to Rick the cop was always on duty. Like Rick would ever forget, but still. Rick helped Frank in the barns and Marshall would lend a hand so he didn't feel like so much like a third wheel, but he could feel the head hand's disgust at having the cop at the ranch. From what Marshall could tell, Frank liked Rick, treating him like a son. Breakfast and lunch were in the guest house but supper was always at the main house at Nana's insistence. Marshall was included, of course, and he couldn't help but notice how strained the meal was, especially between the two cousins.

"Why do you put up with this, Rick?" Marshall asked curiously on Sunday. This supper had been particularly rough. Ian had returned home and had made it perfectly clear he didn't want Rick anywhere on the ranch, much less at the same table as the rest of the family. The argument Nana and Ian had had could be heard all over the house and had left a sour taste in Rick's mouth. He was silent until he and Marshall had returned to the guest house.

"I put up with it just for Nana. Hell, Marsh, I know what everyone thinks, I'm not stupid. 'Cause of the Knights, I'm guilty until proven innocent, instead of the other way around," Rick shrugged philosophically.

Rick turned away, but not before Marshall noticed the faint shine of tears in Rick's eyes. The cop just stared as Rick walked slowly to his room and softly shut the door. It wasn't long before Marshall heard the steady thumping of Rick going at his speed bag. As Marshall fell into an uneasy sleep later, the sound hadn't slowed, even though it had been over two hours. *Lord, help me get through this*, Marshall prayed as he closed his eyes to the faint thump-thump-thump from the other room.

Chapter 23

Monday morning dawned chilly and frosty. Shivering despite his winter jacket, Rick waited on the porch for the twins to arrive at Glencrest, wanting to talk to Jordan just one last time. He'd begged Marshall to turn a blind eye, just this once, so he could see Jordan. *I don't wanna talk to her, Marsh. Seeing her isn't wrong, is it?* Rick had begged. Sighing, the cop agreed, even though it was technically breaking the court order.

Rick knew he couldn't or shouldn't speak to her, but he could at least see her. He needed to know she was okay. No one would tell him how she was doing, so he needed to see for himself everything was fine, because if she wasn't, court order, or no court order, he was going to go back to school to protect her. He melted into the shadows on his porch as Mickey's truck pulled in and parked, music thumping from the speakers.

Mickey got out of his truck and sauntered up to the front door, his boots echoing on the deck. Rick heard Megan greet her boyfriend and, once the door closed behind them, Rick moved swiftly, knowing he was breaking the judge's order, but not really caring. He had to talk to Jordan. Keeping an eye out on the main house, in case Mickey came out sooner than expected, Rick sped over to the truck and rapped on the window, even though he was positive Marshall was watching. He didn't care anymore.

Jordan jumped at the sudden noise. When she saw who was at her window, she rolled it down. "Rick, are you insane? Mick'll kill you!" she whispered, frantically trying to shove him away, even though she wanted to pull him close.

"I don't care, sweets. I had to see you one last time. The judge told me I can't go back to school until they know who did this, but I had to tell you I didn't hit you. I had to make sure you knew," Rick said just as softly. He reached up and gently touched her healing face. Jordan didn't need Rick to tell her he hadn't attacked her. She knew.

If only Daddy could see him now, Jordan thought sadly. *Then he'd understand.* Suddenly, she felt Rick's hand tense, and he dropped to his knees. A fist swung wildly over Rick's head and Jordan could see the fury in Mickey's eyes. Rick rolled away from the truck and jumped to his feet. Mickey followed, his anger and hatred clear. Without thinking about the danger she was putting herself in, Jordan threw open the door and dashed between the two.

"Jordan, move!" Megan screamed from the porch. Nana was rooted in the front door, mute for the first time in Megan's memory.

"Mickey, STOP!" Jordan shouted. She placed herself directly in the path of Mickey's oncoming fist.

Rick didn't hesitate. He knew Mickey couldn't stop the punch. It had too much momentum behind it. If that punch connected, it would shatter Jordan's jaw, and he'd get blamed for it. Springing forward, he knocked her sprawling and Mickey's punch sailed harmlessly overhead. Rick landed on top of Jordan as they sprawled in the dirt. Mickey didn't even seem to notice he had almost flattened his sister and not his "enemy".

"Mickey, enough!" Nana cried, finding her voice and striding from the house.

"You just couldn't wait until we got to school, could you, boy? You had to lie in wait for her here!" Mickey shouted. He stood over Rick, fuming. Megan joined him and stood, glaring at her cousin, hands on her hips.

"Mick, stop it! He only wanted to say good-bye!" Jordan said shrilly as she struggled out from under Rick.

"Good-bye?" Mickey said, puzzled.

"I'm surprised your old man didn't tell you. The case was dismissed, but the judge ordered me out of school. He said Tony couldn't figure out what was going on if I was there 'cuz nothing would change. This way, there's a chance. I just wanted to see her one more time," Rick said wistfully. He hadn't bothered to get up. He figured it'd make Mickey feel better to tower over him.

"Good. Maybe we'll have some peace and quiet," Mickey snarled, and grabbed Jordan's arm to lead her back to the truck.

She wrenched away and ran back to Rick. Kneeling, she kissed him and whispered, "Thank you. I love you."

"You're welcome, sweets. Now go, before he comes and drags you away," Rick encouraged her. One last hug and Jordan stood to walk back to the truck without a backwards glance. Mickey didn't say anything as his sister climbed in, but Jordan knew he was furious.

"What'd that prove, lad?" Nana asked sadly, extending her hand to help him up.

Rick took the offered hand and pulled himself up. He watched the light of his life drive away. His throat tightened, but he didn't look away nor answer Nana until the truck was completely out of sight. He sighed, ran a hand through his hair and turned to face his grandmother. There was pain in his voice, but his face didn't show it.

"I didn't wanna prove anything, Nana. I just wanted to see her one last time. You know Seamus is never gonna lemme near his daughter again, even if I'm cleared," Rick said finally. He turned and walked slowly back to his house. The door closed softly behind him, but to Nana it sounded like the slamming of a jail cell door. *Now what?* she wondered as she strolled to the barn. She needed a long ride to help clear her head.

Mickey was silent all the way to school. He was fuming at Rick's arrogance. He was furious at his own lack of control. But most of all, he was furious with his sister. He couldn't understand why Jordan wouldn't dump Rick. He was trouble and everyone but Jordan could see that.

Jordan, for her part, sat on her side of the truck, silent tears streaming down her face. Megan sat between them, trying not to be noticed. This was one time she knew she had to keep quiet. Neither one was exactly right and neither one was wrong, and Rick was the root of it.

As they pulled into the parking lot, Mickey had to swerve to avoid the black and silver sports car which darted suddenly into his path before parking nearby. As he stared at it, he thought how much it looked like Rick's. *Naw*, he thought, *it was Rick. I know he ran me off the road*. Even though Mickey tried to stop and talk, Jordan didn't wait for the others. She just dashed into the school, ignoring her brother's cries to wait. Mickey finally caught up with her at the entrance to Homeroom.

"Jordan, wait. Please?" Mickey begged, catching her arm. "What's wrong, sis?"

"Let me go, Mick. You're not my brother." With those words, Jordan stumbled to her desk. Tears continued to flow as she tried not to sob out loud.

Stunned and hurt far more than he cared to admit, Mickey followed his sister slowly into Homeroom and sat down in his usual spot beside her. He wasn't really surprised when Jordan got up and moved to a desk on the far side of the room. *She may not think I'm her brother anymore, but I don't care. I will protect her*, Mickey vowed. *Dad's counting on me*. Homeroom seemed to last forever and History and English were no better. By lunch, both Mickey and Jordan were thoroughly miserable, each for very different reasons.

As the three teens headed for the cafeteria, Mickey couldn't handle the silence anymore. With a quick whisper, he sent Megan ahead a bit, knowing he was taking a chance, but he needed to talk to Jordan. Alone. Pulling his sister into an empty hallway, Mickey spoke urgently.

"C'mon, sis. Don't do this to me. I'm sorry. Alright? Please?" Mickey begged.

"No, it's not alright. It's not gonna be alright until I can be with Rick. All he was doing was saying good-bye and you weren't even willing to let him do that. Why can't you and Daddy get it through your thick Irish skulls? I love him! Now, he's not coming back, thanks to you two. Why can't you just leave us alone?" Jordan cried and fled to the cafeteria. Mickey and Megan followed her a moment later, sitting at the far end of the table.

Near the hallway the trio had just left, the Knights couldn't believe what they had just heard. "Confirm what the Irish chick said, Brain. If Moneyman's out, we'll need to change our plans," Blade ordered. Brain nodded and sauntered off to the office.

"Wha'cha thinking, Blade?" Crank wanted to know as he leaned against the wall and crossed his arms.

"Don't know, man. Gonna depend if Moneyman's out fer good or just a couple of days," Blade said, thinking and wondering what was really going on. Pup handed his cousin a pop and a chocolate bar the smaller boy had managed to lift from the canteen. Blade nodded his thanks and downed both, still thinking.

"Ya got some fer me, kid?" Crank growled. With a sneer, the younger boy tossed over another can and bar.

Blade paced restlessly. It didn't take long before he had his knife in his hand and was playing around with it. Crank and Pup both prudently stepped out of Blade's line of sight. They didn't want to be near their leader if he got angry. He was frighteningly accurate with that knife. The three waited in the gloomy hallway until Brain returned.

"He's out fer good!" Brain called gleefully.

"Well, Blade, what's next?" Crank asked yet again.

"Brain?" Blade turned to the thinker in the group. "Gimme somethin' good, man. I wanna break the bastard this time," Blade growled.

"We'll have to lay off the physical stuff, man. That's not gonna work if he's not here," Brain began thoughtfully. He paced for several minutes, his brow furrowed in deep thought. Blade pulled out his knife again and began tossing it up and catching it. He knew better than to bother Brain no matter how impatient he was for answers. Brain whirled suddenly, his eyes lighting up with excitement.

"Okay, here's what we'll do." Brain took fifteen minutes to outline his new plan. "We just gotta pick one and focus on 'er," Brain finished. He preened as Blade nodded his approval.

"Good, Brain. That'll work fine. Find out where he's crashed and then we'll figure out who to go after. Leave 'em fer now," Blade ordered.

The other three split for class, leaving Blade alone in the hall brooding. Brain almost felt sorry for Moneyman. The look of hatred on Blade's face made Brain shiver and he *knew* what was going to happen. Pity Rick didn't. It would almost be more fun to watch Rick worrying about who, when, where and, more importantly, how. He already knew why.

The week was far too long for Mickey. Jordan refused to speak to her brother at home or school and even Megan was feeling the tension between the two. Teachers, parents and other friends tried to get the twins back together, but nothing worked. Jordan was just as stubborn as her brother and father and was determined to hold out until they listened to her. The only thing everyone noticed that week was the lack of attacks on the girls. That just proved Mickey's point. He was certain Jordan would now see things his way. Unfortunately, when he pointed this out to Jordan, she definitely didn't see it his way.

"Sis, I know you hate me, but have you noticed you're not being bothered now that Rick's not here?" Mickey said at lunch one day.

"What's your point?" Jordan asked coldly.

"That *is* my point, sis. Now that Rick isn't here, you aren't getting attacked," Mickey reasoned. Megan nodded in agreement. Neither was prepared for the violence of Jordan's reaction.

She jumped up from the table, sending food and dishes flying. The shattering glass stilled the usually loud cafeteria and everyone turned to stare at their table. "How many times do I have to tell you he didn't do anything?" Jordan shouted.

"Jordan, lower your voice! Everyone's staring," Mickey hissed angrily, embarrassed by his sister's actions.

"What do I care? Rick did NOT attack me! Why can't you believe him? Hell, why can't you trust me? He's at Megan's and nothing's happening to her. Just leave me alone!" Jordan cried and fled from the cafeteria. Stunned, Mickey and Megan followed more slowly.

On the other side of the cafeteria, Blade and Brain finalized their plan, almost dancing with glee at the way things were going now. It took the gang the rest of the week to put their plan together and into action. All Blade could think of was how much fun it was going to be to blame all of this on Rick. *You'll break, little man*, Blade gloated to himself. *You'll beg me to stop.*

By the following Monday, Megan began to relax. She was able to concentrate on school. She was proud of her excellent marks and was determined to stay at the top of her class. She worked just as hard to get Mickey and Jordan talking again, but it didn't take long before she realized that effort was wasted. She decided to leave them alone and prayed they never made her choose between them.

Her good mood was shattered when she got home that Monday night. As always, Martha had gathered the mail for Nana to sort and her grandmother had left Megan's on her desk. Megan found several letters and a couple of magazines waiting for her. She glanced through the letters and smiled since most of them were from her friends back home. One was from the youth center about an upcoming session she thought was interesting, and one had no return address.

The last one puzzled her the most. She turned it over to see where it came from, but there was no stamp and the envelope had been typed out with only her name. It was plain white and looked like every other envelope she'd ever seen. Even more puzzled, she stared at it and wondered who had sent it. With a small letter opener, Megan slit it open and removed the contents. She put the envelope aside and wandered over to her vanity bench, where she sat down to read.

As she skimmed along, she became more and more angry. *What's he thinking, threatening me?* Megan thought furiously. She was prepared to rip up the letter, but as she read it a second time, she paled.

"Hey cuz," it began. "I hope ya had fun at school last week. I know I did. I loved watchin' ya tryin' to get Mickey Mouse and my Jor talkin' again. I laughed every time ya tried. It was priceless. She was so frickin' mad at him. I loved the look of despair on Mickey Mouse's face. I wonder how long it'll take Mickey Mouse to get to ya if I decided to take ya out. It's not like ya live all that far from me. Take yesterday, for example. Ya looked so sweet in yer black jeans and white shirt on that pretty little filly. It would be so easy to get ya off her. I can't wait to put my hands around yer neck and squeeze, just like I did with Jor. Are ya mad yet, Megs? Scared? No? Just remember I can get ya wherever and whenever I want. Sleep well, Megs. I know I will."

It was signed with Rick's stylized M's.

Megan shook. With anger or fear, she didn't really know. Nor did she care. Rick couldn't do this! She called Tony at the station.

"Sorry, miss. Constable Whitefish isn't here right now. He's at the youth centre," the front desk sergeant said.

"Thank you," Megan replied and quickly dialled the youth centre.

"Whitefish," Tony said smoothly once Megan was connected to his office. He was leaning back in his chair waiting for Rick. He wasn't prepared for the frantic phone call from Megan.

"Do something about that punk or my dad will!" Megan cried. The anger was gone and had been replaced by panic. She couldn't control the shaking any more.

"Meg? What's wrong, kiddo?" Tony asked. He sat up quickly at the terror he could hear in her voice and knocked over his coffee. He muttered a curse as he mopped up the mess. *What now?* he fumed silently. *What else am I gonna have to get him out of?*

"He's threatened to strangle me. He talks about watching me at school, when he's not even supposed to be there and yesterday when I was riding Mystique. He clearly described what I was wearing. Tony, he even admitted choking Jordan. I'm beyond scared, Tony. I'm terrified!" Megan's voice shook as she realized what could happen. With her father doing so much travelling for Nana, Megan realized how vulnerable she was. After all, Mickey couldn't stay with her all day, every day.

"Meg, calm down. Please. Keep the letter and envelope. I'll talk to Rick, but you realize he's just gonna deny everything," Tony said casually. His mind worked furiously and he suddenly recalled the phone calls he received from his partner every night.

Marshall reported in every night to Tony before he called in to Seamus. Marshall felt so far out of his league trying to deal with Rick he knew he had to tell Tony about everything that was happening. The kid would spend hours sitting and brooding, or going hard at his speed bag. Marshall noted nothing seemed to help and it was worse if Rick saw Marshall watching. Every night Tony would ask Marshall if he had ever let Rick out of his sight, since Tony knew how sneaky Rick could be. Every night Marshall responded in the same way.

"Hey, partner, I know my job and I don't wanna lose it. The kid's never outta my sight for more than a couple of minutes and that's while he's in the john. Rick only leaves Glencrest when we come to see you. Trust me, Fish," Marshall protested hotly.

Now Tony wondered if his partner was covering for Rick so the kid could slip away to spy on Megan and the twins. Marshall hated being Seamus' spy and Tony wouldn't be surprised if Rick had talked Marshall into letting him do just about anything.

Blast it, boy, are you trying to get yourself locked up for good? Tony swore silently. Then his common sense reasserted itself. Spy or not, unwelcome or not, Marshall wouldn't put his career or his honour on the line. He would've called Tony as soon as he knew Rick was gone. Tony could tell there was stress and tension at times when Marshall called, so he knew his partner wouldn't lie to him.

"Tony? You still there, Tony?" Megan's panicked voice brought Tony back to reality.

"I'm here, Meg. Look, just stay in your room until I can talk to Rick and come and see you. Don't touch the envelope or letter any more than you already have, alright? It'll be okay," Tony reassured her.

"Okay, but Tony, something has to be done. This has to stop! If it isn't Rick, then find out who's doing this. If you don't, I'm sure Seamus will. Or Mickey'll solve all of our problems once I tell him what's going on, but either way, I just can't stand it anymore," Megan said as she finally broke down. Tony tried to soothe her some, but he could tell it wasn't working.

He hung up and stewed, trying to figure out what was going on. He didn't like where his thoughts went. Rick came in a couple of minutes later, laughing with someone who was outside. As soon as Rick turned to face his friend and counsellor, he could tell something had upset Tony and he was about to pay the price for it. *Great, now what?* Rick wondered angrily as he hesitated just inside the door.

"Hey Tony, what's up?" Rick asked. He began to clench his fists when Tony didn't answer right away. Now Rick knew something was really wrong.

"Sit, Rick. I have to talk to you," Tony said finally, motioning to Rick's chair. Rick hesitated a long time, before he finally sat and waited, trying hard to keep his legs from jumping. Tony grimaced. *Man, he's already upset and I haven't even said anything*, Tony mused. *How do I do this without setting him off?* he wondered.

"Rick, I just talked to Megan. She's very upset right now. With you," Tony began after the silence had stretched to several minutes.

"What did 'I' do this time?" Rick sighed. Now that he had an inkling of what was wrong, he took a deep breath and stilled his legs. *I'm not guilty*, he repeated to himself over and over.

"Before I tell you, remember I believe you and I haven't been out to see Meg, nor talked to her in great detail. I will believe you," Tony said soberly.

"Tony, what's happened to Megs?" Rick demanded impatiently. "Is she okay?"

Tony had moved around to perch on his desk and looked at Rick. "Yes and no. She's received a threatening letter. She says it talks about what she did last week at school and what she was wearing yesterday while she was riding. Guess who signed it?" Tony asked pointedly.

Rick sighed gustily. "I don't need to guess. Me. Uncle Ian hates me enough and now this. I'll be lucky if he doesn't kick me off the ranch, no matter what the judge wants. Crap," Rick said dejectedly.

"Yeah. So I need to ask. Did you threaten Megan?" Tony asked. He knew the answer before Rick said it.

"No," Rick denied softly as he struggled not to show any emotion, but Tony could see how much the new accusations hurt. He made a snap call. Rick didn't need him – Rick needed Bob.

"Okay, Champ, head to the gym. No counselling today. You need to "talk" to Bob. I'm gonna head to Glencrest and talk to Meg. Just pray I can convince her you didn't do this. If not, she's probably gonna call Seamus and have you arrested again, and that's if her father doesn't beat her to the punch. Where's Marsh?" Tony asked as they both stood. He motioned for Rick to lead the way out of the office. The one thing Tony failed to mention was Megan's threat to tell Mickey and let him deal with Rick. *Not that Mick'd have any kind of a chance with the Champ, but hey, let him dream,* Tony thought as he opened the door.

"Outside, waiting. We've kinda come to an understanding and I'm not so leery of having him around anymore. Besides, we figured I didn't need two cops to watch me. After all, it's not like I can take a cop down, right, Tony?" Rick grinned back over his shoulder. The accusations rankled, but he knew there was nothing he could do. He had to trust Tony.

"Get out of here, boy!" Tony laughed, miming a swing at Rick's head, who ducked easily and dashed away, laughing. "Watch out for him, Marsh. He's sneaky," Tony said, half serious, half joking. He motioned for his partner to call him later. Marshall nodded to both suggestions and followed his charge off to the gym.

"He's not a bad poker player, either," Marshall called back. "He beats me all the time and you know how good I am."

Tony laughed as he headed to Glencrest. He thought about the "letter" and how it got to the house. *What's going on now?* he wondered. As he pulled into the driveway, he saw Megan just heading back from the barn, dressed for riding. Alone, Tony noted immediately. *Not smart after that threat*, he thought. Tony honked his horn to get her attention.

"Hi, Tony," Megan said wearily as she climbed down from Mystique and tethered her to the porch. Her eyes were red from crying and she was still shaking. She kept glancing over her shoulder as if she expected to be attacked at any moment. Not what Tony wanted to see. Ian was gonna freak.

"Hey, kiddo, how're you holding up? Told your dad yet?" Tony asked, climbing out of his car and giving her a hug. He could feel her shaking and didn't know how to fix any of this.

"No, Tony. Daddy isn't home yet, but I showed it to Nana, and I'm not holding up very well. I'm scared," the young girl said, wiping away fresh tears.

"Easy, lass. We'll get through this. Trust me. Now, where's the letter?" Tony asked as he released her.

"Nana has it in her office," Megan said. She led Tony back into the house and to Nana's office, where she sat behind her mahogany desk, working on one of her many projects. She smiled at Megan and shooed her granddaughter out with the admonition of "Get. Go ride Mystique and don't come back until supper, lass."

"But take someone with you, Meg. Hello, Nana," Tony nodded as Megan slipped out of the room. "She was ready to go riding alone?" Tony asked incredulously.

"She wouldn't take anyone. She's just as stubborn as her cousin and her father. Tony, we're in big trouble. I know Rick didn't send this, but the signature's his," Nana began, as she handed over the letter.

Tony read the letter and then looked at the envelope. Nothing caught his eye. The envelope was plain and everything except the signature was typed. Tony was puzzled. This wasn't like anything Rick had ever been accused of doing before. Even the one note which had been slipped in Megan's book bag weeks earlier was nothing like this. This one was threatening whereas the other one had been written just to annoy her. Something was off, but damned if he could figure out what.

Why would Rick do this? It just puts Meg on guard and really pisses Ian off, Tony wondered. *It serves no purpose. Rick's smarter than this. He wouldn't try to frighten her first. He'd just attack. Like the attack on Jor. Honestly, that's more like Rick than this.* "Something isn't right," Tony muttered as he flopped into a chair.

Nana shook her head. "I've never believed my grandson was behind any of this. Someone's after my boy and I want him or them or whoever found, Tony. You and I both know it's those horrible Knights. Prove it! Do you hear me?" Nana demanded. Tony raised an eyebrow at her anger, knowing she wasn't really that angry at him. Just frustrated at the whole situation.

"Loud and clear, Nana. Please, be careful. Keep an eye on Meg, and by the Creator, do *not* let her go riding by herself. Something's just beginning but I can't figure out what. And do me a favour, if you can. Please make sure Mick doesn't find out, especially from Meg. That boy's Irish temper always gets the better of his common sense," Tony said with a snort. The cop left, taking the letter and envelope with him. He'd fingerprint and analyze things in the morning, but he was positive there'd be nothing to find.

An hour after Tony left, Rick and Marshall pulled into the driveway. For the first time in a very long time, Rick felt relaxed and ready to face the challenges of home. Ian was in the yard with Megan putting Mystique through a difficult dressage workout, under Ian's watchful eye, and even from here, Rick could tell he was angry.

Rick slowed his car carefully and parked in front of the house. He knew not to spook the horse. "Any bets on how long it takes your uncle to jump on you?" Marshall asked dryly. Rick only shook his head. He knew not to take that bet.

"Richard, come here!" Ian snapped from the front porch as Rick climbed out of his car. *Not long at all*, Marshall snorted to himself.

"Yes, sir?" Rick said. *Like I don't know what's about to happen*, Rick thought sourly. He stopped at the bottom of the stairs and waited.

"Tell the truth, boy. Did you threaten my daughter?" Ian demanded after staring at his nephew long enough to make the boy start to fidget.

"No, sir," Rick replied firmly. He waited for the hammer to fall and when it did, it was only what he really expected.

Yeah right. Like he'd admit it if he had, Ian thought sourly and frowned. "Martha'll bring your supper over from now on. Better yet, why don't you learn to cook for yourself? That way we don't have to deal with you at all. I don't want you near the main house. Understand me, boy? Hell, if I had my way, you'd be on the street and to hell with the consequences." Ian dismissed his nephew with a flick of his hand.

"Son, what the hell was that?" Nana demanded from just inside the door as Rick stormed away.

"I'm just trying to keep my daughter safe, Mother, and right now, I don't trust him any further than I could throw him. I know, I know. We can't prove anything, but I just don't want him anywhere near my daughter until Tony finds out what's going on and arrests him," Ian replied over his shoulder as he watched Megan work with Mystique. "Megan, grip tighter with your knees and control her! That part's slow and deliberate," Ian called to his daughter, who flushed and did the manoeuvre over again.

"Ian, why must you and Seamus accuse Rick without any proof? And stop calling him 'boy'. He has a perfectly good name and you'd better start to use it. It's bad enough Seamus does it. I don't want to hear it on this farm ever again. Understood?" Nana asked as she came to stand by her son who nodded resignedly. He stood quietly for a minute then spoke.

"Mother, you've always told me to trust my instincts when it comes to the horses, right?" Ian asked, turning to look at his mother. At Nana's sharp nod, Ian continued, "Well, I'm trusting those same instincts right now with Rick and they tell me he's up to no good. And, if you are right and it's not Rick, then someone's playing a very dangerous game. Someone's gonna be hurt and I just don't want it to be my baby," Ian finished and walked down the stairs to talk to his daughter.

"Stubborn old fool. Just like your father," Nana muttered darkly as she watched Rick and Marshall saunter into their house. Tomorrow she'd make sure Rick had enough food to cook decent meals with. She knew he'd learned a long time ago how to cook, simply out of self-defence.

"Does that happen a lot, Rick?" Marshall wondered aloud as they entered the kitchen. Rick took stock of the food and quickly pulled out the makings for steak and potatoes. Marshall immediately grabbed the potatoes and started to peel them, while Rick worked on a rub for the steaks.

"All the time, Marsh. Remember I'm guilty until proven innocent. Johnny's seen to that," Rick reminded him wryly as they worked.

Later that night, before they sat down for their nightly poker game, Marshall called Tony before he contacted Seamus. "Hey Fish, it's me," Marshall said when Tony picked up.

"Hey, Marsh," Tony said wearily. It had been a long day with nothing to show for it. He was bone-tired of dodging Seamus and fighting for Rick. Ian had called the inspector and Seamus had immediately tried to have Rick hauled in. It took some fancy talking to convince Seamus to let it lie for now.

"You, my friend, sound wasted. What's up?" Marshall asked. He sat at the kitchen table and cracked a pop.

"Rick tell you 'bout the letter 'he' sent?" Tony asked dryly. He had lit some sweet grass and inhaled deeply, trying to relax.

"Yeah. He also denied sending it. Fish, what the hell's going on now? And how long before Seamus demands Rick's head on a platter?" Marshall asked. It hadn't taken long for Rick to earn Marshall's sympathy and respect, once they finally talked and came to an understanding about Marshall's presence. Anyone who had put up with as much crap as that kid had in his short life would not resort to a campaign of psychological terror. He'd come after you straight up.

Tony detailed what had been in the letter. "Somehow I've managed to convince Seamus to leave it for now, so he's not gonna be banging on your door, at least not tonight. I can't guarantee anything about tomorrow. So once again, I have to ask, Marsh. Did you let Rick out of your sight long enough for him to slip up to the school and spy on the girls?" Tony asked with a sigh. He knew the answer before it was even given.

"Dammit, Fish. You know me better than that! You *taught* me better than that! If that kid had been out of my sight for more than five minutes and I couldn't've found him, I would've called you right away. The last thing I want is to be responsible for getting Rick locked up again! I don't think he can handle much more," Marshall snapped, irritated at the constant question. *I know I can't,* Marshal didn't add, but he wondered if Tony actually knew that.

"Easy, Marsh. I knew the answer, but I had to hear you say it again. Okay, next question. Did you see anyone hanging around the ranch who shouldn't be there?" Tony asked curiously.

"If you mean, did I see any of the Knights – nope. Rick would've let me know. He seems to have a sixth sense when it comes to where they are. Take yesterday, for example. Rick wanted to get away, so we drove downtown to eat before counselling. We drove to his favourite pizza joint. Fish, it was weird. He just stared at the building. I was half way to the door before I realized he hadn't even left the car," Marshall said.

"And?" Tony asked. This was interesting. Rick had never mentioned anything like this before.

"I came back, asked him what was wrong and he said, "The Knights're inside. Let's blow." I climbed back in the car, but didn't leave right away. His shoulders were shaking, and he was clenching his fists so tight. I didn't wanna be moving if he needed to bail and hit something, y'know? Anyway, sure enough, a few minutes later, Blade and Crank sauntered out. Trust me, Fish, if the Knights had been here when Rick was, he'd have known and he would have let me know," Marshall said quietly.

"Hell, I don't know anymore, Marsh. Those punks've almost become saints at school and that has me worried. Delaney says they haven't done a bloody thing to the girls, never mind attack anyone else at the school. They're attending classes, behaving themselves. Everyone's waiting for the hammer to fall on either Jor or Meg. I'm missing something in that bloody letter, I just know it," Tony worried. Marshall couldn't believe the strain he heard in Tony's voice.

"Easy, Fish. You're scaring me, man. I've never heard you this stressed before. Meditate tonight. Call on, um, Black Eagle, isn't it? Ask for some help, some guidance. Hell, ask for some sleep. I know you're burning out trying to be friend, counsellor and dad all rolled into one with Rick. That can't be easy day after day. You're the sole investigator on this since Seamus put me here in this prison. It'll come to you once you've reconnected with yourself. Speaking of the boss, I'd better call him," Marshall said dryly as he glanced at the clock.

"Thanks, Marsh, for keeping him as level as you can. I owe you, buddy," Tony said. He reached for another bundle, this time sage, to burn while he prayed to the Creator. He knew he needed help and he didn't have time to go home to visit his shaman.

"We're partners, man. I've got Rick's back and yours. Later," Marshall said, and after hanging up, he dialled Seamus.

"Well, it's about time, Constable," Seamus barked loudly. "Anything?" He made Marshall feel like an errant school boy.

"No, sir. Nothing. I haven't left him alone for more than a couple of minutes and that's in the washroom. He doesn't have time to contact anyone, let alone slip away to spy on the girls at the school. I would've contacted Tony immediately if had he slipped away, I swear to you. Sir, perhaps you could tell me what I am supposed to be looking for?" Marshall finally asked point blank.

"If I have to tell ye, then yer not as ready for that promotion as ye thought ye were," Seamus yelled and slammed down the phone. Marshall hung up and stared at the far wall of the kitchen. *I think I just screwed up*, Marshall thought dryly.

"O'Reilly not too happy with you, Marsh? Lemme guess – no incriminating evidence, no promotion?" Rick drawled. The teen pushed himself away from the door where he'd been leaning. Marshall took a deep breath and tried to still his pounding heart.

Rick chuckled at the look on the cop's face. "Sorry, man. I was coming to get a drink before our game and I couldn't help but overhear what Seamus said. He's very loud on the phone," Rick apologized. He wasn't really sorry, but knew he had to say something. He grabbed a couple of pops and joined Marshall at the table. Silence fell as heavy as the darkness outside.

"Do you know why Seamus hates you so much?" Marshall finally asked. He had finished the first pop and stood to get another. A glance at Rick showed the teen had polished off his first drink just as quickly and had slouched in his chair. As Marshall got another drink for both of them, he noticed Rick's leg twitching. Slightly. The run-in with Ian had made him angry. Marshall prayed the kid could hold it together until he decided to hit the bag.

Rick took a long pull at his pop and shook his head. "Honestly, I don't know. Never have. I think it has to do with the Knights. I've always known O'Reilly didn't like me dating Jordan. But, other than the Knights, I can't think of any real reason and you'd think he'd be happy with me getting out. Funny thing, though. Tony asked me the same question a while back. Specifically, he wanted to know about anything I said or did that would make O'Reilly hate me. Couldn't think of anything then and still can't. Did you hear about the attack on Jor?" Rick asked.

Marshall nodded. "I helped Tony interview her after it happened," he replied quietly. He couldn't get the terror in Jordan's eyes out of his head and didn't think he ever would.

"Then you know O'Reilly told Tony not to look for any other suspects. O'Reilly wanted to pin that attack on me no matter what, just to get me away from her. Evidence or no evidence. Nana laid into him after the case was dismissed. Threatened to report him to his bosses if he didn't lay off me. Tony admitted in open court O'Reilly ordered them to focus on me. He hates me and I don't know why," Rick finished. He stood up, stretched lazily and grabbed the cards from the drawer and dealt the first hand. He lost easily since his mind wasn't really on the game, but on Blade.

Tuesday dawned silent and frosty. Rick rose early and padded to the kitchen. He made his breakfast and ate at the table, enjoying the quiet of the morning. In the summer, at least in town, he would take his breakfast onto the front porch and listen to the neighbourhood wake up. It was too cold to do that at the farm right now, but he knew summer would come soon enough.

Marshall came in about 20 minutes later and fixed himself a cup of coffee and some toast. "What's the plan today, kiddo?" he asked as he settled across from Rick.

"This morning I'm gonna help Frank clean the barn and repair some stalls. My tutor is coming after lunch. I'm thinking of going for a ride, but that depends on how long it takes to get done in the barn. I'm not sure about supper. Ready to get dirty, Marshall?" Rick stood up and brushed the crumbs from his hands. Marshall smiled at Rick's enthusiasm. It took a lot to get him excited about anything these days. More often than not, he was a beaten and defeated boy.

The day passed quickly. Nana came and helped at the barn while Ian was working at the store. The ride was scrubbed when Marshall told a small lie and said he didn't ride. The truth was he rode like the wind, but he knew it would be too tempting for Rick to slip away and ride over to the O'Reilly farm. Once Seamus saw Rick could do that, he'd put a padlock on the barn for sure.

No one noticed anything unusual. No stray visitors. No unusual noises, yet, by the time Megan got home, another mystery letter had appeared. It was placed on her pillow with a single blood red carnation – her favourite flower. Megan knew Martha didn't put it there. Mail was always left on her desk. Now she had someone breaking into her room. What next?

Megan read the newest letter and cried, proving she wasn't as strong as she thought. She dried her eyes and left the letter in her desk drawer. What was the point of telling anyone? It only made Rick bolder. *If it was Rick*, her conscience nagged her. Tony kept pointing that out to her. *Prove it was Rick*. She always fired back at Tony to prove it wasn't Rick. After composing herself, Megan went down to the barn and took Mystique for a long ride. Frank rode along since no one wanted her to be alone.

The letters continued all week, getting more and more detailed. Each one left her in tears, but nothing could make Megan tell anyone about them. What worried Megan was whoever was sending these letters, if it wasn't Rick, seemed to know she was too scared and upset to tell anyone. Her stalker seemed to take great delight in Megan's misery. Thursday's letter really played on that.

Y'know something, Megs? I'm havin' a ton of fun watchin' ya when ya open my letters. Ya struggle not to cry. I know yer upset, and I know yer dad thinks I've only sent ya the one letter. I dream 'bout gettin' my hands on ya. I've been workin' out so snappin' yer neck'll be so easy. It's only gonna get harder fer ya and easier fer me. Keep an eye out behind ya, cuz. Ya never know when I'll be there. Sleep well. I know I will.

Megan felt better Friday when she got home and found no letter waiting for her. She took her time changing into her work clothes. Since she was on the second floor, she didn't bother to pull the drapes. Besides, she loved how the afternoon sun warmed the hardwood floors, even in the winter. She had just finished re-braiding her hair when her private phone rang.

"Hello?" Megan said, cradling the phone against her shoulder as she worked.

"Hey, Megs," a voice said. Megan frowned. It had Rick's lazy drawl, but yet it really didn't sound like Rick. Despite that, it still sounded vaguely familiar.

"Rick? What do you want? Daddy doesn't want you talking to me," Megan said firmly. Her hands shook and she struggled not to drop the phone.

He chuckled evilly. "Like I care what yer old man says. I do whatever I want. Haven't y'all figured that out by now? Y'know something, cuz?" he continued smoothly, "ya looked really cool today. That blue sweater fit really nice. Ya looked so sweet at lunch, snuggled up to Mickey Mouse."

"What were you doing at school, Rick?" Megan demanded. *And why're you never seen by anyone?* she wondered. *How do you hide?*

"I do whatever the hell I want, Megs. Haven't y'all figured that out by now?" he said again. "I like watchin' ya change, cuz. Ya really should close those drapes. Ya never know who's watchin'. Say, Megs, must be damn lonely in that big house without Daddy 'round to protect you," he said harshly. In the background, Megan could hear someone laughing.

"What do you mean, Rick?" Megan whispered, terrified. *Why didn't Daddy tell me he was leaving this morning?* she thought in a panic.

"I watched yer dad load up the SUV today and pull away. He loaded at least one suitcase, so he's gone fer a couple of days at least. It's so damn easy to get into yer room. I've done it before. I've even watched you sleep. It would be so easy to reach down and squeeze....."

Megan slammed the phone down before he could finish and flew to the window. She yanked the drapes closed. This was more than she could handle. She fell across her bed and sobbed into the pillows like her heart was broken. She couldn't take the strain anymore. She cried so hard she didn't hear Nana coming up the stairs until she knocked on the door.

"Megan?" Nana said, opening the door.

"Oh, Nana, I didn't hear you come up," Megan said as she quickly swallowed a sob and dashed away her tears.

"Lass, what's wrong? What's happened to ye?" Nana asked as she gathered her granddaughter to her.

Megan struggled to control her crying but she couldn't. Sobbing, Megan finally told Nana about the phone call and the letters. It felt good to talk about it, but Megan was sure her stalker would know and it would only get worse. Nana let Megan cry herself out and then went to the phone. Pressing a couple of keys, Nana tried to find out the last number that had called.

"Damn," Nana swore softly. Whoever it was, was smart. He had blocked his number from being detected. He knew Nana couldn't prove Rick hadn't called.

"Lass, go. Take Mystique for a long ride. Take Frank," Nana ordered.

It was a very long weekend for Megan. She received two more calls. Nana finally called Tony on Sunday and gave the cop as much information as she had. Tony listened as patiently as he could while Nana ranted and raved over this new attack. Finally, even Tony's legendary patience snapped.

"Look, Nana, I know everything points to Rick, but there're no prints on the letters. The calls sound like Rick, but yet they don't. We can't trace the calls, and Rick denies everything. So what the hell do you want me to do? Hound him like Seamus? Stop believing in him? Abandon him like Meg and Mick have? Drive him away like Seamus is trying to do with Jor?" Tony demanded.

He sighed and looked down at his hands while he waited for Nana to answer. He was holding an eagle feather his shaman had blessed and given to him the last time he had returned home looking for some help. The shaman said it would give him guidance and strength. So far, Tony wasn't getting much of either.

He got up and paced the room. He was upset at these latest attacks and getting very frustrated at the apparent frame-up of Rick. He was trying to do some investigating on his own time into the Knights, but nothing was panning out. Now, knowing what was going on, the cop was struggling to decide if he reported the threats to Seamus or just keep going on his own. Since the letters always arrived in the afternoon and the calls were being made right after school, Rick was either in counselling or in the ring, and under the watchful eyes of one cop or the other. Yet, Tony knew Rick would ultimately be blamed. It was beginning to be very frustrating.

Nana's shoulders slumped in defeat. She was sitting behind her large mahogany desk at the ranch. She looked around the room at the bookshelves as she brooded over her family. *What a mess*, she thought as she continued to stare at her library. Her collection of hardcover books ranged from Shakespeare to modern classics, all bound in leather and cared for by a retired librarian and a rare book dealer. The warm sunlight poured through the window making everything glow with a soft haze.

Tony said nothing as he finally sat across from Nana. Martha had brought some tea when Tony had arrived, but neither one drank. "Well, Nana?" Tony asked after a few minutes of silence. "What do you want me to do?" he asked again.

"I don't know, Tony. What does Rick say when you ask him?" Nana asked, curious.

"He denies everything, of course, but if I ask him who he thinks is doing this, he just clams up," Tony said quietly. "It's like the old gang loyalty's kicking in. He refuses to talk about who's behind this, if he really knows. We argue about it every session." Tony just shook his head.

"Who do you think is doing this?" Nana demanded. "You must have some idea,"

"I have my suspicions it's the gang. But I can't *prove* anything. That's the real problem, Nana. Nothing points to anyone else. Everything points to Rick. I'm getting damn tired of defending him, but I can't stop now. Someone has to stand up for him, and by the Creator, that's gonna be me! Now, Nana, I have a different question for you," Tony continued quietly. He always felt he had to be quiet in Nana's office since it reminded him of a library, and you never raised your voice in a library, no matter how angry you got.

"Something's wrong, Tony. What do you need to know?" Nana asked bluntly. She leaned back in her office chair and tapped her fingers on the arms. She hated it when someone beat around the bush.

"Do you know Carlos Mendez?" Tony asked.

"I've never heard the name before. Why do you ask?" Nana replied.

"Has Michael ever asked you for money without telling you why he needed it?" Tony asked instead of replying.

"Heavens, all the time. He claimed it was for bills he was behind on," Nana said. "What's wrong, Tony? Get to the point," Nana demanded.

"You could say Michael was behind on some bills. We think he's several *thousands* of dollars in debt to Mendez. Maybe even hundreds of thousands. Mendez's a bookie. Do you know what that is? No? He places bets on sporting events for gamblers at a high rate of repayment and it's very illegal. He's normally not nice to people who get behind on paying their debts," Tony said finally.

"Amazingly enough, for some reason, he has yet to lay a finger on Michael. As far into debt as Michael is, he should be dead by now," Tony finished bluntly. Nana was shocked.

"Is there any danger to my family from this Mendez character?" Nana demanded.

"We don't think so. That's not usually the way Mendez works, but I thought you should know anyway," Tony shrugged philosophically.

"Is there any chance that Mendez is the one behind the letters and calls?" Nana wondered.

Tony shook his head immediately. "Compared to what Mendez's known to do, the letters and calls are very childish. No, that's someone Rick's age. And before you say anything, Nana, trust me. I will find out who's doing this, no matter how long it takes me," Tony swore as he left.

Chapter 24

By Remembrance Day, Megan was tired of the constant barrage of letters and calls. She struggled to keep everything quiet, since she really didn't want Mickey and Rick to fight, and she knew her boyfriend would find some way of confronting her cousin. She woke that morning to find it had snowed again, just as it had almost every night over the past week. It was clear and cool, but not cold. The sun was shining and the snow sparkled as if it had been covered in tiny diamonds. *Time for some exercise,* Megan thought.

She bounced out of bed, took a quick shower, dried and braided her hair then dressed warmly. She grabbed her sunglasses to cut the glare as she left to join her dad and Nana in the breakfast nook. Megan kissed each of them on the cheek and sat down in her usual spot at the table. After grabbing toast, milk, juice and some fruit, Megan began to eat enthusiastically, drawing smiles from the two adults.

"Was it something we said, lass?" Ian chuckled mildly.

"No, Daddy. Why?" Megan replied, puzzled.

"No reason, lass. You're just eating like your pants're on fire, that's all," Ian smiled. It was good to see her happy again.

Megan giggled, but slowed down. "Sorry, Daddy. I'm thinking of going skiing through the woods. I've been feeling a little down and I need to clear my head," Megan explained. The threats of the last week seemed so very far away.

"Just remember to keep an eye out behind you and be back before dark," Ian warned. No one really thought the danger would be brought to the house, so no one thought to insist someone go with the teen. She couldn't go as far on her skis as she could on her horse, after all.

"I need you to do some work with the new show jumpers first, lass. Your father and I need to finish evaluating them," Nana said. "Please?" she added when Megan's face fell.

After breakfast, all three went to the barn where the two newest members of Nana's stable waited outside. Under Nana's watchful eye, Megan put each horse through their paces on a lunging rein. After Nana and Ian were happy with what they saw, the horses were groomed and loaded into a horse trailer to be taken to a nearby farm which had an indoor arena. There they would begin their training with Nana's most trusted trainers.

"Mother, when're *we* building an indoor arena?" Ian wondered as all three returned to the house for lunch.

"In the spring, son. I've been without one for too long," Nana said.

After a quick lunch, Megan dressed warmly and pulled her cross-country skis out of the storage shed near the barn. She strapped the skis on and, with a wave to Frank and Ian, strode off, her father's warning to watch out still ringing in her head.

She flowed effortlessly into the woods behind the barn. The silence was broken only by the sound of Megan's skis swishing through the snow and the occasional chickadee calling. As she skied, Megan noticed a couple of deer grazing in a small meadow, but at the sound of her approach, the doe and her fawn dashed into the underbrush and were quickly gone from view.

As Megan travelled deeper into the woods, she noticed the sudden silence, unnatural in the woods. There were no longer winter birds chirping or calling in the trees. Even the wind seemed to hold its breath. She paused at the far side of a second meadow to rest. She looked around and, in the gloom of the far trees, she thought she saw someone staring at her. Megan shook her head. "Great. I've become paranoid," she muttered out loud. The sound of her voice seemed unusually loud in the deafening silence.

Megan resumed her course and began to circle back towards the farm. Without warning, she heard several twigs snap behind her. The sound was close enough and sudden enough to make Megan panic. She began to ski faster, desperate to escape her pursuers.

Someone was chasing her, Megan was positive of that. Megan risked a glance behind her and saw a shadowy figure running behind her, driving her towards something. As Megan glanced behind her again, something caught her across the chest and knocked her flat.

Megan landed hard, forcing the air out of her lungs. She gasped as she struggled to catch her breath. Something told her to get back on her feet and quickly, too. She kicked off her skis and was on her knees when the first blow fell. It was a solid kick to her ribs. Once again, Megan's breath was gone. More blows fell on her back, legs and ribs. It was like someone was trying to kick her to death. Finally, after what felt like an eternity, the attack stopped, leaving Megan gasping on the ground. She struggled to breathe. Every icy breath was a painful stab to her lungs and she prayed the attack was over.

No such luck. Megan was dragged to her feet and shoved up against a large tree. Her gloves were lying on the ground along with her hat and sunglasses. The sun glaring off the snow made her squint and her eyes water. She could feel the rough bark on her back, even through her coat, as her attacker wrenched her arms back and tied them behind the tree. Her shoulders were screaming with pain and Megan was no longer sure what caused her eyes to water more, the pain from the sun or the pain from her shoulders.

No matter which way Megan wrenched her head, though, she couldn't see anyone. She could hear voices behind her, laughing, encouraging the attacker to finish it. She finally had enough breath to scream for help. Once.

A solid cuff across her head brought further tears to her eyes and choked off the scream. Another blow fell, knocking Megan's head back into the tree, dazing her. Into her blurred vision swam a young man about 17. To Megan's battered brain, he was the same height and weight as Rick. She saw a black and silver jacket and there was a bandana covering the lower part of his face which struck Megan as odd. She knew damn well that stupid bandana was supposed to be over Rick's hair, not his face. But it was the piercing blue eyes above the bandana that caught Megan's attention. They were the same as her cousin's.

More blows rained down. The ropes which held her hands prevented her from falling completely to the ground, making it easy for her attacker to land blow after agonizing blow. Finally, her battered body could take no more and she slumped, consciousness fading fast.

"Rick, please," she begged softly. "Please." Only one thought skittered across her bruised mind. *After all of the threats, why hadn't she brought someone with her?*

One final blow across the back of her head sent Megan spiralling down into darkness. As she slipped away, Megan heard the sound of crazed laughter and, just as she faded away completely, she thought she heard the sounds of another fight. Finally she knew no more. Her battered body hung limply from the ropes while her bruised and bloody head lolled against her chest.

As Megan hung against that tree, Rick was wandering through the same woods. He, like Megan, was trying to clear his head. He had to make a choice before someone got killed. Sitting in the house, going crazy from being spied on, wasn't helping him think. He had slipped away by telling Marshall he was taking a long soak. Rick then eased out of the back window of his bedroom, while Marshall was talking on the phone. He had even run the bath to make things seem right.

Rick felt bad as he slipped past the barn, hushing Mystique and Cherokee. He knew Marshall would be in trouble for letting him escape, but Rick couldn't help that. *Oh well,* Rick shrugged philosophically as he stomped through the woods. *I need the space. I can't think in there anymore. It's not home – it might as well be jail.* He relished the silence which reigned in the woods. There were no birds chirping and most of the animals were hibernating or gone. It was oddly silent and yet somehow the silence still seemed normal.

On the edge of a meadow, Rick came across a fallen log. Just as he sat down, he heard a sudden crashing through the bushes. *Must be a startled deer*, Rick thought. He returned to thinking about his problem; his choices were simple, but he didn't know which way to go.

Feeling the cold, he was startled to find he'd been on that log for over an hour and a half. He stood up and stretched. He had done some serious thinking and had reached a very hard decision, one no one, especially Tony, would like. It was both right and wrong, but he'd have to live with it even though it wasn't the best idea he'd ever had in his life.

He continued to toss around different ideas in his head as he meandered back towards the farm. His mind may not have been on the world around him, but his ears definitely were. He stopped when he realized the silence was no longer natural. It was deafening. Glancing at the darkening sky, Rick proceeded quietly through the woods. Something was clearly wrong.

Meanwhile, Ian was in a panic at Glencrest. Megan hadn't returned yet and she'd been gone for over four hours. After searching the barns and the woods right around the farm, Ian broke down and called Tony.

"Afternoon, Ian. What's up?" the young cop asked lightly. He was sprawled on his couch catching the end of an entertaining hockey game, after being at the cenotaph for Remembrance Day services. At Ian's next words, though, Tony bolted upright, sending his remote flying.

"Megan's missing. She went skiing about one this afternoon and she's not back yet," Ian began tersely.

"You let her go out alone? After the threats?" Tony demanded incredulously. He almost asked Ian if he was nuts, but Ian was upset enough.

"Don't beat me up any more than I already have, Tony. I can't believe I let her go alone. What the hell was I thinking? How stupid could I be?" Ian cried. Tony calmed Ian down and promised to drive out immediately. He had hardly hung up the phone when it shrilled again.

"Tony, he's gone!" Marshall cried before Tony could even say hello.

"What do you mean? Rick's gone?" Tony demanded. His heart sunk. He prayed Rick was long gone, but he knew he wasn't. Rick would've said good-bye.

"He told me he was gonna take a bath. I never noticed how long he hadn't been around until just a few minutes ago. Tony, he's been gone for at least two hours. O'Reilly's gonna kill me!" Marshall babbled.

Tony's mind worked furiously. He knew Rick was probably innocent, but if Ian or Seamus found out Rick had been missing for any part of the time Megan was, especially after the way Megan had been threatened, the kid's name would be mud. *Gimme strength*, Tony prayed.

"Did he take his car?" Tony asked.

"No. It's still out front," Marshall replied after taking a quick look.

"Good. Then he's not far. Does Ian know?" Tony pressed.

"Not that I know of," Marshall replied, calming slightly as he talked to his partner.

"Keep it that way, 'cause Meg's missing too. I'm on my way." Tony hung up and dashed out to his car. All the way to Glencrest, Tony was thinking in two directions. Darkness was falling quickly and the temperature was dropping, making speed vital. The longer Megan was missing, the greater danger she was in from hypothermia. On the other hand, though, the longer she stayed missing, the better it was for Rick. That way, Tony stood a greater chance of finding his young friend before anyone else did. Tony drove faster.

As Tony slid into the driveway, he saw Ian had the farm hands organized into two search parties. Everyone was dressed warmly and carried powerful flashlights. Ian had two sleds loaded with blankets and hot chocolate.

"Ready, Ian?" Tony asked as he strode up to the group. He nodded a greeting to Marshall, who offered to stay behind in case Megan came home on her own.

Ian nodded. "Frank's taking one group around the pond to the west, since that's usually the way she comes home. You and I'll follow her tracks around the barn to the east."

"Let's go. The longer we take, the more trouble Meg may be in," Tony said and winced at his choice of words. *Please lemme be wrong about this*, he thought.

Rick had continued his trek carefully in the silent woods, unaware Megan was missing, but knowing something was wrong. Unaware, that is, until he heard the strangled scream of someone just ahead. What was worse was the sudden silence which followed. Swearing, Rick began to run as fast as his winter boots would allow, knowing time was running out for someone.

He burst onto a scene from his worst nightmare. Megan hung from a tree while someone wearing what Rick thought was his Knight's jacket pummelled her. As Rick stood there, frozen in disbelief, the final blow fell across Megan's head. She slumped, unconscious, her battered body hanging limply by the ropes which held her to the tree.

He launched himself at her attacker, while someone else laughed just out of sight. Rick knew that laugh as he continued to struggle with Megan's attacker. The bulky jacket he wore restricted his movements, but at least it protected him from the blows that were thrown in his direction. At the sound of Megan's name being called in the near distance, a sucker punch to Rick's head sent him flying, slightly dazed, and the attackers made a clean getaway.

Rick hesitated before he got up. Again, he had a choice and neither option was good. The right choice would be to help Megan down from the tree. Unfortunately, that'd mean he'd probably be found at the scene and then, of course, he'd be accused of beating her. The other choice would be to leave now and try to sneak back into his house. He dismissed that one almost immediately, even though he knew that by now Marshall would've reported him missing and O'Reilly would probably come and arrest him personally.

Either way, Rick was in trouble. Sighing, Rick knew he couldn't just leave Megan hanging there. No matter how she felt about him, Rick cared about his cousin. She had to have been missed at home by now. *But where was everyone?* Who knew how much longer it would be before the searchers found her?

Rick approached the tree. He could see the brutality of the attack. Megan's face was swollen and bloody, not to mention what damage must have been done to her shoulders to be wrenched back like that. He shook his head. The Knights had done their work well and Rick swore they'd all pay and pay dearly. Based on what he saw, they obviously didn't want Megan talking any time soon. He pulled out his knife and carefully cut the ropes holding Megan. Before he could catch his cousin, she landed in a heap at the base of the tree.

Rick rolled Megan over and made sure she was breathing. He'd just stood up and was getting ready to step back from her when Ian and Tony crashed through the brush and onto the scene.

Chapter 25

Tony and Ian stared across the silent meadow at Rick. Rick just stared back. He knew what they were thinking. Ian's face was contorted with rage and hatred. Tony was just disappointed, looking at Rick like he was an errant son. Rick could almost hear Tony's disbelief in what he was seeing. Rick just sighed in resignation. No one would believe him this time. *So much for my freedom*, Rick sighed quietly. In the silence, he swore he heard someone snickering.

"I didn't do this, Uncle Ian," Rick said quietly as he backed away from his cousin's lifeless body. "Believe me, I did *not* do this."

"Megan!" Ian cried. He dashed over to his daughter. As he held her, Ian could see the amount of damage to her face. Even Tony couldn't believe the savagery of the attack. Yet, from where he stood, it looked like mainly cuts and bruises.

"What'd she ever do to you, boy?" Ian shouted. He dropped Megan's head back into the snow and rushed at Rick.

Rick just stood there. He let his uncle grab him and shove him against a tree. He knew letting his uncle get mad at him was the only way Ian would feel better. Tony, watching them out of the corner of his eye, directed the other members of the search party to wrap Megan in the blankets and secure her to the sled. As they worked, several of them muttered about no good hoodlums and Tony reprimanded them sharply. He didn't want Rick to hear that – it would only set the teen off even more. Once Megan was secure and the rest of the team had been sent back to the farm, Tony turned his attention back to Ian and Rick.

Ian still had Rick pinned against the tree with one arm shoved against his throat. Tony saw Rick wasn't struggling (although his face was turning a spectacular shade of purple), and every time Ian asked him why, Rick would croak "I didn't do it." It was only when Tony saw Ian pull back to take a swing at his nephew that he finally intervened.

"Ian, stop it!" Tony growled and pulled at Ian's arm.

"He attacked my baby!" Ian shouted and shoved his arm tighter against Rick's throat, causing Rick's vision to fade. Rick batted weakly at his uncle's arm, but anger made Ian stronger. Rick's arms dropped to his sides as he struggled to maintain consciousness.

"Lemme deal with him. Go back and take care of your daughter," Tony ordered as he realized Rick was about to pass out.

Ian finally let Rick go. Rick dropped to his knees, coughing, gasping and shaking his head, trying to get his wind back and clear his vision. Ian just glared at him in disgust and strode off. Tony stood over Rick for a long time, then offered a hand to help him up. Once he was finally on his feet, Rick looked around. Any evidence that had been there was probably long gone, beaten into the snow. Tony followed his glance and realized the only things left were Megan's skis and the rope used to tie her to the tree. What Tony could gather up, he did.

A soft cry in the distance made Tony look up. In the gloom, somehow, he saw Black Eagle. He was circling slowly, crying almost sadly. *Sorry, old friend. I just might not get him outta this one,* Tony said softly. *Give us both strength and everyone else patience.*

Then, silently, Tony led Rick back to the farm. All the way, Rick wished Tony would just talk to him. The silent treatment from someone who was supposed to be his friend hurt more than Rick wanted to admit. He could feel Tony's anger and frustration, and knew Tony was upset, to say the least. Rick just wasn't sure if it was because of him sneaking away from Marshall or because of what he'd found in the woods. *I'm sorry,* Rick wanted to say, but somehow the words wouldn't come out.

By the time the two of them arrived back at Glencrest, cold, wet and miserable, it was obvious Ian had called both the ambulance and O'Reilly, since Seamus was standing in the driveway, yelling at Marshall like he was a teenage shoplifter who had been caught at the local mall, instead of in class. The paramedics had finished stabilizing Megan and were loading her in the back of the ambulance. Ian climbed in beside his daughter while Nana climbed into her truck to follow them.

"Why did ye let him escape, Constable? Don't ye want that promotion anymore?" Seamus shouted. The older cop was furious and Rick swore he could see steam coming out of Seamus' ears. He would have giggled if the whole situation hadn't been so tense.

Marshall paled under the constant abuse, but did nothing to defend himself. Tony finally stepped forward. He couldn't bear to see his partner getting yelled at. "Look, Inspector, Marsh wasn't here at a judge's order. You chose to lock him up here. Rick didn't have to clear anything with him. He only put up with it because he thought it'd make you and Ian feel better. If Rick chose to leave for a while, it was because he should've been allowed to do so from the start. Don't blame Marshall," Tony defended his friend.

Rick tried to remain out of Seamus' sight, but Seamus' roving eyes finally found him.

"C'mere, boy!" Seamus yelled. *Once, just once, couldn't he just speak to him instead of yell?* Tony wondered idly. He stood beside Rick, waiting, knowing what he was going to have to do and dreading it. The longer it took for Seamus to order Rick to be arrested, the harder it was for Tony to believe what his eyes had seen. His common sense had finally re-asserted itself and Tony knew deep down Rick had nothing more to do with Megan's attack than with Jordan's. The kid just had some incredibly bad luck to be found at a second crime scene over a second beaten and unconscious girl.

Rick stiffened. He knew no matter what he said, Seamus wouldn't believe him. So he chose to say nothing. Nor did he move. Seamus' face turned even redder, if that was possible.

"I told ye to come here, boy!" Seamus roared.

"No. I'm not gonna talk to anyone but Tony," Rick said softly. He turned to Tony. *Help me,* Rick wanted to say.

The cop hesitated. He was so unsure of what he should do. Every instinct Tony had said Rick didn't do anything, but instinct didn't cut it in a court of law. Evidence did and the evidence, he was certain, was going to point right at Rick. Tony sighed loudly in the sudden silence. He didn't have to say how much he hated this – everyone knew and everyone except Seamus understood. He motioned for Rick to turn around and slipped the cuffs on. Quietly, Tony reminded Rick of his rights and led the boy to his car.

After securing Rick in the back seat with a promise they'd talk as soon as they got going, Tony turned to Marshall and said, "Seal his house, Marsh, and I'll send the team over to check it and the clearing we found Megan in for what evidence we can find once I get Rick back to the station. Oh, and Inspector?" Tony said almost as an afterthought.

"What?" Seamus growled again. Tony smiled grimly. Seamus was acting like an old bulldog. *All bark and no bite,* Tony thought.

"Knowing how you feel about this suspect, I strongly advise you let others who are not so influenced by personal feelings handle this investigation," Tony suggested blandly. Seamus just nodded, his arms folded across his barrel chest.

Tony climbed into his car and took off for the station, trying to figure out what to do. "Off the record, son, why'd you slip away?" Tony finally asked. He couldn't stand seeing the hurt in Rick's eyes. He knew he should've said something before now, but the memory of Megan lying in the snow at Rick's feet wouldn't go away, and made it impossible to talk to Rick until Tony'd calmed down somewhat.

"I was tired, Tony," Rick replied shortly.

"Next time take a nap!" Tony snapped back.

"Stuff it, Tony, alright? I was tired of being stared at. I was tired of being spied on. That's what Marsh was really doing there – spying for O'Reilly. As if you didn't know, being his partner and all. O'Reilly even threatened to take away Marsh's promotion if he didn't find some incriminating evidence. How could O'Reilly do that, Tony? It's not Marsh's fault he couldn't find what doesn't exist. He's gonna lose his promotion because of that and it's not fair," Rick groused. He took a couple of deep breaths before he continued.

"Dammit, Tony, O'Reilly's made my home a prison cell! That house was supposed to be a place where I could go and get away from everything. A place to leave my problems behind and he took that away from me, too. Now I really have nothing," Rick snarled.

"I was tired of fighting," Rick continued bitterly, "both with Johnny and my family. I'm not allowed at Nana's because Uncle Ian doesn't want me there. He doesn't care that Nana does. What he says, goes, just like with O'Reilly. Do you have any idea how lonely that is? Do you?" Rick demanded hotly. He brushed angrily at the tears which had started to fall. He suddenly felt completely alone.

"No, Rick, I don't. I've no idea. None. Even at its worst on the reserve, I still had family who believed in me and loved me. Even those who hated me trusted me. They always believed I did what I did because it was right. If there was no one else, my elders and my shaman were always there. They'd always listen when I needed someone to talk to. You don't even have *that*. You have no one left to lean on except Nana, Bob and me and it's pretty damn hard to talk to Nana when you're banned from the main house," Tony said softly. His heart went out to the scared teen in his back seat. Like Marshall, Tony was beginning to wonder how much more Rick could handle before he broke completely.

"I was so damned tired of it all, Tony, and I needed a break. I needed to get out of my prison, so I went for a walk. To think. To clear my head. I just wanted to spend some time alone. Is that too much to ask?" Rick cried hoarsely.

Tony winced at the pain in the teen's voice. "For most people, Rick, no, it's not too much to ask. For you, it's impossible to have," Tony replied.

Rick fell silent as Tony navigated the traffic. After a few minutes, Rick finally asked, softly, "Know what I decided while I was walking, Tony?"

Tony didn't answer right away. He had pulled into the alley behind the station and wasn't at all surprised to see Owen waiting for him with Nana by his side. Tony knew this wasn't going to be an easy interrogation. *Give me strength,* Tony prayed for the millionth time since meeting Rick. *Someone, please, get both of us through this.*

"Tony?" Rick asked again softly. The cop came around to let the youngster out.

"Tell me inside, okay, kiddo?" Tony replied and squeezed Rick's shoulder. Rick nodded and let the cop lead the way to the same break room he held their last interrogation in.

"Make yourself at home, Nana," Rick said flatly, nodding toward the couches.

"Okay, Rick, talk to me. What'd you decide while on your walk?" Tony asked after removing the handcuffs and sitting across from the teenager.

Rick lowered his head. *Tony's gonna be so mad at me,* Rick realized suddenly. *He's tried so hard to help me. But I can't do this anymore.* Rick stared at his hands on the scarred table top for the longest time. He was struggling to get the words to come out of his mouth.

"Rick?" Tony said softly. He didn't like the sudden dead feeling in his stomach. Something told him he wasn't going to like what he heard.

"I decided I'd be better off with Johnny," Rick whispered hoarsely. He lowered his head all the way to the table and his shoulders shook with almost silent sobs. He knew he had just let Tony and Jordan down. The worst part was Blade was right.

He was a Knight for life.

Chapter 26

Tony was stunned at Rick's admission. He'd expected anything but that. But the more he thought about what Rick was going through, the more Tony understood. Every time Rick turned around, he was getting beat down, not physically, but mentally and emotionally, and Rick just couldn't handle it any more. It was the worst case of abuse Tony had ever seen and Tony had seen quite a few, both on and off of the reserve.

Nothing Rick tried to do would ever make him acceptable to Seamus, especially after the fight Seamus swore had happened three years ago. Rick had no support anymore except for Tony and Bob, since Seamus was doing his level best to keep Jordan away from Rick. The only family who believed him anymore was Nana, and Tony figured Ian believed Rick had somehow manipulated his grandmother into giving into him. Michael didn't want him. Rick didn't know where his mother was and no one could convince Nelson to come home and take care of his little brother. Nelson was too busy running from his own past.

The worst part was the lack of any support from kids his own age. Seamus had built such a huge wall between Rick, Jordan and the inspector it'd take ages to break it down, if ever. Mickey never really liked nor trusted Rick from the first time the two boys had met, and if Rick really had beaten up Mickey's best friend to get Michael's attention, then there was nothing for the trust to build on. Megan would never feel safe around her cousin again, even if he was innocent. Once again, Tony realized how screwed up Rick really was. But for now, he had to convince Rick the decision he was thinking of making was wrong. Dead wrong.

"Rick, son, look at me. You know that's not the answer. You know that. Yeah, sure, you might stop the attacks and the girls *might* be safe. Yeah, you'd have those four guys who would fight for you and with you. Yes, they'd be your 'family'. Problem is, if you're back in the gang, you'd be no closer to getting Jor and you'd still be in trouble with Delaney and Seamus.

"You'd be fighting alright, but you wouldn't be the pride of the youth centre's boxing club. Man, Coach is so proud of you! You should hear him talk about you! He brags every chance he gets and he doesn't care what you did before you came to the club. Rick, you'd still be so angry, dangerously angry. You'd be that coiled cobra I met a couple of months ago, and frankly, by now you'd've probably killed someone with your reactions. You'd be in so much trouble you wouldn't see the outside of a jail cell until you were a little old man," Tony said intensely.

Rick didn't even react. Tony knew he wasn't getting through to him and was suddenly desperate for some kind of response. He hesitated. Maybe it was finally time for Tony to admit to Rick how important the teen was to him. "Rick, if all this hadn't happened, right from the start, you'd never have been assigned to me, and I'd be working with some other kid. There would've been no counselling, no teaching, no learning from each other and definitely no friendship. I never would've had the chance to get to know you. Rick, believe this, if you believe nothing else. You're more like a little brother than a counselling assignment to me now. I've learned a lot about helping kids from talking to you and that's made me a better person and an even better cop. You're important to me and I'd be devastated if you went back to the Knights," Tony said with conviction.

Rick sobbed even harder as he listened to Tony's admission. He finally admitted to himself how much Tony had given up for him and nothing Rick could say or do would ever get that back. Personal relationships had been sacrificed for him and it hurt to know that. For a long time, the only sound was Rick and his heart-wrenching sobs.

Tony didn't know what else to do. It had cost him a lot to admit Rick was important to him and Rick didn't even seem to care. Yet somehow he had to get Rick to believe in himself again or everything they'd worked so hard on in the last couple of months would be wasted.

Finally, Nana couldn't stand hearing her grandson cry anymore. She came over to the table and sat down. "Rick, lad, look at me," Nana commanded softly. Rick lifted his tear-streaked face and looked at his grandmother. She reached over and wiped away his tears, like she'd done so many times when he was younger.

"Look, lad, I should've stood up to Seamus when he put that guard on you. Marshall's a nice guy and all, but there's always someone at the ranch even when your uncle Ian and I aren't. You weren't under house arrest. You should've been free to move around. That house was supposed to be a haven for you, not a cell. I'm just as much to blame as anyone for what happened today. I'm sorry, lad," Nana finished quietly. Rick shook his head quickly as if trying to deny what his grandmother had said.

"We've all made mistakes lately, Nana," Tony pointed out. "No one's hands're clean anymore. Look, Rick, we've gotta go up in a few minutes, but not until you've spent some time with Owen. Go over your story with him before I get back. But I want you to think about something before we go."

"What, bro?" Rick gulped back his tears and stared up at the only person he could call a friend, father and brother. Tony smiled slightly as Rick managed to acknowledge what Tony had admitted.

"By even *thinking* about returning to the Knights, Johnny's won. Do you really want that?" Tony waved Nana out of the room with him so Rick could talk with Owen.

"Nana, how's Meg?" Tony asked urgently.

"Not good. Whoever beat her did a good job. She has a couple of broken ribs, several cracked ones and both shoulders're badly strained, but not dislocated. She may have a cracked skull in the back, and most definitely a concussion. There may be internal damage, but I don't know. There're lots of cuts and bruises to her face. Fortunately, she's still unconscious, thank heavens, or she'd feel all the pain she no doubt is in," Nana said sadly.

Tony's shoulders fell. "That bad, huh?" Tony said, leaning wearily against the wall.

"It's bad enough, Tony. She didn't even get a chance to defend herself. Jim says there're no defensive wounds, only offensive, whatever that means," Nana said, exasperated.

Tony smiled his first real smile of the night. Nana never liked not being able to understand something. "It means that, if Meg had fought back, her knuckles'd be scratched or bruised. She would've scratched at her attackers and maybe had skin under her nails. All the wounds on her are strictly from someone else hitting her. Offensive, like you said," Tony explained as he grinned at Nana.

"Tony, every one of those wounds is offensive to me," Nana snapped back.

"Easy, Nana. This whole mess has been offensive right from the start. I'm getting very tired of people picking on my little brother in there. He doesn't deserve this," Tony grated, nodding towards the closed door.

"Little brother? Tony, what're you talking about. Why're you calling him that?" Nana asked puzzled. "He's not your family."

"No, Nana he's not blood, but he's also no longer just a counselling assignment I chose to take on either. I've had a chance to get to know him like no one else does, not even his own family. Certainly Jor doesn't know him as well as I do now. He's become something I never had – a little brother. I'm the youngest, and I have seven sisters, or eight mothers. Take your pick. He's taught me more about myself than anyone, including my shaman, has ever done. I've *tried* to tell myself over and over I have to back off. That I have to treat him no better than any other teen I've counselled, but I can't. Not anymore. I meant it when I said he was important to me," Tony said softly. Nana squeezed his arm in understanding.

"Tony, do you really think he did this?" Nana asked.

Do I? Tony wondered. Even after what he'd just admitted, did he believe Rick had attacked his cousin? "We'll have to wait for the evidence, Nana. Go home. I just pray Seamus listened to me and left everyone alone at the ranch. I suggested he shouldn't be there to oversee the investigation. And with Megan still unconscious, there's really no point in going back to the hospital. Before you go, though, say good-bye to Rick. Let him know you love him and you believe in him. Make him believe it, Nana." Tony let Nana back into the room where he could hear Owen and Rick talking quietly.

Ten minutes later, Owen led a very subdued Rick out. Nana had said her good-byes and gone to see Megan at the hospital. She told Tony on the way out she'd see him back at the ranch. They both knew he'd be there after he talked to Rick, no matter how long that took or how tired Tony was. Tony led the way up to where Rick was once again booked in. Once in the interrogation room, Tony pulled out the tape recorder and set it on the table. Rick sighed.

"I know, little brother, I don't want to do this, either, but let's go through this just once. Then I'll leave you alone," Tony said formally. With another sigh, Rick told Tony what had happened from the time he had left his house until Tony and Ian had arrived on the scene. Tony didn't interrupt once; he wanted Rick to get it all out.

"I swear on Pop's grave, I didn't do this, Tony. I didn't," Rick protested, getting more and more agitated when Tony didn't seem to believe him right away.

"Calm down, Rick. While the counsellor has no problem believing you, the cop's gotta wait for the evidence to say he believes you, 'kay? Now, I want you to take a couple more minutes and think very carefully. Is there anything, any detail no matter how small, you remember that could point to someone else?" Tony urged.

Rick closed his eyes and replayed the scene. Nothing stood out right away. "You won't find anything from them on the rope," he said suddenly. "He was wearing black gloves. I wasn't wearing any, and I know I grabbed the ropes to cut her down," Rick finished.

"Little brother, I said something that would point to a different suspect, not incriminate you," Tony snorted. Even Owen smiled.

"Sorry. Tony, I know I didn't get to look at Megs in any great detail, but I didn't see any marks on her neck. Was she strangled?" Rick asked suddenly.

"Nana never mentioned anything, kiddo. Why?" Tony replied after reviewing what Nana had already told him about Megan's injuries.

"Now, the letters said a lot about how much fun it'd be to strangle her. Don't you find it strange 'I' beat her up but didn't strangle her at all?" Rick pointed out.

Surprised at Rick's understanding of the whole situation, Tony nodded and made some notes. "What else struck you as odd, son?" he encouraged.

"When I got there, at first there was absolute silence, even though someone was still beating on Megs. There was no noise. No encouragement, and trust me, it would have taken a lot to keep Johnny quiet. He loves to encourage those guys to pound on people. There was none of that at first, but I remember hearing someone laughing in the trees when I was fighting with the one who I saw hit her. There was definitely someone else there," Rick said confidently.

"Unfortunately, Ian made a right mess of that crime scene when he went after you," Tony pointed out. Rick shook his head quickly.

"It was no one I could see, Tony. They were in the trees. In the shadows. Hiding. Enjoying every minute of it. Watching. Waiting..." Rick's voice faded away as he stared off into space. Tony remembered something Marshall had mentioned in one of their early conversations.

"Rick, who was it?" Tony asked softly. Owen leaned forward. *How would Rick know who it was if he didn't do it?* the lawyer wondered.

"It was the Knights. They were there," Rick whispered. "I could feel it. They were laughing at me. Especially when Uncle Ian had me pinned against that tree."

After a few seconds of uncomfortable silence, Tony snapped off the tape recorder and stood. Rick shook his head to clear it. "Okay, Rick. That's enough for now. I'm gonna join the team at your house. Pray I don't find anything," Tony said grimly.

Once again, Rick was led to the holding cell. This time, though, no one offered to bring Rick any supper, nor did Rick ask for any. He lay on the lower bunk with his stomach in knots. He just continued to think about what had happened. *How's anyone gonna believe me anymore?* Rick wondered. Faintly he heard the sound of metal jangling. It took him a long time to realize it was his trembling legs making the bed shake. It was definitely going to be a long night.

Tony shared that thought. He'd sent a team to Glencrest when he had first arrived at the station with Rick in tow. Now, once again in his uniform, Tony drove out to see what they had found. As he pulled up, he could see Seamus hadn't left, nor had Marshall.

Typical Seamus, Tony thought, disgusted. *With your history and how much everyone knows you hate this kid, why'd you stay? Won't you ever learn?*

Just as Tony parked, a member of the team came out of Rick's house, holding a black and silver leather jacket. Tony groaned as he sat in the car with his head in his hands. *No, not that,* he begged. *Anything but that.*

Seamus chuckled. "Good work, Josh. Bag it and tag it. We've got him this time," Seamus said gleefully. He was acting like a kid in a candy store.

"What've you got, Seamus?" Nana asked as she, too, pulled up to Glencrest.

"We found this jacket shoved into the bottom corner of the second bedroom closet, ma'am," the crime scene investigator said, holding up the black jacket.

"Seamus, I believe it was suggested you not be part of this investigation. Do I need to file a formal complaint?" Nana said pointedly. "After the last time, how can I be sure you didn't plant that jacket in that closet?"

Seamus paled. "Megan Attison, are ye accusing me of planting evidence?" he thundered.

Gimme patience, Tony thought yet again. It seemed to be his mantra these days. "Enough, Nana. Inspector, no one's accusing you of anything, but you know what happened last time Rick was accused. Besides, it's perfectly natural for Rick's jacket to be in Rick's house. It's not at the spot where Meg was attacked. Now, boss, go home and let the team do its job. We'll see who the evidence points to," Tony said, trying to placate his boss.

Seamus, reminded of the informal complaint Nana had already filed, turned abruptly and strode to his truck. He sped out of the driveway, spraying rocks everywhere. *Idiot*, Tony thought, shaking his head.

"Nana, just let me finish up here and then I'll stop in to see you," Tony said.

Turning back to Josh and the rest of the team, Tony motioned to the tech holding the jacket. Tony snapped on some gloves and looked at the jacket. His heart sunk as he could make out the stylized M's that had been sewn into the lining. It was Rick's, all right. The one piece of evidence that could really put him away for good, even if it wasn't found at the crime scene. Not what Tony wanted to see right then.

"Okay, boys. It's bad, but we've seen worse. Marsh, I need you to head back to the station. Keep an eye on him. Keep looking, boys. I need someone to go back to where we found Meg. There might be evidence of someone else there, especially outside of the original scene. Maybe in the trees. I may've missed something in the rush to get Megan back to safety. Photograph, bag and tag everything you think may be helpful. Be thorough. We don't want to do this again," Tony said firmly. Everyone left for their assignments, but Tony's night was far from over.

He walked up to the porch and stood at the rail, looking over the ranch. Overhead, the stars glittered and the moon light was weak. He could see the search lights moving in the distance as his team looked for evidence in the woods. It was such a peaceful night he couldn't believe a sweet, innocent girl had been viciously beaten that far away. He could just hear a quiet neigh of one horse to another in the barn. Somewhere in the distance, a coyote yelped and another one answered. Tony's breath steamed in the cool night air as he let his thoughts wander. He needed some peace before seeing Nana. *Before I have to be a cop again,* Tony thought sadly.

"Tony, come out of the cold," Nana said softly from the door.

Tony smiled and followed Nana into the house. The house seemed to glow softly and its warmth soaked into Tony's weary body. He gratefully accepted a cup of strong black coffee and a plate of sandwiches from Martha. He and Nana settled into chairs in the library.

After devouring a pair of sandwiches, Tony asked, "Any change in Meg, Nana?"

"She opened her eyes. She didn't wanna talk until tomorrow so I made her father promise not to let anyone disturb her. That included your boss. So, Tony, please tell me you have nothing on my boy," Nana begged.

She looks old and tired, Tony thought. "I don't know yet, Nana. The coat's definitely Rick's. The fact it was found in his house isn't good, but the one plus is it was found in the closet in the room Marsh was using. No one, not even your stubborn son, is gonna be mad enough to accuse Marsh of helping Rick attack his cousin. The other plus is it's been found at his house and not at the crime scene in the woods. However, unless he attacked Meg, rushed back to his house, put the coat in Marsh's closet without Marsh seeing him, then went back out and found his cousin, I don't know how the jacket's gonna help Seamus lock him up," Tony said as he finished another sandwich.

As Nana nodded, Tony continued. "I mean, you saw the bright down-filled coat he was wearing. I doubt it even registered with Seamus or Ian. Rick swore to me, right after Jor's attack, he'd thrown all the gang wear out and anyone could've grabbed the stuff outta the trash. He remembers garbage wasn't picked up until late the next day," Tony said with a grimace. How much more of Rick's gang wear was in someone else's hands, Tony didn't want to think about. He put down his plate with a thump and began to pace.

"Has anyone ever talked to those awful boys in his gang?" Nana asked finally.

"I've done some quiet investigations into the Knights on my own, interviewing other kids at the school and such, but so far nothing. I can't find a single piece of evidence that doesn't point to Rick," Tony said bitterly. "Right now, it's Rick's word against theirs and we both know Seamus doesn't believe Rick. If he knew of just one person who could put the blame squarely on Rick, he'd have the statements in the judge's hands by now."

"And my boy'd be gone," Nana finished, heartbroken.

Tony nodded without answering. He didn't need to. He knew Nana was right. *What else can happen to this family?* he thought, grimly. He let his gaze wander around the library. A warm fire was crackling in the fireplace. The books glowed in the flickering light. It was warm and safe here. There was no time and no enemies. Tony sighed as he stood in the firelight, fingering one of his long braids.

"What's wrong, Tony?" Nana asked gently. It didn't take a rocket scientist to figure out something was bothering the young cop.

"I'm tired, Nana. One hundred per cent bone tired. I've run outta energy. I'm tired of fighting with Rick against Seamus. No one should have to go through what Rick has! I desperately wanna believe him, but I don't know what to believe anymore!" Tony cried. Nana remained quiet. It was the first time Tony had ever given into his own anger and frustration with all of this.

Thankfully, Nana realized Tony wasn't mad with Rick. He, like her grandson, just needed someone to vent to every now and then.

"Worst of all, when I look in the mirror, I see a monster," Tony finished lamely.

"A monster?" Nana said, puzzled. "Why a monster? I don't understand."

Tony was quiet. "Maybe monster isn't the right word, but I don't know what else to call myself. Hypocrite, maybe. You've never had to wear two hats in this mess, Nana. You've always been able to support Rick. You've been able to love him unconditionally. There've never been any strings attached to your commitment to him. I can't do that; I *have* to try to keep some professional distance between us," Tony said absently.

"Take tonight, for example. By the Creator, please make tonight go away. Tonight, when he really needed a champion to stand up for him, to be on his side, I had to be a cop. I had to arrest him, interrogate him and treat him like a common criminal. Believe me, I know he's anything but. I don't believe Rick attacked Meg any more than I believe he attacked Jor. It's not like him. He's not the kind of person who would try to scare you first. He'd come after you straight up. You might not see him coming but thankfully, you'd never feel it after the first punch.

"I can't see him punishing Meg like she was beaten tonight, but as a police officer, I couldn't stand beside him and support him. I had to go with the evidence and it all points right at Rick. Yet I'm still his counsellor and, if there's one thing I have learned the hard way since this all began, it's that Rick needs one person, just one, to always stand beside him and support him. I can't ever abandon him or he'd be completely shattered. He'd have nothing left to live for and he'd become just as cold and unfeeling as Johnny is. Not even Jor'd be enough. Do you understand?" Tony asked softly.

At Nana's thoughtful nod, Tony continued. "My other problem *is* the counselling. I wasn't kidding when I called him 'little brother.' He's family, Nana, not by blood but by other bonds that are far, far stronger. I'm so close to Rick now I really shouldn't investigate anything involving him. I can't be objective any more. Hell, let's be honest, Nana. I don't wanna be objective when it comes to him and I don't dare leave him to someone else. It'd just send him back to square one and he'd probably run, screaming, back to the Knights in a heartbeat if I gave up on him too. And I believe him when he blames Johnny. I've seen his kind of work before. Johnny's vicious and cruel. He thinks nothing of hurting someone like Meg. She's a distraction to the gang. So is Jor," Tony said quietly.

It was several minutes before Tony could go on. "But every time I think of getting Rick a new counsellor, I think of that day at the gym when he took me down. The absolute panic in his eyes when I refused to listen to his side of the story about Mick's truck's something I never wanna see again. God, the pain there was horrible. He thought I had bailed on him like everyone else," Tony said and shook his head at the memory.

"He's scared, Nana. Now more than ever. He knows he's not gonna get outta this very easily, if at all. Even if he's found innocent, Ian and Meg'll never trust him again. That's why he made the comment about the gang. Sure he'd stop the attacks, but Johnny would push him every time he turned around, just to make Rick prove he was loyal to the Knights. Johnny was trying to turn Rick into a smaller version of himself, I think, and if Rick returned, I don't think he would be able to stop it," Tony said grimly.

Tony's fear was very real. Rick had talked, once, about returning to the gang right after Mickey had almost flattened Jordan at Glencrest. It'd be for the best, Rick had explained. It had taken a long, long time but Tony had finally made Rick see Blade would push until Rick was just another Blade, mean, vicious and cruel. Evil.

All Tony had to do to prove to Rick he'd never survive in the gang again was to ask Rick if he would enjoy beating up someone small and defenseless. Would Rick enjoy watching them suffer from constant pain? Could Rick live with damaging someone to the point they had to have constant nursing? Rick had been physically sick at the images, and Tony had thought they were done with the issue of Rick going back to the gang. *Apparently not*, Tony thought sourly.

Now, as he stood by the fireplace, Tony knew he should get back to the station before Seamus or Ian got a hold of Rick, but he couldn't bring himself to leave the warmth of Nana's library. He stared into the flames and felt safe. The library reminded him of the warmth he often felt when he visited his shaman's tent. He smiled slightly then frowned. He was still worried about the boy sitting that jail cell at the station.

"What should I do, Tony?" Nana asked finally. The silence had dragged on for too long.

"About Rick – love him unconditionally, no matter what Ian tries to get you to do. If he gets outta this, he's gonna need that sanctuary over there more than ever. Give him what his father won't and what Ian refuses to. About Meg – just get her healed and don't let her father railroad Rick into jail. My gut tells me this isn't played out yet. About Michael – get him as far away from your family as possible. Mendez's hunting for him now, but Michael has darted down a deep, dark hole," Tony replied absently. He didn't turn away from the fire yet.

"Oh, hell. I'd forgotten about that," Nana muttered darkly.

"I hadn't. Mendez's still looking. From what we can find out, Michael owes him about a hundred grand and it grows daily. I'm surprised Mendez hasn't gone for the business yet. I've received assurances from several different, and reliable, sources on the street that Mendez has promised he won't come after you, but Michael's business should be fair game. For him to have left it alone this long is very unusual for this guy," Tony said, stretching, as he finally forced himself to turn away from the mesmerizing fire. He felt his back crack and some of the tension in his shoulders left. He sighed again as he glanced at the mantle clock.

"I'd better get back, Nana. We told Seamus to leave the investigation alone. We didn't tell him not to return to the station. He's probably got Rick pretty worked up by now," Tony chuckled dryly.

"Tony, I know this isn't easy for you, but please don't back out on Rick. He needs that father figure in his life, and you're the closest thing he's got to one. Ian won't, not now, and Michael never was," Nana said, resting a hand on Tony's arm.

I think I already am, Tony started to say, but the shrill ringing of the phone forestalled any reply Tony might have made.

Nana answered, listening quietly for a moment. Tony watched her face grow dark. "We're on our way!" Nana slammed down the phone and motioned for Tony to follow. "That was Marshall. Seamus and my son got to Rick. Apparently, there's a fight going on."

Chapter 27

Tony sped into Collingwood, lights flashing and sirens blaring. He screeched to a stop and pounded into the station, Nana right behind him. They could hear the fight as soon as they opened the door. When they ran into the squad room, the sight before them chilled them both to the bone.

In a circle of cops, some of whom were trying to break up the fight, Rick lay on the floor, gasping for air. But only for a moment. He sprung back to his feet with a move that would've made a gymnast proud and swung at his opponent. Nana could see Rick had several cuts on his face and a split lip, but otherwise he seemed unharmed. His hands flashed so fast Nana could hardly follow them. Rick's opponent couldn't follow them either and was soon on his knees. Rick deliberately backed off and gave his opponent time to rise, instead of kicking him while he was down. Horrified, Nana realized it was Ian and was too shocked to move. Thankfully, Tony wasn't. By the time he got between the two, Ian was back on his feet and Rick had swung again.

Tony reacted with pure instinct. Somehow, his hand shot up and caught Rick's punch before it could land. From the trembling in Rick's hand, Tony knew that if that punch had landed, Ian would be out cold on the floor. "Rick, no," Tony said softly. He could see the rage in Rick's eyes, but, then again, Tony could understand why.

Rick shook his head, surprised to see Tony between him and his uncle. Taking several deep breaths, he lowered his hand. He dropped his head and closed his eyes, muttering under his breath. Finally, under control again, he raised his eyes and stared at Tony. Tony looked back, unafraid, all of his trust and compassion there in his dark eyes.

"Sorry, Tony, but he started it," Rick shrugged philosophically.

Tony chuckled. "I understand, little brother. I really do. Hey, at least you didn't lose yourself this time. I was able to get through to you. You're getting better," Tony praised. Rick stood a little straighter. *Even that small bit of praise was enough to boost his spirits after the horrible night he just had,* Tony realized and promised himself he'd do it more often. Without a backwards glance, Tony led Rick back to his cell and Marshall guided Nana and Ian to an interview room while another cop got some first aid for Ian.

Tony could see the evidence of a fight inside the cell, too, and grimaced. "Where the hell's Seamus? Why didn't he stop this?" Tony groused.

"Because he allowed it to start, Tony," Marshall said, coming up from behind. He tossed Rick a towel and a bottle of water. The teen guzzled about half and then dumped the rest on his head to cool off. He began to stretch and work out the kinks which had already developed.

"What do you mean, he allowed it to start?" Tony demanded incredulously.

"That's what I said. Seamus brought Ian in, opened the cell door, pointed and said, "There he is," and walked back out. Every time someone tried to stop the fight, one or the other would tell us to back off or take a swipe at us. That's why I called you. We couldn't stop them without using force and I didn't wanna make the call on that," Marshall said.

Great, Tony snarled to himself. *How're we gonna fix this? Nana's gonna have a field day with the boss.* "Thanks, Marsh. Rick, physically, you okay?" Rick nodded as he stretched. "I'll help Nana get Ian calmed down and out of here. Why am I always in charge?" Tony mock growled. Rick's answer stayed with the cop for a long time as he walked away.

"'Cause you believe in me, Fish," Rick said quietly.

Tony glared good-naturedly at his partner for telling Rick Tony's nickname. Marshall just chuckled. At least now Tony knew

Rick had accepted all Tony had done for him. He was the only person Rick knew as a father or big brother and, by the Creator, Tony was going to live up to that. No matter what the cost.

When Tony walked into the room where Nana and Ian were, Nana was scolding her son.

"....and then I come in to find you fighting with your nephew. Badly, I might add. Now you tell me Rick provoked you and Seamus allowed it. What a fine example you are for your daughter. You do remember her? Young thing, lying in the hospital, badly injured. You're no better than Michael!" Nana said sarcastically.

"Now, wait a damn minute, Mother! I'm twice the father Michael ever was. All you have to do is look in that jail cell to see that. All I wanted was some answers from that boy as to why Megan? Why couldn't he leave my baby alone? Why, Mother, why?" Ian cried. He had a towel loaded with ice wrapped around his hands and blood had dried on his cheek where one of Rick's punches had cut him.

Tony closed the door softly. "Ian, only one person has that answer and I don't think it's Rick. Look, I understand you're upset. You're not the only one. Frankly, I don't think any of this would've happened if we'd been allowed to investigate Jordan's attack properly. Now we have to live with the results. I'm not even gonna pretend to know how you feel. I can't. I'm not a father. All I can ask for is time and patience. Let us do our job. Rick claims he's innocent and, until he's found guilty in a court of law, he *is* innocent. How about we let the court try him? Please, Ian? For Megan?" Tony asked softly.

"Yeah, right, he's innocent, Tony. Seamus told me about the jacket," Ian snapped back, unwilling to calm down.

"Did he also mention it was found in Marsh's room in the house at the ranch, not where Meg was attacked?" Ian shook his head slowly. "Didn't think so. So, unless you're willing to accuse Marsh of helping Rick attack your daughter, and you'd better be able to back that up with solid physical evidence, the jacket's purely circumstantial. It wasn't found at the scene, it was found in Rick's house – a perfectly natural place for Rick's jacket to be.

"Until I talk to Meg, alone," Tony continued before anyone could question him about the jacket, "I'm not pointing fingers and you shouldn't either. Until and unless Meg can positively say it was Rick and can say for certain the jacket we found was the jacket he was wearing when he threw the first and last punch, it's all circumstantial evidence. Lemme do my job, please," Tony said again.

Silence fell as Ian struggled with everything Tony had said. Finally, Ian nodded. His shoulders slumped in defeat and he sat heavily in his chair. *My baby's hurt and I can't help her,* he thought miserably.

"C'mon, lad, let's go home," Nana said, laying her hand on Ian's shoulder and squeezing gently in support. Ian struggled to his feet and stumbled towards the door. Everyone in the squad's bullpen sat silently at their desks as they watched the normally proud and strong man shuffle along as if he had suddenly aged fifty years.

"Thanks, Tony," Nana said as she followed Ian out.

"Just doing my job, ma'am. Get him through this, Nana, and he'll be stronger for it. Owen'll be here in the morning?" Tony asked as he escorted mother and son out of the station. He stood by as Nana climbed into the driver's seat of Ian's SUV.

"Along with a formal complaint about Seamus. Has he got rocks for brains right now?" Nana said, disgusted.

Tony didn't answer. He watched the two drive away and again just stood in the cool night air trying to regain his focus and patience with the world. It was a long time before he could force himself back inside. He returned to the cell to find Rick working out the last of his frustrations on the mattresses from the beds. He had leaned them against the wall and was using them as a modified heavy bag. Marshall was inside the cell and just watched in amazement.

Tony smiled and closed his eyes, listening to the rhythm. He found his toes tapping and saw the sun setting in the meadow by the river. He could almost see the drummers on the far side warming up as he got ready to begin the most challenging dance of his life. He took a deep breath, stepped into the meadow and….Almost painfully, Tony pulled himself back to the present. That dance at his middle sister's wedding celebration had been one of his best.

"He's good, isn't he?" Tony asked with a certain amount of pride.

"I've seen him a couple of times at the centre, sparring with Carl, but never in an actual fight. I know his sparring's totally different than what I saw tonight. I was wondering how he put you down, man. Now, I see," Marshall said in wonder and knew how much it had cost Rick not to swing at him the entire time he'd been at the house.

"Was he getting mad again?" Tony asked. He knew Rick hadn't been, but he needed someone else to tell him.

"Naw. Said he had some extra energy to burn," Marshall shook his head. "Said you stopped him before he could finish," Marshall smiled. Tony snorted.

Tony watched for another minute or so, then rattled the cell door lightly. Rick finished up in a flurry of punches and looked up. "Looking good, Champ, but time to crash for the night," Tony said lightly.

"Okay. Hey, Fish?" Rick said suddenly.

"Yeah?" Tony replied after letting Marshall out and relocking the door.

"How's Megs? She gonna be okay?" Rick asked.

Tony wagged his hand back and forth. "A lot of damage, son. I won't lie. Broken ribs, wrenched shoulders, concussion for sure, maybe even a cracked skull. Cuts and bruises, like you saw. Whoever did this really wanted to send a message," Tony said gravely. *Did you get the message, Rick?* Tony wondered.

"Message received, Tony," Rick said and turned his back. Tony could see his shoulders tense, then relax. By himself, Rick got back in control. *Message received loud and clear, Johnny, but*

I'm not coming back, Rick vowed as he straightened up his cell and flung himself down to try to sleep.

Chapter 28

Marshall and Tony both decided to sleep at the station that night and left a wakeup call with the night sergeant for 6:30 am. They wanted to be with Rick when Seamus showed up for his 7 a.m. shift. There was no way either cop was leaving him alone with Rick. Marshall sat on a chair outside the cell, working on detailing all the evidence collected to date. Tony stayed inside with Rick, finishing up his report about finding Rick at the scene. They managed not to wake Rick up as the night sergeant said he hadn't slept most of the night.

Seamus sauntered in right at seven and glanced at the two officers. "Back to yer desks, constables. He doesn't need to be baby-sat. Ye have a case to prepare," Seamus growled.

"We're working on it now, sir, but, after last night, we're not leaving Rick alone," Marshall said shortly, not looking up from his paperwork. *Especially with you in the office,* he didn't say. *Yikes,* Tony thought as he listened to the tension in Marshall's voice. *Guess I should've asked Marsh if* he *was okay.*

"Given up hope of that promotion, Constable?" Seamus asked idly, leaning against the cell with his arms folded across his broad chest.

"We both have, sir, but that doesn't change our minds," Marshall said with finality.

Seamus didn't say anything for a long time. He just stood there, staring at the two best investigators he had worked with in a very long time. He had taken both of them under his wing and had trained them personally. He had been to the reserve and watched Tony dance many times. He had been to Marshall's brother's wedding just last summer. He knew both families very well. He was so proud of these two young cops, yet he couldn't say it to them, especially not right now.

He knew who they were guarding Rick against. Him. He knew last night would be the final straw for Nana. He still didn't know why he had let Ian into the cell and let him go at Rick. No doubt sometime today that formal complaint Nana had threatened to file last time would arrive at Regimental Headquarters and he would face an inquiry – maybe even a suspension. But hang it all, he was only trying to protect the ones he loved.

"Standing over us, glaring, isn't gonna change our minds, Inspector," Marshall grated. He hated being stared at as much as Rick did.

Ouch. When'd I lose his respect? Seamus wondered as he stomped off to his office. The inspector already figured out when he had lost Tony's. Now he had to figure out how he'd ever get their respect *back*.

Marshall jumped a foot when a hand came down on his shoulder from inside the cell. "Easy, partner," Tony cautioned softly.

"Dammit, Tony, you trying to gimme a heart attack?" Marshall demanded loudly.

"Shh," Tony cautioned again as Rick tossed on his bed with a soft groan, responding unconsciously to Marshall's anger. They waited until Rick settled back down.

"That's not what I meant, Marsh. What's happened to you, man? You've never snapped at the boss like that," Tony murmured.

"This is wrong, Fish. That kid in there's gone through hell, and half of it's my fault. Even once we had an understanding about me being at the ranch with him, he hated having me around. I had to stand in his door and watch him work out, because I couldn't let him outta my sight, Seamus said. It made him madder and I know that came out in your sessions with him, so don't even try to tell me it didn't. What the inspector's made me do has tainted everything I used to believe in and stand for in

- 350 -

this job. Quitting'd be too damn easy. Now I just want justice," Marshall said harshly.

It was worse than Tony had thought. He'd just thought Marshall was mad about the fight the night before, not that he felt like a bad cop. Marshall was one of the few cops in the station who was allowed to call the inspector 'Seamus' to his face in front of the other officers. Even Tony usually called the elder cop Inspector, or at the very least boss, in front of everyone else, although it was Seamus when the two were alone. It was a sign of respect Seamus allowed Marshall that freedom. Now that was gone.

"Marsh, listen, no matter what happens in that courtroom today, I have to pull outta the investigations as much as possible. I can't think clearly about Rick any more. I've become too close to him. I know him too well," Tony began.

Marshall interrupted roughly. "You've become the only dad he knows, Fish, admit it," Marshall said.

Tony looked back at Rick. Even while sleeping, the teen's face was haggard and drawn. He was so tired, Tony could tell. He twitched slightly, groaning softly once again and Tony figured he was reliving the fight from last night. But Marshall was right.

"If not a dad, then at least a big brother. A substitute for Nelson. I told him last night I considered him more of a little brother than an assignment," Tony admitted quietly. The more times Tony said it, the more he believed it.

No kidding, Marshall thought. *You spend a hell of lot of time with him.* "Fish, you want out? Really?" Marshall asked instead of pushing Tony on the subject.

"Want to? No. Need to? Yes. If I don't, I'll be as guilty as Seamus for obstructing justice. Marsh, you want that badge to mean something again? Get justice for Rick and the girls?" Tony continued quietly.

"Yes," Marshall hissed. Rick tossed on his bunk again, almost as if reacting to Marshall's anger.

"Quiet, Marsh, don't let him hear that anger. Not today. I don't have time to calm him down if you get him worked up.

Look, I want you to take over the lead. I'll help as much as I can, but you need to be the one in charge from now on. For your own reasons," Tony advised.

"I'm not as good as you, Fish. Hell, Jones has more experience than I do. What if I screw up?" Marshall wondered.

"The girls won't like having a stranger talk to them. They know you and they'll trust you far more easily than they would Jones. They'll be more likely to tell you something that might point at Rick before they'd tell Jones. Something to Jones that is clear evidence of guilt, to us is simply another piece of the larger puzzle.

"As for screwing up," Tony continued as Marshall chewed over what Tony had just said, "how could you screw things up any more than Seamus already has?" Tony asked philosophically.

"You really think I can do this?" Marshall asked quietly.

Tony smiled. *So unsure of himself, just like Rick,* Tony thought. "I know you can, Marsh. I'll still be along for the ride, so you won't be alone," Tony assured him. How many times had he said those very words to a certain teen sleeping on the bunk behind him?

"I'll do it," Marshall agreed after a long moment of silence, and finished his paperwork in a much better mood while Tony sat back down beside Rick and just stared into space. It was the right thing to do, but how Rick would take it was anyone's guess.

Precisely at eight, Rick rolled over and sat up. He was tired and grouchy, but awake. Sleep had been elusive for most of the night and when he did sleep, it was filled with dreams. He frowned when he saw the two cops. "What're you guys doin' here?" he asked, rubbing at his eyes.

"We're here voluntarily, little brother," Tony said. He tossed Rick an apple. "Seamus duty," Tony said cryptically.

Seamus duty? What the hell's that? Rick wondered as he munched on the apple. He stopped wondering when he heard the inspector bellowing for someone to bring him something. "Lemme guess, he came into the office ticked off," Rick said glumly.

"Toast, kiddo?" Tony asked instead of replying. He passed Rick two pieces when he nodded.

"It's just gonna get worse. Your grandmother's probably gonna be filing a formal complaint today after that little dust up last night," Marshall said from outside the cell.

Great. O'Reilly's really gonna flip on me, Rick swore silently. *Thanks, Nana.* He finished up his toast and stood up. He did a full body stretch and sighed with relief when he felt his back pop again. It was becoming a regular occurrence and always seemed to relieve some of his tension. He began to do some of his warm-up stretches to work the rest of the kinks out. Tony just watched as Rick worked out, every now and then correcting a stretch.

"Don't want you tearing anything, kiddo," he said when Rick looked at him funny.

By 8:30 a.m., Rick was up and pacing restlessly. He was ready to go, but Owen hadn't arrived yet. "Hey, Tony," another cop called suddenly.

"Yeah, Jonesy?" Tony yelled back as he watched Rick.

"The kid's lawyer just called. Said he's running late and to meet him at the courthouse," Jones called back.

"Thanks, Jonesy. Let's go, Rick. You doing okay?" Tony asked quietly.

Rick nodded. He stood with his hands behind his back, but Tony swung him around. "No cuffs, Rick. Even though it violates every rule in the book, no cuffs. I trust you. No, *we* trust you," Tony said firmly while Marshall smiled.

With Marshall in front and Tony behind, Rick left the station and walked to the courthouse, head held high. *Tony trusts me*, Rick thought, elated. *He doesn't think I've failed.* Rick felt better than he had in days. At least *someone* still trusted him.

The trio met up with Nana and Owen just outside juvenile court. Nana looked like she hadn't slept all night. Owen didn't look much better. Both smiled at Rick, however and projected outward calm. A calm Owen really didn't feel. He didn't think today was going to go well at all. Nana, remembering Tony's advice from the night before, gave her grandson a long hug.

"I love you, Rick. More importantly, lad, I *believe* you," she whispered in Rick's ear.

Rick returned Nana's hug and whispered back, "Thanks, Nana. Love you, too."

Clapping Rick on the shoulder, Owen said, "Let's go, Rick. They've called our case." Without a backwards glance, Owen led the way, trusting Rick would follow.

Once inside the courtroom, Rick sat at the all too familiar defendant's table. *How much more can one boy take?* Owen wondered as he got prepared, absentmindedly greeting the prosecutor.

The judge read over the charges silently. It was the third time Rick had faced him and Rick could see he wasn't impressed. "Why can't you stay outta my courtroom, son? Do you like jail that much?" the judge asked rhetorically. Rick remained stubbornly silent.

"How do you plead this time?" the judge asked once again.

"Not guilty," Rick replied after the slightest of hesitations. No one noticed except Tony. His eyes narrowed. *Not yet, Rick*, he thought silently. *Don't you dare give up on me yet.* Rick had considered, for a brief moment, of pleading guilty just to put an end to everything, but he wasn't quite ready to give up. Not yet. Tony had been right. *Give up now and Blade's won.*

"Constable Whitefish, what evidence do you have at this time?" the judge asked. Tony put his hand on Marshall to stop him from rising to speak. Until Tony had cleared it with the judge, he was still lead investigator.

"Right now, your honour, mainly circumstantial evidence. I haven't talked to the victim, since she was unconscious for most of the night. The defendant, once again, was discovered standing over the victim, but there're no witnesses to him throwing a single punch," Tony replied. Frowning, the judge made some notes as Tony continued to outline the sketchy evidence. Even the prosecutor didn't look happy. Seamus had led him to believe the evidence was much stronger and this was an open and shut case.

"Is it true this boy was under police supervision?" the judge asked suddenly.

"Yes, your honour, that was my detail," Marshall said neutrally as he stood up. *How the hell'd he find out? Nana?* Marshall wondered.

"Why? He was ordered released. The previous charges were dropped. There was no reason for anyone to be watching over him," the judge said angrily. "Constable, it makes me wonder how much of what happened yesterday was your fault," he finished with a glare.

"I understand completely, your honour. I've asked myself that same question many times since Miss Attison was found and haven't come up with an answer that satisfies my own conscience, so I don't have an answer for you, either. As to why I was assigned to Richard, you'll have to ask Inspector O'Reilly, sir. I only do as I'm ordered," Marshall replied stiffly.

"Believe me, Constable, I will. Okay, Richard. I know you say you didn't do this, but in light of everything that has been happening, with the letters, the threats and the phone calls and the brutality of the crime, I'm ordering you remanded into custody. You'll be held at the juvenile detention centre until your preliminary hearing on January 10. Constables, make sure you go over all the evidence in both assaults again. If the evidence points to Richard, fine. We'll set a trial date in January. But don't you dare exclude all other suspects this time. Understood? Next!" The judge banged down his gavel and a stunned Rick was led away in handcuffs.

Tony hurried up to the bench while the next case was being set up. "Can I have a moment, your honour? In your chambers?" the cop asked quickly.

"On or off the record?"

"On. That way Inspector O'Reilly can't argue," Tony decided quickly. The judge waved to the court reporter to join

- 355 -

them in chambers and apologized to the next defendant as they left. He promised this wouldn't take long.

As Tony settled in the nearest chair, the judge looked him square in the eye. "Now what's so all fired important you couldn't say it in open court while Richard's case was open?" the judge wanted to know.

"I didn't wanna blindside him with some of what I'm about to say. This is going to be tough enough on him. You may not've noticed, your honour, but he hesitated right before he pled not guilty. It was just long enough for me to notice, although I'm sure no one else did. Your honour, he was ready to quit and give up today, just in the faint hope it'd all go away. As you ordered after his first case, he's been in counselling at the youth centre. I chose to be his counsellor. What you may not know is, after the second or third session, I had him join the boxing club there. His anger can't always be talked out until he's physically exhausted," Tony began.

"I heard he knocked you flat, Constable," the judge chuckled. Tony wasn't surprised the judge knew about the attack. It was almost like this judge had taken a great interest in knowing what happened with Rick Attison. Tony wasn't sure if that was a good thing or not.

"He did, your honour, but I really did provoke him, no matter what anyone else might've told you. I did the one unforgivable thing with him. I accused first. I didn't even give him a chance to explain what had happened. It wasn't until after he stormed out of my office I found out he had been accused of vandalizing Mickey O'Reilly's truck – which I already knew – and a couple of the other boxers reported seeing him get into a fight with one of the Knights on his way to the centre for our session, which I hadn't known," Tony explained.

"Interesting. Didn't know about either of those," the judge said softly and made a note on his day timer.

"Your honour, please, don't add those to the list of things he's accused of doing. You never heard about the vandalism because I've already cleared him of it," Tony said wearily.

"Why didn't you Taser him the night he hit you?" the judge asked. "You put at least four other people in danger by not doing so," he pointed out.

It was a reasonable question and one Tony had a ready answer for. "A danger they willingly put themselves in, your honour. They wanted to help me. Besides, I thought tasering would be too dangerous to him physically. By the time he got to the parking lot, he'd been pounding away at the heavy bag for over two hours. His heart was racing, both with anger and adrenaline. Tasering him would have sent a shock into his already overworked heart and it could've been fatal. I didn't want that on my conscience. I was gonna mace him, but I never got the chance," Tony defended himself and his actions.

"Get to the point, Constable," the judge ordered after glancing at the clock.

"Speaking as his counsellor, not a cop, it is my professional opinion it'd be a disaster if his boxing was interrupted while he's in custody. He'd have no way to vent his physical anger. Emotional, mental, spiritual problems – those he could still talk out, but only if I remained his counsellor. He's made some great progress, in the last month especially, but I don't think anyone wants to see him become that violent, angry, destructive teen again. His self-esteem is extremely fragile. He's finally developing a self-image which doesn't revolve around the Knights, but it's still shaky at times. He has no self-confidence to speak of," Tony explained.

"There are counsellors at the detention centre," the judge reminded Tony.

"Yes, sir, and for a normal young offender, I'd say that's fine. However, in this case, it'd send Rick back to square one. It would destroy everything he has worked so hard on in the last couple of months," Tony protested.

"Constable, if he's made so much progress, why's he still in my courtroom? Why'm I still hearing stories about him?" the judge wanted to know. Tony just shrugged and avoided the question. Someone wanted him in constant trouble and in jail, but Tony had nothing but a gut instinct to go on.

"Your honour, even with my notes from all of our sessions, the counsellors would have to start over. You'd have to find someone there who's at least as big as Marshall and even then I don't think they'd be able to contain him if he ever broke out of a session room and that's always a very real danger. I'm not always sure I can hold him. Putting him in with a total stranger is probably gonna lead him to be sedated and so drugged up he won't know his left from his right. That's how someone new is gonna deal with that ticking time bomb!" Tony said vehemently.

"You sure of that?" the judge asked quietly. It wasn't something he agreed with either.

Tony nodded. "I talked to the head counsellor at juvy the last time Rick was sent there. That's exactly what they wanna do to him, no matter what I say. Put him on downers the minute he walks through the door so they don't have to worry about him. Everyone's so damn scared of him they don't wanna take a chance. They don't even wanna know why he's like he is. They don't care. And that's not gonna do that boy one damn bit of good. Look how long it's taken me to gain his trust. I've been his counsellor since the beginning of October and he just now feels comfortable enough to tell me almost anything. I still have to push and ask the right questions, but once I do, he'll talk for hours. Those other counsellors don't have that kind of time," Tony pressed on.

"And you do?" the judge asked. He was certain Tony hadn't fully made his point.

"I *make* the time. Inspector O'Reilly doesn't like it, but he's learned to live with it. Those counsellors would spend what, an hour a week with Rick. I spend at least two hours a *day*, five days a week with him and I still can't always work with him," Tony continued relentlessly. "And that doesn't include the times he'll phone me late at night to talk because he can't handle the nightmares he's been getting."

"Is that where the boxing comes in?" the judge asked shrewdly.

"Yes, your honour. Sometimes it's only after he's completely physically exhausted I can get him calm enough to talk. Even then, he sometimes gets mad enough by the end of the session to take a swing at me. Now, do you really think those counsellors would put up with that at all, never mind session after session?" Tony reasoned. The judge shook his head. Tony knew he shouldn't put up with it at all either, but he did it for Rick.

"Do you believe him, Constable?" the judge finally asked quietly.

After weighing everything he had seen, heard and learned about Rick, Tony made up his mind, once and for all. "Yes, your honour. I believe him," Tony said firmly.

"How're you gonna maintain objectivity in this investigation?" the judge asked.

"I can't. I've known that for a while, I just needed to force myself to see it. My partner, Constable Andrews, has agreed to take over the lead in the investigations. I'll help any way I can. I'll make sure Rick understands the normal counsellor-patient privacy rules don't apply in our case. I'll still be the liaison between Inspector O'Reilly and the team. I'm getting used to being yelled at. No one understands the inspector the way I do," Tony said cryptically.

Now what does that mean? the judge wondered as he stared off into space for a second. Finally he nodded. "Very well, Constable. You've convinced me. You're no longer the lead investigator when it comes to any case involving Richard Attison, but you may remain available for Andrews to consult with. Rick continues his boxing and his counselling with you. I want you to make sure the detention centre understands the kind of prisoner who has just walked in there. It's gonna be your job to keep that boy under control no matter what it takes. That means if he has to be sedated, you *will* do it. Do you understand me?" the judge demanded.

At Tony's resigned nod, the judge continued. "No matter what time of day, no matter what you're doing, if he's about to go off, *you're* the one who's in charge of calming him down. Now, I'm late for that case sitting in my court. Don't worry. I'll cut the orders here in the next hour and send copies to everyone involved," the judge reassured Tony as he hesitated to leave.

"Thank you, your honour," Tony said. He nodded to Marshall who had waited outside the judge's chambers. His partner sighed. They could do it.

"Owen, Rick. Hold up, guys," Tony called as he spied the court officers leading Rick around the corner. They stopped and waited for the partners to catch up.

Tony strode up to the group. "Rick, I'm out," Tony began. He never got to finish his sentence as Rick immediately began to panic.

Rick froze. *Not Tony. I'm lost without Tony*, Rick thought wildly. *No. No. NO!* "Tony, no! Look, I'm sorry. I'll go back and plead guilty. Okay, Tony? Don't leave me, Tony! Please don't do this! God, no! Please, no!" Rick begged. His eyes widened. He began to shake uncontrollably and Nana could see how frightened he was. *Tony, what're you doing?* Nana wondered. *Don't do this to him now. He needs you.*

Marshall and Owen wondered the same thing as everyone watched Tony struggle to calm Rick down. Now, unwittingly, everyone was going to see what it was about Tony that made him a good counsellor and, in Rick's case, the only one that could deal with him.

"Whoa, Rick, easy, son. I'm sorry, I didn't mean to scare you. Rick, I need you to listen to me. Calm down. Breathe. Don't panic, son, listen to me. I'm not leaving you alone. I promised I wouldn't. Little brother, please. Listen to me," Tony said softly, insistently. Marshall just led the two court officers away, explaining Tony would deal with Rick. This was normal, he insisted. At least Marshall hoped this was normal. Tony didn't see or hear anyone else. He was focused solely on Rick and what he'd just done to him.

"Rick, look at me," Tony commanded quietly. He gently forced Rick to look at him. Tony didn't like what he saw. The despair and panic were incredible and he had promised himself he would do everything in his power to never put Rick through that again. With two simple words, he had almost shattered Rick's fragile self-esteem. Without ever breaking eye contact, even though the cop was sure Rick wasn't really looking at him, Tony guided his friend to a nearby bench and knelt right in front of him.

"Rick, take a couple of deep breaths. Look at me, son. Easy. Calm down. That's right," Tony soothed, always looking right at Rick. The teen managed a couple of shaky breaths that seemed to help a bit, but his panic still overwhelmed everything.

"Tony, I'm sorry. What did I do? I'll fix it, I promise. I'm sorry! I didn't mean to do it! Just please don't leave me! I don't have anyone else! Please, don't do this to me!" Rick sobbed, tears falling. His shaking hadn't even started to ease and Tony quickly removed the cuffs so Rick had his hands free. Otherwise, Tony didn't know what else to do to get through to Rick.

"Rick, please calm down and listen to me. You have to listen. You didn't let me finish. What I started to say is I'm out of the investigation, little brother. Marshall's gonna be lead from now on. Rick, please. I can't help you if you don't calm down and listen to me. I'm still with you, son. I promised I wouldn't leave you alone. Rick, please listen to me," Tony said urgently. *Crap,* Tony thought desperately. *Now what? He won't listen. You frightened him too damn bad, you idiot.*

Rick took several more deep breaths and let Tony's words sink in. "You're...you're not leaving me?" he said hopefully. He sniffled and brushed away the tears.

"No, I'm not leaving you. I promised you last night I wouldn't. Look, I've convinced the judge of something very important in your case," Tony said. He never took his eyes off Rick. He had to make sure Rick was calm enough that it was safe to leave him alone.

"My innocence?" Rick's heart jumped.

"Hey, I'm good, but not that good, son," Tony chuckled dryly. Rick smiled hesitantly. *Good, he's finally calming down,* Nana thought, relieved. She and Owen watched the drama unfolding before them, while Marshall just stood back.

"I've convinced the judge to keep you in counselling with me and in boxing. I'll be there every day just like we've been doing the last couple of weeks, but I'm also gonna arrange for Bob and Carl to come and train with you at juvy five days a week. How does that sound, Champ?" Tony asked. He never moved. He could still see some hurt and fear in Rick's eyes. *Come on, buddy, calm down. I can't go back to work unless you do,* Tony urged silently.

"Why not use the counsellors at the detention centre?" Owen asked curiously.

"It would send Rick back to square one. He doesn't have time to learn to trust another counsellor. The *kids* in that centre don't have time for him to learn. He'd become angry and violent almost right away if I wasn't there. No one needs him losing everything he's worked for. Besides, I promised my little brother here I wouldn't leave him alone. The next couple of months're gonna be hard enough on him without someone he trusts to talk to. I trust him and I believe him," Tony said as he finally rose to his feet.

"Do you really believe me, Tony?" Rick asked quietly.

Tony looked down at Rick. His shoulders were hunched over and Tony knew he wasn't totally calm, but Tony just didn't have any more time to work with him. The court cops were beginning to fidget and Tony knew they wanted to get Rick to the detention centre before anything else happened. He was calm enough he would be okay until he could get together with Bob that afternoon.

As Tony stared at the teen, he didn't see a confident 17-year-old young man. He saw a scared six-year-old kid whose mom had run out on him and whose dad didn't love him or want him. He saw a frightened eight-year-old always fighting in school just to get attention. He saw a vulnerable 14-year-old boy pushed by an idiotic fight with Seamus into a violent gang in the hopes he'd finally found a family.

Most importantly, Tony saw a determined 17-year-old kid who, despite being beaten down all the time, was trying to get his life back on track. That kid had almost succeeded, until last night when everything got derailed again. Now, that same 17-year-old kid desperately needed someone who believed in him.

"Yes, little brother. I believe you," Tony said finally. Marshall echoed his partner's words as he stood behind Tony.

"So do I, lad," Nana said, smiling at Rick.

"Me three, Rick," Owen said with as much conviction as he could. The lawyer knew this little bit of belief would go a long way in keeping Rick sane for the next couple of months.

"Trust us, Champ, you're not alone," Marshall vowed. "We'll see justice done."

Rick digested what they were saying. Nana reached over with a tissue and dried his eyes. He stood up, held his head high and his muscular shoulders back. He looked at the adults as Tony put the cuffs back on. There was no more fear or panic in his eyes. He was confident he could beat this, no matter what happened.

"Thanks, everyone, for believing me. Johnny may have won this battle, but I'm gonna win the war," Rick said confidently.

Chapter 29

Marshall and Tony watched as Rick was led away, followed closely by Nana and Owen. *He's gonna be okay. For now*, Tony thought as he watched Rick disappear. Despite the noise around them in the hallway, silence settled around the partners, each lost in their own thoughts.

"Let's get the team together and get going, Marsh. We only have two months to save that boy," Tony exclaimed.

The two marched back into the squad room and called their team together. As a goodwill gesture, Tony even included Seamus, so he didn't have to tell the judge's orders twice. "Here's the deal, guys. Rick's been remanded," Tony began while a couple of the other cops muttered.

"Good," Seamus barked.

Tony and Marshall just glared. "Yeah, boss, you got your wish. Rick's off the streets. For now, at least. We have until January 10 to get the evidence. Now, due to me counselling Rick, I've pulled myself as lead on the investigation," Tony continued.

"Why?" several officers demanded loudly. "You're the strongest investigator we have! We don't care Jonesy has more experience, you're better than anyone!" Tony waited until the protests fell away before he spoke again.

"Because I feel, and Rick's judge agrees, I can no longer be objective when it comes to him. Face it, guys. You've all seen it. I'm too close to him. However, I'll still be the liaison to the inspector. We...understand each other, don't we, sir?" Tony said mildly.

Seamus squirmed but nodded curtly. "Who do I appoint in yer place, Constable?"

"*You* don't. I've already agreed to take over and the judge seems to agree, *Inspector*," Marshall spoke up sharply.

"Still hoping to get that promotion, Constable?" Seamus asked sarcastically as he leaned back in his chair. Inside he was cringing at the thinly veiled anger in Marshall's voice. *Thank God I don't suspect him or Tony of being on Mendez's payroll,* Seamus thought bitterly. *I know it's someone in this room, but it's not them. I don't think I could bear it if it was.*

"No, sir, not anymore. I'm in this for *justice*," Marshall snapped back. Seamus frowned. *What've I done to make him so mad at me?* the inspector wondered as Marshall continued to brief the team.

"Like Tony said, we have until January 10, folks," Marshall said, turning everyone's attention back to him and off Seamus. "The judge has ordered us to go over everything in both assaults again to ensure we didn't miss anything or there's nothing new," Marshall said over the groans. He handed out the assignments. "I know, guys. You know and I know we didn't miss anything forensically in Jordan's assault, but let's go over all the evidence and retest everything. Go over the interviews you've already done and re-interview if you think someone might've remembered something new. At least when we find nothing new, the courts'll agree," Marshall said dryly.

"Let's do this one by the book, boys. No mistakes this time," Seamus said as the team left the room.

"This wouldn't have happened if you hadn't made mistakes last time, Seamus," Tony muttered bitterly as he helped Marshall gather up their notes.

"Easy, Fish. You'd better help me question Megan. She knows you better than she knows me, so she'll be more relaxed if you're in the room," Marshall said. Tony nodded and went to gather what they would need.

They arrived at the hospital half an hour later and were directed to a room protected by two private security guards. The guards took their job seriously and actually called the station to verify the partners' badge numbers with Seamus.

"Seamus organize this?" Tony asked, surprised.

"Ian," was Marshall's terse reply.

The two officers knocked on the closed door and entered. Mickey was sitting with Megan, talking quietly and Jordan was sitting in a chair by the window, trying her best to ignore her brother and best friend. The tension between the twins was obvious. Tony shook his head, amazed at how stubborn the Irish were. There was nothing anyone could do to heal the rift between the twins until Rick was cleared or at least until Mickey gave up this stubborn obsession to make Rick guilty of everything since the fall of Rome. Even then, Tony figured it would take a long time for Jordan to forgive Mickey.

"Hey, guys," Tony said cheerfully.

"How's it going, Tony?" Mickey asked as Megan just smiled tiredly.

"Not bad. Look, Mick, can I ask you to wait outside for a while? We need to talk to the girls. Alone," Tony said firmly.

Mickey hesitated, then nodded. He could trust two cops, couldn't he? He leaned over and kissed Megan gently. She smiled up at her boyfriend and raised a hand to touch his cheek. Mickey brushed a stray hair back out of Megan's eyes and whispered, "Love you, lass."

"Love you too, lad," she whispered back.

"Go easy, Tony. She tires quickly," Mickey warned as he left the room. Tony nodded distractedly, but his eyes were on Jordan. The instant Mickey had leaned over to kiss Megan, Jordan had stood up and turned her back on the pair.

At Tony's glance, Marshall nodded toward Jordan and whispered "Romeo and Juliet." They could see the despair as clearly in Jordan's eyes as it had been earlier in Rick's. It wasn't fair, they knew, but what could be done?

Once Mickey was gone, Jordan slouched back in her chair, Marshall took the second one and Tony sat down gently on Megan's bed. He could see the cuts and judging from how dark it was in the room, she definitely had a concussion. But as Rick had pointed out, there wasn't one single mark on her throat.

"How're you feeling?" Tony grinned at Megan.

"A better grade of lousy than last night. He really did a number on me, Tony," Megan said truthfully.

"Who did, Meg?" Tony asked quickly. The whole case could hinge on Megan's reply. Megan was silent for a long time, thinking.

"Daddy wants me to say it was Rick. Mickey, too. I'm pretty sure Inspector O'Reilly has already made up his mind. Jordan says Rick didn't do it, and I just don't know for sure, Tony. It happened so fast," she said softly. "There was something wrong about the whole thing," she added.

Tony nodded thoughtfully. They let Megan rest while they talked with Jordan, who couldn't remember anything new about her assault. As Jordan fell silent, Tony turned to Megan and asked if she was ready.

"As ready as I'll ever be, I guess," Megan replied, trying not to wince at the prospect of facing the memories of her attack.

"Okay. Now, Megan, think very carefully about this question before you answer," Marshall asked quietly while Tony let him take control. "What was the threat in each of the letters?"

Megan didn't hesitate. "He always said he couldn't wait to get me alone so he could put his hands around my throat and squeeze. Just like he did with Jordan," Megan said indignantly.

"Did whoever beat you up, in fact, choke you as well?" Marshall asked in an almost lazy tone as he wrote in his notebook.

"Well, of course not. You can see that," Megan snorted with derision.

"In your experience, when Rick says he's going to do something, does he do it?" Tony asked, hiding a smile. This was going exactly like he and Marshall planned.

"Of course," Jordan replied immediately.

"Always," Megan replied more slowly. She wasn't sure where Tony and Marshall seemed to be heading with these questions.

"Did your attacker have an opportunity to strangle you?" Tony inquired.

"Yeah, he did. He tied me to that tree," Megan replied.

"Did he strangle you?" Marshall asked.

"No, he didn't."

"Did he try to?" Tony asked.

"No, Tony, he didn't," Megan realized.

"So even after threatening you three times, he didn't even try to strangle you, even though he had the chance?" Marshall asked.

Megan couldn't answer him aloud; she simply shook her head, horrified at the implications.

Keeping Marshall's point in mind, Megan thought once more about everything that had happened to her. Two things really stood out. One was the silence, except for the laughter. "I've never heard Rick laugh like that. It was high pitched, almost crazy laughter. Like he was enjoying something way too much. And the one hitting me never said anything. Just like Jordan told me what happened when she was attacked. It was like there was someone else there just out of sight," Megan said softly.

"What's the other thing you remember, Megan?" Marshall asked gently. He had filled several pages with notes and was feeling very confident.

"Well, it's what he looked like. He had the same colour eyes as Rick and the same hair colour, but the hair style seemed wrong. Too perfect, like he was trying too hard to be just like Rick. He also seemed too short to be Rick, but maybe they just tied me higher on the tree. I don't know, Tony. I just can't say for sure," Megan said, shaking her head. The more Tony asked, the more unsure she became. The interview was interrupted by a sharp knock on the door. Ian and Nana entered to see Megan.

"Good, Constables. I'm glad you're here. Megan's told you who did this, right, Megan?" Ian said with a warning in his voice. One eye was a spectacular mix of purple, green and yellow and he walked very gingerly. *His ribs must hurt like hell*, Marshall thought gleefully. *Serves him right.*

"Actually, Ian, she can't say for sure," Tony said without blinking.

"What do you mean, she's not sure? You were sure this morning when I was here," Ian demanded. Megan flinched at the anger in his voice.

"Actually, Daddy, *you* were sure this morning. I told you then I didn't know for sure and I still don't," Megan said wearily. It sounded to Tony like Megan had been fighting this battle for a long time already and Ian wasn't going to let it go. Just like Seamus and Jordan.

"What's it gonna take to put that boy away for good?" Ian demanded, exasperated.

"How about some real physical evidence? Scratch marks on Rick from Jordan's attack, since she remembers scratching her attacker deep enough to leave marks. Bruising on his hands from punching them. Gloves or not, his hands would still be bruised. Physical evidence like blood or fibres, especially on Rick's clothes. A witness who doesn't get cold-cocked would be a definite help. Got any video?" Marshall snapped, sarcastically.

"What're you saying, Marshall?" Nana asked while Ian stewed over the cop's harsh words.

"In both attacks, we have some physical evidence, that's true. Rick's bandana at Jordan's attack and now his coat. Remember, though, the coat wasn't found at the scene of the attack. It was found in my closet at Rick's house. But that's it. There's nothing else," Marshall shrugged, then glared at Ian. "And unless you plan on accusing me of helping Rick attack your daughter and you had better be able to prove it, I suggest that you don't even look down that path, much less travel it," he snapped.

"Nothing else? Marshall, he was found standing over both of them, for crying out loud!" Ian protested.

"Did anyone see him throw a single punch?" Tony demanded immediately.

"What's your point, Tony?" Ian said sourly.

"I've seen Rick with both Meg and Jor. He's gentle, kind and attentive. Yes, he can be a bit over-zealous when it comes to protecting them, right, girls?" Tony chuckled as the three shared a private memory.

"But in all the times I've seen Rick with anyone smaller or less able to defend themselves, he's never been violent. Rick's told you about Tom, hasn't he, Nana?" Nana smiled and nodded as Tony continued. "Thought so. When the Knights attacked Tom, Rick wouldn't lay a finger on him. Blade tried to force Rick again, right at the beginning of the school year, the same day Rick was arrested for damaging the playground equipment. Rick couldn't do it.

"I asked Rick once, if he went back to the gang, if he could beat up someone like Tom. He was physically sick at the mere *thought* of doing something like that. He hates it. He very rarely did more than give Jor a gentle hug and an even gentler kiss. He's always treated her like she was made of glass. Rick would never lay a hand on a female, never mind someone he cares about," Tony said with finality. Jordan nodded in agreement.

"I've spent time with Rick at his house. Not willingly, I might add. I've seen him going at that speed bag of his and I've watched him in the ring. If he'd hit either of these girls, they would've been killed. Probably with one punch. Definitely dead if he'd hit them more than once. He has that much power. When he's fighting, he doesn't hold back. He can't. He doesn't know how. I don't think if he was attacking someone, he'd be *able* to hold back. You know that, Ian. He wasn't holding back during that little altercation at the station. You're bigger, so you were able to roll with the punches," Marshall agreed as he stood up. He snapped his notebook closed with finality and motioned to Tony.

Tony rose as well. "Look, Ian. I'm not saying Rick isn't a suspect. He is and he knows it. But we're not done with our investigation. Hell, we've just started. We're taking this one nice and slow so there are no mistakes," Tony said. "We'll review everything that's happened since September. We'll re-do interviews. Reprocess evidence. Everything. You have my word on it," Tony swore.

"And if the evidence clearly points to Rick?" Ian asked quietly.

"I don't think it will, but if it does, then the prosecutor'll be able to make his case and Rick'll go to jail," Tony shrugged indifferently. *And I'll nominate the bugger for a Best Actor award,* Tony snorted to himself.

"Either way, guilty or innocent, Rick'll always know he has one person who believes him. Me," Tony said harshly, striding from the room. Jordan followed, closing the door while Ian stood there, stunned at the ferocity of Tony's tone.

"One last thing, Megan, and then I'll let you rest," Marshall said as he approached the bed. "Does any of this look familiar?" He placed several photographs around her.

Megan looked at each one carefully. "This is the jacket, I think," Megan began, pointing to one picture. "I don't see the bandana. Either way, I can't say for sure. It all happened so fast," she apologized. "With the sun in my eyes and all the blows to my head, I just couldn't see anything clearly. I'm sorry, Daddy," she sniffled.

Marshall nodded. As he turned to leave, he noticed how tired she was. "Rest, Megan. I promise you, everything'll be fine," the cop assured her and left her alone.

In the hall, Marshall found Tony talking with Jordan and Mickey. Rather, Tony was talking and the twins were listening. Mickey, as usual, was defensive and Jordan, as usual, supported anyone but her brother.

"How can you not blame Rick? How could she not? I just don't get it, Tony. Look at everything he's done," Mickey said stubbornly. Jordan just snorted. *Stupid, pigheaded Irish fool,* she thought.

Tony shook his head emphatically. "No, Mick. Look at everything he's been *accused* of doing. You give me one, just one, real witness who saw him do anything and I'll march them to the prosecutor's office myself. Have you ever stopped being stubborn and actually tried to get to know Rick?" Tony asked, exasperated.

"Why should I?" Mickey shrugged. "I don't give a damn about him."

"Because at least you'd understand what Rick's gone through," Jordan said hotly.

Tony motioned for everyone to follow him down to the cafeteria. Once everyone was settled, Tony looked at Mickey. "Understand something, Mick, right now. What I'm about to tell you comes from my sessions with Rick and is strictly confidential, but I think you need to hear some of this. Not one word gets back to your dad. Not one single word. Promise?" Tony asked. "If Seamus finds out any of this, I'll haul your butt to the detention center, lock you in a room with Rick and set him loose. Understand?"

Having heard about the fight between Tony and Rick, Mickey paled and nodded. "What's all this about?" he wanted to know.

Tony took a deep breath and gave Mickey a brief version of Rick's life story, with certain editing. The fight with Seamus was not something Mickey needed to know. Jordan listened carefully, since most of this was new, even to her. By the end, Mickey had a funny look on his face – like he had a mouthful of sour grapes and didn't know if he should swallow or spit them out.

"Can you confirm any of this?" Mickey asked finally.

Tony nodded. "His mom filed for divorce two months after she left. Rick was six. She signed over her parental rights and left Rick and his brother with Michael. The drinking, gambling and women never even slowed down. Nelson, Rick's brother, left when he was 15 and Rick was only nine. He couldn't stand it anymore. Rick hasn't seen him in years, but Nelson's happily married and living in Australia. He travels a lot for his company, so Rick gets gifts from all over the world. He's got a niece and a nephew he's never met.

"Rick doesn't know his mom's happily remarried, and he has two half-sisters. I think if he really wanted me to, I could get her to come and be with him. The poor kid's been an orphan since he was six. He just didn't know it," Tony said sadly.

"Tony, I don't believe it. That boy's cold-blooded and hot-headed. He doesn't care about anyone except himself," Mickey protested. *I don't wanna believe it,* Mickey whispered to himself.

"Mickey, you're just as stubborn as the inspector," Marshall said, exasperated. Mickey blinked. *What happened there?* Mickey wondered. *What the hell did Dad do to Marsh? He's never called him anything but 'Seamus.'*

"Look, kids, I'm not saying Rick hasn't made some mistakes. He has, and he knows it. Before you judge him anymore, I want you to think about some things. One – you've never had a dad who didn't love you, nourish you and protect you," Tony said intensely.

"Protects some of us too much, if you ask me," Jordan muttered darkly. Tony and Marshall chuckled. Even Mickey grinned.

"Rick's never had that. Never will. He wouldn't know a dad if one slapped him in the face and I'm sure Michael's done that a time or two. Two – you've never been beaten down so much you can't get up anymore. That's what's happening to Rick. At the first sign of trouble, people jumped ship faster than rich people off the Titanic! In the space of three months, he's lost his dad, his home, his gang, what few friends he had, his family and his girl, although Jor would protest that, I'm sure. Now he's lost his freedom. Trust me, you two, it's one of the worst cases of abuse I've ever seen, and I've seen quite a few. The verbal abuse from Michael alone probably would've been enough to pull Rick from the house, had Social Services known about it. That doesn't include any physical or mental abuse Rick won't talk about.

"Know what he said to me yesterday, before we began to question him about Meg's attack?" Tony continued quietly. The twins shook their heads. "He said he'd be better off with Johnny." Tony just sat back. Stunned silence fell. Marshall just looked away. How much of that feeling was his fault, he could only guess.

"After all the work he's put into trying to get out, now he thinks he should've stayed?" Jordan asked, horrified. Even Mickey was shocked.

"Think about it, sweets. He'd still have his home, his gang and his friends. Sure, he probably wouldn't have the girl he loves, but at least you and Meg'd be safe and he wouldn't be alone," Tony said. "That's the worst part right now. He's alone. He has no one. Jor, you may love him, but you can't be with him. No matter what happens, Meg'll probably never trust him again and Mick never has. *He is alone!*" Tony emphasized.

"One last thing I want you to think about, Mick, and then I'll go. I don't want an answer. I just want you to think about this. Why's Rick not allowed to change? He asked for a chance and you promised to give that to him. One little scratch was all it took to break that promise. He's made every effort to change and neither you nor your dad have let him. To top it all off, you've tried to drive such a wedge between him and Jor, it's backfired on you. Be careful that it doesn't end up blowing up in your face, youngster.

"Instead of loving Rick less, she loves him more. Instead of driving them apart, you've driven them closer together. If you're not careful, you're gonna drive her right into juvy hall just to be with him. And in doing so, you've driven her from you. Don't think I don't know what's going on. I've heard stories from your dad and the other kids at school. You're gonna end up hurting your sister so bad the wound'll never heal. If either of you had ever bothered to look at Rick and Jor, you would've seen a loving couple. Just think about it, son. Think about it."

With that, Tony and Marshall got up and left the twins sitting there in stunned silence.

Chapter 30

"You got the coat and bandana, Marshall?" Tony asked on the way to the car.

"No. It's still being processed at the station. Why?" Marshall asked as he slid his large frame behind the wheel.

"I've got a session with Rick later and I wanna see how he reacts." Tony smiled as Marshall gave a short bark of laughter. They both knew how Rick was going to react.

That afternoon, Tony pulled into the young offenders' centre for his session with Rick. In a non-descript brown paper bag, he carried the jacket and bandana collected at the ranch. The cop signed in and was directed to the gym. He'd already made permanent arrangements for a small office to be available and one without a lock on it had been cleaned out. Tony dropped the bag in the room and put an "Occupied" sign on the door.

Tony followed the sounds of cheering and found the gym. In the ring, he could see Rick and Carl sparring. At least, Tony thought they were sparring. But by the way the other boys were reacting, Tony wondered if Bob had decided to try a match-type situation, just to prove a point to some of the other inmates. Sure enough, when Tony got closer, he could tell the two boys were going at it like they were in a real match. Tony leaned against a nearby post and let his eyes wander around. He spotted a group of boys to one side who all looked like they had second thoughts about going a couple of rounds with the former gang member. *Atta boy*, Tony thought as he watched Rick connect solidly with a couple of quick jabs. *Make 'em realize you're not fair game.* He nudged one of the boys standing around the ring, cheering.

"How much time's left?" Tony wondered idly.

"About a minute in the final round," the kid replied excitedly.

Tony watched intently. There was no sign of rage on Rick's face, just fierce concentration. Carl tried a couple of body shots Rick easily deflected. Suddenly, Rick lashed out with two quick rights to Carl's ribs and followed with a solid left uppercut which dropped Carl like a stone. Bob waved Rick over to a neutral corner and counted Carl 'out' as Carl looked up and grinned. The bell sounded, ending the match and the crowd cheered their approval as they dissipated.

Bob was helping Carl to sit up as Rick walked circles around the ring. Tony hopped up and waved Rick over to him. He untied Rick's gloves and began to strip off the tape. "Hey, Champ. Looking good in there. What's happening?" Tony said as he fought with the tape.

Rick pulled out his mouth guard and unsnapped his helmet. He shook the sweat out of his eyes and pulled his hands away long enough to reach for a towel. "Bob asked me to go a couple of actual rounds with Carl," Rick said. "For the first time, it felt like I was really a boxer, Tony. Could I really make a living at this? Fight for money?" he wondered.

Tony handed Rick a bottle of water as he chuckled. "You could, Rick, but I think Nana has other plans for you. Keep moving or you'll stiffen up," Tony advised. Rick nodded, slipped out of the ring and began his cool-down stretches.

Tony went around to the other side of the ring where Bob was tending to Carl. Carl kept shaking his head to clear the stars as he listened to his coach explain where it had gone wrong. "So you see, when you picked your hands up without stepping into him, Rick popped you twice in the ribs. You still hadn't stepped into him, so when you dropped your hands to help defend your ribs – *wham* – you're on the deck," the trainer said as he showed Carl how his hands had moved in response to Rick's attack.

"Okay, Coach. I think I got it this time," Carl chuckled as he, too, went to do his stretches. Knowing how much Rick needed to hear praise, Carl took the time to congratulate Rick on the fight and they dissected every blow as they stretched. Tony was very glad Carl had never cared what Rick had done, or almost done, to Tony or anyone else, for that matter. All Carl wanted was a sparring partner who could give as good as he took.

Bob nodded to Tony as the two boys stretched. "How much did you see, Tony?" Bob asked as he joined the cop.

"The best part. The last three shots," Tony grinned while Bob chuckled. "He's good, Bob. Good idea to let the rest of the boys see what he's capable of. There're some boys who looked like they wanted to take on Moneyman," Tony said with a snort.

"I know. I saw them standing over by the far side of the ring, watching. Thanks for the call this morning. It gave me enough time to get all of this properly set up. Thank God you convinced the judge to let him keep doing this. When I got here, Rick was nervous, uptight and angry. He should be ready for you now," Bob promised. With a nod of thanks, Tony figured it was time for him to start earning his paycheque.

He walked over to Rick and tapped his friend on the shoulder. Rick finished the stretch and looked up. "Cooled down enough, little brother?" Tony asked. Rick smiled and nodded. "Hit the showers and meet me here in ten, okay?" Tony said. With another nod, Rick dashed off and soon was following Tony to an office for their session. Tony put a large "DO NOT DISTURB. COUNSELLING IN PROGRESS" sign on the door and motioned for Rick to grab a chair. The teen continued to sip his water and rub a sore muscle or two.

"Okay, Rick. Here's the situation. Y'know that what you say normally in a counselling session's *supposed* to stay between you and your counsellor, right?" Tony asked. He'd perched himself, as usual, on the corner of the desk. At Rick's nod, Tony continued.

"But I'm also a cop. Even though I'm no longer leading the investigation into Meg's attack, I'm still on the team. I have to warn you right now that anything you say to me which might incriminate you – in any way – could be used against you if you go to trial. Do you understand?" Tony warned.

"Sure, Tony. Really, I do. You're looking for someone who's attacked two girls and hurt them bad. If I say something that proves I did it, you've gotta tell Marsh," Rick agreed. He leaned down suddenly and grabbed at a calf muscle. He muttered a curse and started to rub.

Rick's reaction was not what Tony expected. Acceptance, not anger, was really out of character for Rick and threw Tony for a loop. To cover up his confusion, Tony plunged into counselling. "Bob said you were upset today when he got here. What happened?" Tony asked.

"New kid in the cell block, Tony. Y'know how it is. It's just a little rough at the start, that's all," Rick tried to shrug it off, but Tony could see how much being in here was already bugging him. "Nana told them I'd be keeping my speed bag in my room. It wasn't even a request since she knows how much it helps. I've been warned I'll have a guard on me the instant anyone even *suspects* I'm getting upset. The head counsellor even threatened me. Told me if I don't keep it under control, judge's order or not, he'll knock me out. Everyone's been warned about me," Rick said gloomily. He stared at his hands, which he had clenched in his lap. Tony could see a faint tremor in Rick's legs, and his jaw was clenched slightly.

He's starting to get upset, Tony realized. *I'm getting better at seeing the signs earlier.* "Hey, c'mon, Rick. Don't start getting uptight already. Relax. Keep your spirits up. You knew these next couple of months weren't gonna be easy. But look at it this way. You'll get to work on your schoolwork to keep from falling behind. You've got your speed bag to take your frustrations out on. Use it every day, as much as you need to. You still get to box with Bob and Carl every day. You've shown the other inmates not to mess with you, especially after that little demonstration today. Trust me, kiddo, that's gonna go a long way in keeping the other inmates off your back. Maybe the counsellors, too. And, last but not least, you get to talk to me instead of someone new. What more do you want?" Tony said with a mock growl.

"Besides, I have a message for you." Tony handed Rick a folded piece of paper. It was a short letter Jordan had slipped to Tony at the hospital. Tony gave Rick some time to read it. By the end of the letter, Rick was smiling again. *Thanks, sweets,* he thought. *I needed that.*

"See, Romeo, your Juliet hasn't jumped off the balcony. Don't give up on her," Tony said, almost hiding a smile.

"Now, for the rest of today, I wanna go over your story again. I wanna make sure we've missed nothing," Tony said. He slipped off the desk and sat down behind it. He pulled out Rick's file, a note pad and pen and made Rick go over his story several times to make sure he had everything down.

"Rick, one last time. Did you attack your cousin?" Tony asked pointedly.

"Tony, I've told you! No! I'd never hurt Megs. Jor, neither," Rick protested loudly.

"Does this ring any bells?" Tony asked quietly as he dumped the paper bag on the desk.

Rick paled. There, on the desk, was his only gang jacket. He stared at the black leather and hesitantly reached out to trace the silver stitching on the hem with his finger. He knew this coat so well. It was custom-made and had cost him a lot of money. He'd worn it every day for almost two years, rain or shine, warm or cold, day or night. With a groan, he shoved the jacket across the desk, praying it would go away. But there it sat, silently accusing him. Tony wasn't going to believe him anymore, no matter what he said. Rick's head swam.

Tony didn't say a word for the longest time. He just sat behind the desk and let Rick struggle. He knew, especially here, Rick was going to have to learn to deal with some of this on his own, and if he couldn't calm himself down, the head counsellor would indeed sedate him. Tony watched Rick's face. He knew the conclusion the youngster had just jumped to. *Keep your cool, kiddo,* Tony urged silently. *I'm not leaving you.*

"We found that jacket and this bandana in your spare bedroom closet – Marsh's room – tossed on the floor in the back corner. That's the semi-bad news," Tony said blandly.

"What's the good news?" Rick croaked. He couldn't drag his eyes away from the most hated piece of clothing he had ever owned.

"It wasn't found at the scene of Meg's attack. Also, there's no blood, no hairs, not one piece of trace evidence has been found on that coat. It's been wiped clean, too clean, the techs said. Meg also couldn't identify the coat as the one her attacker wore. Whose coat is this, Rick?" Tony pressed on relentlessly.

"Mine," Rick whispered. Tony could actually feel the desk shaking from Rick's legs bouncing just out of sight. *I'm toast*, Rick thought miserably. *Nice knowing ya, Jor.*

Tony suddenly smiled and eased up. "Relax, Rick. Calm down. Remember, no matter what happens, I'll believe you," Tony reassured him. Rick was able to pull his eyes away from his coat only after Tony grabbed it and shoved it back into the bag.

"Tony, if my coat was found at the scene, O'Reilly'll lock me up for good," Rick said after a long moment of agonized silence.

"It was found at your house, son, not the scene and that's a perfectly normal place for your coat to be. Remember that. It was also found in Marsh's room, not yours, and no one's even remotely *hinting* at the thought Marsh helped 'you' attack Meg. I've one more question. The lab tech found a single piece of paper in your left pocket. There wasn't a single print on it. She said it had one word typed on it. 'Remember.' Do you know what it means?" Tony asked.

"It's gotta be from Johnny. Remember who I am or at least who I'm supposed to be – a Black Knight. He's been saying it to me in one way or another since this all started, but he could've put it there ages ago," Rick said. He sighed and slouched in his chair. "I'm beat, bro. Are we done?"

"Yeah, little brother, we're done for today. Get out of here and keep your hopes up. Remember to keep hitting the books, too. Keep your mind busy," Tony said quietly. *Don't let this place get to him,* Tony begged as he watched Rick leave the office. His shoulders were drooped and his head hung low as he shuffled along. He hadn't been in the centre a day and he was already feeling pretty defeated.

Tony slowly gathered up his notes and threw the bandana in with the jacket. He finished making his notes on the session and what he thought Marshall needed to hear, then just sat in the office and fretted. Unless he found some new evidence to the contrary and quick, Rick would be a permanent resident of the detention centre and he'd end up a broken and bitter young man. *Please, Black Eagle, give him strength. Hell, give me strength. Don't let him break,* Tony grumbled to himself as he finally left. He felt the world owed too much to Rick to fail him now.

Chapter 31

By the end of November, Rick was becoming an increasingly angry young man. He knew he hadn't done anything wrong, but here he was in jail while the Knights roamed free as birds, doing whatever they wanted. The investigations were at a standstill. The team could find nothing new, but the judge refused to move the preliminary hearing up, wanting Rick to learn a hard lesson. And because of this, Rick would continue to stew in his jail cell for over another month.

Tony didn't know if he could handle another month of these brutal sessions, let alone if Rick could. Rick's workouts no longer seemed to help, and, more often than not, that anger came out in his sessions with Tony. Rick would rant and rave, yell and scream, or say nothing at all, sitting in the office in cold silence. Occasionally, he would take a swing at Tony in frustration and desperation. Through it all, Tony remained calm and unmoving, taking it all in stride, making Rick even angrier.

"Rick, c'mon, kiddo. Let your anger out. Get it all out, son. If you really wanna hit me, little brother, we'll go at it in the ring and I don't care if you flatten me. If that's what you need, then fine, son. I'll be happy to let you do it. Pound on your speed bag for hours if you have to. Just don't keep that anger inside," Tony urged time and time again.

At first, Rick would do everything Tony suggested, except fight him in the ring. He didn't trust himself. He was afraid he'd kill his friend before he could stop himself. But it just galled the young man to see Tony sitting across from him, taking the abuse Rick dished out day after day. Somehow Tony would shrug it off, even though Rick was deliberately cruel at times, just to get a rise out of the cop.

After almost three weeks of these antics, though, Tony decided to give as good as Rick was dishing out. He was suddenly tired of being Rick's whipping post, no matter how much he'd encouraged it in the first place. Tony hoped it would finally wake Rick up to the kind of person he had become.

"Rick, enough, dammit. Stop acting like a little kid. I'm sick of it," Tony snapped during one session in December, finally letting some of his own frustrations show.

The two were sitting in their office decorated for Christmas. Everywhere Tony looked, the detention centre was trying to make the jail feel festive. It wasn't working, at least not for Rick. And if Tony had to admit the truth, the decorations were pretty lame. No wonder Rick wasn't able to get in the "spirit" of the season.

"Tony, I'm mad, alright? Mad at the system for putting me though this. Mad at Johnny for doing this. What the hell did you expect? Happiness and joy just 'cause it's Christmas? I won't get to see Nana Christmas morning. I don't get to give Jor her present. Hell, if Seamus had his way, I wouldn't even be allowed to think about her!" Rick snapped back.

Bingo, Tony thought. Suddenly he realized what was going on and what had been missing from their last few sessions. *He hasn't even mentioned Jordan in a couple of weeks. I can't believe I missed that,* Tony realized. "Okay, Rick, I'm sorry, man. I get it. You're not really mad at me. You're mad Seamus won't let you see Jor. That's what the past weeks've been about and I've been too tired to really see it," Tony said amicably.

Frowning, Rick got up and paced like a caged tiger. His shoulders were tense and he was developing another terrific headache, something that was becoming an almost daily occurrence. As he paced, he thought about what Tony had said. It made a lot of sense, but knowing it and accepting it had done nothing to calm him down. Stopping finally in front of the door, Rick stared blankly ahead. He faintly heard Tony shift in his chair as if to spring over and slam the door if Rick tried to leave. He continued to stare through the door, not really seeing it. He could just see her. She was there, just out of his reach.

C'mon, Rick, think about it, Tony urged silently. *Admit what's wrong and we can deal with it.* It was never easy to watch Rick struggle, but Tony had learned that as long as he gave Rick his support, silent or vocal, Rick could take all the time he wanted and needed. Tony tried to set the pace, but usually let Rick decide when and where they would go in their sessions. It was always up to Rick, no matter how long it took.

This time, however, Tony decided to try a different approach to see if he could get a different reaction, other than anger, out of Rick. Tony got up from his chair, walked around the desk and leaned against the door so he could see Rick's face. Rick didn't even move. His face was so blank it could've been a mask. Knowing Rick was staring off into space and probably wouldn't see him until the cop said something, Tony watched Rick carefully. He noticed a tightening of the jaw and the smallest frown on Rick's forehead. His hands clenched tightly and Tony thought he heard something crack.

"Rick, what's wrong? Do you see something?" Tony asked softly. It was interesting to watch Rick's eyes moving as if watching someone or something moving just in front of his face. *What's going on in that head of yours, son?* he wondered, curious.

Without moving, Rick replied, "It's like a slide show, Fish. I see her eyes. Ever since grade three, those eyes're the first thing I see when I think of her. They shine when she smiles at me, and they turn black when I screw up. They snap when she's angry. I see them in my sleep and wherever I go." His voice was so quiet Tony strained to hear.

"Keep going," Tony whispered. *This is really interesting*, Tony mused. *I wonder what else he's 'seen' in our sessions. What isn't he talking about?*

"I see her lying on the floor with her hair spread out around her head like a halo. She's so still, Fish, I can't even tell if she's breathing. There's little traces of blood at the corners of her mouth. I can see the hand prints around her neck. I wanna help her, but someone's holding me back." Rick's voice got louder and louder. "He won't let me help her! Why, Tony? Why won't he let me go? Why?" Rick shouted as he pounded on the door until his hands were sore.

Finally, Rick sagged to his knees as he sobbed wearily. Watching Rick carefully, the cop slid his long frame down the wall to sit beside Rick. He didn't know what to say. Nothing would help since he knew it was Seamus Rick begged, and it would be a cold day in hell before Rick would ever get permission from the boss. *What a mess*, Tony thought for the umpteenth time, as the glimmer of an idea began to form.

"Rick, if I could arrange it, would it help you to see Jor, even for just a minute?" Tony asked as silence descended on the office.

"Get serious, Tony. Don't play with me. Not today. I'm not in the mood," Rick snapped, exhausted. His knees were killing him, but he just didn't have the energy to move. "Besides, O'Reilly won't let her. You know that."

"There's an old saying, kiddo. 'It's better to beg forgiveness than to ask for permission.' Or something like that. Lemme work on the logistics, but I'll try and sneak Jor in here before Christmas. Do you have a gift for her?" Tony asked, hiding a smile. *Seamus might not let her, but what he doesn't know, won't hurt her. Not yet*, Tony amended.

"Nana has it. She asked me what I wanted to get everyone the last time she was here and promised to take care of everything," Rick said. He rubbed his hands. They were sore, but not sore enough for Coach to excuse him from training. *Besides, I really need to hit something*, Rick grumbled to himself.

Tony let Rick rest for a few minutes while he planned his little manoeuvre. He knew what he was planning would be tricky, but he knew he had to try something. He finally nudged Rick so his friend would look at him.

"Okay, Rick. Today's been hard. Harder than we've done in a while, but we're not quite done. I need you to do a couple of things for me. First, and most importantly, don't let this place get to you. It's gonna be hard, I know, but don't break. You've gotta fight, son and fight hard. You're stronger than this, I promise you," Tony said as Rick snorted.

"Second, I want you to start writing some of this stuff down. Whenever the mood hits, 'kay? Day or night. Don't wait for our sessions anymore, even though they're daily. You don't have to show them to me if you don't want. Make 'em letters to Jor if you want. She may not see them, but write them anyway," Tony said.

"Why?" Rick wondered where Tony was going with this.

"You're not dealing with the anger in our sessions anymore so much as just trying to find ways to contain it and stay calm," Tony explained. "That's not doing you any good. You *have* to get the anger out if you want to survive in this place, and I think by writing the stuff down it'll help. 'Kay?" Rick nodded thoughtfully. "Then let's go. Coach should be here by now," Tony said. He sprung to his feet and held a hand out to Rick.

Rick stared at Tony for the longest time, then grabbed at the offered hand as if he were drowning. The cop hauled him to his feet and opened the door, wincing slightly at the damage Rick had done to the door and knowing he'd have to pay for it. Talking quietly, the two meandered to the gym where Tony handed Rick over to Bob with the recommendation to make him sweat.

It didn't take long for Tony to track Jordan down. Mickey had dropped her off at home on his way to Glencrest with Megan. Jordan refused to go, saying it wasn't fair to her to have to sit with a couple while her boyfriend was locked away. Mickey always used the drive home afterwards to try to convince Jordan Rick was nothing but trouble and they'd end up fighting.

Jordan was in her room studying when the housekeeper knocked on her door. "Come," Jordan called distractedly, concentrating on her Chemistry.

"Sorry, Miss Jordan, but Constable Whitefish to see you," the housekeeper said, poking her head in the door.

"Show him in," Jordan said with delight and laid her books aside.

"Hey, sweets, how's it going?" Tony asked as he sauntered into the room and planted a kiss on her cheek. She giggled.

"Hey, Tony. Same grade of horrible. Mickey's over at Glencrest mooning over Megs," Jordan said, disgusted.

Tony raised his eyebrows. "You two still fighting?" he asked, surprised.

"Yes. If you call what we do fighting. Fighting would imply I actually talk to him. I try to have as little to do with him as possible. Daddy, too. They watch me like a hawk and won't let me anywhere near Rick. I just wanna talk to him," Jordan said sadly.

"Well, now, I think I can help with that if you don't mind deceiving Mick and your dad a bit," Tony chuckled.

"What've you got in mind?" Jordan asked curiously, her eyes narrowing to a squint. Tony leaned closer to the young girl and talked quietly for several minutes as he outlined his plan.

"Know this, though, Jor," Tony warned softly. "When, not if, but when your dad finds out about this, it'll only cost me my job, but you'll pay a higher price. You'll lose your dad's trust. You still wanna do it?" He stared at Jordan for several long minutes while she thought about what could happen. Tony grimaced as he could still see the deep bruise around her larynx as she was thinking. He wondered if it would ever really heal.

"Even if it costs me my life, Tony," Jordan finally said.

Tony winced inwardly at her choice of words. "Be ready Friday at noon."

By Friday, Tony managed to get Rick's gift for Jordan from Nana and deliver it to the detention centre. He made arrangements for Rick to have a special visitor on Friday and most importantly, Tony managed to arrange to have Friday and the weekend off. He told Seamus he was burning out with all the investigations going on and he needed some time to get his head back in the game. Fortunately, it wasn't far from the truth. Tony was bone tired and he really needed some rest, physically and spiritually.

"Good idea, Constable. Yer head hasn't been here fer a long time," Seamus snorted as he granted both Tony and Marshall a three day weekend. *Neither has yours, boss*, Tony thought as he cleared his desk Thursday night.

Jordan managed to keep Tony's plan a secret, even though Mickey kept trying to get her to talk to him. She'd just ignore him and go on with her day. By Friday, she was a bundle of nerves, but excited nonetheless. She dressed carefully, and slipped downstairs for a strained breakfast with her family. As usual, Seamus warned Mickey not to let his sister out of his sight and soon the twins were on their way to Glencrest to get Megan.

"You're in a good mood this morning, sis. Something up?" Mickey asked. Jordan jumped slightly as she realized she had been humming.

She didn't hesitate more than a moment. "Not really. The day's nice. School's almost out for Christmas and I'm just happy," she said as she smiled at the thought of seeing Rick that afternoon.

"Happy enough to quit treating me like I have a disease?" Mickey asked quietly.

"Only if you're ready to admit you're wrong about Rick," Jordan snapped back.

"Nope. I still say the guy's bad news and you're better off with him in jail. Look at how things've calmed down at school since he's been gone," Mickey pointed out.

"Then your name's still mud, brother," Jordan sneered. Mickey winced, but didn't push his sister as they pulled into Glencrest. He knew she would eventually come around to his way of thinking. It just might take a couple of years.

Things were calm for Megan and Jordan, but the Knights were still causing a lot of trouble. Lockers were being destroyed, food and drink were stolen daily from the canteen, teachers were being abused and fights were becoming regular events. Mr. Delaney was struggling to maintain order in his school and failing miserably. He was ready to call the police and have them in the school permanently, he was that desperate.

Everyone knew what was going on, but no one had the courage to press charges and follow through with them. There was a rumour going around school a student named David MacDonald had seen Pup stealing from the canteen. The rumour also said David had threatened to go to the police, but changed his mind when he was threatened at knife point in his home at 2 a.m.

In short, the Knights were holding Colonial High hostage and no one was able to do anything about it.

That is, until a new group of boys had shown up. It started with four boys – Tom, Carl and two others from the boxing club. They, too, had an outfit that marked them as a "gang" – blue jeans and grey shirts with "Grey Angels" emblazoned on them. The four boys varied in size, and all but Carl had been targets of the Knights at one time or another and were tired of being victims. Carl had seen what the Knights had done to Rick once and didn't want it to happen to anyone else.

At first, no one, including the teachers or principal knew what to make of these four, but it didn't take long for them to make their presence known to Blade. The four had come around a corner to find Blade and Crank picking on a slender Grade 11 girl, new to the school, who had made the mistake of looking at Blade and asking him directions.

The two Knights had sent her books flying and had pinned her to the lockers. Blade had his hand raised as if to hit her when the Angels arrived. Without a second thought, they shoved their way past the two Knights and stood there, as if daring Blade and Crank to take a swing at them. Tom had his arms around the trembling girl, holding her while she sobbed with relief.

The two Knights hesitated, then walked away, laughing. While two of the Angels stayed with the terrified girl, the other two gathered up her books, then all four escorted her to her next class. One of the Angels had that particular class with her, so he stayed right beside her while the other three reported the incident to Mr. Delaney.

The four took to roaming the halls with Delaney's blessings, always ready to step in when the Knights tried to start something. They arranged to be an escort to anyone who wanted one, especially anyone who had already been targeted. Their numbers seemed to grow almost daily and there was only one criteria to join. You had to want to take Colonial High back from the Knights.

Every morning since the Angels had first shown up, a day after Rick's arrest for Megan's attack, Jordan had been met at the front doors by one of the Grey Angels who would escort her wherever she wanted or needed to go. And he would tell her the most amazing stories about Rick. Rick had saved Tom's life, at least twice, in his eyes. The first time had been when Rick had stood up to Blade in the computer room and the second time had been when Rick had got Tom into the boxing club. No matter how many times Tom told the story about the day in the computer room, Jordan never got tired of hearing it.

This morning, Tom was waiting for Jordan in his usual spot, leaning against the wall with his arms folded. He greeted Megan and Mickey politely and then followed Jordan towards her Homeroom. He nodded soberly to a couple of other Angels as they showed up to escort Megan to her Homeroom, leaving Mickey to trail miserably behind his sister. *Some boyfriend I am,* he thought as Megan left. *I can't even protect her in a crowded room.*

"Tom," Jordan whispered with a glance over her shoulder to see where Mickey was.

"Yeah?"

"You willing to help me?" Jordan asked.

"Anything, Jordan. You know that," Tom said earnestly.

"Good. Come to English 11 in second period about five minutes before the lunch bell. Tell Mr. Robson you've been sent to get me because I've an interview about my attack. Will you do that?" Jordan asked quietly.

"What's up, Jordan?" Tom asked just as quietly. She told him in a hurried whisper and swore him to silence. Since it involved Rick, Tom readily agreed to help with the plan. With one change – he made her agree to tell Delaney in case Mickey followed or checked on her.

True to his word, about five minutes before the end of English, Tom knocked on Mr. Robson's door. The teacher had a hurried conference with the lad, then called to Jordan. "Jordan, you're wanted at the office right now. There's someone there who can't wait five minutes for class to end. Go on, now. Don't keep them waiting," the teacher ordered, exasperated.

"Jordan?" Mickey hissed. He reached for her as if to grab her back. She tossed her hair back over her shoulder and glared at her brother. She left with Tom escorting her down the hall.

As soon as the pair were out of sight of the classroom, they broke into a run and dashed out the front door. Tony waved frantically for Jordan to get in the car.

"Tony, give this to Rick," Tom gasped and pressed a thick envelope into the cop's hand.

"Go, Tom, before you're seen," Tony urged.

Tom returned to the office and reported to the principal. "I hope she knows what she's doing," Delaney muttered as Tom nodded thoughtfully.

Without a word, Tony drove to the detention centre and signed in. Jordan was registered as a guest and the two walked to the office Tony used for Rick's counselling.

"Wait here. I'll go get him," Tony said gleefully. He put the DO NOT DISTURB sign on the door as he headed out. Since it was lunchtime, he headed straight to the cafeteria. *He's gonna be so surprised*, Tony laughed to himself.

The cop stopped the first kid he saw in the crowded room. "Have you seen Rick Attison?" he asked.

"Yeah, poor little Ritchie Rich's over by the atrium," the kid pointed with a sneer.

"Thanks," Tony said with a small grimace. *He's still not making any friends here*, Tony realized. *It's gotta be tough on him and that nickname's not gonna help either.* Tony looked in the direction the kid pointed and saw Rick sitting by himself. He was toying with a slender box brightly wrapped in Christmas paper.

"Hey, son," Tony said as he approached.

"Hey, Fish. Jeez, you're early," Rick said with a glance at the clock. *Why'd he give this to me?* Rick wondered again as his gaze returned to the box in his hands. *It's not like I can give it to her.*

"Yeah, I know. Talked Seamus into giving me and Marsh a three-day weekend. Told him my head needed a break and it didn't take much for him to agree. I'm burning out taking care of you, kiddo. Wanna talk early today? You don't look like you're eating anyway, and I've gotten you excused from your afternoon classes so we don't have to rush if we don't wanna," Tony said, noticing the tray of untouched food. While his face betrayed no emotion, inside Tony was dancing with glee. He knew his "gift" would make life a little better for Rick. For a while, anyway. Nothing short of getting out of here would make life perfect for Rick.

"Sure. Stuff's crap, anyway." Rick dumped his tray and followed Tony out. His feet knew the way to the office from any part of the centre by now, so his mind wandered back to where it had been before Tony arrived – Jordan.

He was thinking about her so hard, that, when Tony first opened the door to the office and Rick saw her sitting there, he thought he was dreaming. But when the soft scent of her perfume reached Rick, he knew he wasn't dreaming.

"Jor?" he whispered, stunned.

Tony pushed Rick gently into the room and closed the door. He turned his back so the two could have as much privacy as possible, since he wasn't allowed to leave Rick alone with anyone. Glancing quickly over his shoulder he could see Rick holding Jordan tightly as if, by letting her go, she would disappear.

"Rick, love, you look terrible," Jordan said finally. She had pulled back and was staring at Rick's face. She frowned, not liking the dark circles under his eyes nor the haunted look in them. *What've they done to you in here?* Jordan thought. *What's happened to the boy I fell in love with?*

"This place sucks the life out of you, babe. Besides, there's not much joy in my life right now," Rick said truthfully.

They spoke quietly for several more minutes as Jordan told him the news from school. Rick began to laugh when she told him about the Grey Angels and how Tom and Carl had formed them. The best part for Rick was the part about Tom being Jordan's daily escort. Nothing would've annoyed Blade more than seeing someone he had attacked come back so strong.

"Tom?" Rick said incredulously and shook his head. They were still lost in each other, but, as Tony moved around behind his desk, they seemed to let him into their circle, so it wasn't awkward. Tony just sat down and let them talk, since he didn't need to have Jordan back to school until almost two.

"They formed the group shortly after Meg's attack. Told Mr. Delaney they were tired of no one standing up to the Knights. Tom's been in two fights with the blond one – what's his name again?" Jordan asked.

"Brian," Rick shrugged nonchalantly, but inside he was seething at the thought of the Knights taking over his school. *If it wasn't for Tony...* he thought angrily.

"That's what I thought, but I wasn't sure. Well anyway, Tom's beaten him. Twice! I guess he's learned how to box from your trainer and he's doing almost as well as you. At least according to Carl. He's Meg's escort, even when Mick's around. And let me tell you, love, that doesn't sit too well with my brother," Jordan said emphatically.

"Heh! Mick's gotta be mad," Rick chuckled in agreement.

"Tom also told me to tell you he'll be kind and attentive, but very respectful of your girl. He also said to tell you that as long as I'm your girl, Johnny isn't laying another hand on me," Jordan said softly.

"Are you saying Tom believes me?" Rick asked, stunned.

"Tom believes you. I believe you. You know Tony and Marsh believe you. Rick, believe this, I trust you, with my life," Jordan said firmly. Somehow, Jordan knew she had to make Rick believe her.

"Why?" Rick wanted to know.

Tony held his breath. Jordan's answer could very well save Rick in this place or drive him over the edge. He watched, sitting as still as possible, as Jordan took Rick's hand and looked at his face, studying it as if seeing it for the first time.

"Simple, Rick. I love you." Jordan's eyes never left Rick's as she leaned forward and gently kissed him.

"I love you too, Jor. Sweets, I swear I didn't hurt you. Ever. Please believe me," Rick begged. He reached up and touched the same bruise Tony had noticed.

"With all my heart," Jordan replied softly, wincing away from the tender spot. Rick frowned as he realized he had just hurt her.

Tony couldn't help himself. He began to chuckle. He tried to keep quiet, but the harder he tried, the harder he laughed. The two of them looked at him, their spell broken.

"Tony Whitefish, what *is* your problem?" Rick snapped, annoyed at the interruption.

"Would you two like a stack of pancakes under all that syrup?" Tony chortled. He wasn't only laughing at that. He was laughing due to sheer relief. Rick had finally been convinced Jordan believed him and she would defend him, no matter what else happened. *Now if only I could get two stubborn Irishmen and a hard-headed Scot to believe him, we'd be getting somewhere,* Tony thought as he continued to laugh.

Jordan snickered. Then she giggled. Finally, she laughed out loud. Rick looked at both of them like they were crazy and then, as he thought about the conversation, he realized what he and Jordan had said to each other and began to laugh. He admitted to himself it was pretty sappy.

Finally everyone calmed down enough to talk. Jordan just sat back and listened while Tony and Rick had their session. She learned more about Rick in that hour and a half than Rick ever wanted her to know. There was one particular discussion which showed the young girl more clearly than anything else what Rick's life had been like before the Knights. It started with an innocent query from Tony.

"Rick, remember about a month ago, I asked you to think back to the one act that got Blade to take you into the Knights?" Tony began, sitting back in his chair.

"Yeah, and I think I know," Rick replied. He hesitated and turned to Jordan. "Sweets, this won't be easy for you to hear, but I think you should. If you hate me after this, then I'll understand, but when you hear this, I think you'll know me better than you ever wanted to."

Rick looked back at Tony and continued. "It took me a while, but I finally remembered the day Johnny got me. It was the day I creamed Colin Falher," Rick said softly. He hung his head. Just over a year ago, he hadn't even thought about it, but he finally felt ashamed of what he had done.

"I remember that fight. I started it," Jordan said sadly. She refused to let go of Rick's hand, even though she could feel him shaking.

"What makes you say that, Jor?" Tony wondered. He was writing furiously.

"Colin had asked me to a movie, for probably the tenth time. I thought it was well known around school that I was Rick's girl, and yet, Colin kept asking me out. I think he did it because he was Mick's friend and he knew Mick wanted me away from Rick. Problem was, I loved Rick from an early age and I haven't stopped," Jordan explained.

"What happened?" Tony asked intently. *I'll bet Seamus doesn't know about Jor's role in this,* Tony thought.

"I thanked Colin, and gently, but firmly, told him for the last time I was Rick's girl and I wouldn't go out with anyone but him. Colin looked so crushed I gave him a hug. Just as I was stepping back, but with Colin's arms still around me, Rick sauntered around the corner. I've never seen him so angry, Tony," Jordan said with a shiver. She refused to look at Rick, as she realized, in an obscure way, she had actually driven her boyfriend into a gang which had nearly destroyed him.

"All I knew was Colin had his arms around my girl. I had warned him, and this time I wanted to teach him a lesson he'd never forget," Rick grated. Even now, Rick got angry at the scene he remembered. He just wasn't sure if he was more angry at himself or at Colin.

"God, Tony, he was half my size! He didn't have a quarter of my strength, and you know how strong everyone's told you I was even then. I always hated how Johnny went after the little kids, and here I was going after the same kind of kid! To this day, I don't know why I didn't walk away. Later, it made me sick to think about what I did to that poor kid, but at the time, I didn't care."

"Easy, Rick. It's just a memory. Tell me what happened," Tony urged softly.

"I came up behind Colin, pulled him away from Jor and threw him to the floor. The look on her face was one of disgust, but I really didn't care. I just wanted everyone to understand Jor was off limits. Colin pulled himself to his feet and came at me. My fist slammed into his face, and he fell over. I know I beat him up pretty badly, Tony, I just don't remember any of it. That first punch is the only thing I remember until Jordan pulled me off of him. He just lay on the floor, not moving. I could've killed him, Tony," Rick said flatly. His eyes stared straight ahead and Jordan could see they were dark with pain. Mickey had kept tabs on Colin after that fight and Jordan knew he had never really recovered from it.

"What happened after that?" Tony asked intently. *Now I'll know if Seamus really fought Rick that day*, Tony thought.

"I walked outside, leaving Jor trying to get some help for Colin, and Mick crying like a baby. I was so proud of myself," Rick muttered darkly. "Johnny caught up with me just off school property. He tossed me my first leather jacket and told me I was in. I must've given him a really puzzled look, because he explained I was now a Black Knight. He told me I'd never be alone again. I couldn't get that coat on fast enough, Tony, and once I did, I finally felt like I belonged. I had a family, something I hadn't had since Mom left. The Knights made me feel like I was worth something. After that, I headed home with my head held even higher than when I left the school. Johnny and I hooked up with the rest of the gang the next day and I was officially in," Rick said softly.

"Did you meet anyone on your way home?" Tony asked curiously. *This isn't going the way Seamus said it did*, Tony realized with a sinking heart. *Something tells me he didn't fight Rick that day.*

"Nope. No one. I stuck to the back alleys and side streets. I know at least three, maybe four different routes home from the school and, to this day, I don't use the same one two days in a row. Johnny's taught me too well how to watch my back," Rick said, puzzled.

"Rick, as high as you were from the fight and getting into the Knights, is it possible you met up with, say Seamus and had another fight, but don't remember it?" Tony pressed as his heart sunk even further. *Seamus, who the hell did you fight that day if it wasn't Rick?* Tony wondered.

"I know Mick called Daddy right after the fight, but if Rick says he didn't meet up with my father, or anyone else, then he didn't!" Jordan spoke up quickly in Rick's defence.

"Easy, sweets. Tony, you got a reason for asking me that? Something you wanna tell me?" Rick asked casually, but he stared at his friend with narrowed eyes until Tony shifted uneasily in his chair.

"No," Tony lied quickly and snapped Rick's case file closed. Rick frowned as he realized Tony was lying, but decided not to press the issue. He wasn't in the mood, but Tony's question had made him think. *Was it possible I blanked something else out from that day? It took me a long, long time to recall the fight with Colin. Is it possible I forgot something else? If I did, it'd explain why Brian always told me I could take Seamus*, Rick thought as he just sat there, continuing to stare at Tony.

"Jor, do me a favour over Christmas, 'kay?" Rick said, taking her hand again as Tony wound up the session.

"What, love?" Jordan asked cautiously. She had an idea what Rick wanted and she wasn't sure she could do it.

"Tony's told me about the fights you and Mick've been having over me. I know he doesn't trust me, but I'm not worth that. He's too important to you. If I've learned nothing else from Tony, it's that if I had had someone like Mick, someone who had loved me and wanted to protect me, I might not be here now. Please, sweets, promise me you'll patch things up?" Rick begged.

"I can't, Rick. He refuses to see any good in you," Jordan protested.

"That's because, to Mick, there is nothing good about Rick. Rick's a punk, a trouble-maker and a violent gang member. Everything Mick isn't," Tony shrugged as Rick flushed in shame and hung his head. "It's up to you, Jor, to *make* Mick see the good in Rick."

"Just try one thing, sweets," Rick suggested, picking his head up and looking at his girl.

"What, Rick?" she replied sourly. Rick smiled at her attitude.

"Tell Mick as long as you both promise not to talk about me, you're willing to become his little sister again. Make me a forbidden topic and try to work things out. For yourself, and not for me," Rick said gently.

Jordan sighed. That promise, at least, would be easy to do. Since Mickey refused to talk about Rick unless it was to condemn him, they just had to avoid talking about him. "That I can and will do, love," Jordan promised.

Right before they left, Jordan and Rick exchanged their gifts. Jordan bought Rick a guardian angel on a gold necklace. "For all the times Tony can't be there," she said as she put it around his neck. Her name and the year were on the back. He smiled as the cold metal sat against his chest.

Rick's gift was a delicate gold and diamond i.d. bracelet. On the back were the words *'Think of me'*, but Rick's name was nowhere to be found.

"That's so you can tell your dad anyone but me gave it to you, and he can't make you get rid of it," Rick explained as he slipped it onto her slender wrist.

"One last thing, Rick," Tony said, and tossed over the card from Tom.

"I'll read it later, Fish, and tell him I said thanks," Rick promised.

After a tearful good-bye at the front door, Tony and Jordan left, with Rick watching the car fade from sight. He returned to his room and opened Tom's letter. The card was a comical Santa and reindeer, complete with a crazy saying and had been signed by all of the guys in the boxing club. Rick smiled and put it on his night stand. It was the only Christmas decoration he was going to allow in his room.

Tom's letter took Rick an hour to read. The details of the Grey Angels and how it was formed was amazing, but the more Rick read, the more worried he became. The Angels sounded too much like a gang for Rick's comfort. He sat propped up on his pillows and re-read the letter. He thought about it all through training and supper. Finally, right before lights out, he picked up a pen to write back.

"Hey, Kid, thanks for the card. Although I see Coach and Carl every day, I miss the rest of the club. Glad to hear your headaches're going away and your vision's improved. I've heard how well you're doing in your training, too. Coach brags about you about as much as he brags about me, I guess. Keep it up.

"By the way, thanks for looking out for Jor and Megs. I really appreciate it. Jor laughed every time she told me about how you've become her Guardian Angel and how you helped her today. Thanks. Just keep it buried or Mick'll cream you. Remember, Kid, she's a good friend, too.

"Tom, I've read your letter several times and it scares the crap out of me. I know the Angels were started as a response to the Knights, but be very, very careful. If you fall, it's difficult to get back up. I should know. I'm still trying.

"If things continue the way they are, when you're not watching, the Angels're gonna turn into a gang. A vicious gang that justifies what it's doing by saying it's just protecting those who can't protect themselves. The good you're doing now could be completely wiped out if you get someone like Johnny who likes to hurt, not help. The Angels're fighting, aren't they? And don't tell me the Angels don't challenge Johnny for no reason 'cause I know they do. I know *I'd* love to, especially if I'd been attacked by the Knights like you.

"Please, Tom, keep the Angels going. They sound like a great group. But talk to everyone and remind them they got together to *stop* Johnny and the Knights, not to become them. The Angels should escort people like Jor from class to class. Use the Angels to clean up and reclaim the school. Use the Angels as Delaney's eyes and ears. But for my sake, don't let the Angels fight Johnny unless they have to.

"Don't go looking for fights, Tom. Get the Angels into the boxing club if they wanna fight. Just please, don't go looking for Johnny or the Knights. The instant you do, you'll be no better than Johnny, and I don't think you wanna be like someone who's willing to come up behind someone who's smaller than you and smash him in the back of his head.

"Every time Johnny or one of the other Knights challenges you, remember me and ask yourself if you wanna be here. Remind the Angels of what happened to you, for God's sake. And, Tom, think – what're *you* willing to lose?"

Rick signed it and put it in an unsealed envelope. He'd give it to Bob tomorrow so he could pass it onto Tom. He just prayed Tom would get the message.

Chapter 32

As Rick tried to deal with being locked up for Christmas, Nana was dealing with a few annoying issues of her own. Despite being warned at Thanksgiving, Michael had continued to ask for money and Nana continued to refuse, knowing now what it was for. Because of Michael, Nana spent hours going over her estate with Owen, making decisions that would affect her family forever, including one that at least one member wouldn't be happy with. Owen agreed the changes were probably for the best and agreed to have his team get everything ready by Christmas. That allowed Nana to concentrate on getting Glencrest ready for the holidays.

By the last Saturday before Christmas, Nana had the ranch looking like a winter wonderland in the hopes it would help ease the Christmas sorrows. The main house was covered in lights, Glencrest ice blue this year, in stark contrast to the white house. Megan loved how the house glowed blue at night when all the inside lights were turned off. A large fir tree, lovingly decorated by all three and swarmed under with presents, dominated the formal living room. Everywhere you looked, there was Christmas; holly, mistletoe, evergreen boughs, candles and Christmas cards draped across strings hanging from the ceiling.

While the house was filled with the signs of Christmas, there really was no joy. It would be Megan and Ian's first Christmas without Diane, and Megan, especially, was taking it hard. There was no laughter in her eyes, especially since her attack. She was still sore, and tired easily, so she said, but she had healed physically for the most part. The nightmares were easing; and Ian had begun to allow her out of his sight, although it was very reluctantly. He'd come way too close to losing her once and he didn't want to go through that ever again.

Nana was sad because she didn't have all of her grandchildren home. Nelson hadn't been home in years, but he always sent a card complete with a long, loving letter and a special gift for both Nana and Rick. Michael he ignored. This year the parcel had come from Germany where he was working and his letter said he would be back in Australia with his wife by Christmas Day if Nana and Rick wanted to call. Also in the package was something special for both Ian and Megan, since Nelson knew they had moved in with Nana. Rick was in juvy and, as far as Ian was concerned, the boy was about as welcome at Glencrest as a swarm of locusts.

"Ian, lad, I need to talk to you and Megan, privately," Nana said. "Let's go into the library," Nana suggested, asking Martha to bring them some apple cider.

After everyone had sat, Nana spoke. "I've been doing some thinking over the last couple of weeks and I've made some decisions, very hard decisions I might add, neither of you're gonna like," she began.

"Goodness, what's wrong, Nana? You sound as if the world's gonna end," Megan said. She had settled herself on a stool by the fire and was warming her back. She stretched like a cat and every joint in her spine popped.

"It may. First of all, lass, I know you've been invited to the O'Reillys for both Christmas and New Year's Eve. I'd like you to decline Christmas Eve, please," Nana began.

"Why?" Megan asked curiously. "You didn't object last week when I told you they'd invited me."

"I still don't, but I've made arrangements for all three of us to go see Rick on Christmas Eve," Nana said and sat back for the fireworks.

"Never!" Ian shouted.

"Nana, no! Please! I can't!" Megan cried. She stood up and knocked over her cider Martha had just set on the table. Megan grabbed for some napkins and mopped up the mess, her tears falling as she tried not to sob.

"Mother, he attacked my daughter, your granddaughter, and you want me to be nice and celebrate Christmas with him? Never!" Ian cried again.

"Enough! Both of you, calm down," Nana snapped. "I know perfectly well what my grandson's been accused of doing. I'd like to stress *accused*, Ian. Unlike you, I get weekly updates on the investigations, and so far there's been nothing to convince the police, let alone me, Rick's guilty of anything except maybe making some bad choices when he was younger. There's absolutely *no* physical evidence other than that bandana and the jacket to link him to any crime and there's been no forensic evidence found on either one of those items to tie them to Rick, other than association. Nothing! Do you hear me? And your own daughter has been unable to say with absolute certainty Rick was the one who attacked her. Until that happens, he's *innocent until proven guilty!* Do you understand me, son?" Nana snapped. Ian's fury subsided with a sharp nod.

"Besides, he's still family and he's alone in that horrible place. Unlike you, lass, Rick doesn't even have a father who loves him. Michael abandoned that child without a second thought and Lord knows where Kara is. Nelson won't come home and now you've both decided to treat him as if he was a disease. Remember Christmas is also a time of forgiveness. Please, if nothing else, do it for me," Nana begged. Her face fell as her son shook his head.

"No. I'm sorry, Mother, but I can't. I won't. Until a court clears him and, even then, until I can forgive him, no. Absolutely not. I won't," Ian said firmly. Megan nodded in agreement as she dried her eyes once more. *How could Nana even ask me to do that?* Megan wondered as she returned to her seat.

"Very well. If that's your final decision, then you two'll stay here at home and have a quiet night. Alone. And I expect both of you to stay here. If you won't come and see Rick, then you don't see anyone," Nana scolded. She took a deep breath and continued.

"My second decision's final and I won't accept 'No' for an answer. Michael'll be joining us for supper on Christmas Day. I've an important announcement to make and Michael needs to be here to hear it. He's arriving at five and he's agreed to be gone by seven, whether supper's done or not. Ian, can you be civil to him for two hours?" Ian nodded at Nana's demand. "Good. Now go. I'll see you both at supper," Nana said and dismissed them with a wave. As Megan slowly left, she swore she saw Nana crying.

"Daddy?" Megan called softly as she stood by the door.

Her father turned back. Megan had stopped outside the library door and was listening intently. "What is it, lass?" he asked, puzzled.

"Daddy, I think she's crying. I think we've really hurt her feelings," Megan whispered as she motioned her father closer.

Ian put his ear to the door and listened carefully. Megan was right. Over the crackling of the fire and the carols playing in the background, Ian heard his mother's quiet sobs.

"Daddy, maybe we should reconsider," Megan whispered hesitantly.

Ian led her to the dining room where they sat at the table. "Could you really do it, Megan? Could you sit in the same room as the boy who's been accused of beating you and Jordan and pretend nothing happened? Think hard now, lass. Could you do it?" he asked.

"No. Not yet, Daddy," Megan finally replied after thinking for several minutes. She sighed. "My head says he did this. Maybe the evidence will too, I don't know. But my heart says he didn't." As Ian began to protest, Megan raised her hands to stop him. "No, hear me out, Daddy. I've done a lot of thinking since the attack, mostly at Tony's urging. Ever since I met him, I've always trusted Rick somehow, deep down. That first day of school, against Nana's wishes, he introduced me to Johnny, but he's also shielded me from him as best as he could. Despite how he knows Mickey feels about him, Rick also gave me my boyfriend. It was like Rick knew we'd hit it off right away. Daddy, honestly, I have to wonder if my constant accusations of Rick stem from Mickey's hatred of him. He's the first to blame Rick and, I might've just followed along this time without really stopping to think about it.

"Daddy, the whole attack just didn't seem like Rick. It was too brutal. It took too long. Rick's not like that. If he did it, it'd be one punch and all over. There's this kid at school, Tom Shelley, who's become Jordan's protector, even when Mickey's around. He's always there, watching Jordan's back, to use one of Rick's phrases. He's taking the same boxing training as Rick does. Apparently Tom asked Coach if he thought Rick could attack someone like Jordan or myself, Coach told Tom Rick wouldn't just knock us out. He'd probably kill us," Megan said quietly. She was a little frightened that she knew someone with that kind of power.

Ian was shocked. "He's that strong?" he asked incredulously. "He must've somehow held back when we fought, then, because he creamed me."

"He's that strong. And no, Daddy, he probably didn't hold back. It's just you're bigger and stronger than Jordan or I, and you'd be able to handle it. So you see, Daddy, somehow, I can't blame Rick. I just don't know if he did it. Does that make any sense? I know I can't go to see him, Daddy, but I think we could've found a better way to tell Nana," Megan said thoughtfully.

Ian nodded. "You're right, lass. Let's go," he agreed.

They walked back to the library and knocked. They noticed Nana hadn't moved. Seeing the tears still on her grandmother's cheeks, Megan knelt beside her and touched her knee. In her hands, Nana held a photo of happier times – the four teens, lounging on the porch in early September, laughing. *Clearly one of the few happy days in the past four months,* Megan agreed thoughtfully as she smiled at the photo.

"Nana, I'm sorry. We're sorry for reacting the way we did. We should've been more thoughtful. I still can't agree to see Rick, but I'd like to make an offer," Megan said in the silence. It was something she had thought of on the spur of the moment.

"What, lass?" Nana asked, drying her eyes.

"How about I tape a letter for Rick? Maybe Jordan could too. You could add something if you wanted. At least this way he could hear Jordan's voice, since I know Mr. O'Reilly never lets them talk. I know it's not the same as going and seeing him, but I'm just not ready to face him yet, whether he did this or not," Megan said softly.

Ian nodded in agreement. "I'm not ready at all, Mother. It's not just a trust issue. It's an I-need-him-to-be-cleared-by-the-courts issue. Even then, it's gonna take a while to trust him completely. We just reacted badly. We should've thought about your feelings, not just ours. I keep forgetting how small this family really is and how much you've always enjoyed having us around. Please. Forgive us, especially me. I should've known better," Ian said huskily. He, too, had knelt down in front of his mother to beg for her forgiveness.

Nana smiled and reached out to put her hand on his head. "Of course I forgive you, son. Have I ever not forgiven you?" she asked quietly. "I was just shocked you wouldn't want to spend time with family, no matter what they've done, but I guess I understand," Nana said.

She looked at Megan. "Your idea's a good one, lass. It'll be good for Rick. He needs all the help he can get. He's struggling to get by right now and only time will tell what's gonna happen," Nana predicted. With that, the family went their separate ways for the night.

On Monday, with the school holidays begun, Megan rode Mystique over to the O'Reilly farm. It felt good to be riding by herself again and not feel like she had to look behind her all the time, or to have to have someone riding with her. In her saddlebag was a tape recorder and some blank tapes. After slipping her horse into her stall in the barn and removing her gear, Megan grabbed the recorder and sauntered up to the house.

"Hi, Mr. O'Reilly," she called as the housekeeper let her in.

"Hello, Megan. Feeling better?" Seamus said coming from the living room to give her a careful hug.

"A bit more every day, sir. Unfortunately, I have to turn down your invitation for Christmas Eve. Nana's asked me to stay home with Daddy," Megan said. She winced at the small white lie. *Well, it's mainly true,* she amended to herself.

"That's okay, lass. We'll still have you here for New Year's," Mickey said from behind her. *And that's the most important day anyway,* Mickey said to himself. He wrapped his arms around his girlfriend and gave her a hug.

"Come on, Megan. Jordan's waiting." With a wave to Seamus, Megan followed Mickey up the stairs to his sister's room.

"Hi, Meg," Jordan greeted her best friend cheerfully as if they hadn't just seen each other two days earlier. She reached over to the stereo and turned down the carols.

"Hey, Jordan. Ready for Christmas?" Megan asked. The twins nodded as all three flopped on the double bed.

"You two seem to be talking again. I'm glad. School's a drag when your best friend won't talk to you because you're dating her brother," Megan giggled as Mickey pulled her against him in another warm hug.

"We made a promise to each other. As long as we don't talk about Rick, I won't condemn him and she promised not to shut me out," Mickey shrugged. He didn't understand the sudden change in her, but he wasn't going to argue.

"Christmas is a time of forgiving, a friend pointed out. So I forgave him. I had to. I couldn't stand the pain anymore." She brushed her hair back with her right hand and Megan noticed the new bracelet.

"Where'd you get that, Jordan? It's beautiful," Megan asked, examining the bracelet when Jordan held her arm out at Megan's silent request.

"She won't say, lass, so don't bother asking. Trust me, I've tried," Mickey muttered.

Jordan laughed. "So what's up, Meg?" the youngest O'Reilly asked.

Megan quickly outlined the discussion she had with Nana two days earlier and her idea. "I can't see him yet, not until I've figured out in my head if he actually did this, even though Nana wants me to, but I thought hearing our voices might help him.

Yours especially, Jordan. I know how your dad doesn't let you talk to him. Since he loves you so much, maybe hearing your voice will help him make the right choice and admit anything he's done. Nana's says he's struggling right now and even Tony and the boxing isn't helping much anymore. What do you say, Jordan? Will you do it?" Megan asked, pulling out the tape player and the tapes and laying them on the bed.

"Dad'll freak if he finds out, sis," Mickey warned. Jordan didn't even hesitate.

"'Tis better to beg forgiveness than to ask permission, bro. Gimme the tapes," Jordan said and held out her hand.

Over the next few days, Jordan "talked" to Rick. She talked about the farm and what she was doing over the holidays. She talked about school as if their meeting hadn't happened. She talked about the Angels and how they were doing. Mostly she talked about the way they'd changed. She was so worried about Tom. She was beginning to have déjà vu. He reminded her of an early Rick – angry and violent, willing to do almost anything. He was still so sweet and attentive, but he was scary at times with how extra protective he'd become. Most of all, she talked about how she felt about Rick.

At the end of the tapes, Jordan talked about their visit, praying her dad never found out. "I kept my promise, love. I forgave Mick. You're right. He's too important to me to hate him over something silly, even if it's you. I'm trying to get him to see the good in you, but it's an uphill battle. Unfortunately, Daddy may never see the good, but I do, and maybe, just maybe, I can get Mick to, as well. Think of me often, Rick. Don't let that place get to you or Johnny wins. I love you. I trust you and I believe you. Love always, Jor."

She snapped the recorder off and removed the final tape. She labelled it carefully and put it with the other two she had already filled. Mickey had promised to take them to Megan in the morning so Nana could take them to Rick Christmas Eve. Jordan just hoped they would help.

Jordan's fears her dad wouldn't find out were futile. Shortly after she had began the first tape, Seamus had overheard her dictating her letter and had begun lurking outside of her bedroom door. He was furious she'd disobeyed him and even more shocked to realize she'd somehow slipped away from school and seen that boy. Enough was enough.

Seamus strode down the hall to his son's room. After a perfunctory knock, the elder O'Reilly swung open the door and marched in, much to his son's surprise.

"Hey, Dad. What's up?" Mickey asked, annoyed. He put down the book he was reading and reached over to turn down his stereo.

"Son, have ye and yer sister been keeping secrets from me?" Seamus demanded.

"Secrets? Not me, Dad," Mickey protested mildly. *Little sis, what've you done now?* Mickey thought, amused, although his amusement didn't last very long.

"Do ye know anything about yer sister seeing that boy earlier this month?" Seamus demanded again.

"No," Mickey replied slowly. "Dad, what're you talking about?" *That day at school*, he babbled to himself, schooling his face into calm indifference. *No one wanted to talk to her about the attack. She tricked me!*

"What about these tapes she's making for him?" Seamus demanded yet again.

Mickey froze. "Dad, have you been eavesdropping on Jordan?" Mickey asked quietly.

"As long as she lives in me house and under me roof, she'll obey me rules! Now answer me question, boy!" Seamus thundered as he towered over his son.

Mickey had never seen his dad so angry. *If this is what Rick's had to face all these times, no wonder he hates my dad*, Mickey thought. A tense and uneasy silence fell in the room while Mickey decided what to do and how to calm his dad down. Mickey may not have liked Rick, but he'd always loved and sheltered his baby sister. He protected her from everything, even things she didn't think she needed protecting from. He just never thought he'd have to protect her from her own father.

"I'm waiting, Mickey Liam O'Reilly," Seamus said, his voice deathly quiet.

Mickey winced. His dad never called him by his full name unless he was really mad. "Look, Dad. I don't know anything about any visit. You'll have to ask Jordan about that. The tapes, I could tell you about, but I'd be betraying Jordan's confidence and I'm no snitch," Mickey said softly.

"If she thinks she's gonna send those tapes to that boy, she's got another thing coming," Seamus snarled as he marched to the door. Mickey jumped up and put his hand on the door so his dad couldn't leave.

"Dad, wait. Listen for a sec." Mickey grabbed his dad's arm. "Fine, I'll tell you about the tapes. First of all, the tapes were Nana and Megan's idea. They're worried about Rick right now. Nana says Rick's struggling and Tony's counselling isn't helping. She thought hearing some tapes of Jordan and Megan might help. Who knows, Dad? Maybe he'll hear something on those tapes and confess. So don't yell at Jordan for them.

"Secondly, you've forbidden Jordan from seeing him. You never said she couldn't write to him or send him something like this. God, Dad, since when does *she* live in a prison? I know for a fact she's been keeping a diary ever since they hooked up three years ago and definitely since Rick told us he was out of the Knights. That was back in September. She writes in it every day, telling Rick what's been happening, even if he was there.

"Third, Tony pointed something out to me. Dad, the more you and I push Jordan away from Rick, the faster she's running towards him. Your anger's driving a wedge so far between you and Jordan that it's never gonna heal. I finally got her talking to me again, but only by agreeing to not talk about Rick. It's the only way she'd speak to me and even now, it's fragile. One wrong word and she'll stop talking to me altogether and I'll never get her back. She loves him more now than she ever did and it just seems to keep growing, no matter what we do. If she did sneak off to see

Rick, you can bet she did it to annoy you as much as it was to spend time with him. She doesn't care about what we want for her anymore," Mickey said. He paused and looked at his dad.

Seamus pulled his hand away and yanked open the door. He was still angry. Mickey could see that. But something told Mickey his third point had scored. Seamus loved his children almost unconditionally and nothing would ever change that.

"Anything else, son?" Seamus growled.

"Yeah there is. C'mon, Dad, please, it's Christmas. If you wanna freak on Jordan, fine. But could you at least wait until after Christmas? Please? Don't ruin our holiday by jumping on her about this stuff now. Let her send the tapes. They won't harm anything and they might do some good. Then talk to her – *talk*, Dad, don't yell – after Christmas," Mickey urged quietly.

"Okay, son. We'll do it yer way. For now." Seamus slammed the door on his way out.

Now it was Mickey's turn to be mad. He had just covered for his sister. He'd probably just lied for her and he wanted an explanation. He opened the door carefully and listed for his dad. Seamus was down in the living room watching TV. *Good, I have time,* Mickey said to himself. He hurried to Jordan's room and knocked.

"Can I come in, sis?" he called quietly.

Jordan opened the door. She was in her dressing gown, ready for bed and was in the process of brushing out her long, red hair. "Have a seat, Mick. I'm almost done," she said as she sat back down at her vanity.

Mickey watched his sister for a long time. He remembered Jordan spending hours brushing her hair until it shone. He smiled sadly as he remembered their mother doing the same thing until her hands became too crippled with the onset of arthritis. He sighed. *Happy Christmas, Mom,* he thought.

"Remembering Mama?" Jordan asked, looking at her brother in the mirror. Her hands pulled the brush through her hair in a mesmerizing rhythm.

"Do you realize it's been over six years since we lost her, sis?" Mickey asked quietly. He didn't stop watching Jordan brush her hair. He could almost see his mom standing over Jordan's shoulder.

"I miss her every day, but especially at night, when I'm brushing my hair. Oh, the hours we'd spend sitting and brushing," Jordan sighed happily. The brush continued its mesmerizing pattern.

"The hours I'd sit and watch you. To this day, I still don't know what it was about watching the two of you brush your hair that would capture me, but I never missed an opportunity to sit and watch," Mickey chuckled. "Y'know, sis, sitting here watching you, I almost thought you were Mom for a second. Do you know how much you look like her?" Mickey asked suddenly, his voice husky.

Jordan put down her brush and turned to face Mickey. Her brother never talked about their mom unless something was wrong. It was his way of saying something was hurting him badly. She studied him. He had stretched out on her bed, his long legs crossed at the ankles. He was leaning over onto his right side and his hand held up his head. He was dressed in jogging pants and a muscle shirt with a plain gold chain Megan had given him glistening in the light from the candles Jordan had lit around her room. His hair was still slightly damp from his earlier shower and his eyes reflected the candle light, too. All in all, he seemed relaxed, but ever so slightly she noticed that his jaw was clenched.

"What's wrong, Mick? You never talked about Mama unless you're upset," Jordan asked bluntly.

"Jordan, you keeping secrets from Dad?" Mickey asked lazily. He watched his sister out of the corner of his eye.

"Why do you ask?" she asked immediately.

"Dad's been listening outside your door and says you snuck off to see Rick. Is that true?" Was it his imagination or did Jordan just jump slightly?

"Why's Daddy listening at my door?" she demanded hotly.

"I don't know, sis," Mickey said honestly. He sat up and shifted to sit at the end of the bed facing Jordan. He looked at her intently.

"Look, sis, I may not like Rick, but I think I understand why you did it. I think, knowing how much Megan means to me, if she were locked away, and I was forbidden from seeing her, I'd probably sneak away, too. Did you do it?" Mickey asked again. He so wanted her to deny it, but somehow, he knew she had.

"And if I did?" Jordan asked quietly. She now understood what Tony had meant. He might lose his job if, – no, *when* – her father found out who helped her visit Rick, but she'd probably just lost her father's trust and love.

"Then I'd say duck, because Dad's gonna go freak if you did. Jordan, he wanted to take the tapes away from you," Mickey continued. He couldn't stand the sudden pain in Jordan's eyes. *Dad's a blooming idiot*, Mickey grumbled to himself. *Tony's right. We're gonna drive her away.*

"The ones for Rick?" Jordan paled at the thought of all her hard work being destroyed.

Mickey nodded. "The bracelet's a gift from Rick, isn't it?" he asked softly. He ran his finger over it, catching the diamond on a rough patch of skin.

Jordan nodded miserably. "Mick, what'll I do? Daddy wasn't supposed to find out anything," she whispered. The tears she had been struggling to hold back started to fall.

"Nothing, sis. Dad's agreed to wait until after Christmas. We've got time to figure something out," Mickey soothed as he gathered his sobbing sister into his arms. As he held her tight, he realized Jordan was in deep trouble with their dad. *What a mess*, he thought as Jordan continued to sob. *What a bloody mess.*

Chapter 33

Nana was the only one to come and spend a quiet Christmas Eve with Rick at the detention centre. Not even Tony came to visit his friend. It was hard for both Nana and Rick, but listening to the tapes Nana, Megan and Jordan had made helped Rick get through the day somewhat. Even Ian had sent Rick a small gift and wished his nephew a good Christmas.

"At least he understands it won't be happy or merry," Rick said sourly as he put the tapes aside.

"I know, lad, it's hard being in here, but you have to be patient. Tony's gonna get you outta this and outta here," Nana said confidently as she passed over the gifts.

Rick smiled as he opened the beer stein Nelson had sent from Germany. "Well, I guess I'll drink pop in this until I'm legal," Rick said, laughing at the letter in which his older brother told him about the family in Australia. "I always forget he's married now. Cherie and Matthew sound like they're growing faster than Nelson would like. He's missed a few things this year and he's gonna talk to his company and tell them he'd like to either quit travelling or get a transfer back here. Does he know about me, Nana?" Rick asked as he folded the letter. He put the family picture on his nightstand and sighed. They looked so happy.

"Yes and no, lad. I've told him you were in a gang and managed to get yourself into a little trouble with the law, but I didn't want him rushing back here. There's nothing he can do after all, so I didn't give him full details," Nana said carefully. She didn't want Rick to know exactly how much she had told Nelson and how mad his big brother had been. It had taken some fancy talking to stop Nelson from rushing home to confront Michael.

Rick continued to open his presents. Megan had bought him some new jeans and several new cds, all from his favourite bands. Ian's gift was a new watch. Nana had found several movies she knew Rick had seen and liked, as well as a couple of new books to keep at the centre. She told him about the new furniture added to his house, confident Rick would be coming home in January.

The evening came to an end all too quickly. With a sigh, Nana picked up all the gifts but the two books, the tapes and the cds. The centre did not allow anything else to stay, not even the new clothes. "Merry Christmas, lad," she said with a lump in her throat as she held her grandson tight.

"Merry Christmas, Nana," Rick said thickly. He watched her drive away, then went back to his room. There he spent the rest of the night pounding on his speed bag, trying to get rid of the all-consuming anger he felt building rapidly.

Megan woke early on Christmas morning. Silence dominated the house. "'Tis Christmas morning and all through the house, nothing is moving, but this little mouse," Megan whispered to herself. *How many times had she woken her parents up with that little poem?* Megan wondered as she left her bed. She sighed sadly as she remembered this year, it would only be her father she would wake. *Merry Christmas, Mama,* she thought. *I miss you.*

Shivering in the pre-dawn chill, she went to her window and grinned. The lights from the house sparkled on the snow below. Barely discernible in the dark morning were the falling snowflakes. It was seven in the morning and snowing on Christmas Day.

Megan pulled on her robe and slippers and padded down the hallway to her father's door. Putting her ear to the door, Megan could hear his deep breathing. *Good, he's still asleep. Time to wake him up,* Megan giggled to herself. She eased the door open and slipped silently into his room. She let her eyes adjust, although she knew she could move unerringly to her dad's bedside in total darkness if she needed to. Once Megan determined where her dad was, she stepped carefully to his side.

Little did Megan know that her father was wide awake. He'd heard his daughter slip into his room and knew what time it was. He, too, remembered the poem and he, too, wondered how many times they'd played this game. *The first one was in Dundee,* he recalled suddenly, *the year before we moved back home and Megan was four. Diane, how your little girl has grown up these past months. You'd hardly recognize her,* Ian thought sadly as he mourned again for his lost wife.

"Daddy, 'tis Christmas morning and all through the house, nothing is moving," Megan began whispering in Ian's ear.

"But my little mouse!" Ian said. He grabbed Megan around the waist and flipped her over onto the bed with a squeal. Then, mercilessly, he began to tickle his daughter as she continued to squeal with laughter.

A throaty chuckle from the doorway joined in. "Can't an old lady get some sleep around here?" Nana demanded good-naturedly.

"Merry Christmas, Mother," Ian said as he rolled out of bed and threw on his robe.

"Merry Christmas, Nana," Megan's muffled voice echoed from underneath the comforter Ian had thrown on top of her.

"Merry Christmas to you both. Come now. Let's open presents." Nana beckoned and led the way to the living room.

An hour later, all the presents were opened and the paper piled for recycling. Megan admired the elegant writing set Rick had given her. He knew how much she enjoyed writing long letters to her friends. She also received several new outfits from her mother's family and a beautiful portrait of Diane, painted by a friend of her Grandma Edna.

"It looks just like Mama, doesn't it, Daddy?" Megan's eyes filled with tears as she stared at the picture. Ian could only nod, as he, too, tried not to cry.

There was new tack for Mystique, done in black and gold, as well as a new riding outfit for Megan. Ian gave his daughter several new cds and movies, new perfume and a new winter bomber jacket. Jordan had given her friend a set of Irish folk songs as well as a new gold chain with half of a Best Friends charm on it.

A note included with the gift said Jordan had the other half. But it was Mickey's gift that blew Megan away.

Ian handed Megan a slender box with no card or ribbon. She looked at him, puzzled. "This is from your lad. He said to tell you it's part one of two and you'll get the other part on New Year's Eve," Ian explained.

Megan eagerly slit open the paper and removed the jeweller's box from inside. She opened it, gasped and promptly dropped the box, sending the item skittering across the floor. Ian picked it up and held it out to his daughter. It was a necklace like none she'd ever seen. Even Nana gasped when she saw it for the first time.

It was 24K gold, of that she was sure. Along the tiny box chain were alternating tiny diamonds and emeralds. In the firelight, Megan looked like her throat was wrapped in emerald fire.

"Megan, it's beautiful," Nana said finally. Megan couldn't say anything.

The phone suddenly shrilled, making everyone jump. Ian answered it with a cheerful "Merry Christmas" and then listened for a moment. "Yes, she did. Of course, she's right here. Hang on." Ian beckoned to Megan. Still reeling from the gift, Megan could hardly walk to the phone.

"Hello?" she somehow managed to croak.

"Merry Christmas, lass. Do you like it?" Mickey's sonorous voice came back to her.

"Do I like it? Mick, it's absolutely gorgeous! It must've cost you a fortune," Megan gasped finally.

Jordan's chuckle came over the extension. "Actually, Meg, the necklace's a gift from both of us and it didn't cost us a cent. That necklace once belonged to our mother," Jordan said. Megan could hear the sadness in her best friend's voice.

"Jordan, I can't keep this! You should have it," Megan protested.

"Don't worry, Meg, I already have one. Mom had two made for a family portrait we had done over in Belfast 10 years ago. I've been adding the extra links she had made for me ever since. It was the last family picture we were able to have done before she died four years later," Jordan said. Mickey took a shuddering breath and sniffled. Megan could hear the unshed tears in his voice and realized she wasn't the only one who had lost a mother at a young age.

"It was Mom's dying wish that her necklace be passed onto the next lady to come into our family, whether it was someone Dad loved or me. I asked Dad if I could give it to you," Mickey continued, his voice thick with emotion.

"When did you ask, Mickey?" Megan wanted to know.

"That day we met, lass. That very first day. You got under my skin the instant Rick introduced us, but Dad made me wait until I was sure I loved you," Mickey said so softly Megan could barely hear him.

"Do you?" Megan asked pensively.

"Absolutely," Mickey replied with a grin.

"My gift wasn't nearly as nice as this, Mickey," Megan giggled. She had given Mickey an i.d. bracelet, similar to the one Jordan wore.

"Yours is absolutely beautiful, lass. It's never coming off," Mickey vowed.

The rest of Christmas day passed quickly. Everyone put their gifts back under the tree and went outside where Frank had hooked up a team of horses to the sleigh. After picking up the O'Reillys, the two families drove around the countryside visiting other families to sing carols and spread some Christmas cheer.

By four o'clock, Megan, Ian and Nana were back at Glencrest to prepare for supper. The house was filled with the smell of roasting turkey, potatoes, stuffing and all the trimmings, and a table set for seven. Megan knew once the meal had been served, Martha was leaving to go and spend the rest of the night with her family in Collingwood, while Frank and the rest of the hands had their own turkey dinner in their bunk house.

"The O'Reillys are coming over," Nana explained after Megan tracked her down in the library. "There's no point in cooking a full turkey meal for three in two separate houses, after all."

Knowing that her friends were coming over, Megan took great care in dressing for the evening. She chose an emerald green velvet dress that flowed and swirled when she walked. She left her hair loose so it cascaded down her back, except for two thin braids she did up at her temples and pinned at the back of her head with a small barrette. Delicate dance flats dyed the same colour as her dress were slipped onto her feet as she adjusted her new necklace so the clasp was in the back. She finished off the outfit with a pair of diamond earrings that had belonged to Diane, a slender gold bracelet and a simple gold watch.

She emerged from her room at the stroke of five to hear Michael being admitted into the house. Ian and Nana met him at the foot of the stairs just as Megan reached the top, where she paused to make her entrance. All three adults turned to watch the teen glide down the stairs, with her hand resting lightly on the railing. Ian reached up for Megan's hand just as she reached the bottom few steps and helped her finish her descent.

"An entrance fit for a queen, lass," Ian chuckled.

"Shall we adjourn to the library? Our other guests won't be here for a while and I have some family business I'd like to get outta the way before they arrive." Nana turned and led the way to the library. Once everyone was settled in front of the crackling fire in the fireplace, Nana opened the leather portfolio laying on the table beside her.

"Michael, Ian, I've done some very hard thinking these past couple of months. This family's having no end of troubles and I'm beginning to wonder if we'll ever see something resembling normalcy again. Ian, you've lost your lovely wife, and now, very nearly your daughter. I've decided you won't be doing any more travelling for me. It's just too dangerous. I've hired someone else," Nana began.

"You're not upset at how I did things, are you, Mother?" Ian asked, even though he was relieved to be able to stay at home with Megan.

"Heavens no, lad. I just realized if something happened to me or Megan and we had to try and find you when you're travelling, it'd be very hard. So you'll stay home and focus your energies on the training and breeding programs here. Specifically, I want you to focus on the rodeo and ranch horses. Those seem to be in far greater demand in the area than the show jumpers, so I'm going to eliminate that portion of the breeding program once the current batch of colts are trained up and sold," Nana said. Ian nodded and sat back.

"I've also made a decision about my estate. I know Christmas's really not the time to be discussing my death, as it's supposed to be a time of joy and rebirth, but in light of certain events in the past couple of months, I decided these changes couldn't wait any longer. I've changed my will, effective immediately and it's non-negotiable." Nana paused for a long time, staring at Michael.

"Michael, I don't know what kind of mess you've managed to get yourself into, and frankly, I no longer care. Just as you've disowned Rick, I'm disowning you. You no longer have a place in this family. What money problems you have are far too great for me to fix. So I've changed my will to reflect the following: Ian, as ever, will be my executor. That won't change. Should he predecease me, that unfortunate chore'll fall to Megan. The estate'll now be divided as follows: Ian'll receive 40 percent, Megan 30 percent, and Rick 30 percent, minus a few special bequeaths I've set aside for special gifts for people like Martha, Frank and the clinic.

"As per Nelson's request, I've set up trust funds for Cherie and Matthew. He's also asked for a couple of special pieces of art he gave me and, if he chooses to come home in the near future, a section of land I own that he's had his eye on for several years. Otherwise, he asked me to give his portion to his little brother, as he's done well enough in his own business pursuits and investments, he doesn't want anymore. A very generous young man, is your eldest son, since I know you'd never do anything like that, Michael. Again, should Ian be so unfortunate as to pass before I do, his 40 percent shall be split between Megan and Rick, 30 percent/10 percent. And this was not an easy decision to make, let me tell you, but it was one both Owen and I felt was necessary. And Michael, it's all been filed with the courts. This will's irrevocable. I don't suggest challenging it," Nana warned as she sipped at her glass of sherry.

Michael was speechless. He wasn't expecting this. Even though his mother was in excellent health, he had counted on getting the money eventually. Now, he'd been shut out completely. "Mom, I don't get it. What're you saying?" Michael finally demanded.

"I'm saying what I said at Thanksgiving, Michael. The Bank of Mother's now closed. Permanently. You'll never get another penny from me," Nana said firmly.

"Mom, don't do this. I'm in real trouble here. I need the money. Give me my term deposits at least. You didn't take those away, did you?" Michael asked, panicking at the sudden implications. Without that money, he was as good as dead.

"I did, Michael. It's all in Rick's name now. If he goes to prison for life, all of it'll end up in Cherie's and Matthew's names. It's all gone, Michael. You've made your bed. Now lie in it!" Nana snapped.

"NO! Mom, you can't do this to me! I need that money! Please! Give me the term deposits and I'll never ask for another penny! I swear!" Michael begged.

"How much money do you need, Michael?" Ian demanded, puzzled by his brother's panic and his mother's ruthlessness.

Michael started to say it was none of Ian's business, but Nana spoke first. "At last estimate, he owed Mendez over $250,000 and it's growing every day," Nana said viciously.

"Mendez? Who's this Mendez?" Ian asked, even more puzzled.

"His, uh... bookie, I believe the term is," Nana said even more viciously. She knew she was being hard on her eldest son, but Michael needed to be brought back to reality.

"A bookie? You're gambling? How could you be so stupid?" Ian demanded.

"Look, just give me the damn term deposit and I'll do anything you want. Just don't hang me out to dry," Michael growled.

"Michael, that's over $2 million dollars! If I gave you that, you'd just gamble it all away. The answer is no. The bank's closed for business. Period. Now get out and don't ever set foot on any of my property again, and that includes Hollyhock's," Nana said with finality.

"But....but...."Michael stammered.

Ian hauled his older brother up out of his chair. "You heard Mother. Get out!" Ian snapped, grabbing Michael's arm.

"Get your filthy hands off of me, Ian," Michael snarled and wrenched his arm free. He stumbled to the door, then turned and glared at the rest of his family. When he spoke, the venom in his voice was unmistakable.

"Mark my words, all of you. One day, I'll make you pay for this. You'll beg me to take the money when I'm through with you," Michael growled and stormed from the room. They all heard the front door slam behind him.

"And a very Merry Christmas to you too, Uncle Michael," Megan said sarcastically, raising her glass in a salute and sipped her cider.

Megan, Ian and Nana sat quietly in the library until the O'Reilly's arrived at six for supper. Martha led the family into the library for drinks while she finished getting supper ready. Mickey greeted Ian and Nana distractedly, but only seemed to see Megan. As he stood beside her with a hand extended to help her to her feet, his dark grey slacks and white shirt seemed to be a perfect complement to Megan's emerald dress.

After a lively supper, the two families retired to the living room for drinks. The tree was glowing and Nana had lowered the lights in the room to match the mood. A fire crackled in the fireplace. Megan had sat in her favourite wing-back chair near the fireplace. Her necklace glowed in the subtle light. Mickey sat at her feet, looking up at her while they talked quietly. By an unspoken agreement, there was no outward showing of how they felt about each other.

"Ian, your camera. Quick," Nana said softly. She nodded toward the two in front of the fire. Ian snagged his camera from the table where he had left it earlier that morning.

He waited patiently, knowing the shot would be worth the wait. He raised the camera to his eye when Mickey raised his head and smiled at something Megan said. The young man had one hand on his girlfriend's knee and the other was supporting his weight as he lounged at Megan's feet. The instant Megan returned Mickey's smile, Ian snapped the picture.

"Perfect," he whispered.

Several minutes later, Ian noticed Jordan had joined the couple. She perched herself on the arm of the chair and all three were holding hands, almost as if Mickey and Megan were trying to give her their unquestionable support. Ian shook his head and felt incredibly sad as he snapped the picture. While Megan and Mickey almost shone with their love for each other, Jordan was the picture of heartbreaking sorrow.

Chapter 34

Two days after being disowned, Michael was drowning his sorrows at East Side's, just like he'd done the night before and the night before that. It was the only way he could deal with what his mother had done. Unfortunately, the more he drank, the fewer ideas he came up with to get the money he needed to pay off Mendez. And he needed it soon. His bookie was starting to make noises about taking the brokerage and making Michael work for him.

"Rye and Coke, Michael?" the bartender called out as Michael walked in right before supper.

"Gimme a steak sandwich, medium rare and keep the rye flowing, Greg," Michael said grimly as he sat down.

By 10 pm, Michael was well passed drunk. The bartender came over and put his elbows on the bar. "Michael, something you need to talk about, man? This is the third night in a row you've come in, hell bent on getting as drunk as you can as fast as you can. If you don't slow down, I'm gonna have to cut you off," he warned.

"Hell, Greg, don't do that. I'll slow down. Don't cut me off, man, my old lady's already done that," Michael said mournfully.

"Your mother?" Greg asked incredulously.

"Snap. Just like that, I'm outta her will, outta the family, outta her life and outta money, man," Michael said, snapping his fingers. He slammed down the rest of his drink. Greg put a plain coke in front of him and just shook his head.

"What'm I gonna do, Greg? Mendez's gonna kill me," Michael slurred.

"Christ, don't bring that maniac down on me, Michael. Don't know what you're gonna do, but that's the last booze you get for a while. Ease up," Greg said and walked away.

In the dark corner behind Michael, another patron laughed quietly. Blade had recognized Michael the instant he had walked in, and had set himself up near him in case Michael said something about Rick. This was so much better. He waited for several minutes while Michael downed a couple of more cokes and then begged Greg for another rye.

"Hey, man. I couldn't help but overhear ya," Blade said, sitting down beside Michael. He motioned to Greg for a drink and the bartender, with a slight hesitation as he looked around for the undercover cops who frequented his bar, dropped a beer down in front of the teen and left them alone.

"Do I know ya, kid?" Michael slurred, as he tried to get his bloodshot eyes to focus on the shadowy figure across from him.

No, but I definitely know you, man, Blade thought gleefully. "Name's Johnny and ya look like ya could use a friend. I'm a friendly kind of guy," Blade said quietly. He looked around and noticed there were too many people around for them to talk comfortably.

He led Michael over to the darkest part of the bar. The table was poorly lit and far enough away from the noise the two of them could talk without being overheard. Over the next couple of hours, Blade kept Michael just drunk enough to keep him easy to manipulate. Michael was definitely indiscreet enough that Blade got the whole sordid family tale and, inwardly, the teen was roaring with laughter. The plan was working perfectly. Rick would come crawling back.

But the more Michael talked, a different idea started to emerge for Blade. He thought he saw a way to get rid of Rick, permanently. It was no longer enough for Blade to break Rick. He wanted the only Knight who had ever left the gang gone forever, so no one would ever think of leaving again. The one thing Michael kept coming back to was he needed money quickly or Mendez was going to come after him with guns blazing.

"Look, Michael, ya gots a big problem. But I think I've gotta solution fer ya," Blade drawled as he leaned back away from the stench of Michael's breath.

"You do?" Michael said surprised.

"Yep. See, I gots a couple of good friends who, fer a small fee, will help solve yer problems. Permanently," Blade whispered to Michael.

Michael sobered quickly as he figured out what Blade was possibly suggesting. He frowned. "Look, kid, I'm too drunk to think straight. Call me at this number after New Year's," Michael growled as he scribbled on a napkin. "We'll talk then."

Chapter 35

New Year's Eve was magical, at least for Megan. She spent the day with Nana and Ian, but the evening was going to be spent with the O'Reillys. She was nervous since her necklace was only the first part of her Christmas gift from Mickey. She could hardly wait for the rest.

When Ian dropped her off at the O'Reilly's on his way to a New Year's Party, she noticed Jordan's eyes were bloodshot, tears were falling down her cheeks almost non-stop and she refused to look at her father. As Megan greeted Seamus distractedly, she noticed the bracelet Jordan had been wearing was gone, and her wrist was bandaged.

"Mickey, what's going on? What happened to Jordan?" Megan whispered as she greeted her boyfriend.

"We had an awful argument this morning, me, Dad and her. About Rick. Somehow, Dad found out about the tapes and she's apparently managed to sneak off and see Rick at the detention centre at least once since his arrest. She refuses to tell Dad how and who helped her, and now I'm not allowed to let her out of my sight. Dad's turned our house into her jail cell, and I'm her jailer," Mickey said with a small growl. He was standing behind Megan with his arms around her and Megan could feel his arms tighten with anger. Both watched as Jordan moved quietly around the living room to sit on the farthest side away from her father and brother to stare out the window.

"She's close to breaking, Mickey," Megan said softly.

"I know, and I can't help her anymore, dammit. I've already paid my own price for this, and I can't keep covering up for her, no matter how much I love her," Mickey said as he turned Megan around. He pointed to a bruise on his cheek. Megan was shocked and reached up to touch it gingerly, not surprised when he winced and moved away.

"What happened?" she demanded, horrified at what was happening to the family she loved as much as her own.

"Dad hit me. No, don't worry, lass, he only did it because Jordan's hell-bent on defying him. He took his anger at her out on me, thank God," Mickey said defensively. His ears had rung for a long time after his dad had hit him, and he shuddered to think what would've happened if his father had hit Jordan.

Megan looked at Jordan again and then Seamus. He was standing at the door with his arms folded and glaring at his daughter, as if staring at her long enough would eliminate everything that had gone so wrong. Megan wondered if he really knew how close he was to driving his daughter over the edge.

"Mickey, I need to talk to your dad," Megan said and slipped away from Mickey's embrace. Someone needed to stop this before it got way out of hand. *If it hasn't already*, Megan thought sourly. She approached Seamus carefully because she knew his temper matched his fiery red hair.

"Mr. O'Reilly, sir, may I talk to you for a moment?" Megan asked finally, after standing in front of the cop for several minutes waiting for him to acknowledge her. "Privately?"

"Certainly, lass. Keep an eye on yer sister, son. We wouldn't want her to slip away from us now, would we?" Seamus said with thinly veiled anger. The twins both flinched as Seamus led Megan to his office nearby. He gestured for Megan to take a seat and then sat down across from a young lady he considered his second daughter. He knew what was coming and had his arguments ready.

"Mr. O'Reilly," Megan began hesitantly.

"Megan, I think ye know me well enough by now to call me Seamus," Seamus interrupted gently.

"Very well...Seamus, I noticed something today when I came in. Jordan's been crying, she looks like she's been hurt and Mickey has a black eye. I know you're mad at her, but you need to understand I asked Jordan to make the tapes for Rick. She didn't decide to do them on her own. She was doing it for me and for Nana. Please don't be mad at her – be mad at me," Megan said nervously.

"Look, Megan, me daughter knows when I forbid me children to do something, that's the end of it, no questions asked. She broke the rules, whether ye asked her to do it or not. She knew she was breaking the rules and she didn't care. She's not to have anything at all to do with that boy," Seamus replied hotly, his temper already rising.

"And when those rules're so ridiculous they push her to break them, what then, Seamus? Don't you understand? The harder you push her away from my cousin, the faster she's running towards him. Tony's been trying to tell all of us that for months now," Megan said passionately.

"As long as Jordan lives under me roof, she'll obey me and me rules. End of story," Seamus said stubbornly.

"And when she can't handle that anymore and she leaves, then what, Seamus? Will you hunt her down like a common criminal and haul her back in handcuffs? Will you lock her away like a princess in a tower? Is it so important to punish Rick, even if he's not guilty, you're willing to risk not only Jordan's love, but Mickey's and mine as well? Be very careful, Seamus O'Reilly. You know I care a great deal about your son, but I've also come to care about you and Jordan. As important as that is to me, if you continue to punish your family for someone you hate, you'll lose the people you love. If Jordan wants to leave this farm, I'll help her and not think twice about it. Think very hard about this, Seamus. What are *you* willing to lose because of one boy?" Megan's words lingered as she left Seamus sitting alone in stunned silence.

Jordan, too, was sitting in silence, just as miserable as she could be. She was as far away from her brother as the room allowed, even though she knew deep in her heart he was only doing what their father wanted. Still, he didn't seem to stand up for her as he once did. She sat on the window seat in the large bay window and stared at the frozen world before her. Gently, she cradled her wounded wrist as silent tears continued to fall. *I wonder what it would take to get sent to the detention centre*, she wondered. *At least then I'd be with Rick and maybe having some fun.* Her thoughts wandered back to the fight that morning.

It had started like any other day. Jordan got up, showered, dressed and came down to breakfast. Around her right wrist was the bracelet Rick had given her. She never made any attempt to hide it since she firmly believed her dad didn't know who gave it to her. When she arrived at the dining room, the door was closed, but it didn't stop her from hearing the argument between her dad and Mickey. *Well, if Daddy can eavesdrop, so can I,* Jordan decided and placed her ear to the door. She almost wished she hadn't.

"... and I can't understand why ye let her visit him, boy!" Seamus yelled. Jordan flinched as she heard the anger in her father's voice. Why he was so mad at Mickey, Jordan didn't know, but he was absolutely furious with his son.

"Don't call me 'boy,' Dad. I'm not Rick!" Mickey shouted back. "Besides, until a week ago, she wasn't talking to me. What the hell was I supposed to do? Tie her to me so she's never out of my sight? I'm her brother, for crying out loud, not her damn jailer!"

"Yer whatever I tell ye to be! Yer responsible fer her when she leaves this house and ye know that! Do you hear me, boy?" Seamus shouted back, even angrier than he had been when he'd cornered his son in the dining room to confront him.

"I told you not to call me that!" Mickey shouted again.

Jordan heard a loud crack and then deadly silence. She couldn't move at first. Their father rarely used physical punishment anymore, as he had far more effective methods. If he ever spanked them, it was only because these other methods had failed and they had pushed him too far. He had never, ever, slapped either of them. Jordan knew then she was in deep trouble, but she had made her choice and now she had to live with it. She pushed open the door and marched into the room.

At the far end were Seamus and Mickey. Jordan could see the red welt already forming on her brother's face where their father had struck him. The look of shock on Mickey's face was clearly matched by the one on Seamus'.

"Mickey, son, please. I'm sorry. I didn't mean to," Seamus begged, holding his hand out in apology. Disgusted with his dad, Mickey turned and faced his sister.

"Look, Jordan, I've done my best to protect you, but we both need to know. Did you sneak off to see Rick?" Mickey asked. His eyes begged her to deny it, but Jordan wasn't sorry she had done what she'd done. She loved Rick and nothing would keep her from seeing him whenever she could.

"Yes," Jordan replied without flinching. Mickey's shoulders dropped. There was nothing he could do for his sister now.

"After all me warnings, ye dare to defy me, girl?" Seamus growled, his face getting redder and redder from the anger he could barely contain.

"Daddy, we have names. Use them!" Jordan snapped. Her patience was finally gone. If her father wanted a fight, then, by heaven, he was about to get one.

"Why did ye disobey me, Siobhan Jordan Colleen O'Reilly?" Seamus yelled, shaking with anger. He couldn't believe what he was hearing from his daughter.

"Because I love him! Just as much as you loved Mama! Nothing you say or do to me's ever gonna change that! Why can't you get that through your head? I love Rick Attison and I won't abandon him! Ever!" Jordan shouted back.

"After everything he's done, ye still love him?" Seamus sneered at his daughter.

"I've said it before and I'll say it again, Daddy, *you can't prove he's done anything!*" Jordan cried shrilly. "Dammit, like every other criminal in this bloody world, Rick's innocent until proven guilty in a court of law! As a cop, you know that!"

"Watch yer language, young lady! And what do I need with proof? Ye were told not to have anything to do with that boy. Ye're not to see or contact him and now ye've done both. Explain yerself. Who took ye to see him? It certainly wasn't yer brother," Seamus growled.

Remembering Tony's warning about losing his job if Seamus found out he helped her, Jordan remained stubbornly silent. The longer she stayed silent, the angrier Seamus got. He ranted. He raved. He shouted. He threatened. Mickey began to worry Seamus was about to start breaking furniture if Jordan didn't answer soon, if he didn't keel over from a massive heart attack first. He was about to intercede when Seamus caught a glimpse of the bracelet on Jordan's wrist and shifted his focus to that.

"Did he give this to ye?" Seamus demanded, catching Jordan's wrist in a vice-like grip. He squeezed the bracelet into her wrist so hard, she cried out in pain. Mickey jumped to his sister's defence immediately.

"Dad, stop it! You're hurting her, dammit!" Mickey yelled as he struggled to pry his father's hand off and not caring about being punished for swearing. His patience with his dad was long gone.

"I'll hurt her a lot worse if she doesn't answer me!" Seamus continued to squeeze, not caring how badly he could feel the bracelet cut into her wrist.

"So what if he did give it to me, Daddy? Are you gonna cut off my hand so you can get rid of it?" Jordan demanded through her tears. She forced herself not to struggle in Seamus' grip, but it hurt like hell.

"Ye'll take it off and throw it out. That's what's gonna happen!" Seamus said furiously.

"No," Jordan replied softly.

Both Seamus and Mickey were stunned. "What did ye say?" Seamus demanded incredulously, staring at Jordan like she'd just grown a third head.

"I said no. I won't take it off. I won't throw it away. You can't make me," Jordan said defiantly.

Seamus shoved her so hard Jordan stumbled backwards and would've fallen against the table if Mickey hadn't grabbed her and steadied her. He glared at his father while Jordan cradled her injured wrist. Mickey could hear her sobbing and saw the blood dripping from where the bracelet had cut her. He was mad as hell and immediately shoved Jordan behind him to protect her as he stood up to their father for the first time in his life.

"What the hell's wrong with you, Dad? You're acting just like Rick, you know. Is this how you treat your cops if *they* defy you?" Mickey demanded.

Seamus didn't move for the longest moment. He took several deep breaths and tried to calm his pounding heart. *What's wrong with me?* Seamus wondered as he continued to stare at his children. It was only a bracelet, after all, but the fact his daughter had willingly broken one of his cardinal rules was driving him insane. He stepped closer. Never had these two made him so mad he became irrational, but something about the bracelet was driving Seamus around the bend.

He leaned in close enough neither teen had any trouble hearing him. His voice was low, hard and full of anger. "Get this straight, Jordan. From now on, ye'll remain in either mine or yer brother's sight at all times, here and at school. Ye'll not wear that cheap piece of costume jewellery ever again. If I see it on ye, I swear I *will* cut off yer hand if I have to, mark me words. You will *not* write to him, call him or visit him. I had better not find that diary of yers, either, 'cause if I do, I'll burn it right in front of ye. Disobey me just once, me girl, and ye'll rot in that room of yers!"

With that, Seamus strode from the room. The twins heard the front door slam and the sound of Seamus pacing on the front porch. Mickey just held his sister for a few minutes as she cried broken-heartedly. Once he had her calmed down, he took her to the bathroom so he could take care of her wrist. She cried out a couple of times while Mickey eased the bracelet out of the cut, but fortunately, he didn't think it was bad enough to require stitches. She washed off the bracelet and locked it away in her jewellery box, then hid her diary even better than before.

Now Jordan was forced to live under a microscope. Mickey had indeed become her jailer and there was nothing either teen could do while the slightest hint of suspicion fell on Rick. Somehow, some way, Jordan had to convince her dad Rick wasn't a threat to her or anyone else.

As miserable as Jordan was, Mickey was even worse. He couldn't believe what their father had done that morning and nothing was going to change anytime soon. He'd tried to talk to Seamus again that afternoon, but his father just reiterated Mickey wasn't to ever let his sister out of his sight. At least in the living room, he could give her as much space as he could while still technically obeying his father. He felt Megan's hand slip into his as she came back from her talk with his father, and from the sigh that escaped from her, Mickey realized she hadn't had any more luck than he had.

"What a miserable New Year's Eve," Jordan muttered out loud. She jumped slightly as Mickey touched her shoulder.

"Is there room for two more, sweets?" Mickey asked. He knew it was Rick's special endearment for her and it nearly broke his heart to see the fresh tears welling up in his sister's eyes.

Jordan shifted around and her two best friends sat on either side of her offering their silent comfort. Mickey pulled his sister closer so her head rested on his shoulder. It was so much like the way Rick would hold her Jordan couldn't help herself. She burst into tears again and Mickey just held her tighter.

"Sis, you know I can't change Dad's mind, so we're just gonna have to live with this until Rick's cleared. When that's happened, well, even though I don't like him…." Mickey paused.

"What, Mick?" Jordan's sobbing began to quiet.

"If you truly wanna be with him after everything's said and done, if he's cleared, then I'll stand behind you. Even against Dad," Mickey vowed. Unknown to the three teens, Seamus stood behind a door near them. He winced to hear his own son promising to stand up against him.

What's wrong with me? Seamus wondered again as he returned to his office. He thought back to a conversation he had overheard between Tony and Marshall a few days earlier. Tony had been talking about a session he had had with Rick and how

Rick had admitted the fight with Colin was what had got him into the Knights, but Rick couldn't remember fighting with Seamus. *Something that important in his life, and he can't remember doing it?* Seamus thought incredulously. *Maybe that's what's made me so mad.*

In the living room, Mickey continued to try to soothe his sister while she cried. He finally managed to convince her a snowball fight in the front yard would do wonders for her, so she and Megan teamed up against Mickey. They still lost. Twice, in fact. Wonderfully exhausted, the trio went for a wander around the farm, talking and planning their next year. Megan was glad to have such wonderful friends.

Megan and Mickey tried to make Jordan feel welcome, but Jordan couldn't help but feel like a third wheel. No one liked having their little sister hang around when they wanted to be alone with their girl. Jordan knew there had been several occasions when Mickey had wanted to be alone with Megan. But, since Seamus had shackled the twins together, Mickey couldn't slip away with Megan. Mickey refused to let Jordan stay in the house with their father since he didn't trust their father's temper if he had Jordan alone. All in all, it was a thoroughly miserable night for Jordan.

At midnight, despite all their differences and the fighting, the family stood together to welcome the new year. At the stroke of twelve, with his father watching and smiling softly, Mickey slipped a simple gold band onto Megan's ring finger.

"Megan, lass, I know we've only known each other for four months, but, from the moment I met ye, I couldn't help wanting to be beside ye all the time. I know ye figured that out the first day I took ye home. The more I got to know ye, the deeper I fell in love. Yer smile makes me weak-kneed and the sound of yer laughter gives me goose bumps. This is me official request – would ye be me girl?" Mickey asked. He had turned to face Megan and was looking down at her. His Irish accent, normally almost non-existent, had grown thick as he waited for Megan to say something.

No words were necessary, in Megan's opinion, as she kissed him in agreement. Jordan turned away. She couldn't help the tears that had welled up again, and, with a strangled sob, she fled to her room where she cried herself into an exhausted sleep.

Chapter 36

Rick's New Year's Eve wasn't much better than Jordan's. He was sulking in his room while the other inmates were in the lounge, eating, talking, and either watching television or playing pool – badly in Rick's mind – and he'd been tempted to grab a pool cue and embarrass every last one of them. That wouldn't've made him any friends. Not that he had any now, but still, he didn't want to isolate those few who might become friends.

Generally, they were having a good time. Rick, on the other hand, was sulking. There was no other word for it and he knew it. He was miserable and he wanted out. He was tired of being locked up for something he didn't do.

He stared around his room and finally focused on the tapes Megan had thought would help him get through this. It had only made things worse. Instead of being happy to hear Jordan's or Nana's voice, even Megan's, Rick became more and more upset the more he listened to them. Jordan was so near and yet so very far away. He couldn't even listen to the ones Nana and Megan had made, because they reminded him so much of Jordan's.

Rick sprung up from his bed and went over to his speed bag. As his hands flowed automatically into the rhythm of the workout, his mind drifted back to the day before.

Ian and Megan had shown up unexpectedly. Tony had just left Rick in the gym with Bob. It had been one of those days where Rick had been too angry and beat down for the counselling session to do any good. After only fifteen minutes, Tony had broken it off. "You need to hit something very badly, little brother," Tony said, irritated.

"Do you have Seamus hiding anywhere close?" Rick had asked sarcastically as the two had walked to the gym. Tony just laughed, even though he knew Rick was serious.

Tony had just walked out of the gym to get a cold drink when he spied Ian and Megan signing in. "Ian. Megan. What're you doing here?" Tony asked, surprised. *Like I don't know,* Tony thought and suddenly he was more than just irritated.

"I need to see Rick, Tony. I really need to hear from him he didn't do this. I'm sorry," Megan replied, a little shakily. Tony could see the last remaining cuts on her face had healed and the scars were a vivid white against her slight tan.

"What brought this on so suddenly?" Tony asked, since Tony knew not a week earlier she had refused to spend any time with her cousin.

"I got a phone call last night. From my attacker. When I asked him who it was, he said, 'Ya know it's me, cuz. Moneyman.' I could hear that laughter again in the background. They described my attack in detail and took great delight in making me cry. It was a pay telephone, so I don't know where the call came from," Megan said quietly.

"Easy, lass. It wasn't Rick," Tony said with a small sigh. *Thank God they used a pay phone, or Rick would've been in deep trouble*, Tony thought. "There're no pay phones on site and no one's allowed off site without an armed escort. Never at night, and never without good reason. Phoning someone from a payphone isn't a good reason," Tony explained.

"That kid's slipperier than a wet saddle, Tony," Ian said disgustedly. "He could've been in and out before anyone missed him."

Tony looked at the two standing before him. Ian was still mad about the attack and Megan was just plain scared to be in this place. Tony sighed. He was going to have to do some fancy talking to try to get these two to leave without talking to Rick.

"First of all, Rick's a special case. After supper, he generally stays in his room and he usually has a guard on his door. Most other places would call it a suicide watch. I call it anger management. Secondly, the only door that isn't locked down 24/7 is the front door. The emergency exits are all alarmed, and if they *are* somehow opened, they set off an audible alarm and a light on a map in the guard's control room that is also monitored 24/7 and right by the front door. If Rick had slipped out any one of those doors, he would've been caught long before he could've made it to the nearest pay phone, which is over 10 blocks away from here. Trust me, guys. I've seen it happen. There's always one or two who try.

"Besides that, today's not a good day to try and talk to Rick. I'm not only speaking as his friend, but as his counsellor. I haven't been able to get him to talk today, so he's trying to work off his anger with Bob first," Tony warned.

"What's so special about today?" Ian asked angrily.

Tony hesitated, then decided these two needed to know what was happening to Rick. Otherwise, they weren't going to leave him alone. "Rick gets moody in here, and it's slowly been building to the point where Rick can't control the anger any more. No amount of talking or boxing's doing him any good and it's begun to take a heavy toll on him. He's angry, hurt and worried. He doesn't know what to do about any of it anymore and he can't control himself most of the time. He's almost needed sedation a couple of times.

"Since neither of you've ever spent any time in a juvenile detention centre, let me explain something about this one. This place has one goal in mind when these kids come in – break 'em and do it quick. The counsellors here're overworked and understaffed and they swear you can't do anything with most of these kids until they have their spirit broken. Literally broken. There's nothing left to work with. They don't care about finding out why a kid does the things he does; they only care about getting them so broken down they can't get back up. Only then, the counsellors swear, can they be reformed," Tony said with some heat.

Tony had argued with the head counsellor on this point several times since Rick had arrived. Even with the judge's orders, the counsellor had still wanted to sedate Rick to the point where he wouldn't be able to function.

"Rick's been able to resist that so far, but it hasn't been easy. And his resistance's slowly being eroded. It's helped that the court ordered him to keep up with his boxing and his counselling sessions with me. I've become his verbal punching bag and Bob's been working on his physical punching bag. Despite all of that, Rick gets in a foul mood every now and that leaves him restless, angry and very bitter," Tony repeated.

"If he'd just admit to attacking the girls, then things'd be easier," Ian said stubbornly.

"You sure you're not related to Seamus?" Tony asked sarcastically. "My point is," Tony continued before Ian could answer, "today's one of those really bad days for Rick. I broke off counselling after only fifteen minutes and sent him to the boxing ring. I *might* be able to get some counselling done if, and only if, Bob wears him down completely he has nothing left physically, but I doubt it," Tony finished with a grimace.

"Tony, please, I need to see him," Megan begged.

Tony shrugged and tried to hide the frustration he felt. "Okay, but I warned you," the cop said and led the way back into the gym.

Rick was working at the heavy bag under both Bob and Carl's watchful eyes. Carl was holding the bag, while Bob was trying to give Rick advice. "Placement, son, placement. See that spot as Carl's ribs. Just like the practice rounds. Placement, Rick. C'mon, Champ! Placement! Okay, Rick, stop. STOP!" Bob yelled finally. Rick looked up, his eyes clearly unfocused. Bob moved in close to Rick and said something that popped Rick's eyes wide open.

Uh oh, Tony thought. *I got him here too late. He's got that look in his eyes.* Tony tensed, waiting for the explosion.

It never came. Whatever Bob muttered quietly to Rick seemed to work. Carl continued to hold the bag as Rick went back to work. Tony could see the difference in the punches Rick was throwing, though. Now they were crisp, clean and focused. Before they had been all over the place and, while they may have had power, there was no strength or Rick's usual finesse.

"Look at him, Ian," Tony urged, turning back to face Megan's dad. "Can't you see the anger in those punches? Don't you remember the fight you had with him? If even *one* of those punches had hit Meg, she'd be dead. You know that. You know much damage there was to her face, so imagine if Rick had hit her more than once. Is he holding anything back, Bob?" Tony asked as the trainer approached.

Bob looked back at Rick and nodded. "Yeah, finally. We're trying to go for strength and control today, not power. So he's holding back a little, but not as much as I'd like. He's trying to see the bag as Carl and is supposed to be working on body shots right now, when I can get him to focus on what he's supposed to be doing which isn't very damn often. Placement, Rick! Focus!" Bob bellowed across the gym. Rick waved in acknowledgement and resumed punching. Bob watched Carl correct Rick's stance and then returned to the conversation.

"Have you ever seen Rick hold back in a fight, sir?" Megan asked timidly. Even though she'd been told about how strong Rick was, seeing it really made her realize there was no way he attacked her. Now she just wanted to hear it from him.

Bob shook his head. "He can't, not yet. Not in a real fight. Carl ended up with a great set of bruises from a match I set up between the two of them when Rick first came here. Carl couldn't figure out why he was still having trouble breathing a couple of weeks later until we found out Rick had actually broken one of Carl's ribs in that match. No, miss, Rick doesn't hold back in a fight. He doesn't know how," Bob emphasized.

"If Rick was to hit my daughter, what would happen?" Ian finally asked.

Bob cleared his throat. "Hmph. He'd kill her. End of story. I'm just now getting him to the point where I can get him to pull some of the power from his punches. Otherwise, fight or not, he's gonna kill someone sooner rather than later," Bob replied.

Tony pulled the trainer away. "They wanna talk to Rick. Have you got him calmed down any yet?" Tony asked urgently.

"No, and there's no way you're gonna be able to talk to him at all today, he's that angry. Hell, Tony, I know exactly who that is and if she asks him that one question you know she's going to, it's gonna drive him over the edge. How soon's his preliminary hearing? If he doesn't get out of here quick, he's gonna break," Bob urged.

"It's not until the tenth and there's no new evidence against him. The judge refuses to move the prelim up, no matter how much I ask. I'll try to get these two to leave," Tony said softly. As Bob walked back towards Rick, Tony just stood and watched. He could see the tension in Rick's face as he failed to hold his anger in check. This was not the day Tony wanted to have this confrontation.

"Tony?" Megan asked, touching his arm.

"Meg, do you really wanna do this to him?" Tony asked, still looking at Rick.

Megan winced at the tension she could hear in Tony's voice. "Tony, I know in my heart he didn't do this. I understand now what you've been saying about how strong he is, but I just need to hear him say it. I need to have him say to my face he didn't hit me," she replied quietly.

"Do you have any idea what that one question may do to him? He's barely hanging on and that one simple question may break him. He'll probably end up sedated. Do you understand the chance you're taking? Do you really wanna be responsible for that?" Tony pleaded, as he turned to face Megan.

"Tony, my daughter wants to talk to Rick. Period. Why's that so damned difficult?" Ian said brusquely.

Tony continued to argue with Ian and Megan as Carl struggled to hold onto the bag Rick was pounding on. "Coach, I can't get him to focus. Tony talk to him yet?" Carl grunted as Rick continued to push him all over the place.

Bob just shook his head as he watched the best boxer he had ever trained fight a losing battle with himself. "Rick, let's stop for a while, 'kay? Rick, you hear me?" Bob asked quietly. It was something Tony told Bob to do. Sometimes, it was the only way to force Rick to listen. Thankfully, it worked.

"What's wrong today, Champ? You can't stay focused for more than two minutes," Bob said, throwing a kindly arm around Rick's shaking shoulders. Bob could feel the anger simmering just below the surface. Carl followed close behind, just in case.

"I'm not sure, Coach. My mind keeps wandering and I can't focus on the bag," Rick shrugged. He took a long pull at the water bottle Carl had handed him.

The trio stopped in front of the large windows on the far side of the gym. Rick's eyes immediately snapped forward and focused on something only he could see. "What do you see, son?" Bob asked quietly, again following another one of Tony's suggestions.

Rick's jaw tightened and his shoulders tensed even more. The anger was no longer just below the surface. "O'Reilly," he hissed. He tried to shake Bob's arm off, but his coach wasn't letting go. "I just wanna see her, but he's keeping her away from me. I can't focus on this. I just want to see her!" Rick's voice rose in frustration. Out of the corner of his eye, Bob saw Tony break off his conversation with Ian and Megan and hurry over towards the window. Megan and Ian followed more slowly.

"Easy, Rick, easy. I think I understand. I've given you a task too hard for you right now. Listen to me, son, this is what I want you to do. Go back to the bag and just pound away at it. I still want you to control your punches, just like you've always done, but I don't want you moving from that bag until you've let that anger out. Carl, watch him," Bob ordered and shoved Rick gently back to the bag. Rick stumbled blindly back to the bag and started pounding away, even before Carl got there.

"What's wrong?" Tony demanded immediately.

"He saw Seamus and said he was blocking him from her. He can't focus on anything. There's no way you're gonna talk to him today," Bob said seriously, ignoring Tony's question.

"I'm sorry, sir, but I have to. I need to," Megan insisted.

"No. Please, miss, I know what you wanna ask him, but it's not gonna do him a damn bit of good. You might be the one thing that causes him to end up sedated," Bob said angrily. *Why can't everyone just leave the kid alone?* he wondered.

Megan and Ian were both firm. Ian didn't care what it did to his nephew as long as his daughter got the answer she needed so desperately to hear. After arguing with them for another few minutes, Bob just sighed. "Enough. Tony, it's obvious that they're gonna insist on this. If you can get him calmed down enough to talk to these two, fine. Just don't let him get any angrier. He'll really hurt himself if he doesn't calm down. Get him back here as soon as you can," the trainer warned. Tony just nodded as he warily approached Rick.

"Hey little brother, I need you to listen to me for a second. Rick, son, look at me." Tony continued to talk softly and soothingly until Rick's punches began to slow. It took several minutes before he could focus on his friend, and when he did, he was shocked to see Megan and Ian standing behind the cop.

As Rick stood there, dumbfounded, Tony stripped off the gloves while Carl got Rick some water and a towel. Rick did some stretches and Tony did some massage on the teen's legs and shoulders. "Okay now, Rick?" Tony asked finally.

"Maybe," Rick replied shortly, still wondering what was going on. Silently, Tony led the way to the office. The 'COUNSELLING IN SESSION' sign went up on the door, and Ian and Megan sat down inside while Tony talked with Rick in the hall. He wanted Rick to be prepared for what was going to happen.

"Easy, son. Now I know you're wondering what's going on, especially since you're not supposed to talk to your cousin. Owen's not here to okay this, so you have to decide if you wanna do this. Legally, she shouldn't be here and I really should arrest her. You're not supposed to have any contact with her until either the pre-lim or your trial. Neither Bob nor I think it's a good idea, especially not today, but, against my better judgement, I'm gonna suggest you talk to her. Do you think you can?" Tony asked, continuing to keep his voice low.

"After my crappy boxing today, I don't know, Fish. I'll try, but I'm not gonna make any promises," Rick warned. As they entered the office, Rick tensed up and looked straight ahead, avoiding Ian and Megan's eyes. Tony wanted this contained in the office, so he led Rick behind the desk and stood in front of the door. The cop wasn't going to take any chances on anyone's safety if Rick lost control.

Finally looking directly at his cousin, Rick couldn't help but grimace as he saw the fading scars on her face. He could tell she was scared to be in the same room as him. *Please, just don't ask me that*, Rick prayed as he tried to stop his legs from jumping. His fists clenched and unclenched as he waited for the inevitable question.

Megan took a deep breath. "Rick, seeing you just now, training, I think I know you didn't do anything, but I just need to hear it from you. I'm sorry, I know you don't want me to ask this but...did you attack me?" she asked softly. Neither Ian nor Megan were prepared for the violence of Rick's reaction.

Shaking, his face bright red, Rick shot to his feet. "You just said you know I didn't do this! What more do you want? I cut the damn ropes that held you up! Bloody hell! Why won't anyone believe me?" Rick shouted, as he struggled not to fly around the desk and actually hit his cousin.

He spun away from Megan and swung a wild punch, connecting solidly with the metal filing cabinet. At the sound, Tony hoped Rick hadn't broken his hand again. He barely ducked a second punch that again connected to the cabinet as he grabbed onto Rick and pinned his arms to his sides. Struggling to hold Rick against the wall, Tony shouted at Ian, "Get her the hell outta here!"

Stunned at Rick's violent reaction, Ian hesitated for a long moment, then grabbed Megan and dragged her out the door. Tony could hear Megan sobbing "I'm sorry, I'm sorry," as she fled the room, and Ian thought he heard something crack as Rick's head connected with Tony's chin.

"Don't you two dare leave this centre until I have a chance to talk to you, Ian Attison. This is your fault, but *I* have to deal with it," Tony growled as Ian closed the door behind them. It took Tony almost 20 minutes to get through to Rick and to calm him down enough the teen was able to go back to the gym without wanting to hunt his cousin down.

Chapter 37

Now nearly midnight on New Years' Eve and over 24 hours since his outburst in the office, Rick was going hard at his speed bag. Rick wondered what Tony had told his cousin and his uncle. It had taken Rick almost two hours before he had calmed down enough to think instead of just reacting. Even after Bob finally left, Rick had spent another hour or so slamming at his speed bag.

Hell, this isn't working, Rick cursed silently as he lost the pattern of his workout for probably the tenth time. If anything, he was angrier than he was when he had started. He knew thinking about Megan's visit had set him off again and he needed to deal with it. He picked up his phone and called the guard on duty at the front desk.

"Yes, Mr. Attison?" she asked politely.

"I'm angry and frustrated," Rick said abruptly.

Samantha, like all the other guards at the centre, had been warned about Rick. He was to be treated with kid gloves, not because of who his family was, but because of his anger. Rick knew everyone had been told about the night he took Tony down and how it had taken five others to get him under control. His anger, he knew, was to be contained at all costs, even if it meant locking down the rest of the centre while Rick was in the gym by himself.

"Did you try your speed bag?" Samantha asked immediately as she scanned the board to find the only guard who could possibly handle this kid.

"Already did, ma'am, for over an hour. It didn't help. I'd like to go to the gym and work out, please," Rick said. He could hear the tension in his voice and wondered if the guard did.

"That bad, eh, son?" Samantha said soberly.

"Yeah. Can I go, please?" Rick begged.

Samantha didn't hesitate. "Go ahead. I'll have a guard meet you at the end of your hall," she said as she paged the guard and Tony. *Standard procedure with this kid,* she thought sadly as she wondered how much more one kid could handle. *Page a guard and page his counsellor.* "Thank you, ma'am," Rick said and hung up. He felt slightly better as he strode off to the gym, not even noticing the guard who met up with him at the end of the hall.

Rick was still there an hour later, going hard at the bag, when Tony arrived. He was so focused on what he was doing he didn't even bother to acknowledge his friend. Tony watched Rick for several minutes, trying to figure out what was going on in the kid's head. Finally, he waved to the guard.

"Evening, Officer," the guard said quietly, never taking his eyes off of Rick.

"Evening. Everything quiet tonight?" Tony asked idly.

"Until about an hour ago, yeah. That kid has some *power*," the guard said admiringly.

"I know. Trust me, I know," Tony chuckled dryly, rubbing his still-aching chin where Rick's head had cracked him the day before. "What's up?"

"Sam took a call from him about an hour ago, begging her to let him come here. Said he was angry. She told him to try his speed bag, but apparently he already had for over an hour. Sam paged me then, since I'm the guard who's usually assigned to him because of my size. I wasn't surprised to hear it was just him. He's alone all of the time, even when he's surrounded by other kids. Officer, he was the only kid not at the New Year's Eve celebration in the lounge and he's still not making any friends. Sorry to ruin your evening, sir," the guard apologized.

Tony sighed as he listened to the guard. "With this kid, I don't have a day off," Tony shrugged philosophically. It had been a boring evening anyway. Something had told Tony he shouldn't go to any party he didn't want to leave, so he had just stayed home and watched television.

"Watch my back, but do *not* interfere unless he looks like he's about to kill me," Tony said to the guard as he cautiously approached Rick. The cop stood there for probably five long minutes, just listening to the rhythm of the punches. Even angry, Rick kept to the same set of punches Bob had started him off with so many weeks earlier. Just like the night at the station, Tony found his toes tapping and he had to force himself to keep from dancing. It was a soothing sound, to Tony at least.

"How long, Champ?" Tony finally asked, pitching his voice just barely loud enough to be heard over the thumping of Rick's fists into the leather bag.

"An hour here and at least an hour at the speed bag, Fish," Rick grunted as he punched.

"Talk to me, little brother," Tony said as he leaned idly against a pillar by the ring. He could see Rick and he was semi-comfortable.

"Why? You don't help anymore," Rick snapped as his punches grew harder.

"Hey, what the hell did I do to deserve that?" Tony asked, stunned. After every insult Rick had ever thrown at him, that one simple sentence hurt Tony the most.

Rick dropped his hands and hung his head. He was suddenly ashamed, especially now. Tony had done so much for him and had given up his own life to make sure Rick got through this and now Rick had basically told his one friend to take a hike. He just stood there, defeated. *You win, Blade*, Rick thought. *You win*.

"Sorry, Tony, it's just that talking isn't working anymore. Nothing's working," Rick sulked. *I've turned into a bratty six-year-old again*, Rick thought angrily.

"What set you off this time? Still being teased, son?" Tony asked as he pulled himself up onto the edge of the ring. Rick had mentioned in several sessions how he was called the "poor little rich boy" and several other unflattering names, including the hated Ritchie Rich.

"Not anymore. Not after taking out the leader of the Pack," Rick said, referring to a fight in the lounge with one of the long-time residents of the centre. It was the same kid Tony had noticed during the first time he came to the centre standing off to one side as Rick and Carl fought. The other kid had started the fight, and Rick had only been defending himself.

"No, Fish. I just don't have any friends. The special treatment I get with the boxing and having special stuff in my room's isolated me and so now I just get ignored. I don't know what set me off," Rick continued to sulk.

"That's bull, and you know it, son," Tony said good-naturedly. "Relax. Take a couple of deep breaths and clear your mind. Think about it. Only when you're calm will the answer come to you," Tony soothed. It was a mediation technique Tony had been taught when he was a boy and he often thought of using it with Rick. Tony was certain he knew what was wrong, but Rick had to admit it, otherwise nothing would change. It didn't take Rick long to calm down and find the answer.

"Yesterday, why'd Megs do that? I was already upset and I know she could see that. Yet she still pushed me. Why?" Rick finally demanded.

Tony didn't have to ask what Rick meant. After leaving Rick with Bob, Tony had torn a strip off of both Ian and Megan, and since Tony was still upset at the two of them, he was willing to bet Rick had been stewing over the visit all day long. "You heard her, Rick. She knew you didn't attack her, but she needed to hear you say it. She just picked the worst possible time to ask. You're already wound up over being in here, away from your family and friends, and she pushed you just enough," Tony said reasonably.

Rick stood there, seething. "When the hell'm I getting outta here?" Rick snarled. He whirled suddenly and slammed his hand against the bag. Tony didn't even blink.

"Did it help?" Tony asked mildly.

If only he'd get angry at me again, Rick thought. *Nothing I do makes him angry anymore. Not even if I insult him.* "No," he snapped.

Tony stood and faced Rick. "Look, Rick, I understand your frustration. I won't tell you I know how you feel, because I've never spent a single night locked up and you've been in jail for several weeks now. Just be a little more patient. We're going over the evidence again and the interviews, but right now the investigation's at a standstill. There's nothing new. No evidence. No witnesses. Nothing. I've gone over the interviews at the school again. I've even talked to Tom several times. By the way, nobody'd better accuse you of anything around him. To him, you're a saint," Tony chuckled.

"Yeah. I kept Johnny off him a few months ago. If Johnny had hit him even once, it would've killed him," Rick said softly. He took several more deep breaths and could feel the anger and tension easing. *Tony did it again*, Rick thought in wonder.

"Rick, I know you've calmed down, but this has been building a long time. I don't think Meg's visit was the only thing that set you off. Something else has, I'm sure of it. Do you still listen to Jor's tapes?" Tony asked innocently.

The anger built as quickly as it had dissipated. "Why? So I can be reminded constantly how I can't have the girl that I love? Why bother to lock me away? Just make me listen to those tapes and hold her just out of my reach! You've punished me far better than any jail time could! Damn you, O'Reilly! Damn you!" Rick shouted.

Tony was surprised, to say the least. The tapes were supposed to help Rick, not rekindle the anger towards Seamus Tony thought they had contained. Rick turned back to the heavy bag and was swinging wildly. *Time to defuse my time bomb again,* Tony sighed and stood up. He approached cautiously as the bag was swinging around wildly.

"Rick, son, I know you're angry and you need to hit something, but you're gonna hurt yourself," Tony cautioned gently. He was sure Rick could barely hear him over the sounds of the gloves hitting the bag, but he didn't raise his voice. "Back off for just a couple of seconds, Champ. C'mon, son. Listen to me. Step back and get some control over yourself."

Rick continued swinging wildly as if he hadn't heard Tony at all.

"Rick, listen to me," Tony continued. "Step back. You're gonna hurt yourself if you don't."

Rick finally listened long enough to step back and let Tony grab the bag. Then Rick was right back swinging, hard, fast and wild. Tony grunted each time Rick connected. *The power in this kid's incredible*, Tony thought as he fought to hold the bag. Tony looked around for the guard who had been there earlier and waved for him to come closer. As he turned his head to talk, Rick got in a good shot and the bag ricocheted off of Tony's head.

"This is gonna be an all-nighter," Tony grunted as he shook the stars from in front of his eyes. "I'm gonna need strong, black coffee for me, water for him and food for all of us. You might as well stick around and learn something about dealing with an inmate like this." The guard nodded and moved away to make the arrangements.

Tony turned back to Rick. "C'mon, Rick, get it out. All of it, son. Yell, scream, cry. I don't care, but get that anger out."

Rick's arms swung wildly with emotion. "You need to control your punches, though. Don't swing wildly. Carl's gonna beat you next time if you don't get yourself under control," Tony urged.

Hearing that, Rick growled and leaned into the bag, swinging a series of short, sharp punches. "That's better, Rick. Hard, but with control. Get that anger out," Tony said encouragingly.

By the time the guard returned with everything Tony had ordered, Rick was calmer and utterly exhausted. Tony finally thought it was safe for him to do his stretches.

"Does this happen often, Constable?" the guard asked curiously, looking at Rick who had stopped stretching and was staring out of the window.

"Rick? C'mon, little brother, finish stretching. I don't need you cramping up on me," Tony called. He watched until Rick was stretching again, and then turned back to the guard.

"Far too often, I'm afraid. You know his history?" Tony asked.

"Required reading in case we ever get anyone like him again," the guard nodded.

"Pray you never do." With that, Tony began one of the longest, most exhausting sessions he had ever had with Rick.

They talked for hours. That is, Rick talked and Tony just listened, encouraging the teen to get it all out. Rick would yell sometimes, and at others, he talked so quietly Tony could barely hear him. All through the long night, Tony encouraged Rick to get everything off of his chest, to get rid of the anger. By the time the sun had come up, Tony and Rick were sitting on the floor with their backs against the base of the boxing ring, almost asleep, but still talking. The guard had learned more in that one night about dealing with juveniles than he ever would have learned in any training class.

"I remember now, Tony. I remember fighting with Seamus, that day I beat up Colin. I don't know how I got hold of his gun, but I remember pointing it at his head. I dropped it off at the house a week later when I was out at the farm for some reason, but why can't I remember getting that gun in my hands?" Rick cried weakly.

"Son, it's taken you this long to remember the fight with Colin and the fight with Seamus. If I hadn't pushed you to remember, you'd never've figured out what got you into the Knights in the first place. Don't worry about the gun. What did you do with the bullet you kept?" Tony asked, rubbing his eyes. *Man, I'm glad he finally admitted that fight.*

Rick chuckled softly. "I buried it under the rose bush just outside of Jor's room. Once I gave the gun back, I decided I didn't want a souvenir. Johnny wanted me to keep it, but I couldn't. I didn't want any reminder of that fight. Ever."

They fell silent for a few minutes, then Rick sighed. "Jor's told me all about the Angels. Now I have *that* to worry about," Rick said wearily.

"What's wrong with the Angels? I've heard nothing but good things about them from Delaney," Tony said, puzzled.

"Remember the letter you gave me from Tom when you brought Jor to visit?" Rick asked. Tony nodded. "Bro, they've been seeking out the Knights and deliberately starting fights. They've stopped being protectors and are becoming what they were formed to protect everyone against. They sound more and more like how the Knights started, and Tom sounds more and more like an early me," Rick continued. He fell silent again as he mourned the loss of Tom's innocence. *What'd I get you into, kid?* Rick wondered.

"You let *me* deal with that, okay, little brother? You just focus on keeping yourself calm and centred long enough to get outta here. You've gotta keep your cool," Tony said.

Rick sat silent for a few more minutes, then looked at Tony. "Fish, if there's no new evidence, why am I still here?" he asked finally.

"Rick, until your prelim on the 10th, you have to stay here. Didn't Owen explain that to you? Is that what your problem's been these past few weeks?" Tony asked, incredulously.

"No, Tony, he never said anything like that. I guess he figured I knew, but I thought once you couldn't find anything else, you'd let me go," Rick said. He slumped with defeat. *Ten more days? I'll go crazy*, Rick thought.

Tony laughed. "Not my call, son. God, Rick, I'm sorry. I really thought you knew you'd be stuck here until the 10th. That's when the judge'll hear all the evidence against you. If he says there's enough, we'll go to trial and you'll be back here until then. You can't go home until he says you can. Understand?" Tony asked gently. Inside he was berating himself for not making sure Rick understood why he was still in custody. He also made a note to call Owen and give the young lawyer crap as well.

Rick felt like a fool. "I guess I should've figured it out, bro, but I was just too busy feeling sorry for myself and taking my anger out on you," he said with a smile.

"Don't worry, little brother. I didn't know that was the problem and I should've made sure you understood. Feel better now?" Tony asked. He was exhausted, but satisfied. It had been a productive night.

Rick nodded and Tony continued. "Good. Now I have a couple of things I want you to do. First, don't spend all day sleeping so you can keep your days and nights straight. Second, I want to you to listen to Jordan's tapes again, and then write her a letter," Tony said. The exhaustion was making his voice thick and Rick was trying to understand him.

"Why?" Rick asked bluntly when he figured out what Tony wanted. "You wanna undo all the good we've done today?"

"No. Don't just hear her voice and think she's outta reach. Listen to her words. Remember how I asked you a while back to write things down, no matter what time of day it was? Same kind of thing. Listen to what she says and what she doesn't. Talk to her about tonight and everything we've talked about in our sessions. Let her know what's going on in that brain of yours. She may never see the letters, but at least you'll get everything out in the open. Okay?" Tony explained. Rick nodded again.

The two climbed wearily to their feet. Tony managed to steady himself against the ring, but Rick swayed so badly the guard came up beside him and steadied him. Tony could hear the guard murmuring a couple of comments to Rick who replied just as quietly. Rick was shaking, he was so exhausted. He had done several hours of hard workouts and then poured his heart out to Tony. He was glad for the guard's support.

Neither cop nor teen could remember when they had last had a proper meal nor when they had slept last. Rick looked at the cop and realized Tony was probably worse off, since the cop had put in a full day's work before coming to the centre to deal with him. The rest of the world was gearing up for the day and all the two of them wanted to do was crash.

"Tony, I gotta know. What'd you say to Megs and Uncle Ian?" Rick asked as they staggered towards his room.

"I asked them what they thought they proved by provoking you. Like I said, Meg just needed to hear you didn't do it. I can tell you I wasn't really happy with them coming unannounced. You should've had time to adjust to the thought she wanted to see you, but we also should have had Owen here. Legally, she shouldn't have been anywhere near you and if the judge finds out she did come here, it's possible he could throw the case out, evidence or no evidence. Basically, witness tampering," Tony said truthfully.

They stopped outside of Rick's room. Tony looked Rick in the eye and said, "Rick, Meg told her dad you didn't do it. It stopped Ian cold. Your cousin believes in you. For how long, I have no idea, but right now, she believes in you. Hold onto that," Tony said with a smile.

After a couple of minutes of silence, Tony asked, "Little brother, can you hold it together until the 10th?"

"I think so. Tonight helped a lot. Tony, how can I thank you for all of this?" Rick asked honestly.

"Let's get you outta this and prove who's really behind it. Then we'll worry about thanks. Besides, you've taught me as much as I've taught you, little brother. Set your alarm for 1 p.m. and don't go back to sleep until tonight, even if your body screams for it. No naps either," Tony cautioned, pushing Rick into his room. Rick didn't protest. He staggered over to his alarm clock, set it, then fell across his bed.

Tony chuckled wearily as he closed the door. "Out cold before he hit the bed," Tony grinned at the guard.

"You look like hell, officer. You okay to drive?" the guard asked pointedly.

Tony took stock of his body and shook his head. "Got a phone I can use?" he asked. The guard nodded and led Tony to the phone in the guard room.

"Hey, George, get this officer a phone and call someone to watch over Attison. I've been up with him all night and I'm beat," the guard said as they entered.

Tony dialled Marshall directly. "Where the hell're you, Tony? The inspector's been screaming for you all morning. Your shift started two hours ago!" Marshall said.

Tony groaned. "He would be. Marsh, I've been with Rick since about midnight. I've just finished and I'm beat," Tony said. The cop was leaning heavily against the wall and trying hard to not slide down it.

Marshall heard the exhaustion and sighed. "Rick blow?" he asked.

"Just about. I haven't slept since the end of my shift on the 30th and I haven't eaten since supper last night. I just poured Rick into bed and I'm asleep on my feet, trying to talk to you," Tony mumbled.

Marshall didn't hesitate. "Jones! You're with me! Hold on for a few more minutes, Fish, I'll get you home," Marshall said with a chuckle. Tony agreed to meet him at the front doors in fifteen minutes. Seamus was going to kill him for missing a shift, but it couldn't be helped. Rick was always Tony's number one priority.

"Constable? I know Rick's set his alarm, but I've also left a note he's to be woken up no later than 1 p.m. Do you want some coffee?" the guard asked, holding up a fresh pot.

Tony realized the guard was just as tired as he was. The cop shook his head. "I'd better not, and I wouldn't recommend it for you either. As tired as we are, the coffee'll do nothing but keep you awake when you really need the sleep. Thanks for watching my back, though. You may've gained Rick's trust today, and believe me, that's not easy," Tony praised. He made a note of the guard's name so he could get him a commendation for helping.

When Marshall showed up fifteen minutes later, Tony was sitting on the bench in front of the centre, his head in his hands and exhaustion clearly evident. "Fish?" Marshall said, touching Tony's shoulder gently.

Tony surged to his feet and swung a punch. "Whoa! Easy, Fish, it's me!" Marshall said, catching hold of Tony's hand.

Tony blinked and swayed on his feet. "Sorry, Marsh, you scared the hell out of me. I think I was asleep," Tony slurred.

"C'mon, partner, give Jones your keys and let's get you home," Marshall laughed as he held onto Tony. Tony couldn't wait to get home, fall down and sleep for a week. He never wanted to do a session like that again.

Chapter 38

When Tony returned to work almost two days later, Seamus demanded to see him in his office. "What the hell happened you felt the need to spend all night with that boy and miss a shift?" Seamus demanded.

"Look, Inspector, I've been ordered by the court to keep him under control. You know that. I got a call from the centre saying he was losing control and I needed to get my butt over there and calm him down. It doesn't matter if I'm in the middle of a take down or something even more personal, if Rick Attison's about to blow, I'm responsible for him," Tony said hotly.

"You're wearing way too many hats, Constable," Seamus noted sourly.

"I wouldn't have to be, Inspector, if we hadn't botched the investigation into your daughter's attack. If you'd let us do our jobs, the guy who attacked her wouldn't have been free to attack Megan," Tony pointed out before he headed back to his desk.

The guy Tony was talking about was waiting for Michael at East Side's once again. Blade was sitting in a dark corner with his back against the wall, nursing a beer. He watched as Michael walked across the bar to join him.

As he had done the first time they met, Blade wore nothing that indicated he was in a gang. He didn't want Rick's dad to put Johnny together with the black and silver Blade wore.

"Yer late," Blade growled as Michael sat down. A rye and coke appeared suddenly in front of Michael, and he took a drink, his hand trembling slightly. *He's nervous*, Blade decided.

"Unlike you, I have a job, boy. Unfortunately, it's a job that doesn't pay enough," Michael snapped back.

"Did 'cha think 'bout my offer?" Blade drawled as Michael sipped at his rye and coke.

"That depends on what you're offering, Johnny. See, in case I was too drunk to make myself clear the other night, I need money. Lots of money. Mother cut me out of her will and gave the money to my younger brother," Michael said quietly as he waved for another drink.

"I can take care of 'im, if that's wha'cha want," Blade shrugged after the drinks had been delivered.

"No. That would just put the money into my niece's hands and that does me no good either. No, I need you do to do something else. I want you to kidnap my brother and hold him for ransom. I don't care if he comes back in one piece or not, but I know my mother would pay lots to get her darling boy back," Michael sneered.

"How much do ya need?" Blade wanted to know.

"All of it would help," Michael replied with a sneer.

"Y'know, last person I heard of with this kinda money problem owed Carlos Mendez. Heard of him?" Blade asked casually. He had done his homework and knew Michael owed Mendez almost $300,000 and it was growing daily. *This is gonna be fun*, Blade gloated.

Michael stiffened. "Did he send you after me?" Michael hissed.

"If he had, ya'd already be dead, man. No one crosses Mendez. No, word's out on the street ya owe big. Got some free advice, though," Blade continued quietly.

"What would that be? Dive down a deep, dark hole?" Michael asked sarcastically.

"Naw, he'd just find ya and it'd be worse. Tell Mendez Johnny Blade's working on yer problem. Man, yer lucky he hasn't gone fer the business yet," Blade said seriously.

"Can you do it, Johnny? Can you get my brother and hold onto him until my mother pays?" Michael asked.

"No prob. And my cut?" Blade asked. He signalled for another round of drinks.

"Not so fast, Johnny. I wanna make something very clear right now. This cannot be traced to me. Ever. That number I gave you last time's no longer in service and my new one's unlisted. If you know how much I owe, I'm gonna assume you also know where I live and work. I also assume we can make arrangements to meet again," Michael said.

Blade's eyes narrowed dangerously. "Are ya saying ya don't trust me?" he asked quietly. Michael tensed as he thought he heard the hiss of something being drawn.

"Not at all. I wouldn't've agreed to meet you again if I didn't trust you. What I'm saying is if you get caught, you're on your own. Don't write anything down. Don't call me. Don't visit me at home or at my office. We'll meet here on Friday to finalize anything you need. I don't wanna appear to be involved in any way. Understand? If you don't agree to this, then I walk right now. Deal?" Michael asked and held out his hand.

Blade didn't hesitate and shook on the deal. "No sweat, but we can't meet here. We've been here too much. Meet me at the pool hall on Sutherland Road. I got a guy I can pin this on. Me and my boys need to check out yer bro up close first. When and where?" Blade asked.

"Do you know the shop called Hollyhock's on the edge of town?" Michael asked. Blade nodded. "My brother's usually there between ten and noon. Tomorrow shouldn't be any different. Can you handle that?" Michael drawled, mimicking Blade's tone.

"Yeah. Now how much? Ten, twenty million?" Blade leaned back in his chair.

Michael shook his head. "Mom's rich, but not that rich. Six should do," Michael said, hiding exactly how well off his family was. Six would be more than enough to get him through.

"And my cut?" Blade asked again.

"One million." Michael offered with finality.

"Done." Blade slipped out of the booth after tossing a few bills on the table. He nodded to Greg. "Get 'im drunk."

The next day, Blade met Brain at the coffee shop across from Hollyhock's. School was back in, but neither really cared. It was no fun when they couldn't go after the girls, and they couldn't go after them with the Angels watching them every minute of the school day. The Angels were taking all of the fun out of going to school and Blade was furious.

"Yo, Blade," Brain said, sliding into the booth across from his leader.

"What's new in the think tank today?" Blade drawled.

"Word's out. Moneyman's still in juvy, but he should be out by next week. Mendez's contact in the cop shop says there's nothing new, so the judge should spring him. Mickey Mouse made up with his sister, but the old man has her under lock and key. Apparently, she's been talking to Moneyman somehow," Brain grinned.

Blade grunted, but didn't say anything. He knew Brain had something to get off his chest and just waited.

"Look, Blade, y'know I'll go along with just 'bout anything ya want. But I've been thinkin' about this since ya called. What's up with this, man? Ya need dough that bad, I'll get ya some, but this is nuts," Brain said quietly.

"It's not the money, Brain," Blade said softly.

"Then what, man? I've never seen ya this obsessed," Brain said as he leaned back in the booth. *This wasn't like Blade*, Brain realized.

"It's the challenge, Brain. Can we do this? If so, can we move from our little gang to helpin' Mendez? 'Sides, the guy that's paying us is none other than Moneyman's old man," Blade chortled.

"Get out. What's up?" Brain asked.

"Daddy's far in debt to Mendez he should be dead by now. Ya know Mendez doesn't let anyone get more than 10 grand behind, right?"

Brain squinted. "Right. How far behind is 'Daddy?'"

Blade leaned forward, grinning. "Well, our guy's into Mendez fer about 300 grand! I don't know why, but Mendez just keeps letting 'Daddy' bet, so fer a million bucks we get ta have some fun."

Something wasn't quite right, but Brain couldn't put his finger on it. "Is Moneyman gonna take the fall?" he asked.

"Duh," Blade snapped.

"Blade, come on, man, what's this really 'bout? Ya want Moneyman broken and back in the gang, not put away fer so long we'll be little old men before he's out again," Brain protested. For once, Blade's logic confused him.

"I gots a friend in juvy with him, one of the Pack. Seems Moneyman's boxing and he figures he's lost the instincts. He's a pure fighter now and he's no good to me anymore. There's not gonna be any fire left in 'im once he gets out and that makes him useless. Now I just want him gone." Blade's eyes were hard.

Brain shivered. "Nothing's gonna happen until he's out of juvy, y'know?" Brain pointed out. "What if Mendez's cop is wrong? What if Moneyman isn't cleared?"

"Worry 'bout that later. Here comes our guy," Blade said as he compared the picture Michael gave him with the tall, dark-haired muscular man coming down the sidewalk.

Brain looked Ian over. The heavy winter jacket did not fully disguise the strength in Ian's arms. The jeans only emphasized the powerful legs and Brain figured Ian out-weighed them all, even combined.

"Won't work, Blade," Brain said immediately.

"Why not?" Blade stared at Ian. *I'm not losing a million*, Blade thought angrily.

"Look at 'im, man. He's what? 6'3" or 6'4"? Moneyman's only 5'10. That's five, maybe six inches difference. Moneyman's stronger now than he's ever been, but I don't think we can pull it off. It'd take all four of us and leave too much evidence," Brain pointed out.

"So taking him is out?" Blade said disappointed.

"If you want to blame Moneyman, it is," Brain said. They sat silently for a couple of minutes, watching Ian. A Chevy pickup pulled up beside Ian and one of the passengers jumped out.

"What 'bout her?" Blade pointed.

"She'd be perfect. We can get her at school. It'll be easier than last time. But either way, we wait, Blade. This ain't somethin' I'm willing to rush. We leave everyone completely alone, and that includes Moneyman when he gets out. We take our time and we plan. Everything's gotta be done perfectly or we won't get away with this," Brain warned.

"But we can do it, right?" Blade asked again.

"Yep. This is what we'll tell our boss." Brain outlined the new plan for several minutes while Blade continued to stare out at Ian.

Friday night, Michael arrived at the pool hall, looking distinctly out of place as really the only adult in the joint. He found Blade playing pool in the back room with Crank and Brain. Pup was guarding the door and closed it softly behind Michael.

"Johnny," Michael said.

"Finish without me, boys. Gots business to talk 'bout," Blade said. He sauntered to the only table in the room where drinks were already waiting.

"Well, Johnny, what's your plan?" Michael asked as he sipped his drink.

"We gots a problem. There's no way to take yer bro and make it look like someone else did. The person I gots in mind is shorter and maybe lighter. Yer bro's a big dude, man. Sorry," Blade said, not sounding sorry at all.

Michael sat up. "You said you could do this," he accused.

"No. I said I could take care of him. Permanently. Yer the one that wants t' do the ransom thing," Blade reminded Michael.

"Mendez's gonna freak," Michael groused.

"Chill, man. I never set my plans in stone. Too many things can go wrong. However, it seems I know yer niece. One of my boys has classes with her at school. How much is she worth?" Blade asked lazily.

"Megan? Probably as much or more than my brother. Go ahead. I don't care. If you think you can get her," Michael shrugged. "Is it going to change what I pay you?"

"Depends on how much I end up asking Granny for her. But don't worry. I can get her any time I want. Now, from now on, ya won't know when, where or how this is gonna happen. Wha'cha don't know, ya can't tell. Right?" Blade emphasized.

"Fine. We have a deal. Try and have everything done by the end of April," Michael said and left.

"Well, Blade?" Brain asked as his leader returned to the game.

"Take yer time, Brain. I wanna couple of different plans. Workable plans. We gots 'til the end of April," Blade said. He lined up his shot carefully.

"And then?" Crank asked.

Blade exhaled softly and took the shot. The cue ball hit one ball that careened off two more. One struck the eight ball and sunk it in the corner pocket. Blade stood up.

"Then Moneyman will be outta my hair. Fer good," Blade snarled and went back to his dimly lit table.

Chapter 39

On the Friday before his preliminary hearing, Rick woke from a fuzzy dream, restless and worried. Something left over from the dream was bothering him, but he couldn't place what it was. He knew if all went well, sometime next week he would be going home. He should've been elated. Instead, he felt like a caged tiger. Something was off. He could feel it in the air.

He glanced at his clock and groaned. He was going to be late for class if he didn't get a move on. It meant he didn't have time to get rid of the extra energy he had. *Oh well,* Rick thought philosophically. *My bad.* He showered and got dressed, then sauntered down to the cafeteria to grab a portable breakfast he could devour on his way to class.

The restlessness plagued him all day. He got in trouble twice from his teacher for not paying attention in class. He was unfocused and undisciplined all morning, and it was showing. At lunch, he was too distracted to do more than pick at his food. He thought he had hidden his restlessness from everyone, so when the head counsellor sat down across from him, Rick was surprised.

"Do I need to call Tony?" he asked bluntly.

"Huh? Oh no, sir. Sorry. It's restlessness, not anger. I know the difference. I have some extra energy to burn and I woke up late, so I didn't have time to burn it off on the speed bag," Rick reassured the counsellor. *At least, I think it's only extra energy,* Rick thought, puzzled. He didn't understand what was wrong with him.

The counsellor didn't look convinced. "Tony here today?" he asked politely.

Rick nodded. "Around three or so. Coach, too. What's up, sir?" Rick asked.

The counsellor pointed to a very familiar guard. It was the guard usually assigned to sit outside Rick's door when he was angry, but Rick knew him from somewhere else. He just couldn't place it. "Derrick noticed. Suggested I come talk to you before you got too upset," the counsellor said candidly.

Rick took quick stock of himself and stood up. "I'm heading back to my room. I'll try the speed bag. If it doesn't work, can I go to the gym?" he asked after a couple of minutes.

The counsellor nodded and wrote out the pass, and one to excuse Rick from his afternoon classes. He handed it to Rick and waited for the teen to leave the cafeteria. The counsellor stopped beside the guard and muttered some instructions. The guard nodded, spoke into his radio and followed Rick to his room once he was relieved.

Rick returned to his room and changed. He left the door open and began to stretch. As he stretched, he heard every little sound outside his door, so he heard the soft approach of someone who stopped just outside his door. The teen sighed. He hadn't convinced the counsellor and was under a watch again. *Just great*, he thought sourly. *Not what I really needed today.*

"Whoever's out there, you might as well come in and be comfortable," Rick called out, trying to hide his anger.

"Sorry, Mr. Attison, no. You're angry enough with me out here," a disembodied voice replied. "But I'll take a chair. Something tells me you're gonna be a while."

Rick snorted and shoved his desk chair out the door. Then, trying to ignore his watcher, Rick approached his speed bag and began his workout. His hands and arms knew the rhythm and patterns so well Rick would often use this time to think and let his mind wander. Today, however, his mind refused to focus. Finally, Rick stopped and threw in one of Jordan's tapes, putting his tape deck on automatic replay. It was the one detailing the story of Tom and the Grey Angels, one of Rick's favourites. Unlike before Christmas when her voice only aggravated him, Rick now found her voice soothing and he was able to return to his workout, letting his hands punch and his muscles react while his mind focused on Jordan.

Rick was so focused he didn't hear Tony come in. In fact, poor Tony nearly got flattened again when he put a hand on Rick's shoulder and caused a break in Rick's rhythm. Rick reacted automatically. He spun and swung for his opponent's head. Tony saw the reaction and managed to duck the punch by falling to the floor.

"Easy, Champ. It's Tony, man," Tony said from the floor where he had landed.

Rick shook his head to clear it. He snapped off Jordan's tape before replying. "Sorry, man. I didn't hear you come in," Rick apologized as he extended a hand to help his friend up.

"So I noticed. How long you been going?" Tony asked with a chuckle. He knew better than to approach Rick from behind. He was only mildly concerned, since he knew if anything was really wrong, he would've been called by now.

Rick glanced over at his alarm clock and saw it was now 3 p.m. "Holy cow! Over two hours, Fish," Rick said, amazed.

"Let's go talk," Tony said casually. Now he *was* concerned. For Rick to have gone that long without a break wasn't good. Tony's main concern was why he hadn't been called earlier. Rick's guard followed at a discreet distance. Tony had noticed him sitting outside the door, but didn't say anything until Rick was settled in the office in front of him.

"What's with the guard, Rick?" Tony asked bluntly.

"I've been restless all day. Woke up late and couldn't make time for a workout. The guard noticed it and reported me. Now I'm under watch again," Rick shrugged. The workout had done some good, but the restlessness and, more importantly, the worried feeling was back, stronger than before.

"Angry restless? Or when-the-hell-am-I-getting-out-of-here restless?" Tony wanted to know.

"No, Tony, that's just it. There's no anger. Not yet, anyway. It's just I can feel a change in the air, kinda like there's gonna be a storm, y'know?" Rick asked. His legs started to twitch and his fingers tapped idly on the desk top.

Having to talk about this is getting him worked up again, Tony noticed. "Yeah, little brother, I know that kind of feeling. Leave it for now. What's with the two-hour marathon?"

"I was just trying to get rid of the extra energy, Tony, before counselling. I wasn't angry or anything. I threw on my favourite tape from Jor and must have zoned out or something," Rick said. His legs went from twitching to bouncing from the tension he could feel building up. *What the hell's wrong with me today?* he wondered.

As Rick got up to pace, Tony was wondering the same thing. He'd never seen Rick like this. He was pacing back and forth in front of the door as if he was seeking a strong vantage point from which to attack. Tony just watched in silence. There was tension, yes, but no anger. Not yet, but the danger was there.

"You know what, kiddo? Talking isn't going to do you any good today until you get rid of that tension. Let's go," Tony said, and motioned to the door.

Bob hadn't arrived yet, but Tony knew the rhythm of Rick's workout almost as well as Rick did. Once Rick changed into his training gear and began to stretch, Tony approached the guard. It was the same guard as on New Year's Eve.

"Constable," the guard nodded in greeting.

"We never got a chance to introduce ourselves that night. I'm Constable Tony Whitefish," Tony said, extending his hand.

"Derrick Tomonavich," the other replied, shaking Tony's hand.

"Look, Derrick, is the guard really necessary? He's not angry, but having a guard on him just might *make* him," Tony protested in Rick's defence.

"It was necessary for the first little while when he was in his room, but probably not any more. However, until I'm told to back off by the head counsellor here, I have to remain. Sorry. But I've been doing some thinking about him since New Year's Eve. The slightest spark could set this kid off, right?" Derrick asked.

"Yep," Tony replied as he watched Rick stretch. He held up his hand for Derrick to wait while he called out some instructions to Rick, then returned to the conversation.

"Like I said that night, I'm usually the one assigned to watch him anyway and today, I was also assigned to watch over the kids in class. I noticed almost right away he wasn't acting normal. His eyes never stopped moving. His hands were clenching and unclenching. His legs were jumpy and he couldn't pay attention in class. He's really doing well in school, and I didn't want him to get in trouble. So I mentioned it to the Head Counsellor. He talked to Rick and, after agreeing to let Rick come here if the speed bag didn't work, the counsellor 'suggested' I keep an eye on him until you got here," Derrick said with a slight emphasis on "suggested."

Tony sighed as Derrick continued, "Suggested in this case meant keep Rick under watch until he's calmed down. I've gotta stay and watch him work out. If you don't think that's going to cause any problems," Derrick added quickly.

"It won't cause any problems, providing you stay out of his sight," Tony agreed and walked over to where Rick was beginning to work out with his weights. Derrick watched quietly from the far side of the gym, moving when necessary to keep out of Rick's immediate line of sight. Tony was right. There was no anger, but Derrick didn't want to disturb the pair.

By the time Bob and Carl arrived, Rick was ready to switch over to the heavy bag, and Bob decided that it was time to try the exercise which had frustrated Rick before New Year's.

"Carl, come here. This is something I want you to work on as well. We're gonna try that focusing exercise again, Champ. You need to learn how to control your strength without losing any power. Boxing isn't always about who can hit the hardest or even the most power. It's about who can hit with the most control, so you decide when to take your opponent out," Bob said. He put two white chalk squares on each side of the bag, approximately where Rick would hit someone's ribs.

"The goal is this. If you can focus your strength enough to control your power and your placement, you should be able to put your punch in the centre of the square without getting any chalk on your gloves," Bob explained. He slowly guided Rick's left hand into the square to show his student where he wanted the punch to land.

Rick took a deep breath. He knew what Bob wanted. He just wasn't sure he could do it. Bob and Tony noticed the worried look right away. "Don't worry if you don't get this right away. It'll take lots of practice. Don't get frustrated and don't give in to the anger," Bob warned.

While Rick and Tony worked together at the exercise at the bag, Bob took Carl into the ring. Rick would land many punches in the square, but little tell-tale puffs of chalk would indicate more often than not he wasn't succeeding the way Bob wanted him to. As Derrick watched, he got a glimmering of an idea, and quietly left the gym. Neither adult was sorry to see the guard leave.

Tony finally called a halt when he could see the frustration building in Rick's eyes. "Okay, Champ. Hold up a minute. What's wrong?" Tony asked as Rick shook his arms to relax them.

"I can't seem to get what Bob wants and it's getting frustrating," Rick grunted.

"Easy, son. Try to relax. Don't let the anger in," Tony cautioned quietly. Rick straightened his shoulders, took a couple of deep breaths and tried to relax.

"Maybe I can help," a new voice said. Tony and Rick looked up to see Derrick standing off to Rick's left. He was holding a padded piece of something about a foot square. Rick stared at the guard for the longest time and then smiled.

"I remember you now. You were here on New Year's Eve. You watched over me. I even remember you praised me a couple of times before Tony arrived," Rick said.

"Derrick Tomonavich, Rick. I'm also the guard assigned to watch over you every time you get angry, and I'm sorry if I have ever added to that. I learned a lot that night and I praised you because you remind me of my older brother. He's a boxer like you," Derrick said proudly.

"What's that you've got there, Derrick?" Tony asked curiously. Bob and Carl had stopped to watch.

"When my brother first stared training, he couldn't control his strength and power either. His problem was if he controlled the strength, he lost the power and vice versa. So his coach tried this," Derrick said, holding the square out to Tony.

It was two pieces of ½" foam covering a thin piece of glass. "If you do this right, Rick, you hit the foam and only crack the glass. Trust me, my brother went through hundreds of pieces of glass before he got it. Watch," Derrick said. He handed Tony the square, set himself in a boxing stance and struck. Rick clearly heard the thump of Derrick's hand into the foam, but didn't hear anything from the glass, even though Derrick struck several more times. When the foam was stripped away, the glass wasn't even cracked.

"How's that possible?" Rick wondered.

"Okay. Try to hit this with everything you've got," Derrick said, holding the square slightly off to one side.

Rick sized up the position and swung. He put everything into that one punch, much like he did when sparring with Carl. He suddenly found himself on the floor. The square was now held over Derrick's head and was clearly unbroken.

"See, Rick, power comes from your abs and your legs. Strength comes from your arm and wrist, where you've also focused your control. When you have all of your strength thrown into your power point, that is your fist, you have no control over where your punch will really land. So if you miss your punch, you end up over-extended and off balance. Had I been an opponent, your ribs would be awfully sore right now," Derrick pointed out.

Rick pulled himself to his feet, his forehead furrowed in concentration. He thought about what Derrick had said and how sometimes he couldn't figure out how Carl was getting in the rib shots at times. He swung back to face the bag and slowly threw a punch, as if determining how to do it right. He smiled suddenly, and, at full speed, he struck. His fist landed in the centre of the chalk square. Then, before Derrick could move, Rick spun back towards the guard and landed a punch in the middle of the padded square. There was only the faintest sound of cracking glass in the silent gym.

Derrick quickly stripped the foam off and held the glass up for everyone to see. There, dead centre, was a small round crack, the only evidence Rick had thrown the punch. Derrick applauded, while Tony cheered. Even Bob and Carl were impressed and said so. Rick smiled again. For another ten minutes, he worked on the exercise, with Derrick, not Tony or Bob, guiding him. He didn't always land right in the centre of the square, but he made progress and that made everything worthwhile.

Toward the end of training, Bob set Carl and Rick at each other in the ring while the three adults watched. "You ever coach boxing, Derrick?" Tony wondered aloud as Bob bellowed instructions to the two fighters.

"No, but I was my brother's sparring partner. Like Rick, no one wanted to get into the ring with him. I learned everything I could from his coach," Derrick said distractedly. He pointed out a couple of things to Bob, who called out some more instructions to Rick.

"You're good. You should get a program like this going here. The counsellors might find it a novel concept to get the kids to work out their anger, instead of drugging them or trying to break the kids mentally. They need to know why the kids are angry, what makes them tick. That's why so many kids end up back in juvy – they don't know why they do the things they do, so they just repeat them. They don't know how to deal with their problems," Tony said seriously.

As the boys cooled down, Derrick approached Rick. "Feel better, son?" he asked.

"Yeah. I was mad at you before, but thanks for noticing and understanding. Sometimes I still can't catch myself before it gets too bad. By the way, you really helped. Coach couldn't explain what I was doing wrong," Rick said as he stretched to his full height. Derrick laughed at Rick's sigh when his back and shoulders popped.

"You outta here soon, son?" Derrick asked as Rick finished up. He laughed again at the light in Rick's eyes.

"If all goes well, on the 10th," Rick said fervently.

Tony just smiled.

Chapter 40

January 10th was cold and clear. Rick woke early, did a 30-minute workout, showered and cleaned his room. He wanted to pack away everything in the hopes he was going home today, but he didn't want to push his luck. He wouldn't be sorry to be leaving this place, but he would be sorry to say good-bye to Derrick. The guard had worked with Rick all weekend on the training exercise and Rick had progressed well. He had managed to contain the restlessness and worried feelings during his last couple of counselling sessions with Tony, and was feeling pretty good.

Tony and Marshall arrived around 9:30 a.m. to take Rick to the courthouse. Tony noticed the agitation in Rick's eyes and smiled reassuringly at the youth. "Relax, Rick. You know what we've found in the investigations. Now let the court do its job," Tony advised.

"Easy for you to say, Fish. You're not the one who could end up in jail for a very long time," Rick replied sourly. He took several deep breaths and followed the two cops out of the detention centre. Derrick waved good-bye from the guard room at the front entrance. He was confident he'd never see Rick in the centre again.

Promptly at 11 a.m., Rick's hearing began and ended. "Your honour, based on the very limited evidence found in both assaults, and with the victims unable and/or unwilling to place the accused at the scenes, I have no choice but to withdraw all the charges against the defendant, Richard Thomas Attison," the prosecutor stated firmly. Rick was stunned.

"Mr. Blackstone, are you saying the evidence is inconclusive?" the judge asked.

"Yes, your honour. Personally, I never would have filed charges had I not been led by Inspector O'Reilly to believe that the evidence was much stronger. The only real physical evidence in either assault case is the bandana in Miss O'Reilly's assault. The black leather jacket which has been identified as the defendant's wasn't found at the scene of Miss Attison's attack, but rather in the spare bedroom in Richard's home. There is no trace evidence of any kind on either piece of evidence nor on any of the clothing the defendant was wearing at the time of either assault. No blood, no fibres, nothing. Miss Attison also cannot clearly identify the jacket as the one her attacker wore since all the jackets the Knights wear are identical on the outside. It cannot be specifically identified as the one the defendant owns," Mr. Blackstone continued.

"Owned, your honour and please, call me Rick," Rick spoke up quickly.

The judge raised his eyebrows at this interruption, but decided to allow it. "Owned, Rick?" the judge asked.

"Yes, sir. During my first counselling session after Thanksgiving, Constable Whitefish made me understand until I got rid of my gang wear, I wasn't going to be free of the Knights. I threw it all out, your honour. That even included my jeans, tee-shirts, everything. I know I threw them out in the garbage, but, since the garbage wasn't collected until late the next day, it's possible someone may have taken them," Rick said firmly.

The judge chuckled. "You do realize how silly that really sounds, don't you, Rick? It's a little convenient, don't you think?" he pointed out.

"Yes, sir and Constable Whitefish had said the same thing right after Jor's attack, but I can't help that. It's the only explanation I have as to why the stuff showed up at the assaults," Rick shrugged.

The judge fell silent as he weighed all of the evidence against the young man standing in front of him. Somehow this kid was being blamed for something the evidence wasn't able to prove. "Very well, Rick. I have to agree with Mr. Blackstone. There just is no evidence to really link you to either assault. The prosecution also has not been able to provide me with a reasonable motive for either assault. Therefore, I am ordering all charges be dropped against you. If, at some future date, there is more compelling and different evidence, then, Mr. Blackstone, you may reinstate the charges.

"Before I release Mr. Attison completely, I would like to see all parties involved in this case in my chambers, please. This court is in recess until 1:30 p.m.," the judge said and banged his gavel. Rick, Owen, Tony and Marshall followed the judge and the Crown Prosecutor into the judge's chambers. The court reporter wasn't far behind.

"Rick, first of all, I wanna say I've had a full report of your time spent in the detention centre. I have to admit I'm proud of you for holding it together as well as you did," the judge began once everyone sat down.

"Your honour, that's thanks to Tony and Coach. I couldn't have done it without them," Rick admitted.

"Rick, what do *you* think is going on? Does this have to do with the Knights?" the judge asked.

"Your honour, I really wish I knew. Nothing started until after I told Johnny I was out. He told me I'd beg him to let me back in just to end their pain, but, hell, sir, I can't prove anything. The only physical evidence points to me, I know. But I can feel it in my bones, sir, Johnny's behind this. Unfortunately, you can't arrest someone based on my gut," Rick said dryly.

"No, Rick, we can't. Constable Andrews, is there anything, anything at all, to point to another suspect in these cases?" the judge asked Marshall.

He shook his head. "There's only the very weak physical evidence which points to Rick, sir, and you've pointed out there's just not enough to warrant going to trial," Marshall indicated.

"Why's Inspector O'Reilly punishing this young man? He led me to believe the evidence against Richard was far stronger than it really was," Mr. Blackstone demanded.

"Look, sir, I've already admitted in open court Inspector O'Reilly has pushed us to only look at Rick, so if you want any further details about why the inspector's focused on Rick, you'll have to ask him," Tony said firmly. He would not betray Seamus.

"Enough, everyone. Keep digging, Constables, and let me know if anything new comes up. Rick, you're free to go. As much as I'd like to ask you to stay out of school and have no contact with either victim, I can't. You live at the same farm as Megan and I know Jordan is only a five-minute drive away. There's nothing to keep you out of school, since you kept up with your schooling in the detention centre. As far as this court is concerned, you've done nothing wrong.

"However, Constables, I wanna make one thing very clear right now. If Inspector O'Reilly tries to put Rick under house arrest again, I'll make him very sorry he ever came to this country. Rick's allowed to come and go as he pleases. Rick, this is my home number and my cell. If Inspector O'Reilly does do something like before, I wanna hear from you immediately. Do I make myself clear?" the judge said ominously.

"Crystal clear, your honour," Tony and Marshall said. Rick just nodded. All three hid grins at the turn of events.

"Now get outta here. I've a court to run," the judge growled.

While Nana drove Rick back to the detention centre to clear out his room, Tony and Marshall returned to the station. "How long will it take Seamus to violate the judge's order and what should I do if he does?" Marshall grinned at Tony as they walked into the squad room. The rest of the team cheered when Marshall told them the cases had been dismissed. Despite everything the Knights had done over the years, thanks to the investigations into the two assaults, most of the cops had come to like and respect the grit and determination Rick had shown in fighting the inspector and the Knights.

"About ten seconds after I tell him about it," Tony grinned back.

"I don't know, Tony. After the threat the judge made, I don't think the inspector would be crazy enough to challenge him," Marshall disagreed, not really meaning it.

"How much you wanna bet? 20 bucks?" Tony said lazily, throwing his money on the desk. He knew exactly what Seamus was going to do, and the young cop had no idea what to do about it. By rights, if Seamus did decide to violate the court order, Tony was obligated to report his boss. That was the ethical thing to do. Ethics and friendship don't always go hand in hand, however.

"Done." Marshall threw his bill on top of Tony's and went back to the paperwork.

It didn't take long for Tony to be called into Seamus' office to report on the outcome of the hearing. Much to Tony's disgust, Seamus immediately decided to assign Marshall back as Rick's watchdog.

"It's the only way to keep him from Jordan and Megan. He'll have to be watched like a hawk at the ranch, and, yes, Tony, Marshall will be on duty again," Seamus growled.

"Seamus O'Reilly, you are the most stubborn, pig-headed Irishman I know!" Tony grated. "Leave the boy alone! He's been cleared of all charges."

"No, he hasn't. There just isn't enough evidence to send him to trial. If ye'd found the evidence I wanted to put him away, we wouldn't be having this conversation," Seamus said with finality.

"Seamus, let me get this straight. The judge has ordered all charges against Rick dropped and he's allowed to go back to school. The judge has ordered us to keep digging into the assaults and who ran your kids off the road. He's ordered you to leave the kid alone, and yet you *still* insist on putting Marshall at Glencrest to be a spy on Rick. Did I miss anything?" Tony asked sarcastically.

"What's yer point, Constable?" Seamus asked.

"My point, *Seamus,* is Rick has a direct line to the judge. If you put a guard on him, he has the judge's permission to phone him at any time. Seamus, you're gonna lose your job if you persist," Tony insisted.

"If it keeps me daughter safe, then so be it." With that, Seamus strode from his office and dragged a very unhappy Marshall off to Glencrest. What Nana was going to say about all of this, Tony didn't know.

Rick and Nana had just arrived back at Glencrest and were sitting in the living room after having unpacked Rick's things, when Seamus pulled up. The inspector knocked at the front door and then sauntered in with Marshall in tow.

Rick was disgusted. "That didn't take long, O'Reilly," he said dryly.

Nana was furious. "How dare you, Seamus? Rick isn't under house arrest. He's not a suspect. The charges have been dropped. That's it. I'm phoning the judge," Nana said, standing up. Rick held up his hand to stop her.

"Inspector, are you doing this to prevent a crime from happening or to satisfy your own sense of frustration at letting the real criminal get away with these attacks?" Rick asked mildly. He shook his head at Nana ever so slightly. He knew what he wanted to do.

"Ye're still me prime suspect and I will not allow ye to just wander around the country. Ye'll remain in this house until ye are in school. No more of this boxing or counselling," Seamus began.

"NO!" Nana interrupted loudly.

"Nice try, O'Reilly, but the boxing and the counselling're court-ordered from the vandalism and I'm not gonna violate that. But...I *will* make a deal with you," Rick drawled. He had settled into his recliner with one leg thrown over the arm and he was rocking very slowly. Only Marshall realized how tense the teen was.

"What, boy?" Seamus growled.

"I'll agree to have Marsh here on one condition," Rick said politely.

"What?!" Seamus ground his teeth at Rick's impudence.

Rick stood up, face to face with Seamus. "You take the guard off Jor. You let Jor live her life and I'll agree to have Marsh here. But that means, if she's over here, I'm free to see her and to speak to her. It means I can talk to her at school. It means you tell your son to back the hell off and leave me and Jor alone," Rick said quietly, but firmly.

Tony had told him about the New Year's Eve fight between Seamus and his kids. How Tony found out about it, he never said, but Rick knew he must have heard it from Jordan. It galled Rick Seamus was treating the best thing in his life like that.

"And if I don't?" Seamus replied just as quietly. "If I force ye to have a guard without agreeing to those conditions?"

"Nana, start dialling. How long do you think you'll remain in charge of the station, let alone an inspector, or cop even, if the judge hears you slapped a guard on me not two hours after you were ordered not to?" Rick continued. In the sudden silence, Seamus could hear Nana punching the phone numbers to the judge's house.

"Enough, Nana. Very well, boy. Ye've made yer point. I won't prevent ye from seeing me daughter, even though it goes against everything I believe. As long as ye don't sneak away from Marshall. If ye want some time alone, fine, but let him know. Deal?" Seamus said, grinding his teeth at having to make these concessions to Rick. *Me daughter'll be safe enough*, the inspector swore.

"Deal." Rick shook hands with the inspector. Seamus stormed out of the house and drove back to the station.

"Why'd you do that, lad? What'd it prove?" Nana asked sadly. Even Marshall looked unhappy. Rick flopped back into his recliner.

"Relax, Marsh. I'll be okay. Besides, I got what I wanted, Nana. Jor's not gonna be under Mick's watch anymore. She's gonna be free to move around. Marsh's not a bad poker player. It gives me someone to talk to other than Tony. It's a small price to pay," Rick finished softly.

Later that afternoon, as Rick was waiting on the front porch for Marshall so they could go to counselling, the restlessness returned. This time, at least, Rick knew what had caused it. Mickey had just pulled into the yard and had helped

Megan out of the truck. The longer Rick stared at his cousin, the more uneasy he became. Whatever was brewing was aimed directly at Megan.

"Go on, Rick, talk to her. I'll back you up," Marshall said from the doorway. Rick jumped and swore. He had been so focused on Megan he hadn't heard Marshall come out of the house, and that wasn't good.

"Easy, son, I didn't mean to startle you," Marshall said calmly. Inside the cop was shaking. *He could've taken my head off without thinking twice*, Marshall realized. *I'm way over my head with him.*

Rick stayed hidden in the shadows of the porch while Mickey and Megan walked to the front door. He could feel the letters in his jacket pocket he had written after New Year's Eve. Everything Jordan probably didn't want to know about her boyfriend was in there. Rick had poured his heart out to her, just like Tony had asked, but had never really thought he could give them to her himself.

"Okay. Here goes everything," Rick said softly.

He approached the truck carefully, keeping one eye on Mickey and one eye on Jordan. She sat inside, looking thoroughly miserable. Rick tapped lightly on her window and smiled as she rolled it down.

"Are you trying to get yourself killed?" she hissed frantically. "Mick's right over there!" Suddenly, she grinned as she realized she was talking to her boyfriend and he wasn't in jail.

"Free as a bird, sweets, kinda. The judge dropped the charges, but your dad still seems to think I'm a threat, so Marsh's back. We have a deal, though, your dad and I, and it means I can talk to you when you're here. It's almost a truce," Rick replied softly. He grabbed her hand and kissed it.

He tensed as he heard Mickey come thundering up. "What're you doing near her? Get away from her, you punk!" he snapped.

"Mickey, can I talk to you for a moment? Please?" Marshall said, guiding Mickey away from the truck.

Rick sighed and handed Jordan the letters. "Part of my deal's your dad's supposed to get Mick to leave me the hell alone. He's gotta leave you alone too, but that might be a little much for him to ask. Meanwhile, Tony asked me to write these letters. You may hate me after you read them, but they're yours now," Rick said. He could feel Mickey staring at him.

"I'd better not push your brother any further. I'll call later," Rick said as he tried to move back.

Jordan leaned out the window and gave Rick a long kiss that left him weak-kneed. "I'll read the letters slowly, but call me tonight. Please," she said as Mickey climbed in and started the truck.

"Jor, let's agree to only see each other in the lounge before Homeroom for right now. There'll be enough people around, including Tom, and Mick'll feel a little easier you're not alone with me. For a while at least," Rick suggested as Mickey climbed back into the truck.

It wasn't a perfect solution, but Jordan agreed. As Rick stood there watching the twins drive away, the sense of uneasiness came back. He could feel someone looking at him and, when he turned to look at Megan and Nana standing on the porch, the sense of dread was almost overpowering.

"Rick, come on, we're almost late," Marshall said from the Firebird. Rick didn't move. "Rick, what's wrong?" Marshall demanded.

"I don't know, Marsh, but it involves Megs," Rick said grimly as he shook off the uneasiness and slid behind the wheel of his car. To drive around felt good, but it would be a lot better once Tony could put Blade behind bars before he did something else to his cousin.

After a good talk with Tony where Rick let him know about the funny feelings he was getting, a fantastic workout with Coach and the rest of the boxing club, and a semi-comfortable meal with Nana, Ian and Megan, Rick was working on his homework in the kitchen when Marshall led Megan in.

"Hey, cuz, what's up? Did I forget something at the house?" Rick asked as he tidied up his homework and grabbed pops for everyone.

"No. Actually, I have a question for you. Do you have anything pressing to do tomorrow?" she asked as she sat next to Rick.

"Nothing until counselling at four. Why?" Rick replied. He leaned back and stretched.

Megan stared at her cousin for a long time before she replied. The wiry strength she'd noticed when they first met had been shaped into strong muscle. His shoulders were powerful, and his biceps rippled under his straining tee shirt. His dark jeans were snug on his muscular legs, but Megan knew Rick moved with ease. He was very comfortable with his strength and he wasn't afraid to show that. Part of that comfort was knowing he could kill someone. Megan shivered.

"What's wrong, cuz?" Rick demanded immediately. He had seen the shiver.

"Rick, I know I said I trust you. It's just I didn't realize until now how strong you really are. It scares me, to be honest," Megan said quietly.

The longer she sat there, next to him, the more uneasy Rick became. "Megs, is everything okay at school?" he asked finally.

"Yeah, why?" she replied.

"Johnny hasn't been bothering you? No unexplained notes, calls, trips? Nothing like that?" Rick continued to press.

"Rick, you're scaring me again. What's wrong?" Megan asked dryly.

"This may sound crazy, but all week I've been feeling uneasy all week," Rick said.

"So what's that gotta do with me?" Megan asked.

"Everything, cuz. Everything. Every time I've looked at you today, heard your name or even just thought about you, the feeling gets stronger. Cuz, just do me a favour and watch your back, please. Whatever Johnny's started is focused on you, I know it," Rick said emphatically.

Megan nodded. "Okay, Rick. Personally, I think you've been cooped up too long, but I'll trust your warning. Speaking of cooped up, can you ride the fence lines with me tomorrow?" she asked, getting to the point of her visit.

"Sure. Where?" Rick asked with interest.

"The lines up towards Morgan's Peak. Seems there's been a few moose going through the area and Nana wants someone she trusts to check it out. She and Daddy have a meeting with a buyer for the last couple of show jumpers in the stable and Frank's down with the flu. There's no school tomorrow, so Nana asked me to do it. Will you come with me?" Megan asked again.

Rick grinned. "I haven't ridden Cherokee in months. And since I can't go without Marsh, how about it, partner? Do you ride?"

Marshall groaned. "Rick, I haven't ridden much in years. You're gonna kill my butt, y'know."

"Be ready at eight, you two," Megan giggled and left them alone for the night.

The next morning, Marshall and Rick dressed warmly, but comfortably. Marshall made some hot chocolate and sandwiches to throw in one of the saddle bags. Rick grabbed a hunting knife, just in case. Ready to face the day, the pair stomped down to the barn, where they found a very sick Frank trying to direct the rest of the ranch hands in the morning chores.

"Morning, Rick, Marsh," Frank managed to croak before he started coughing harshly.

"Frank, get back to bed. Megs and I know how to saddle the horses and I'm sure we can find an easy ride for Marsh. You're gonna make everyone else sick," Rick scolded as he grabbed Cherokee's tack down from where it hung.

"I'll get Poppy Juice ready and then go back to bed," Frank said as he began coughing even harder.

"That's it, Frank. We're dropping you off at the clinic on the way to our meeting," Nana said as she led Megan and Ian into the barn.

"Okay, lass. I want you to head towards Morgan's Peak, but don't go any further than three hours out. Turn around by noon and be back before dark. Your cell phone charged? Call every hour, okay?" Ian said, giving Megan a hug.

"Yes, Daddy. Fully charged. Of course," Megan said dryly.

"I'm doing it again, aren't I?" Ian asked softly as he watched Rick bring out Poppy Juice and Cherokee.

"Yes, Daddy, you are. I trust him," Megan said firmly.

It didn't take long to saddle all three horses and stow the food and hot chocolate in the saddle bags. Megan and Rick swung up easily into their saddles, but Marshall groaned as he settled into his. "Rick, it's been over six years since I rode for any length of time. Do we really have to do this?" Marshall asked plaintively. He settled Poppy Juice in behind Cherokee, who was breaking the trail.

"Marsh, you can blame your sore backside on Seamus O'Reilly. If he hadn't insisted on you being here, you would've been at your desk with Tony. Uncle Ian doesn't want Megs doing this kind of stuff alone and since he's busy and Frank's down with the flu, it's up to me to watch her back. Now suck it up," Rick said mercilessly.

Thanks a lot, boss, Marshall thought as the trio rode easily through the snow. Fortunately, while it had been a long time since he had ridden any great deal, Marshall had been an excellent rider and it showed.

Megan called in to Martha every hour as they rode the fence. By the time Megan called the second time, Frank had been sent to the hospital with pneumonia, and Ian and Nana had already come home. Megan ended that call with an additional promise they would turn around at about 11:30, and there was no damage to the fence.

Despite being in Megan's constant company, Rick's feelings of unease weren't getting any stronger. It was more like a constant throb in the back of his head. He had fallen silent almost as soon as they had left the farm, brooding and worrying about Megan. He could feel his shoulders tensing and he gripped the reins tighter and tighter. Whatever was wrong with the rider was always communicated to the horse. Cherokee began to fidget.

"Rick, what is it? What's wrong?" Marshall called from somewhere behind him.

Rick had stopped his horse in a clearing and was just sitting there, letting Cherokee fidget. Guiding Mystique up beside Rick's black stallion, Megan reached out and grabbed Cherokee's reins. She crooned at him until he settled down, but one look at Rick's face was enough to make her gasp.

Marshall, on the other side, knew something was very wrong, but didn't really know how to fix it. "Rick, listen to me. It's Marsh. Tell me what you see," Marshall urged softly. He glanced at Megan and motioned for her to keep quiet.

Rick's voice was low and raspy. "That's just it, Marsh. I don't see anything. It's only a feeling. She's in trouble. He's coming after her again, but this time it's different. He's more dangerous. I won't be able to get to her in time," Rick said frustrated. Cherokee began to fidget again until Megan crooned at him.

"Who's he after?" Marshall continued to probe.

"Megs. No one's gonna see this coming, I'm sure of it. I don't know what Johnny's planning, but it's all focused on Megs. She's so still," Rick's voice trailed off and he just stared into space.

"Marsh, what's going on? He's scaring me," Megan said. The panic in her voice was the only thing that got through to Rick.

He took a deep breath and tried to calm himself. "Stand, Cherokee, easy. I'm sorry, cuz. It's something that started at the centre during my sessions with Tony. I'd become restless. I'd pace, like a caged tiger. At first Tony just let me be, because eventually, I'd settle down and come back to the sessions," Rick said as he climbed down from his horse and sat on a fallen log.

The other two joined him, passing around the hot chocolate and the sandwiches. "Did you actually see anything?" Megan asked, curiously.

"Yes and no. At first, there was nothing really to see. Then, I'd see something resembling a snapshot. Something I would remember from early in the school year. You know, Jor laughing, you riding Mystique. The four of us just hanging out together. Even Mick standing behind you, protecting you.

"Then it shifted. It was only Jor I would see. Her smile. Her face. Her eyes. Then it shifted again. All I could see was her, lying on that floor in the classroom, just like I found her after her attack. Lying there. She was so still," Rick whispered.

"Rick, focus," Marshall said calmly.

"One day, Tony changed his tactics. I had been complaining about not being able to see Jor and I was pacing. I stopped in front of the door and stood there, staring at it. It was the first time Tony ever asked me what I saw," Rick continued softly. "And I told him."

Megan sat there. "It's almost like you've got a sixth sense, Rick," she said with an encouraging smile.

"Hardly," he snorted. "I guess it's just the instincts Johnny drilled into me. When someone I know is threatened, even if the threat isn't here yet, I feel it. Tony said my face that day was blank, almost a mask. Now, he watches for it and, if he catches it in time, I can usually talk my way through it. If not, well that's what the speed bag is for," Rick continued.

"Megs, I gotta ask. What made you change your mind about me?" Rick asked suddenly.

"Rick, if you had really attacked me, you would've gone after me in that office. There wouldn't have been a damn thing my father or Tony could've done. I got backed into a corner and I was easy prey, but you just turned away. I also realize my love for Mick has blinded me to the fact every time something happens, you're the first one he blames and I just follow along," Megan said.

"Tony made us watch you in the gym afterwards. He said he wanted us to see what we'd done to you. Rick, you were so angry, yet you were crying. Coach wouldn't let you do anything but pound away at that big bag. He refused to let you into the ring, no matter how hard you begged. I'm sorry, Rick," Megan said quietly.

Rick stood and whistled for the horses. There wasn't much more he could say as he pulled himself into the saddle to head back to the farm. But all the way home, all he could think about was how much danger he felt his cousin was in.

Chapter 41

It was a long, hard weekend for Rick. He couldn't stop pacing. He couldn't focus on his homework or his speed bag. Marshall constantly pushed the teen to talk about what was going on, but the more the cop pushed, the angrier Rick became. By Sunday, Rick was unmanageable. Desperate, Marshall called Tony.

"Why can't that boy ever have one of these episodes on days when we have our sessions?" Tony groused.

"What did I interrupt?" Marshall asked.

"A nice romantic dinner and maybe more," Tony sighed. "Try and hold him, Marsh. I'll be there as soon as I apologize to Sheona," Tony said finally.

Marshall hung up to the sound of Rick going hard at the speed bag. The cop winced at the ferocity in the punches. *He sounds like he's gonna break something and tonight, it might be me,* Marshall thought as he walked to Rick's room.

"What?" Rick growled, as Marshall stood in the door.

"Is there something you wanna talk about?" Marshall asked timidly.

"Go away, cop," was all that Rick would say.

Tony arrived in a foul mood. While he knew he had made the choice to be responsible for Rick, he was getting really tired of Rick's lack of control. Especially when Tony had gone through the trouble of making a fabulous meal Sheona would now get to eat by herself. As Tony stomped into the house, he could hear Rick pounding away at the bag, and when he found Marshall just standing outside of Rick's bedroom door, doing nothing, Tony let his partner have it.

"What the hell do you think you're doing? Or not doing," Tony growled.

"He's already taken a couple of swipes at me when I've tried to get him to talk, so don't get mad at me. I've tried everything you told me to do and nothing's worked. It's been like this since Friday. I'm surprised you didn't figure it out in your little session with him. He won't say what's wrong, and the more I push, the angrier he becomes. Get off my back," Marshall snapped back.

"You let this build all weekend? Why the hell didn't you call sooner?" Tony asked incredulously. "No wonder you can't calm him down!" Tony's voice rose.

"Look, I'm trying, alright? He scares the crap out of me. I don't have your experience with him and I have no clue what to do when he gets like this! I'm way out of my league here!" Marshall shouted back. His face was flushed and he had faced Tony with his fists clenched.

Rick stopped. The fight between the two cops hit him like a ton of bricks. These two were not only partners, they were best friends. And they were fighting over the stupidest thing – him. Rick felt sick.

"Tony! Marsh! Stop! Enough!" Rick cried. "Whatever I've done, I'm not worth fighting over! Just stop!" Rick protested loudly.

The two cops stood in the door, both seething with anger. Rick couldn't take the glare Tony directed towards him any longer. He grabbed his coat, pushed past the pair and slammed out of the house. Tony growled low in his throat and started after Rick.

Marshall grabbed his arm. "Fish, wait. He's not going anywhere. He left his keys on the dresser and it's too cold to walk anywhere, even Jordan's. Let him be for a while. I think I'm beginning to get to him again. I can feel the anger radiating from him when I watch him do anything," Marshall said wearily.

"Did Seamus even try to live up to his end of the deal these last couple of days?" Tony asked wryly.

"Not even when Mickey dropped Megan off after school. Jordan could only call him after supper for about ten minutes all weekend. What a mess," Marshall said.

The cops walked to the front door, talking quietly. Through the frost, Tony could see Rick stewing on the front porch. Marshall was right. The kid wasn't going anywhere.

"Coffee, Fish?" Marshall called from the kitchen.

"Lemme check on Rick, first, then I'll be there," Tony called back.

Rick turned his head slightly as Tony opened the front door. His mentor stood in the pale light, leaning against the doorframe with his arms folded. Rick could see Tony was not impressed with Rick's behaviour. Rick waited for the hammer to fall, and when it did, it was worse than he ever imagined.

"I'll be in the kitchen when you're ready," Tony said quietly. There was no emotion in Tony's voice, just the slightest hint of recrimination. The door closed softly behind Tony as Rick just sat there, humiliated.

He got up and paced the length of the porch, trying to understand what was going on in his head. "Richard Thomas Attison, you're an idiot," Rick muttered out loud as he leaned against the railing and looked over the farm.

He was becoming too dependent on Tony for everything, and he knew it. Any time something went wrong, he expected Tony to bail him out, no matter what it interrupted. He knew when he was getting moody or upset, but, more importantly, he knew how to deal with it. Tony had given him all the tools he needed to deal with this.

I'm selfish, Rick decided firmly. *Tony has better things to do than to baby-sit me.* "I can do this," Rick swore quietly. "I know I can."

Rick sighed as he continued to look out at the farm. "Just not tonight."

He knew he needed Tony, one more time. He had let things build too long and he needed someone he trusted to talk him down before he exploded. He slipped back into the house and stopped outside the kitchen to listen to the partners talk.

"It's a good thing Sheona's met Rick and understands his problems a bit more now. Otherwise, that fantastic supper would be sitting on my table getting cold and I'd be getting more than just a cold shoulder. She forgave me, provided I take her out to that new restaurant by the clinic," Tony chuckled.

"Tony, I'm sorry. I just didn't know what else to do. I tried everything, but he wouldn't talk to me. How much longer do you think he'll stew out there?" Marshall asked, sipping at his coffee.

Tony glanced at the clock. "Not long. Something's eating at him and he'll need to talk soon. Did he mention any more about those feelings about Meg?" Tony asked. He poured himself another cup of coffee while waiting for Marshall to answer.

"Nope," Marshall said. He looked over Tony's shoulder as Rick slipped into the doorway and leaned against one side.

"It's about time. Your butt cold? Or do you need some more time to sulk?" Tony asked without turning around. The anger was thinly veiled.

Rick didn't answer right away. He knew what he said in the next couple of minutes could drive Tony away, court order or no court order. He took a breath and let it out slowly. "You must be getting damned tired of these calls, Tony," Rick said finally. He studied Tony's back. Like Rick, the cop was tense.

"You could say that," Tony replied shortly. *What's it gonna take to get through to you, Rick?* Tony thought. *You have to learn to deal with this on your own.*

"Would it help if I said I was sorry?" Rick asked softly.

Tony sat there for the longest time, stunned. Rick had never apologized for anything before. He turned and looked at his young friend. Anyone else would have thought Rick was just leaning lazily against the door and nothing was wrong. Tony knew better. He could see the tension in every line of Rick's body. Especially the eyes that begged Tony to help him one more time.

Tony sighed. "Come on, little brother, let's go talk."

Monday morning, Rick got ready for school, tired and battered. It had been another long and exhausting session, but once Rick and Tony had figured out what was wrong, Tony managed to teach Rick a few tricks on preventing the tension from building up too much again.

As Rick showered, he couldn't believe he was actually going back to school. He'd get to spend time with Jordan and deal with Tom. The more Rick learned about the Grey Angels, the more he felt that they were well on their way to becoming a gang, just like the Knights. Once that happened, Blade wouldn't stop until he had challenged Tom for the right to lead them. Since Blade fought dirty, Tom wouldn't stand a chance.

"Marsh, let's go. I need to get to school early," Rick called from the kitchen where he was making breakfast.

When Rick walked into Colonial High with his shadow, his eyes quickly scanned the crowd of students in the lounge. He tensed as he thought he saw the Knights off to one side, talking, but it was Tom Rick was really looking for and when he found his friend, Rick's heart sunk. Tom was off to one side, his back against the wall where no one could come up behind him, watching the crowd. For what, Rick wasn't sure, but he had an idea or two. Rick had been right. Tom had turned into a younger version of himself. *Whatever happened to that innocent kid?* Rick wondered. Deep down, he knew the answer. The Knights had happened. It was time to stop this.

Tom's face lit up when he saw Rick coming towards him. "Hey, Champ, good to have you back," Tom greeted Rick with a slap on the back. He really wasn't paying attention to Rick, but to the crowd in the lounge. His eyes began to roam again, seeking trouble.

"Tom, we need to talk. Now," Rick said firmly and guided Tom to a bench. Marshall stood where Tom had been while the two teens straddled the bench. Tom's eyes continued to roam the room, watching, seeking, searching.

"Kid, you've become hard," Rick said bluntly.

"What do you mean?" Tom asked, puzzled, snapping his eyes back to focus on Rick.

Rick reached up and tapped Tom's temple. "It starts with the eyes, Tom," Rick said seriously. He wanted to frighten Tom so badly the Kid would step back and take a good long look at what he had become. "Eyes that won't stop moving. Your eyes seek the escape route and're always looking for someplace to put your back when you fight. Your eyes start evaluating the next boy in line. What's his weakness? Can I take him?" Rick spoke quietly, forcing Tom to listen.

"What the hell're you talking about?" Tom demanded.

Rick leaned forward. "I'm talking about you, Tom and the anger you've built up inside. Once you give in to that, just once, you're in trouble. Once your eyes harden, do you know what happens then, Tom?"

Rick broke off and tensed. Over the noise of the students, he heard them approach. He felt them standing behind him, waiting. Rick stayed still, then, sensing the movement behind him, he dove to one side of the bench, dragging Tom with him. Blade's knife thudded into the bench where Rick had been sitting.

Rick came to his feet and waved Marshall off. He was ready to fight. Tom came up behind him, ready to back Rick up, if needed. *Hell, Tom,* this *is what I'm talking about,* Rick cursed silently. *How do I explain you've become just like Johnny?*

"Hey, Moneyman. Yer back," Blade drawled as he retrieved his knife, sliding it back into its holder.

"What do you want, Johnny?" Rick asked quietly. He was amazed he didn't feel any anger. Just that same feeling of unease as strong as ever.

"You," Blade snapped and rushed Rick.

Rick sidestepped his former leader with ease and let the force of Blade's rush carry him on by. Rick had no intention of taking a single swing. Tom and the rest of the Knights stayed out of the fight. It was between Rick and Blade. Blade came back, swinging wildly. Rick blocked each punch with ease, but didn't return a single one.

"C'mon, Moneyman," Blade grated. "Who's chicken now, boy?"

He rushed one last time, swinging for Rick's head. Rick ducked easily and swung back for once. As his punch rushed towards Blade's jaw, he could see Mr. Delaney striding for the lounge. Instead of dropping Blade like he wanted, Rick pulled the punch and only tapped Blade insultingly on the cheek.

"That's enough!" Mr. Delaney's voice cut through the noise.

"Richard, you haven't been back an hour and you're already fighting," Mr. Delaney said. "Johnny, I've had just about enough of you. You're suspended until the start of the new semester. As for the rest of you, leave Richard alone and get back to your classes. I doubt very much your father would like it if I suspended you for two weeks, Brian," the principal pointed out.

Seething, Blade stormed out of the front doors while the rest of the Knights slowly walked to their classes. Rick just sighed. "Thanks, Delaney. That's gonna make the rest of my school year just ducky," Rick snapped.

"Come see me after Homeroom, Rick. We have a few things to discuss," the principal said as he left. Rick just sighed.

"Rick, finish what you were gonna say. What happens when my eyes become 'hard'? I don't understand what you mean," Tom begged as Rick watched the principal walk away.

Rick turned back to Tom and stared at the boy for a long time. "You become hard and get the gang reflexes, Kid. The reflexes that don't let anyone come up behind you. You get jumpy and tense. The more tense you are, the angrier you become. You become a tool to be used by someone like Johnny. Once you get those reflexes, you're prime game for a gang. Once you're in, you're in for life. Those reflexes never leave, Tom. Look at me. How long have I been out of the Knights? But I heard them approach over the crowd and I could tell when Johnny was going to throw his knife. I could hear him pull it out of its sheath. If I didn't have those reflexes, I'd have been dead by now. Those reflexes never leave, Tom," Rick said harshly. He was less than two inches from Tom's face.

Tom paled as he digested what Rick was saying. "Are you saying I've become just like Blade?" he asked horrified.

"Congratulations," Rick said sarcastically.

"What do I do, Rick?" Tom asked desperately. "This isn't what I wanted. This isn't what I created the Angels for!"

"Simple. Don't let it control you. Don't give in to the temptation to stand with your back against the wall and constantly scan a room, looking for the weakest link. Don't ever give into the temptation to fight, just because you can. Every time you do, think of Johnny and ask yourself if that's what you really want to be," Rick said. As he stood talking to Tom, he tensed. The uneasiness was back.

"Megs," he whispered as he searched the front door for his cousin. Tom didn't even notice the interruption.

"I get it, Rick. Think of you and stop before I go through the same thing you did," Tom said as they walked towards the front door.

Rick stopped and looked at Tom. "Don't get me wrong, Kid. The Angels're a great idea. Just keep one thing in mind. Did you form the Angels to stop the Knights or to *become* the Knights?" Rick asked directly.

He glanced at his watch and realized there was less than two minutes until Homeroom. He grimaced. So much for Seamus' promise to let him see Jordan. He turned away from Tom and nearly knocked Jordan down.

"Careful, sweets," he chuckled as he grabbed her arm to steady her.

"Hi, Rick," Jordan said breathlessly.

"Good morning, babe. How're you?" he asked, giving her a kiss. He slipped his hand into hers, his fingers automatically seeking the bracelet he had given her.

It wasn't there.

"Daddy won't let me wear it. He said he'll throw it out," she said when he glanced at her. They stood there in the middle of the sea of students holding each other tight, knowing it was the only time they would be allowed together.

The bell for Homeroom interrupted them. "C'mon, Jordan. We'll be late for Homeroom," Mickey said gently. Jordan nodded and looked up at Rick for the longest time.

"See you tomorrow," she said softly.

"Love you, sweets," Rick whispered back. He bent down and kissed her good-bye. Then she slipped away with Tom guarding her back. Carl nodded to Rick as he escorted Megan to her Homeroom.

Rick stood there for some time after the bell went, his fists clenched tightly. Into his hand, Jordan had slipped the bracelet. At least if she couldn't wear it, this way Seamus couldn't throw it out if he found it.

"C'mon, Marsh. Let's go see Delaney. Not that I really want to," Rick muttered and led the way to the office.

"Good morning, Richard," Mr. Delaney said sourly as he motioned for Rick to join him in the office.

Rick sighed inwardly as he sat down in the all too familiar chair. It was going to be one of *those* meetings, was it? "Look, Delaney, as hard as I've fought to get back into the school, do you really believe for a second I'd start a fight as soon as I walked back in?" Rick protested hotly.

"No, Rick, I don't, but we do need to talk," the principal said as he settled into his chair. He sorted some paperwork as if looking for something specific.

He held up a letter for Rick to see. "This is a letter from Seamus O'Reilly. A declaration of war, so to speak. In it, he demands you be removed from this school, since you have not yet been cleared of all charges, they've only been dropped for lack of evidence. Now, I have a very serious problem, son," Mr. Delaney said, leaning back in his chair.

"What would that be, sir?" Marshall asked.

"On the one hand, the courts say Rick is cleared of all charges, since there's not enough evidence to convict him. That means, unless the school board can come up with some other compelling reason, such as poor marks, he can come back to my school, in the general population with no conditions. Since he kept up with his school work in the detention centre and, in fact, has greatly improved his marks, that's no longer a consideration," Mr. Delaney said firmly.

"And on the other hand?" Rick drawled lazily.

"Stop that! You sound like Johnny!" Mr. Delaney snapped. "On the other hand, I have the chief of police demanding you be kept away from the other students, specifically his daughter, or he's pulling his kids out. He's also threatening to go public with how you beat the rap for both attacks," Mr. Delaney said.

Rick looked down at the bracelet in his hand. The gold seemed tarnished somehow. One-handed, Rick managed to clasp it around his wrist. It barely fit. "I should've known better than to trust Seamus. He gave in way too easily," Rick snapped suddenly.

"Rick agreed to have me as a bodyguard, against the judge's order by the way, in exchange for Seamus letting Jordan live her life. Which was supposed to mean Rick and Jordan could see each other in school. It seems Seamus is reluctant to live up to that deal," Marshall explained when Delaney looked puzzled.

"I think I understand. Rick, I have a compromise I think may work. I have a room just on the other side of that wall that I use for long-term, in-school suspensions, for those kids I want to expel, but for whom expulsion would do them no good." Delaney pointed to the south wall with a large picture on it. "Behind that picture is a window I use to monitor the student I choose to put in there and the only door is through my office here. We'll get you a private tutor to help you finish up this term."

"That's a compromise?" Rick said incredulously.

"In exchange for agreeing to that, I'll talk to Mickey and ask him to have Jordan here ten minutes before school starts. I'll arrange for her to see you before Homeroom and at lunch. Seamus gets his wish, since you won't be in the general student body," Mr. Delaney grinned.

"And Seamus holds up his end of our deal," Rick chuckled nastily.

The last couple of weeks of the first semester weren't easy for Rick. He felt isolated and angry, but he managed to survive, thanks to Jordan. Being able to see her, even if it was only for about an hour a day, helped.

As Rick stood at the front door on the last day of the semester, he glanced out towards the parking lot and saw Blade standing by Brain's car. Rick frowned. He could feel the tension growing inside. He followed the direction Blade was staring and stopped at Mickey's truck. Megan was standing beside it, talking to another one of her friends, while Mickey stowed their backpacks in the truck's jockey box.

Rick shivered. That feeling of uneasiness was almost overwhelming. Whatever Blade was planning, it was big, but it wasn't going to happen soon. As he stared at the Knights, Rick heard someone shuffle up behind him.

Tom was there. "Rick, what's wrong? I've never seen that look on you before," Rick's friend said.

"What look?" Rick asked distracted.

"Your face was blank, but your eyes're angry," Tom said promptly.

"It's starting again, Kid, but I won't be able to save her. She's so still. I'll be too late," Rick said softly and walked away, leaving his friend standing in the door of the school wondering if Rick had just lost his mind.

That night, Rick sat in the kitchen for the longest time, trying to write a journal Tony had asked him to start, but all he could think about was the Knights. Finally, he picked up the phone and dialled a number from memory.

"Yo," a young voice answered. He had to shout to be heard over the pounding music.

"Pup, get Blade. Now!" Rick barked with authority.

When Blade picked up the phone, the music had been turned down, but his anger had been turned on. "Yo, Moneyman, long time no talk," Blade drawled.

"Leave them alone, Johnny," Rick warned softly. The anger in his voice was palpable.

"Moneyman, when're ya gonna learn, boy? I do what I want, when I want. To who I want," Blade sneered.

"Why don't you come after me, Johnny? Let's see who's better and stronger," Rick challenged.

"Tempting, Moneyman, very tempting. But.....no. Yer not ready yet. I haven't begun to break ya. Trust me, little Moneyman, when I'm through with ya, there ain't no one that's going to trust ya ever again. What happened before was just child's play. Practice. If ya don't believe anything else, believe this. When I get done, yer gonna beg me to end it, just to save them," Blade snarled. He slammed down the phone in Rick's ear.

Marshall slowly hung up. He hadn't meant to listen in on the conversation. He had picked up the phone to call Tony and chat, but he had caught the challenge and Blade's response.

How did we miss the evidence? Marshall wondered. *Did Blade really attack the girls and we missed it?* The cop pondered the evidence all night.

Rick sat silently in the kitchen after hanging up the phone. He replayed the conversation with Blade over and over in his mind. The longer he sat, the more he realized his feelings of uneasiness just got a lot worse. Whatever Blade had started in September wasn't over. Not by a long shot.

Join us in <u>White Daze</u> *to find out what Blade has planned for Rick and his friends. This time – it's personal.*

Made in the USA
Charleston, SC
13 February 2016